D0804342

They share a genius for death machines. They share a life of espionage and assassination. They share the love of a woman too beautiful, too secretive, too dangerous to be possessed. They are enemies who share a friendship and a terrible fate. They are about to be killed by their own countries.

———

"Fast-paced . . . THE DEATH FREAK will grip readers until the last bloody page."

—*Bestsellers*

# The
# DEATH
# FREAK

by *"John Luckless"*

Who is also known as
**Clifford Irving**
and
**Herbert Burkholz**

BALLANTINE BOOKS • NEW YORK

Library of Congress Catalog Card Number: 78-8271

ISBN 0-345-28155-1

This edition published by arrangement with Summit Books

Manufactured in the United States of America

First Ballantine Books Edition: July 1979

for Julian Bach and John Cushman

*All this new talk of brotherhood! Does no one remember Cain and Abel? There are good brothers and evil brothers. The man I call my brother is the one who guards my back.*

—JEAN LE MALCHANCEUX
(in the 12th century)

1

In the master bedroom of a half-timbered colonial home in Williamsburg, Virginia, the colonel and his lady glared at each other across the expanse of an oversized bed as white as an arctic icecap. The colonel's lady was young, lovely, and lithe. She was also sore as hell, and when she wasn't involved in glaring she was busily packing the powder-blue piece of luggage on the bed. The colonel himself stood tall and ramrod straight. He was no longer young; his trim military mustache was splashed with silver. He was as sore as his lady, but he worked at concealing it. Concealment was part of his trade.

"There's no need to snap at me," he said mildly. "I asked a simple question. Where are you going?"

"I thought we had an agreement." As she spoke, her strong hands—too strong, really, for such a sensuous body—continued to work in neat, precise motions, stacking cottons, silks, and bikinis in her suitcase. "No questions, either way, remember?"

"Quite so." He nodded his agreement. "But that was three years ago. How many times since then have you simply taken off? Without a word? Oh, yes! 'See you soon.'" He mocked her. "That's just not good enough, Catherine."

"Are you going to bore me with statistics?" She slammed the suitcase shut, snapped the lock.

"I don't find them boring. Quite the contrary. Eighteen times in three years. Add up all the days and weeks. I've done it, my dear. It comes to almost six months that you've been away from home—if you still call it that. And I don't even know where you go. That's not quite the same as a long weekend in Barbados when the weather's rotten and you're feeling blue, is it?"

"No, it isn't." Defiantly, she was ready to admit it. "But that was the agreement, Freddy."

Still mild and cool, he said, "In that case, I think it's time to change the agreement. From now on I want to know where you go, and why."

"The where is unimportant."

"I want to know."

"Just like that?"

"Life isn't static, my dear."

"If you really wanted to know where I went," she said impatiently, "you could have found out long ago. You have the organization for it."

"I don't do things that way."

"The hell you don't. The only reason you haven't done it already is that you don't want the whole department in on your private life. As for why I go away . . . you should be able to figure that out for yourself."

He was silent for a long moment. She was right; he knew. He shook his head, a tired old bull puzzled by the progression of the years. An army brat! It had seemed such a wise, intelligent choice on his part, after his first wife had died. But her father had been a general, and she'd never learned to salute the lesser ranks. At last, he said, "It wasn't always that way, you know."

"Are you going to start *that* again?"

"You didn't know me then. Back in Burma, and Marseille . . ."

"Ah, the war! The best years of our lives! When men were men!" She knew how to plant the barbs.

But he seemed not to have heard her. His voice was lower now, almost indistinct. "It was different then. And I was different. There were so few of us in

2

France, so many of them, and all we could do was—"

"Kill," she finished for him. Her violet eyes were wide and hard. She was breathing rapidly. "All right, go ahead. Will it make you feel better? Go ahead, then. Tell me about all the people you killed. Tell me about the ones you strangled, and the ones you stabbed, and the ones you shot. Tell me about the time you blew the head off the German major with his own Schmeisser. You like to tell that one, don't you? How the blood spurted out of his neck across the room and hit the wall. Go ahead, tell me. You always get a hard-on when you tell that one."

"You're a fool, Catherine. It's not that way at all."

"Isn't it? Do you think I can't *see?*"

"It isn't that simple."

"It is, Freddy. For people like you, it is."

"You know very little," he said softly, "about people like me."

Her eyes flared, and her head shot up, shoulders squared. "People like you. If you can't kill, you can't fuck. It's as simple as that. And when was the last time you killed anything?"

He lunged at her across the bed, fell short, rolled over, and came up reaching. She didn't try to back away. He slapped her twice, then ripped at her clothing and fumbled with his own. He was strong, sinewy. She took the blows silently, bending subtly with them, and when he flung her onto the bed she lay there, waiting. He threw himself on top of her. His hands went around her neck, but she didn't struggle, showed no fear.

"Bloody bitch," he said, and tightened his grip. Her eyes were open; she stared at him calmly, curious.

"Bloody, *bloody* bitch!" And then he was inside her. He said the words over and over again as he moved in her, his hands still clasping her white neck.

"Killer," she said, almost tenderly. "My killer."

The words were a spur. He pumped at her furiously. She accepted all he gave her, but she made no movement. Even her arms stayed at her sides. Only when he climaxed did she arch her body, grunt, and come

3

with him. Only then did his fingers uncurl from the flesh of her neck, leaving the red blotches that would eventually bruise to match her eyes.

He rolled off her, groaning. She rose smoothly from the bed, went to the closet and then to the bathroom. When she came out she was dressed in jeans and a pink cashmere sweater, and she had put her hair back in one thick dark-blond braid. The colonel hadn't moved. His eyes were closed.

"That wasn't bad, Freddy. In fact, it was pretty good."

He opened his eyes to stare at the white ceiling. "Damn your soul. Am I supposed to be flattered?"

"Be what you like, darling. Best of all, be yourself. It doesn't change anything. I'm still going. You understand that, don't you?"

He was silent, drained.

"Don't you want to say goodbye?"

"I thought I just did."

"In your fashion, Freddy. Want to know when I'll be back?"

"You'll be back," he said bitterly, still not looking at her. "That's what matters."

"So far." Then she laughed shortly. "Don't worry. This time too. I'll be back."

He closed his eyes again. He heard her take the suitcase and go lightly down the carpeted stairs to telephone for the taxi that would take her to Patrick Henry Airport. She was tough. He hated that, but he respected it. Lying there, he waited while she waited, waiting through the sound of the taxi's tires on the driveway gravel, the merry chime of the bell, the firm closing of the front door, the squeal of the departure. Birds chirped among the trees in the early-morning February sunshine. Once she was gone he lay there, still waiting although there was nothing left to wait for.

When the telephone rang he ignored it. That was a luxury. But on the seventh ring the movement of light caught the corner of his eye, the regular pulsing of the red light in the base of the instrument. When he saw the light he rolled over at once and picked up the

4

phone. He spoke briefly, then listened for a long time.

"No, Erikson, I don't want you to do that," he said finally. "That program is classified. For O Group only. No technicians. I'll run the printout myself. I just want the five of us there. Clear the printout room and call the others. O Group meeting at oh-nine-thirty. I'll be right over."

The colonel hung up the telephone and went quickly into the bathroom, staring at his face in the mirror.

"Killer," he murmured to himself—far more pleased than shamed. Then he went about the business of returning to his trade.

**2**

## Psychoprofile Series J

| | |
|---|---|
| FOR EYES OF: | Officer commanding Colonial Squad and Closed List O. 5/5 |
| SUBJECT: | Edward Mancuso GS11/58 Substantive |
| CLASSIFICATION: | ARM-1 Weapons Manufacturer |
| ADDRESS: | 410 East 82nd Street New York, N.Y. |
| AGE: | 38 |
| POB: | New York, N.Y. |
| DATE OF PROJECTION: | Immediate |
| PROJECTION VALID FOR: | 90 days |

Subject Edward Mancuso is a specialist in the manufacture of unusual killing devices (UKD's) and has been under continuous contract to the Agency for the past twenty years. He is today considered the leading expert in this field, his reputation being rivaled only by that of Soviet scientist Vasily Borgneff of the KGB (Ref. #U/7924). During the period of his employment, subject Mancuso has supplied UKD's to the Agency in general, and more particularly to the Special Operations Section IV, Technical Services Division (TSD), now known intra-Agency as the Colonial Squad. His products are supplied to the Agency on an assignment basis only, although until approximately three years ago the subject has exhibited considerable personal initiative in the development of UKD's not specifically requested. As policy (Directive 59-A-211), subject is never told the target for his assignment except in the most general terms, and then strictly on a need-to-know basis. Subject is rarely assigned more than three projects per year. He has never refused an assignment. His efficiency quotient, combining quality control and speed of delivery, is 9.6, the highest in TSD.

Although he is primarily noted for his development of the Mancuso Effect (quick-release neurotoxin heart-attack simulator) and the Mancuso Antidote (tablet size and compress inhaler both), he has also been responsible for the following UKD's. Principal but partial list follows:

Mancuso barium chromate and boron fuse.

"Little Devil" blowback silencer for Walther PP and PPK .22 (self-destruct model).

Model R-84 Anaphylactic-shock cartridge.

Mancuso felt-tip pen, Flair or Bic model (containing tiger-snake venom).

Participation in PROJECT GRAVEL MINE and subsequent refinement of PROJECT JELLY FOOT.

Model R-24 miniature detonators.

Mancuso Blow-off Wheel Remover (for all model U.S. cars manufactured after 1967).

Current participation in PROJECT FLASH GORDON.

Educational and cultural background:

Subject is the youngest of four children born to Angelo and Maria Mancuso, both of Genoa, Italy, both emigrated to the United States in 1929. Subject was born on the Lower East Side of Manhattan and was educated in New York City public schools and at Stuyvesant High School, a special-interests school for students of high I.Q. rating and unusual abilities. No formal education beyond high school level. At the age of eighteen he developed, through independent research, the "Little Devil" Blowback Silencer (see above) and offered it for sale to a proprietary corporation (AmerArmCo, Wilmington, Delaware) owned by this Agency, although at the time subject was unaware of this fact. He was eventually referred to Clandestine Services, Langley (ClanServ), which purchased the model and destroyed record of the patent already applied for at U.S. Patent Office by the subject. ClanServ referred the subject to TSD, then located in the Broyhill Building, Arlington, Virginia, and subject was placed under direct control of Agent Richard Wilenski, deceased (Ref. #T/476-d). Since then the subject has worked exclusively for TSD on a contract basis.

When questioned twenty years ago by Agent Wilenski at Camp Peary Training Center about his lack of desire for a higher education, despite his obvious abilities in chemistry and physics and the offer of a scholarship from the Agency, he was quoted as replying: "What could they teach me at Columbia? I already know enough to blow up half of Harlem."

Thus, intellectually, the subject may be described as being streetwise rather than well educated, with an intuitive rather than an empirical mind. Naturally brilliant in his own and closely related fields, he is indifferent to most others. His reading is confined to random periodicals and technical journals, detective novels, men's and sports magazines. Subscribes to *Skin Diver, Sports Illustrated* and *Playboy*. His taste in music runs from hard rock to light classical.

Outside interests include scuba diving (rating: Intermediate), tennis (rated: B player) and basketball. Plays chess and backgammon poorly.

Does not gamble other than minimally. Drinks moderately without specific preferences. Not known to use drugs, and in Camp Peary tests (Series D-2) reacted negatively to Agency-prescribed dosage of LSD (−3); DNT (−2); and cannabis (−.5).

Physical characteristics:

Height: 5'8". Weight: 145–150 lbs. Eyes: brown. Hair: black. Skin: olive. Distinguishing Marks: puckered scar right forearm (childhood accident); transverse furrow left thigh (scuba accident, St. Croix, 1971).

Sexuality: Heterosexual, apparently normal frequency.

No marriages. No known repetitive sexual relationship at present.

Politics: No apparent political preferences. Has never registered or voted.

Highest security clearance granted. (See FBI file: 3/EJM/43219)

Social: Because of the nature of his work, the subject has long been considered totally amoral. Recently, however . . .

The two men walking down Duke of Gloucester Street were dressed in knee breeches and shirts with furbelowed sleeves. Their shoes bore silver buckles, and the white wigs they wore were neatly trimmed to short but effective queues. They might have been the young Burr and the young Hamilton, brooding over General Washington's incompetence, as they walked rapidly and silently, nodding only occasionally to a mobcapped woman in homespun or a portly gentleman in a suit of maroon broadcloth much too heavy for a temperate morning in Virginia.

Keeping up the rapid pace, they turned off Duke of Gloucester opposite the Governor's Palace and skirted the common green past the lowing oxen grazing there, past the smithy, with the clang of the blacksmith's anvil and roar of his forge. Across the green a company of The King's Own Foot, lobsterback uniforms blood-bright in the sun, marched and countermarched in drill. The two men ignored the sight, ignoring as well the band of colonial militia, cocked hats set at everywhich angle, engaged in arms inspection, leathery palms smacking muskets sharply. They were readying themselves for the weekly Sunday-morning battle between the colonial militia and the army of King George. From behind them tolled the bells of The College of William and Mary.

Kelly, the younger and shorter of the two, looked at his wristwatch without breaking stride. "We're late," he muttered. "I hate to be late."

"Can't be helped," Rakow said. "He can't call an O Group meeting Sunday morning on fifteen minutes' notice. I mean, he can do what he pleases, but he can't expect us to be on time. You know where I was?"

"I can guess."

"She didn't like it one bit," Rakow said. "And this time her kid saw me sneak out."

"Well, that was inevitable, wasn't it?"

"*She* didn't think so."

"A fucking flap to the tenth power." Kelly rarely used such language, but he truly hated to be late. It destroyed his image of his efficiency. "Always the same. Run in circles, scream and shout. Like the army."

"You got it exactly. That's why old Freddy does it. He loves it."

The usual mob of casually dressed tourists clutching candy bars and icy beer cans had gathered at the south end of the green to watch the mock battle between the British and colonial troops. Dozens of cameras clicked as buff-coated artillerymen touched linstock to powder hole and ten two-pound carronades roared raggedly at the sky, discharging only harmless air. Kelly and Rakow pushed their way through the crowd, each in his own way cursing the executive decision to relocate Special Operations IV (TSD) behind the seventeenth-century façade of Colonial Williamsburg. The Colonial Squad—that was what the others called them now, with their passion for cute and euphemistic names. At least it was better than the old days when they were known by the button-down crowd at Langley as The Animals. Those smooth, superior bastards, thought Rakow. If we didn't do the dirty work, some of them would be lucky to get jobs as clerks at IBM or the Rand Institute.

Once through the crowd, the two men dropped the pretense of controlled haste and jogged across the road to the street opposite the common green. They were both in fine condition; they barely puffed. Kelly did two miles every morning. Rakow had his barbells.

The row of houses on the other side was typical of the restored area of Williamsburg: frame-and-shingle dwellings neatly made, one with a ground-level shop selling leather goods, another housing a carpenter who

10

advertised his specialty with an oxbow hanging over the door. Eight houses in all, joined together by an impressive facade that neatly masked the activities of the Colonial Squad.

They made for the first house on the right and pounded up the wooden steps to the porch. There was a knocker on the front door, but they didn't knock. They waited. In a moment the door swung open and a tall, broad black man in green-and-gold livery filled the doorframe. He looked like anything but a servant. He looked as if he sorely missed his green beret and his garrote noose. He smiled and greeted them softly.

"*Good* morning, gentlemen. The colonel awaits you in the printout room—and move your respective asses, please."

Kelly, brushing by him, asked, "Can you tell us what it is, Andy? Do you know?"

"I don't get paid enough to have to know those things. All I know is that you're late. Colonel Parker's birds are flapping."

Once inside, the two men hurried through the entryway, elaborately furnished and decorated with period pieces, and into the corridor beyond.

The interior of the house, indeed of all the houses joined in the row, was in direct contrast to the colonial exterior. The guts had been ripped from the eight frame dwellings, and corridors ran through them lengthwise, opening onto offices, meeting rooms, and a small but well-equipped laboratory. The walls and the floors were the ubiquitous gunmetal gray of government issue, and the air, although silent, seemed to be suffused with the steady, monotonous hum of bureaucratic energy.

At the far end of the corridor an elevator dropped two levels below the ground, and the two men ran for it, tearing off their powdered wigs and scratching their itching scalps with eager fingers. First level down: cafeteria and firing range. Second level down: computer plant and printout room.

Kelly and Rakow slid white plastic cards into slots, pressed the tips of their fingers to a pulsing glass panel

11

that automatically checked their prints against their identities, and the door to the printout room slid noiselessly open. The room was long and narrow, pleasantly cool. Banks of printers lined the walls. At the far end of the room, three men stood around an oak table littered with paper files, ashtrays, and coffee cups. They were also dressed in colonial costumes. They straightened and turned as the latecomers entered.

Colonel Frederick W. Parker, tall and erect, with eyes the color of shallow water, fifteen years out of uniform and a colonel in name only now, stared fiercely at them and tugged at the trim end of his mustache. The commanding officer of the Colonial Squad was the only one of the five men to have held high military rank. It was something he was unable to forget.

Red Erikson, the number two in O Group, was even taller than the colonel, but slab-sided and trapped in a perpetual slouch. Amiable and easy-going, his friends found it difficult to believe that the former Green Beret had developed the technique of dropping Viet Cong prisoners from low-flying helicopters as a form of persuasion to interrogation. His only comment when Rakow and Kelly entered was to roll his eyes silently heavenward.

Romeo Arteaga flashed fine and even teeth at them gleefully. The Cuban-born agent and Bay of Pigs veteran was the squad's pet and jester, as well as the office expert on cold steel. In his more active days he had been in and out of Castro's Cuba a dozen times on extraction missions, and now he was the only one who spoke.

"Rakow," he said, "that fox you've got stashed in town is going to dig your grave one of these days."

No one in the room laughed. Everyone there was an expert in unnatural and violent death. They were the top level of the Colonial Squad, the bad boys of the Agency, the superkillers, the ex-Animals. And although these five were no longer active in the field, each had, when an agent, killed, and killed, and killed again. Each knew exactly how many times he had

12

killed—it was the kind of thing no man could ever forget, not even these—and each consciously tried to erase that number from his mind. So that no one laughed. Death was not a particularly funny subject to them. They knew too much about it, had lived with it and for it all their adult lives. Only Arteaga could have made the joke and gotten away with it.

"No shoptalk in the officers' mess," Erikson murmured, and the atmosphere in the room eased.

Rakow's face stayed grim. He rarely smiled or relaxed. He was the only one of the five who had no previous government service before coming to the Colonial Squad. He had been recruited directly from the Boston world of organized crime—a totally unemotional and unimaginative killer who always followed instructions and never failed, no matter who else got in the way. He had proved it to Parker his first month on the job by blowing up a commercial jet in order to kill an agent's wife who was carrying marked money that could have ended the careers of six top men in the Justice Department. The Colonial Squad had many functions. For Rakow there had been no indecision or hesitation; he always did things the easy way.

Melvin Kelly, by contrast, was the other side of the killing coin. A former FBI agent, he had resigned to join the Colonial Squad for the purest of patriotic motives, feeling that he could best serve his country by putting to work his natural talent for murder and mayhem.

The colonel handed each of the newcomers a copy of a printout. "We started without you. You'll have to catch up."

Rakow peered at the top page of his copy.

"Eddie Mancuso? Dirty little Eddie. What's he up to now?"

"Plenty," said Erikson. "Catch up and read on."

Social: Because of the nature of his work, the subject has long been considered totally amoral. Recently, however, it has become increasingly obvious that he has developed a marked distaste for his occupation. Although he realizes that there is no other industry in which he could be so gainfully employed, he is no longer able to reconcile his material benefit with the fundamental nature of his occupation. Moreover, since the subject is generally thrifty (except when he travels abroad on holidays for sport or leisure), does not gamble excessively and has no known expensive habits or sexual abnormalities, it is known that his investment portfolio (Merrill Lynch, Fenner & Smith) bears a current close-of-market value of $76,435. Current balance in his checking account at The Chase Manhattan Bank is $4,136.45. Funds secreted in Switzerland and the Bahamas estimated at between $300,000 and $350,000. Total estimated net worth not less than $380,000. Given the subject's background and mentality, he would consider this a sufficient sum for comfortable retirement.

Mancuso has been involved in the design and personal manufacture of death-dealing devices, both conventional and UKD, for twenty years. Over those years he has been indirectly responsible for the taking of at least fifty and perhaps as many as one hundred lives, a fact of which he is aware. In addition, he felt a friendly affection alternating with hatred for his original recruiter and Control, Agent Richard N. Wilenski, and showed marked signs of distress, however temporary, at the death of Wilenski (along with Agents Robert L. McKay and Graham A. Heuwetter) in Chile in 1972. Subject has no such friendly relationship with his current Control, Agent Stanley T. Erikson.

Mancuso is still a relatively young man. He wishes now that he had continued with his education and chosen some other field of endeavor. This syndrome is not unusual among people who deal with death. Generally, however, it involves only a temporary rejection of the work ethic rarely lasting more than a few months, with a mean projection of 1.7 months. This is not the case with Mancuso. The rejection syndrome has developed over the past five months and shows no sign of abating. The only conclusion possible is that an important social or emotional factor in the subject's life has not been programmed, or has been programmed inadequately, into this Psychoprofile Series J. This factor, for example, might be the death or terminal illness of someone in Mancuso's immediate family (negative), or an association with a woman on such an emotional level as to deepen his sense of the work-ethic rejection past the point of remediable recovery. There is no evidence of any such current important male-female relationship.

Probability that Mancuso may be considering defection to any foreign governments or agencies: 0.02%.

## CONCLUSION:

Notwithstanding the above, the subject, Edward Mancuso, is determined to leave the service of the Colonial Squad, and within ninety days will apply for early retirement.

Indicated possibility of error in this prognosis: 3.2%.

"What a bullshit number," said Romeo Arteaga. Although he had begun before the others, he was the last to finish reading.

Colonel Parker raised his eyebrows, but spoke quietly. "Do you mean the machine's conclusion?"

"Come on, Colonel. We know that CYBER doesn't make mistakes. At least, the old witch hasn't done it yet. I mean Mancuso. What kind of crap does he think he's pulling? His kind of classification doesn't retire. Not in my time, anyway. Not ever. He knew that when he signed on."

Erikson nodded. "Indeed he did. If CYBER hasn't gone ape—which I think we all agree is not very likely —then our Eddie is being a very foolish little boy. With what he knows, he can't walk away. No one can."

"Exactly," Kelly said. "So Romeo is right. Mancuso's no great thinker, but he's not *that* stupid. He knows he can't get away with it. He's got to know."

"Correct. He's not that stupid." The colonel nodded smugly, blue eyes glittering with knowledge. "But he *does* think he can get away with it. Read on and be enlightened. There's a second stage to the printout."

15

As he spoke, the printers started up again, noiseless, calm, probing like a fine scalpel in the hands of a surgeon into the mind of Edward Mancuso.

And while all this went on, the subject cavorted under a sky gray and gritty, playing half-court basketball, two on two, in the schoolyard of P.S. 184, five blocks from his apartment, with three black kids who called one another Martin, Luther, and King. All of these dudes under fourteen, and each has at least three inches in height on Eddie Mancuso, but does that bother Eddie? Certainly not, for Eddie isn't far from the generation that venerated backcourt men—Hy Gotkin of St. Johns, Sid Tannenbaum of NYU: the little guys, the movers and the doers, the guys who got things going in the days before the giants like Wilt and Jabbar stalked the courts. Move, Eddie, move—and Eddie moves, *slap,* taking the pass from Luther backcourt, dribbling, slowly, easily, dancing in his Adidas, giving King half a fake and then taking it back. Luther in the bucket, waiting, nothing fancy, give and . . . *go,* breaking right and charging, jumping and turning on the jump, empty hands clutching, *slap,* it's there, and up—and in! *Two points.*

Good this way, working up the sweat, working out the hate and confusion, because there's a lot of both up there in his head, waves of them rolling around inside, and he's thinking, I've got to get out, got to, got to, *slap,* and fake, and move, and *shit,* right out of my hands! How'd that happen? But they'll never let me do it, never, the bastards, never. On my ass for twenty years, Eddie do this, Eddie do that, Eddie we need a grenade the size of a watch—*cut, Luther, cut!* —way to go, kid! Can do, Eddie? Sure, Eddie can do. Eddie can do it all. Extract a guy from a locked room? Sure, pin-size flechette through the keyhole. *Adios,* General. Bastards don't think I know where they used that one. Blow away some dude while he's driving his car? Certainly, Colonel. Make and model, please. Martin, your feet are too big for your head. Like this, see? Left, and right, and up, and in. *Two more.*

Sure, Eddie can do it, but what happens when Eddie wants out? Twenty years, Christ on a crutch, that's enough, isn't it? Twenty years of mangled flesh, and blood, and broken bones—never saw them, but I know what that stuff does—if anyone knows, man, *I* know—and it's time to get out. Sure, get out. Just try it. Pass, Luther, pass. *Damn!* Just try telling that one to the colonel. Think he'll let you walk away with what you know? Be nice, wouldn't it? Just give you a gold watch and say, Thanks for the twenty years, Eddie. The hell they will. They'll blow you away like a puff of smoke, like all the other puffs of smoke you helped to blow. And they'll be sorry, too. No one better than me. Sorry, Eddie, but that's the way it is. There's no retirement for guys like you. You knew that when you made the contract. Sorry, Eddie. *Adios*, Eddie. Damn, but that King has quick hands. . . .

So you're stuck. There's no way out. One, and two, and *cut*. Stuck for the rest of your life. How many years? That's too long. Except that there is. A way. Out. Oh? You know there is. You've always known it, haven't you? But you're too fucking chicken to think about it, much less do it. *Up*, Luther, *up!* You can make the machines, all right, but do you have the balls to use them? How many, five? Who else knows? Not at Langley. They keep their hands clean at Langley. Yeah, five? it would have to be all of them. Only five. *Only?* All or nothing. Christ, you're actually thinking about it now. Good boy! All right, so it's out in the open. The five of them. The O Group. Hell, it's crazy. A job like that? All five. You? Me? Could it? *Break left*, and up, and in. *Two more.* Could it work? I mean . . .? Sure it could. Sure. Maybe.

### POST CONCLUSION ANALYSIS:

Having concluded that the subject, Edward Mancuso, is determined to retire from the service, his further course of action must now be analyzed.

Given the subject's reasonable intelligence, and his understanding of Agency procedure over a twenty-year period, he is certain to realize that he will not be allowed

17

to retire. His next logical assumption will be that in order to sever his connection with the service he will have to extract the entire top level of the Colonial Squad; in short, the O Group. This assumption stands up under examination. Of Agency officers still alive and on active service, only O Group members have had direct contact with the subject. No one outside of O Group, Colonial Squad, is aware of his function within the Agency. All records of contracts made with the subject, and payments made to the subject, are coded within CYBER and are available only to O Group members. Further, in the event of the elimination of the entire O Group, that part of these coded records dealing with Mancuso would be meaningless to any untrained successor. Therefore, logically, Mancuso must eliminate the entire O Group.

Subject's positive and negative factors relative to this Post-Conclusion Analysis:

Negative: 1) Despite his knowledge of the field, he is not and has never been an active field agent.

2) He is unaware of this Psychoprofile Series J updated and its conclusions.

Positive: 1) His expertise and experience in the production of UKD's, and his pride in his technology, will lead him—after a brief period of indecision—to disregard negative factor #1.

2) He is in excellent physical health, and is theoretically—repeat, theoretically—able to perform many of the functions of a trained field agent.


CONCLUDING ANALYSIS:

Probability that subject will attempt the elimination of the entire O Group: 94.7%

Probability of success: 26.4%


All five men finished reading the conclusion at roughly the same time. An awkward, troubled silence followed, as they stacked and shuffled papers, cleared throats, scratched an ear absently, and reached for cigarettes. Erikson broke the spell.

"Like I said. Dirty little Eddie. My boy! I was like an uncle to him."

"He never liked you," Colonel Parker said flatly. Erikson just grunted. He knew it was true.

*"Hijo de la gran puta,"* said Arteaga. "It doesn't seem possible. It's not even funny."

"CYBER is a lady of great breeding." The colonel spread his hands. "A fourth-generation computer would never lie."

Rakow whistled softly. "Twenty-six percent. It's insulting. It makes us look like a bunch of punks."

"It should be zero," Kelly agreed. "The insulting part is that it's Eddie Mancuso. I mean, it's ridiculous. Maybe he killed a mosquito once. Maybe."

The colonel held up his hand for silence, and got it.

"Gentlemen, let's forget about the personalities for the moment. Concentrate on the situation. We all know what Eddie is and isn't. He may be untrained, but he's a genius with UKD's, and he's after our scalps —or will be soon. The machine says the odds are three to one that he can't do it. Is anyone here willing to accept those odds?"

His answer was a negative rumble. Erikson came right to the point. "But CYBER's analysis makes the odds inoperative, doesn't it? Because now we know."

"Then the next move is mandatory," the colonel continued, nodding at Erikson, pleased. One of his great professional attributes was that he never repeated the obvious, even if it came from someone else. "Immediate extraction. Equally mandatory is that the assignment must be kept within this room. I don't want this bungled by some outsider, and there's no need-to-know for Langley."

Erikson asked softly, "Are you asking for volunteers, Colonel? If you are, then I think you have four of them, willing and eager. That little prick."

Arteaga quickly reached into his pocket and brought out his lucky silver dollar. "Toss a coin? Cut cards?"

"Neither," said the colonel. "I'm assigning this mission." He looked directly at Kelly. "You've been in the field most recently. He's yours. I've cleared you for the lab all afternoon. You know what's available."

Kelly nodded, unsurprised. "How much time do I have?"

Colonel Parker laughed. It was not a pleasing sound. "Kelly, even though that probability was only twenty-six point four, we'll all sleep better if you can get this over within twenty-four hours. Take the evening plane to New York."

# 3

Five thousand miles east of Williamsburg, in the cold, snowy, but pleasant country village of Zhukovka, another colonel, but wearing the uniform of the Soviet KGB, held another computer printout in his hands. He stared angrily at the final figure as if staring could change it or make it disappear.

"Twenty-three point seven percent. Incredible."

"Can there be an error in the probability factor?" asked Major Marchenko.

The tall, thin colonel frowned severely.

"Major, if you think our procurement division has gone to the extraordinary trouble, the expense—and, I might add, the indignity!—of acquiring a computer manufactured in the United States of America, of which not more than thirty exist today even in the West, and if you think that such a computer can then err ... !"

The colonel left his sentence unfinished. One of his slender hands rested almost paternally on the steely gray flank of CYBER. Major Marchenko shrugged.

"The figure is accurate," said the colonel sharply. "And so are the facts. I suggest you read them once again."

Vasily Borgneff
### POST-CONCLUSION ANALYSIS

Having concluded that the subject, Vasily Borgneff, is determined to retire from the service of the Fourth Division of the Second Directorate of the KGB, his further course of action must now be analyzed.

Posit One: The subject 'is a highly intelligent man, a graduate of the Moscow Institute, and a holder of the Order of Lenin (privately awarded).

Posit Two: Having been a serving officer of the KGB for twenty-four years, he is fully aware of Bureau procedure.

Posit Three: Given the first two positions, he is certain to realize that he will not be allowed to retire.

Posit Four: His next logical assumption will be that in order to sever his connection with the Bureau safely, he will have to eliminate the entire top level of Section Nine (now known as the *dachniki*).

Posit Five: He will feel confident of his ability to accomplish this mission in view of his reputation as one of the finest designers in the world of unusual killing devices (UKD's), a reputation exceeded only by that of the American, Edward Mancuso (see file DIVER-77/4).

Posit Six: Subject will be aided in his attempt by the fact that he is now outside the borders of the Soviet Union on a buying mission in Switzerland. Thus, he is not available for immediate apprehension.

Posit Seven: Only members of the Five Group presently have direct contact with the subject. No one outside the Five Group is fully aware of his function within the Bureau. Therefore, Borgneff must eliminate the entire group of five officers in order to survive.

### ANALYSIS:

That subject will attempt the elimination of the entire Five Group: 96.2%

Probability of success: 23.7%

Major Marchenko smoothed the crisp paper of the printout and laid it beside him on the broad desk behind which the colonel sat in his black leather swivel chair. Outside, it had begun to snow again in Zhukovka.

It was easy to understand why for years the Soviet elite had been drawn to Zhukovka. Only twenty-five

22

miles southwest of Moscow, the village perched high on a bluff overlooking the gently flowing Moskva River. The pine groves that surrounded it were rich and resinous, with needle-packed floors, and at the end of the day the light in the sky was the off-white glow of the northern sunset, peculiarly Russian in quality. Stalin had established his *dacha,* or country home, there; so had Khrushchev and, after him, Brezhnev, Kosygin, and Andrei Gromyko. The *dacha* was the first of many status symbols that distinguished the privileged *nomenklatura* from the average Soviet citizen, and to have a *dacha* at Zhukovka was to have a seat at the feet of the communist gods.

Not far from Brezhnev's compound was a long, low *dacha* surrounded by the type of high green fence that Russians learn from childhood to avoid with care. Citizens in the area, most of them members of the Party and the ruling class, had also learned to ignore the unusual number of Zil and Chaika limousines that passed into the grounds daily, the unusual number of stolid-faced servants on duty there, and the odd fact that there was no registered owner or resident for such an impressive building. For in the Soviet Union when property belonged to no one it belonged to the state, and in the case of the *dacha* at Zhukovka the state meant the KGB—more specifically, the Fourth Division of the Second Directorate of Soviet Intelligence.

This division of the KGB had existed under many names, as befitted one of the oldest departments in Soviet espionage. Created by Dzerzhinsky to liquidate the enemies of the Revolution, it had become Stalin's personal instrument for ridding himself of his opponents within the government. During World War II under the name of Bureau One, and at times under the name of SMERSH, it had carried out the scorched-earth policy in the face of advancing German troops. Later, the section of the division responsible for state-sanctioned kidnapping and murder had been renamed Section Nine. In more recent times, when the section was removed from the main KGB headquarters in Moscow's Lubyanka Building to the relative anonymity of the *dacha* at Zhukovka, its members had become known colloquially as the *dachniki*—the boys from the *dacha*.

The meeting of the *dachniki* at Zhukovka bore more than a passing resemblance to the meeting of the Colonial Squad at Williamsburg. Even the physical arrangements were the same. The exterior of the country estate was of conventional stone-and-timber construction; but, as in Virginia, the interior was a maze of corridors, offices, and laboratories. The subsurface division was also similar: two levels beneath the earth serviced by an elevator, and at the lowest level the computer plant and printout room.

The five KGB officers in the printout room had normal Russian names, patronymics, and surnames, but just as Vladimir Ilyich Ulyanov had chosen to be called Lenin and Josef Vissarionovich Dzhugashvili had chosen the harsh name of Stalin, the tall, thin, dark-haired officer in charge of Section Nine was traditionally known as Colonel Fist. The other four were Major Boris Marchenko, Captains Pyotr Suvarov and Igor Durin, and Lieutenant Yuri Krasin. Their ranks were meaningless. Either of the captains outranked any full colonel in the Red Army, and Major Marchenko, with a scrawl of his signature, could have ordered the clandestine assassination of an admiral in the Soviet Navy—and in fact, in 1975, upon reading a section from one admiral's secret memoirs dictated to his wife, had done precisely that.

The power of Colonel Fist was virtually unlimited. He was in charge of murder in the Soviet Union.

All eyes were on the slender colonel now as he shook his head in exasperation and tapped the printout that Marchenko had dropped on the table. Looking directly at Marchenko with his angry charcoal eyes, the colonel said, "Boris, this is *your* man. You've been controlling Vasily Borgneff, if you can call it that. So you will kindly tell me if you are responsible for allowing him to leave the Soviet Union at a time like this."

Marchenko returned the look calmly. A powerful, straw-haired man in his early forties, he had the perfectly chiseled features of a Russian film star and the bland blue eyes of a calculating killer. He was a man not easily intimidated, not even by Colonel Fist.

"Borgneff has been abroad a few dozen times. He has money. He likes women and he likes to ski. He considers himself above most rules. We've allowed that. You know him almost as well as I do, Colonel. And, in addition, he left five days ago." Marchenko tapped the printout himself with a thick forefinger. "Five days before the existence of *this.*"

"Yes, all right." The colonel was more annoyed at himself than at Marchenko, for he considered himself a man who overlooked nothing. He should have known. Sighing, he turned to Captain Suvarov.

"Find out where he is now."

Suvarov, the oldest of the group at fifty, a plump, bespectacled, mild-looking man with a mind only slightly slower than a second-generation computer, pressed a button on a gray telephone. He spoke softly for a few minutes, then waited. The entire room waited with him. No one spoke. Durin smoked nervously and let the ashes fall from his cigarette to the floor. Marchenko hummed absently, a melody from an American musical comedy he had seen recently in London. Colonel Fist drummed his long fingers lightly on the table and then shoved an ashtray across to Durin. Finally, with a grunt, Suvarov hung up the telephone.

"He finished his business in Zurich yesterday. He bought certain chemicals. Nothing unusual—for Borgneff, that is to say. He told our office in Zurich that he was taking the rest of the week off for a skiing holiday. He is in Grindelwald now, skiing."

"And plotting how to kill us," Durin muttered, grinding out his cigarette.

"No, not yet." Once again, the colonel nodded at the computer printout from CYBER. "If that is correct, and we shall assume it is, the thought has only passed through his mind and has yet to find purchase there. Before it takes hold of him, gentlemen, I suggest we end this unfortunate matter and grant Comrade Borgneff's wish for an early retirement. I know your dossiers, but I don't follow you like a bloodhound. We will keep this little matter in the family, so to speak. Kindly tell me, who among you skis well?"

Four hands shot into the air.

"All right, then, who skis expertly?"

Only Suvarov lowered his hand, shrugging. The others stayed casually erect.

"Very well, who skis the best? I don't need heroics and I don't require any gestures of faith. I am asking a question of fact."

Major Marchenko's hand came down immediately, followed then, reluctantly, by Durin's. Lieutenant Yuri Krasin's hand stayed up. He was a ruddy-faced, cheerful-looking man of thirty-six. At the age of nineteen he had assassinated an African premier with a single shot from an SVD Dragunov rifle at a range of six hundred yards, and more recently, he had set a charge aboard a light plane at Vladivostok Airport that caused the mysterious death of three visiting members of the Peking government as well as the Russian flight crew. Now, Yuri Krasin was grinning.

"He's all yours, then," the colonel said decisively. "Major Marchenko will brief you more fully about Borgneff. Captain Durin will arrange transport and whatever else you might need. Get to Moscow this evening and take the first available civilian transport. Travel as an American. Bureau Six will provide the usual papers—Suvarov, see to that, please. And, Krasin—"

"Sir?"

"Make it look like an accident, please, In Switzerland, Comrade Borgneff is known as a distinguished Soviet chemist. A messy death would almost certainly cause a conscientious inquiry. You know the Swiss. An accident, then. A skiing accident would be most appropriate."

# 4

Vasily Borgneff was a happy man. He was happy as he came booming off the outrun of the Faulhorn crouched low over his skis and riding the washboard undulations smoothly, his thighs and ankles happily aching, his ears atune to the happy hiss of snow. He raised up from his crouch and clicked his skis from side to side, slowing himself, working himself into the pattern of colorfully dressed skiers lazily cruising round the chairlift station and the warming hut. A girl cut across his path, poling rapidly, the sleek crimson of her trousers stretched tight to display the chalice of her hips and thighs. He didn't know the girl, but the momentary sight and image brought another girl to his mind, and he decided that he would call her. Tonight? Why not? The thought made him smile, and he was doubly happy. Poling leisurely, he skated on the hard-packed snow toward the warming hut, the thought of tea filling him: hot, strong lemon tea with, perhaps, the one cognac he allowed himself in a day of skiing. The thought of the tea made him even more content. Then he saw Yuri Krasin.

I'm dead, he thought. I'm truly dead.

Muscles flashed messages. His left ankle bent and his right heel slipped over in the beginnings of a move that would turn him away. The movement was in-

27

stinctive. Twenty-four years of service in the world's largest intelligence organization had taught him to disbelieve entirely in coincidence. For Yuri Krasin to suddenly pop out of the snow like an anemone in springtime, dashingly dressed and with shiny new skis on his shoulder, could only mean that he had come to kill.

Me, he thought. They know. I don't know how, but they know. And I'm dead.

But he never completed the turn. Ankle and heel relaxed as he saw the smile on Krasin's face no more than twenty feet away, the killer's face split in a warm and welcoming smile, the friendly arms outstretched, and the voice booming out in perfect Midwest American, "Hey, old buddy, howya been?"

No point in flight. Vasily changed the movement to a turn that brought the two men face to face. He slowed to a stop and looked around him. He was surrounded by skiers busily crisscrossing over the snow, indifferent to the two of them, yet he felt naked and exposed. He had never before met another agent this way: openly, casually, unexpectedly. His insides felt weak and loose, but he knew the words he had to say.

"What are you doing? . . . What is this?" he whispered harshly. "This is against all procedure."

"Not at all, calm yourself," said Krasin in an easy, natural voice. "Something has come up, an emergency. We need your advice in a hurry."

"How did you find me here?"

"The Zurich people. You told them."

"Yes, I did," he admitted, his brain whirling wildly, thinking, Yes, I told them, but the rest is *merde,* and the emergency is *merde.* He's here for extraction. That's his job. He's no courier.

"Take off your skis and let's go someplace where we can talk," said Krasin.

I'm all right here, Vasily thought, bending over to release his bindings. He can't use anything conventional; he has to make an accident. He can't use a gas out here because of the wind, and I'm safe from a spray if I keep his hands in sight. Watch his hands and stay away from anything sharp. And think. Think—my God, I don't even have a pocketknife on me. The most lethal instrument I have is a screwdriver.

He straightened up and put his skis on his shoulder. Together the two men walked to the warming hut and locked their skis into the rack against the outside wall. New Head skis with Samco safety bindings, Vasily noted. The swine, I'll bet he keeps them. A nice bonus for a job like this.

"Where do we go?" he asked.

"Anyplace out here where we can talk safely."

"I want some tea." He knew that he sounded like a small boy complaining.

"Later, after we have talked. Come."

They walked aimlessly over the snow, slapping gloved hands together, stooping at times to stamp their feet like horses in stalls. They walked without conversation for a while. Vasily wondered if breaking the silence would seem like a weakness and decided to wait. Eventually, Krasin said:

"It's an unusual job. That's why we need your advice."

"I'm listening."

"And not just because you're our man on UKD's. There's that, of course, but it's also because you are a skier as well."

"I beg your pardon?"

Krasin grinned at him. "I said it was unusual. You see, we have to take out a man on a ski slope. A place like this. And it has to look like an accident, a skiing accident. You understand?"

Do I understand? Mother of God, he's asking me to plan my own execution.

Keeping his voice steady, he said aloud, "I understand. You're right—it's an unusual job. Does it have to be an accident?"

"Absolutely. Untraceable."

"Can you tell me more? Where and when?"

"You know better than that." Krasin's smile was patronizing. The specialist was never told operational details.

"I see." Vasily rubbed his chin thoughtfully. "No weapons, no gases. How about toxics?"

"Too risky."

"How about heavy metal? Just a drop in his ski boot and three months later he's gone."

Krasin, irritated, said, "You haven't been listening. It has to happen on the ski slope and it has to be immediate."

"Of course. I'm sorry. I'll have to think about this one," he said, and then thought, I have to get him inside and then I need five minutes free. Less—three minutes will do. "How about that tea? I can think just as well sitting down. Better, in fact."

Krasin nodded. "Tea would be good. Remember, no discussion inside."

"Of course."

Inside the warming hut, the odors rose in layers to challenge the tiers of smoke: wet wool and perspiration, beer, tobacco, and tea. They found a tiny table near the door, collected mugs of tea from the counter, and drank it Western style, stirring in sugar and sipping delicately. Krasin wrinkled his nose to show what he thought of the brew.

"Just like Mother used to make," he said sarcastically.

Vasily stood up. "I'm having another. Shall I get you more?"

"Better than nothing. No, I'll come with you."

Cautious, thought Vasily. Not taking any chances on lethal drops in his tea—and if I only had some on me I'd use them. Even chloral hydrate would do.

After the second mug of tea, Krasin looked pointedly at his watch. "Time is passing. Have you thought about the problem?"

"Yes. I have the beginnings of an idea," said Vasily, thinking, I have one hell of an idea and all I need is three minutes away from you. Have some more tea, Yuri. What are you, a machine? Standing out in the cold all morning, and now two big mugs of tea. Don't you ever have to piss? Come on, Yuri, for the

30

glory of the Party and and the Workers' State. Come on, Krasin, go and piss.

"More tea?" Vasily suggested.

"Not for me. If you have an idea, we should go outside and discuss it."

The son of a bitch has a cast-iron bladder, Vasily thought. I'm cooked now, finished.

"All right, let's go," he said. He stood up.

Krasin stood up with him, started for the door, and then stopped. "Nature calls. Wait for me outside," he said, and added sternly, "Don't wander."

"Never fear."

Never fear, comrade; just take a long, relaxed piss and give me three minutes with your skis. Even two.

He was out the door and down the rack of skis, searching, one hand already in the kit at his belt . . . oil, bandages, where? . . . yes, screwdriver, there . . . now where the devil are they? . . . new Heads with Samco bindings . . . *there.* Rate of spring on the Samco something more than a hundred—but that's psi: makes it how much? Multiply by 70.31 into grams per centimeter, say 742—makes it? . . . how are these damn screws set, counter or clockwise? . . . *there* . . . makes it how much? Drop it by half; no, a little more—don't want him walking right out of them. Two turns clockwise does it . . . *there,* and *there.* Screwdriver back. Done. Time? One minute fifty.

He was standing with his own skis on his shoulder and a show of impatience on his face when Krasin came out the door and down the line.

"Why the skis?" asked Krasin.

"It would be easier to demonstrate my idea on the mountain than to explain it."

"Excellent. Business with pleasure."

He wants to go up, thought Vasily. That's where he wants me, and that's where he'll make his move.

Aloud, he asked, "How well do you ski? How high shall we we go?"

Krasin said proudly, "I was first in my course."

Yes, you bastard. KGB Training School Number 311 in Novosibirsk. First in the course, were you?

31

Good. I don't want you slow and sloppy, I want you fast and hot.

"Fine. If you're that good we can go to the top of the lift."

They rode side by side on the double chairlift, rising through the ground mist that still had not been burned away, breaking out of the mist and into the cold, bright sun at fifteen hundred meters, with the snow and the trees far below them. Gaily colored figures dotted the snow, curving and cavorting, and far below and to the right the perpetual snow plume blew from the top of the Eiger. They passed the first station, riding on, their skis lifted clear of the landing stage, and then they were up and rising again, the valley below shrinking to a checkerboard of green and white. Far to their left, like a piece of white paper folded to a sharp edge and then crumpled and thrown on a table, was the razorback outline of the Devil's Ridge. Vasily nudged Krasin, and pointed to it.

"The Devil's Ridge, comrade," he said in Russian. "Can you see it?"

"We are all alone, but speak in English." Krasin frowned. "Yes, I can see it. What of it?"

"A very dangerous piece of terrain. For experts only." Vasily screwed up his voice into an apologetic whine. "I know it is forbidden to ask certain questions, but I must know two things."

"Ask."

"May I assume that the target is an expert skier?"

He could not be sure, but it seemed that Krasin, under goggles and scarf, was grinning slightly. "Yes, you may assume that. What else?"

"Only as far as location. May I assume that the mountain in question will contain a piece of terrain generally similar to the Devil's Ridge?"

Now he was sure of it. Krasin was grinning broadly. "Yes, Vasily Ivanovich, why not? We can arrange it. You may assume that."

"Good. In that case my plan may have some merit."

They left the chairlift at the top station and skied

around the terminal to the left, dropping down and through a tight whip that brought them out onto a gentle trail that edged a meadow of snow. They skied roughly in tandem with Vasily always in front, forcing himself to ski loosely, easily, and telling himself: Stay in front, stay in front. Don't drop back. When he sees you in front he feels safe. Stay up.

Past the meadow the trail dipped down again, and they ran more rapidly now—still not pushing, just swinging with the hill. Then they topped a rise, and below them was the Devil's Ridge. Vasily turned into his stop slowly, slowly, praying that Krasin would do the same. Then the two men stood together viewing the terrain below.

The ridge was a simple drop of two hundred meters connecting two plateaus, a sheer and murderous strip of snow no more than ten feet wide at any point. On either side the ridge fell away into perpendicular ravines. Along these sides the guides had planted pitons in the rock supporting long red flags that marked the acceptable limits of danger. The wind whipped the flags in a frenzied arabesque.

"Red flags," said Vasily. "Appropriate."

"Indeed."

"Frightening, isn't it?"

Krasin grunted. "I've skied worse."

"No doubt you have." Vasily pointed below with a ski pole. "You see how the terrain lies. Only one man can ski it at a time. Or two men in tandem. But not two side by side. Agreed?"

"That's obvious."

"Very well, then. I'm going to make a demonstration. Let us assume that you are the hunter and I am the target. Is that acceptable?"

"Pardon. Did you say that you would play the part of the target?" Krasin fought not to show his surprise.

"Exactly. Now, will your target be armed?"

"I don't think so."

"That's excellent. Neither am I. To continue. I will be the target and I will start first. You will follow immediately after, attempting to overtake me. You will follow every move I make, every turn. Since we are of roughly equal ability, I should be able to stay ahead. Then, at some point along the ridge—I'm not quite sure where yet—I will stop. You will stop also. I will then demonstrate how it will be possible to extract the target so that it looks like nothing more than a tragic accident. Agreed?"

Very casually, Krasin asked, "You'll be ahead of me at all times?"

"You wouldn't want your target behind you, would you? If the man were the least bit aware . . ."

Krasin laughed. "Go ahead then. I'll follow."

I've got him, thought Vasily. The bastard is so intent on killing that he can't see or feel anything else. He's sure of me now; he can smell the meat. He's got me all set up to tumble over the side of that ridge whenever he feels like giving the shove. God, how he must be laughing inside. I set myself up for him and he's having a hard time keeping down the giggles.

And then without allowing himself to think any further he pushed himself over the top of the rise, poled twice deeply, and within ten feet was flying down the spine of the ridge, knees bent and body tucked into a racing crouch. Behind him he heard a grunt as Krasin took off after him, and then he had time only to concentrate on the red flags flashing by, counting their number. Jig right, jig left, the snow hard and firm under his skis, the wind a cutting edge at his nose. Eighteen, nineteen, flag twenty; no way to look back to see if Yuri is following closely, but he has to be, has to, wants to be close, ready to kill. Thirty-five, thirty-six; I hope you're as good as you say you are, Yuri—a real *kanone;* hard and fast, coming up now, forty-eight, forty-nine, fifty, *now.*

At the fiftieth flag he slammed on the brakes, side-slipped right to square with the fall line, and, still crouched close to the snow, dug his edges in to hold. It was a hard, fast check, not too difficult for a top-notch skier, and behind him he heard Yuri grunt as he made the same motion, went into the turn.

Yuri's skis made the turn. Yuri didn't. His safety

bindings, set to pop loose and free his feet at one hundred and seven pounds of pressure, now popped at only fifty-eight. The skis went one way and Yuri went another, the only way he could go: pitching headfirst over the line of red banners, rolling once before he reached the edge, and now dragging his skis by their safety straps after him; rolled once more in a jumble of metal and flesh that turned into a pinwheel tumbling over the side and plummeting down to the stark rocks below.

He screamed once. *Y-y-y-y-y-y-y.* And then he was gone.

Vasily peered after him. He could see nothing, hear nothing.

"That's the way, Yuri," he said softly. *"That's* how you would do it."

Vasily shivered. He felt something rise within him, and he fought it down. It was the first time in his life that he had ever personally killed a man.

But not the last, he told himself. They're after me, and I've got to get out, and the only way I can do it is to eliminate all five of them. Four of them now. Goodbye, Yuri. I wonder if you could have been telling me the truth. Doubtful, very doubtful. And of no significance, because I made the decision a few days ago, and you were on the list. I've just shortened the odds.

Whatever revulsion he had felt at first was gone now, vanished as if it had never existed. How easy it was, he thought. How simple.

But then he shivered again. The rest would not be simple, and it was a task he could not possibly accomplish alone. Anyway, not if I want to live through it, and spend my declining years playing Gauguin, painting brown-skinned girls some decadent Micronesian island. He smiled at this vision.

No, not alone. That decision had been made.

He straightened up, sweating and shivering in the icy wind. He skied the rest of the Devil's Ridge slowly and carefully, but when he came to the far plateau he picked up speed and began the quickest possible descent of the mountain. At the bottom, in the parking lot, he slung his skies and poles onto the rack of the rented Opel and drove quickly to his hotel. In his room he drank three fingers of neat vodka, showered, changed his clothes, and drank another three fingers while the hotel switchboard put through his call to Washington.

"Chalice," he said when she answered—"do you know who this is?"

"Yes, of course." As always, she was calm.

"I must be brief. Have there been any changes in your traveling plans?"

"None. I'm going north tonight to meet—"

"Your other friend," he interjected quickly.

"And then south tomorrow, together."

"The same country? The same places?"

"But you knew all that. Why do you ask? My sophisticated darling, are you finally jealous?"

He laughed grimly. "Not at all. Something unforeseen has happened."

"Something bad. I can tell from your voice."

"Well, that depends." He thought for a moment. "Do you know what I mean when I say the place of the pyramid?"

She was silent, while the transatlantic cable crackled with distant voices. Then, "There are several."

"The magical one."

"Yes, now I know."

"Good. Now listen carefully." He gave her instructions in terse sentences. He said several very serious things, and then some mildly sentimental things as well. He mentioned no names of places or people. When the instructions were finished, he asked, "Are you sure you understand everything?"

"Perfectly."

"One thing more. Your friend should be very careful right now. Very careful indeed."

"In what way?"

"The most important way."

"Am I to tell him that?"

"Certainly not. I mentioned it for your benefit only. Don't get in the way."

36

He said goodbye, hung up, packed his two bags and took them down to the car himself. He removed his skis and poles from the car and locked them into the hotel's rack on the porch. He said farewell to them regretfully. He went inside, paid his bills, left his tips, and pulled away from the hotel less than forty minutes after he had arrived there from the slopes.

Three hours later, he left the offices of the Crédit Suisse on the Paradeplatz in Zurich and went by taxi to the railroad station. He traveled second class to Milan, sitting up all night with two drunken Italian wine salesmen and two chattering American girls from Oklahoma City, and by the time he reached Milan's Malpensa Airport he was weary and red-eyed. Using a Canadian passport, paying in cash with Canadian dollars, he bought a first-class ticket to Mexico City by way of Madrid and Montreal. The 747 was only half full. He explained to the stewardess that he did not want to be disturbed for the movie.

Vasily raised the armrests, stretched out, swallowed a pill, and was soon asleep. He slept easily and without dreams, waking at intervals of several hours. At Montreal's Mirabel Airport he had to disembark. Aboard again, he swallowed another pill.

The final time he awoke, completely refreshed, he saw the snowcapped peak of Popocatepetl through the haze of smog that covered the Mexican plateau.

**5**

Garbage cans clanked in the alley, an oil truck ground through its gears, tires swished on pavement; all these early-morning New York sounds drifted up through the cold February air. In the warmth of his fifth-floor apartment, Eddie Mancuso sat cross-legged on the living-room carpet checking his diving equipment. Eddie heard none of the early-morning sounds. His drifting mind was victim to the nagging unease that had preyed upon it for so long.

All right—so you made your decision and now you've got to make it work. But how? All five of them. How? Think. No, don't. No thinking now. Thinking time starts tomorrow on the beach at Cozumel with Chalice lying there beside you. Christ, I need this. A week of relaxing and diving, and then maybe I can figure this out while I show her Chankanab Lagoon, and then the ruins . . . Palenque, Uxmal, Chichén-Itzá. Maybe then, but not now. Right now all I've got to do is get the two of us on that plane this afternoon. After that there'll be time for thinking.

Although his mind was drifting, he handled the equipment carefully, thoughtfully, with an almost tender touch, refusing to compromise on this one simple and necessary task he had set for himself before the girl awoke. The Scubapro fins, mask, and swivel snorkel were in fine shape; good enough for years to come, for he bought only what he believed to be the best. He inhaled the deep, satisfying smell of good rubber. He inspected the shiny MR12-11 regulator and then, admiring its workmanship and tolerances as only a craftsman could, stuffed it into the big orange dive bag. Then came the pressure and depth gauges, weight belt, wet suit, neoprene boots, modular light, dive knife and sheath, spear gun, the Nikonos and six rolls of Ektachrome, the wrap-around Calypso Compensator and harness.

That task completed, he began a check of Chalice's equipment. Everything passed inspection except the BC vest. It was old and threadbare, dating back to a time before he had known her. Christ, it's practically falling apart, he thought. We get attached to these things and we forget when it's time to throw them away. Then the old reliable pops and lets you down. She'll have to get another one in Mexico.

Then he grinned in sudden decision. Over the past three years there had been precious few chances to buy anything for Chalice. She was very much her own woman, had money of her own, and disliked being gifted. But this was a question of need. There was plenty of time before the plane, and a new Calypso wraparound was a present she could hardly object to.

There was enough time to clear away two brandy snifters, wash and dry them, and return the bottle of Rémy to the bar. Looking around the living room, he decided that it was a great pad and that he was going to miss it. Some good women had crossed the threshold, and no one had ever asked for the complaint book. Least of all me, he thought, and especially not now, not with what's fast asleep in the bedroom. Crazy, wild, but it works, and that's what counts. If it keeps on working, I could stick with this one for a stretch. Tahiti, Bali . . . why not? Dive the Truk Lagoon. *If I get out, if I can do it.* The thought came back to burn him like a match held too long between the fingers.

He went to the closet where his suits hung. He bought them at either Brooks Brothers or Barney's, the choice having nothing to do with the price. It had to do only with whether he felt that day like Eddie Mancuso from Avenue B or Edward J. Mancuso, Director, Manhattan Security Research Systems, Inc. which was what his business card declared. Most of the time it didn't matter. He wore his suits when he went out to dinner or down to Williamsburg for conferences. The rest of the time he wore a duffel coat or a windbreaker, depending on the season, and a pair of jeans faded by wear, not by some Village boutique.

He parted the suits with one hand and with the other slipped a steel key into an almost invisible keyhole in the wood paneling at the back of the closet. The paneling, a metal door with a plywood sheath, swung open smoothly, and he flicked a light switch. Banks of fluorescent tubes illuminated the miniature laboratory, the glassware and burners, the racks of bottles, the cage of white mice, the one lonesome guinea pig, and the busy, buzzing hornets in their plastic nest.

*The laboratory of the mad scientist.* That's what Chalice had named it when he first had shown it to her in a breach of security that would have driven the Colonial Squad up the wall, had they known about it. Not even the Squad itself knew where he did his research. *The laboratory of the mad scientist,* but after the joke she had been deadly serious, wanting to see and understand everything. He had tried to explain as much as he could, but it was hard going. He knew too many things intuitively, and could not articulate them except to other people in the business who spoke his own language. But for all of that, the girl had been an eager listener, and had asked the right sort of questions, her eyes intent and the tip of her tongue working over her lips as he described his wares.

Working quickly and economically, he transferred ether to a gauze pad and killed the mice—a preferable fate to starvation while he was away. He debated over the guinea pig, wondering who might have a use for it. The hornets would survive, and there might be use for them someday. He turned off the light, locked the closet door, and went into the bedroom to look for his Norwegian sweater and heavy gloves. Chalice was a pleasing mound under the electric blanket on the oversize bed, long dark-gold hair swirling on the pillow. He tried to collect the sweater quietly, but she heard the sound of the drawer opening and opened a blurry eye.

"Time to go?" she murmured.

"No, go back to sleep." He bent to kiss her hot cheek. "I'm going out for a while. I'll be back soon."

"Where?"

"Tell you later. It's a surprise."

Both her eyes were open now, less blurred, and she was smiling. She flipped the blanket off her. Her nude body gleamed in the glow of the bedside lamp. "Surprise me now," she said. "Come back to bed."

For a moment he was tempted; then he laughed and said, "When I come back. If there's time."

"Please, Eddie. Now."

He replaced the blanket over her, still laughing. "Later. Go back to sleep now."

He left then, and when she heard the door close and lock she stirred in the bed. She knew that she would not fall back to sleep easily, and she felt a bubble of resentment building. It's not fair, she decided. I wake up feeling all warm, and wet, and all I get is a promise. Maybe later. But I want it now. Not fair, not fair, she repeated, sliding her hands up over her body, relishing the smoothness of her skin. She cupped her breasts and molded them, slid palms over nipples and felt the tactile tissue rise. She knew then that she was going to do it—so unfair to be left that way—and her right hand slid down again from breast to belly to bush, diving fingers first into familiar folds. As the circle of warmth began to spread, she fixed herself on a fantasy, thinking first of Eddie's short, lithe, olive-toned body; and then, the pique of her resentment still with her, she discarded that sight for a vision of Vasily's pale skin and angular grace, his long, narrow cock coming closer and closer, touching her cheek, her lips, her tongue . . .

She was still far from climax when she heard the unmistakable sound of scratching at the front door.

Kelly waited patiently, sitting behind the wheel of the pale-blue Mercury, watching the entrance of the apartment building on East Eighty-second Street. The neighborhood was quiet at that time of the morning. Even the rumble of the traffic from York Avenue was muted. Kelly knew how to wait. To pass the time, he played word games with himself, complicated games involving the letters on license plates. He composed fictional football teams, compiled lists of songs from the Fifties and Sixties, and in extreme times recited to himself the longer poems of Edgar Allan Poe. All this while he watched the entrance to the building and the doorman standing just within the glass doors. He was prepared to wait all day; he had done so in the past. On this particular morning, however, his luck was in. He had been staked out for less than two hours when Eddie Mancuso came out of the building.

He could just be going out for bagels and lox, Kelly thought, and waited.

The doorman stepped out into the street, looking up toward York Avenue. He blew his whistle and waved his arm, hailing a cruising cab. The taxi, on the other side of York, had to wait for the light to change. Then it rolled across the avenue and down the street to stop in front of the building. Mancuso climbed in. The cab rolled away. Kelly grinned happily. That wasn't any bagel-and-lox run. He had the time he needed.

Kelly got out of the car, locked it, and crossed the street. He wore the uniform of an inspector in the New York City Fire Department, and he carried a battered leather briefcase. He stiff-armed the door open before the doorman could get to it, shivering as he passed from the chilly street to the warmth of the lobby.

42

"Nippy today," he said as he came in.

"Yeah." The doorman looked at him incuriously. "So what can I do for you?"

"Malloy, Second Division," said Kelly, and popped out the shield and the ID card with that name on it. Both the tin and the card were legitimate. "I've got some wiring violations to look at. Washing machines on the fourteen floor and the seventh. You have them on every floor?"

"That's right." The doorman rubbed his chin. "That don't mean I let you in, you know? I got to check you out."

"Standard procedure," Kelly said crisply. "Call the Division." He pointed to a telephone number typed on the corner of his ID card. It was in fact the number of the Second Division.

The doorman stared at the number, mumbled it over to himself, and disappeared into a tiny cubicle. Kelly waited with casual ease. He knew exactly what would happen on the other end of the call. There was virtually no limit to the endless chains of interdepartmental cooperation. After a few minutes the doorman came back and returned his card.

"Right you are, Inspector," he said, and waved to the elevator. "It's all yours."

You're damn right it is, thought Kelly, pushing the button.

He took the self-service elevator to the fourteenth floor. He went to the empty laundry room at the end of the corridor and waited there with his usual patience for ten minutes, trying to think of alternative rhymes for "Casey at the Bat." Then he went back to the elevator and took it down to the seventh floor. He did not go to the laundry room. He made for the stairwell instead, racing down two flights to the fifth floor. Out in the corridor he checked the apartments quickly, stopping before the door of apartment 5E. The corridor was empty. He set down the briefcase, took a thin leather case of metal files from an inside pocket, and went to work on the lock.

The scratching sounds from the front door came to Chalice through a fog of self-induced passion, piercing that fog and jarring the image of Vasily Borneff above her, within her, plunging and sliding. Had the scratching come a minute later she would have been too far gone, too far up the erotic curve to have heard them, but she heard them now. Passion froze, and her pumping finger stopped its rhythmic beat. For a moment she lay there, one hand at her breast, the other clamped between her thighs. Then she moved.

She rolled off the bed in a fluid motion, bare feet noiseless on the deep-piled carpet. Three strides took her to the bedroom door, two more to the clothes closet, and then she was inside. In the darkness she felt along the ledge for the strip of steel, the key to the laboratory. Her fingers searched, found it, inserted it by touch, and seconds later she was locked in the lab, shivering in the warm darkness.

Thus secluded, she did not see the front door swing open and Kelly enter. Pistol in hand, he went swiftly through the small apartment checking for occupancy. He checked the living room and the bedroom, the bathroom and all the closets. He checked carefully. Chalice heard the door of the clothes closet open, and then she heard the rustle of the search. She did not hear the sound of the door being closed again. She waited, pondering. Then, slowly and silently, she slid the plywood door open no more than two inches. The closet door was open as well. Her line of sight was narrow but it centered on the carpet just before the front door.

A short, fair-haired man knelt on the carpet facing her. He was dressed oddly, and it took her a moment to realize that he was wearing the uniform of a New York City fireman. An open briefcase lay beside him. From one compartment he took a two-inch canister, green and cylindrical. It looked like the cap of a pen. From another compartment he took a coil of colorless, almost invisible wire. He inserted the tip of the wire into the canister, then, with a firm tug, loosened a small section of the carpeting before the front door. He looped the fine, colorless wire back and forth in a zigzag pattern in front of the door, each loop no more than six inches from the next, burying the wire easily out of sight in the deep pile of the carpet. He opened the door behind him and looked out into the corridor. It was empty. Kneeling again, he snapped a small red button at the head of the canister, then slipped the mechanism under the section of carpet he had loosened. A few carpet tacks had come loose. He took a small hammer from his briefcase and tapped them back into place. Then, with a grunt of satisfaction, he eased himself backward out the open door and shut it.

Chalice, staring in fascination from her hiding place, was unaware that her hand was between her thighs again.

Kelly settled himself once more behind the wheel of the car, turned on the heater and the radio, and waited. On any other type of mission he would have left the scene at once, but this was Eddie Mancuso and he had to be sure. As usual, he waited patiently, playing his games, but also hoping that Eddie would come home soon, soon enough so that after a while he could check the results and then catch the 3:15 plane from LaGuardia back to Williamsburg. Come on, Eddie, he rooted silently, make it quick and I can be home in time for dinner with the kids.

Kelly's luck was still running. No more than half an hour later Eddie bounded out of a taxi carrying a bulky parcel, and vanished with quick, buoyant steps into the lobby of the building.

Kelly grinned his thanks and checked his watch. Ten minutes more, double-check the results, and then head for the airport.

As soon as Eddie twisted his key in the lock and started to swing the front door open with his body weight, he heard Chalice's voice call sharply:

*"Eddie, freeze. Don't come in."*

He froze into total immobility.

"Eddie, is it you?" she called again, this time more shakily.

"Yeah, sure. Who else?" He had not moved an inch. "What is it? Are you okay?"

"I'm all right. Open the door, but don't come in. Do you understand?"

He leaned backward on his heels, then slowly opened the door. He could see Chalice now down the hallway. She wore only a terry-cloth bathrobe, and her face was pale.

"What's the matter?" he said quietly. "Tell me fast."

"I was still in bed . . ." she began, as calmly as she could. She told him then what had happened and what she had seen.

Eddie stood for a few minutes, staring down almost woodenly at the carpet. Death lay beneath it, he knew that. Now that he knew what he was looking for, he saw the faint cylindrical bulge. He gave himself another full minute to work through the possibilities. Then he muttered to himself:

*"Va fongool a barese!* That's one of my gigs. The bastards, they're using my own stuff against me."

And thought, Well, why not? It's the best.

To Chalice, across the space of hallway that separated them, he said, "You saw what he put under the carpet, right? This thing you say looked like the cap of a pen?"

"Yes."

"Tell me what color it was."

"Green."

"You're sure? Not red, or gray?"

"No, green."

"This is important, cupcake. Don't guess. Think about it a minute."

"I don't have to, damn it." She was impatient now. "It was bright green."

"Okay," Eddie said, sighing. "Now do what I tell you. Go back into the lab. In the lower right-hand drawer of the desk, just under the hornets, you'll find a ring of keys. One of those opens the filing cabinet

46

on the far wall. I can't remember which key, you'll have to fiddle around. In the top drawer you'll find two lightweight gas masks. Get them and bring them here, okay?"

Chalice nodded, then disappeared into the closet. He waited, piecing it together, wondering who it had been. The description—short, fair-haired about thirty, very deft—made it sound like Kelly. Yeah, sure, they'd go for Kelly if they didn't want to go outside the O group. But why? Why didn't they just send some outside animal from Langley, or one of the thugs from Williamsburg? They know what I'm thinking, that's why. But how? Not even Chalice knows what I'm thinking.

He was still frowning when she reappeared, carrying the two gray masks of thin rubber.

"Pitch one over here," he instructed. She threw the mask underhand—an easy lob.

"Put yours on," he said. "Watch how I do mine. Fasten it tight. Good. Now, one more job. Go back into the lab and get the guinea pig out of the cage. Go on—he won't bite."

"Do I have to?" she asked quietly. "I really don't like those things."

"Yes, cupcake, you have to. Go ahead."

Chalice went into the closet again and came out holding the guinea pig at arm's length. Even through the mask Eddie could see her expression of distaste. His voice muffled by the rubber, he said, "Put him down on the carpet and let him run."

Through the goggles, he watched the rodent dart forward a few steps from Chalice's hand, hesitate, then dart forward again, tiny nostrils quivering, startled by its sudden freedom and the feel of the carpet. One paw forward, then another, and then the third time touching the fine wire looped in the piling. The unseen canister exploded silently, piercing the carpet, and an odorless, colorless gas spurted up and through the room with the velocity and area coverage of an antipersonnel grenade.

The guinea pig convulsed, blood shot from its ears, and it fell dead with outsplayed, rigid limbs.

Saxitoxin-D, thought Eddie—biological assault with a vengeance. He stepped across the threshold, closing the door behind him. Chalice came into his arms shivering.

"This stuff disperses in about five minutes," he told her. "Open the windows, but keep your mask on for a while."

He collected the guinea pig from the floor and disposed of the body in the lab. Then he checked his watch and stripped off his mask. When Chalice saw him without it, she took hers off as well. He took her into the living room, retrieved the bottle of Rémy Martin, and poured them each a snifter. Chalice put hers down in a lump, then said:

"All right, Eddie. Tell me. Why?"

"Not just yet. Let me think."

Obediently, she accepted that. A long minute passed.

"And what happens now?" she asked.

Eddie looked at her thoughtfully. "Just about now, I would say that Mr. Kelly is sweating it out someplace nearby, wishing he could split, but knowing that just this once he has to come back and check out the job."

"You mean he's coming back here?"

"You can bet on it."

She pulled the robe around her closely, hugging her shoulders with her hands. "What are you going to do?"

"What the fuck do you think I'm going to do?" His voice was heavy and rough.

She licked her lips. "Eddie . . . I don't want a medal for it, but, well, you might say I just saved your life, didn't I?"

He grinned at her; his voice was light again. "I can buy that. You're into me for a big one."

"That's what I mean. You owe me one, right?"

"A big one. Whatever you want."

"Can I collect right now?"

48

"Name it."

She looked away from him, then looked back. Her eyes were bright. "When he comes back. Whatever you do to him, I want to see you do it."

"It won't work that way. It won't happen here."

She was disappointed, but she managed a smile. "Okay. Maybe next time."

Eddie stared at her, unbelieving. "What next time?"

The smile on her face grew.

Kelly gave it an extra five minutes, then walked down the street to the building. The doorman nodded him through the lobby, then turned away indifferently. When the elevator arrived he punched the button marked 5, humming tunelessly. The elevator door slid open smoothly at the fifth floor. Eddie Mancuso stood in front of him, small, compact, dark-eyed, smiling.

"Hello, Kelly," he said, and held out his hand.

Without thinking, only his widening eyes betraying his surprise, Kelly accepted the grip. He shook Eddie's hand. He felt a faint prick, as if he had been stung by an ant. He stared down with horror at his palm. A tiny red mark glowed there, where the pin had entered. Kelly felt his scrotum shrivel and his bowels heave up.

Eddie took a swift step forward. With one hand he squeezed Kelly's forearm; with the other he lifted the car keys from his uniform pocket.

"If you hurry," Eddie said, "I mean, if you really run like hell and you're lucky, and if you can get a cab within a block or two, and if you can get to Doctors Hospital in time, you might just live through it, Kelly." He jingled the car keys. "Don't drive; you won't make it. It's hornet venom. Very new. Still experimental. You wouldn't believe it, but these goddamn hornets come all the way from Brazil and they cost me a buck and a half each."

Kelly's eyes bulged. He listened, fascinated. Eddie still smiled at him darkly. "Doctors Hospital, Eighty-eighth and East End Avenue. You've got about ten minutes. That's the closest, Kelly. You can tell them

49

that the active chemical ingredients are acetylcholine and serotonin, and it mainly hits the myoneural junction. You'll need an injection of epinephrine hydrochloride. Can you remember that, Kelly? You're a pro, you'll remember—but you'd better haul ass. And if you stop on the way to call Williamsburg, you won't make it." He gave Kelly a light, playful shove backward. "Move, baby, move."

Kelly, ashen, sprinted through the lobby into the street. He felt nothing yet except the sting in his palm and a growing numbness in his wrist, but when he looked down he saw that the pinprick was deeper, darker red than before, and his finger looked thicker. Seconds later he spotted the taxi turning off York Avenue, heading his way. Ten minutes; still time. He waved fiercely; the cab slowed, and he wrenched at the door, jumping in.

"Emergency," he gasped. "Doctors Hospital, quick. Eighty-eighth and East End!"

The man at the wheel shot a quick look at Kelly and tromped on the accelerator. He jumped a light at the corner and made the turn screeching. He had gone only three blocks when Kelly's arm began to swell. Two blocks later his fingers looked like *Bratwurst* and his palm had expanded to the size of a purple softball. Sweat came from every pore in his skin.

Less than two minutes. That fucking little wop, he said ten. *He lied.*

The thought of the lie enraged him. Pain shot up his arm into his shoulder, then thrust like a knife for his heart. He bent forward, vomiting, and died.

**6**

The Pyramid of the Magician at Uxmal sat in the low-lying green scrub jungle of Mexican Yucatán. It had sat there for twelve hundred years. The ruin was an oddity when compared with the other survivors of the Mayan civilization. The construction was stark, with a simplicity almost Egyptian, and save for the stone friezes embellished with masks of the rain god Chac, the pyramid resembled nothing so much as the overweight superstructure of an obsolete battleship. The steepness of its sides was frightening; fifty degrees on the eastern side, and a dizzying sixty on the western. Tourists and adventurers came to climb the pyramid, and to aid them a heavy, rusting iron chain ran from top to bottom on either side. Without the chains the pyramid could have been climbed only like a natural mountain, for the steps were shallow—the Mayans were small people, and only the priests, whom the gods protected, were meant to climb—providing little more than a foothold. With the chain, however, the climb was only a difficult exercise, although most of the climbers, after ascending the steeper western side, felt a touch of vertigo and descended on the other. All this climbing was done by day. It was forbidden to climb at night.

Vasily Borgneff sat at the peak of the pyramid in the

darkness of a night lit only by a fragile quarter moon. He sat in the position of a folded stork, his knees drawn up and his chin in the palm of his hand. In the deep gray shadows he seemed a part of the pyramid, a centerpiece provided by the gods to cap their handiwork. He sat as still as a statue, and indeed, if his attitude was reminiscent of Rodin it was a valid comparison and not a cheap imitation, for Vasily was thinking, and thinking hard. Far below him, at the base of the pyramid, the tourist show of Sound and Light was close to completion. Red, gold, violet, and ghost-green lights flashed in the quadrangle of the Nunnery there, playing over the omnipresent masks of Chac with his elephantine snout and the double-headed feathered serpent, Quetzalcoatl. An electronic voice drifted up to him faintly, chanting tales of Mayan legends, of the dwarf hatched from an egg who had built the pyramid under threat of death by the king of Uxmal, and of the seasons of drought and the sacrifices to Chac for the rains of salvation. All this the Russian ignored, his position unchanged, his eyes focused on the nothingness of a darkened horizon. It was only when the lights below blinked out, and the chanting ceased, and the tourists applauded politely and began their way back to their buses—only then did he stir.

He'll be coming now. If she does it right, if she does it the way I told her to, he'll be . . . what's the phrase? . . . champing at the bit, ready to start the forbidden climb as soon as the last tourist is gone. Ready to impress his ladylove with his daring.

He lowered his gaze, staring into the blackness below him. He could see nothing, but with the instinct of the mountaineer he could feel within himself the loom of the pyramid over the jungle. The same instinct told him that no one was yet on the chain.

Stop worrying about Chalice, he told himself. She'll do it, and she'll do it right. Just let him see that sign. CLIMBING AT NIGHT FORBIDDEN. She'll open up those wide eyes of hers and let her nostrils flare. She'll take a deep breath and make herself shiver. She'll thrust out that magnificent bosom. Then she'll say something like "Oh, Eddie, do you think you could do it? Wouldn't that be dangerous?"

He chuckled, and shook his head—half in wonder at the power of this particular woman, half at man's eternal gullibility.

And you? Are you so different? Could she do the same to you?

He considered for a moment, bringing to the question the habits of a lifetime of cold and unemotional analysis.

No, he decided. I admire the woman for many reasons, and in many ways she shakes me and moves me. In bed she is superb. And there's the other thing. But I am not obsessed with her, and he is.

That's the difference between us, Mancuso and me, two totally different types. He is entirely American, with all the brashness, naiveté, and romanticism that the word connotes. And I? I am, God help me, a Europeanized Russian. The worst kind. Older in race and in time than Mancuso, bored, perhaps a touch cynical (a touch!), and just about as romantic as my profession allows me to be. Amend that; Mancuso has the same profession. Very well, as romantic as a steel puddler in Kharkov. Amend further. As romantic as an elderly lecher with a severe case of satyriasis.

He smiled in the darkness, pleased with the word-play in English. He was fluent in seven languages, and conversant with three more. Mancuso, he knew, spoke only English and the bastardized Italian of the New York City streets. He thought of himself as being well read and witty, while Mancuso's reading was limited to magazines printed in the simplest of prose. He was a master at chess; Mancuso was a fumbler. He was an expert skier; Mancuso was an enthusistic amateur.

The list ran on in his head. In every field in which Vasily was adept and accomplished, Eddie Mancuso fell far behind him. Every field except the invention of UKD's. There the man was an untrained genius, but in every other area he seemed unfailingly second rate.

53

It puzzled him that Chalice could be involved with such a man, and indeed, one time in Barcelona he had risked asking her about it. Her response had been an annoyed snort, and then:

"That's a hell of a question to ask me right now. Take your hand off my ass."

With a sigh, he had obeyed; and then he rose to walk across the room and pull open the draperies of their fourth-floor suite. Across the *plaza* from the Hotel Colón bulked the Gothic mass of the old cathedral. Below in the streets hummed the busyness of Barcelona at Christmastime, the broad steps of the cathedral crowded with the stalls of vendors selling trees and ornaments, candles, and cookies and sweets. MEET ME IN BARCELONA FOR CHRISTMAS. A typical summons from Chalice. That was the way she popped into and out of his life: through telegrams addressed to his Swiss bank. Christmas in Barcelona, Easter in Nassau, a weekend in Dublin, once no more than an evening in New York. Only a Russian of the *nomenklatura* could sustain such an affair, he thought wryly. One of the few fringe benefits of my trade. He turned back to face the low, damask-covered sofa where she sat, her clothing disarrayed, her hair slightly tangled.

"Forgive me," he said, with more than a hint of mockery. "I had not expected such reticence."

She tossed her head, leonine hair flying. "Your timing was wrong. We were all set to adjourn to the bedroom and then you start asking me questions about the other man in my life."

"One of the others."

"There aren't that many," she said with a smile that denied her annoyance. "Basically, just you and Eddie."

"Basically. I like that word."

The taut smile stayed on her face. "The two of you are enough for any woman to handle."

"You still have not answered my question. Indulge me."

She looked at him sharply. "If you're looking for a

54

blow-by-blow comparison, you're not going to get it."

"No, something else. I'm not just curious. I'm interested. From all you tell me about him he is so . . . well, what I mean to say is, he isn't . . ."

"He isn't you," she said flatly. "That's what you mean to say, and you're right. He isn't anything like you. He isn't well educated and he isn't witty. He isn't smooth and he isn't diplomatic. He isn't sophisticated. He treats a woman with an old-fashioned, clumsy courtesy. Do you understand what I mean? If you wanted to send me flowers, you would search until you found one perfect dahlia. Eddie would order up six dozen roses. You see?"

"I see exactly. What I do not see is why you remain with him."

"Because, you damn fool, he's a sweet and wonderful guy. He's simple, and uncomplicated, and in many ways innocent, and maybe there's a part of me that needs someone like that. Don't ever ask me to choose between you. I want you both. Just the way it is now."

He inclined his head in a mocking salute. "A friendly providence gave me the intelligence to be content with what I have. But what about Eddie? What if he knew about us? Would he be content?"

"Don't even joke about that." The idea seemed both to alarm and amuse her. "He'd die if he knew. No, I said that the wrong way around. Not die, but kill. If he found out about us he'd kill. First you, then me."

"Very primitive emotions—your simple, courteous, sentimental American!"

"Yes. And I guess that's the answer to your question. In a case like that, you'd laugh and he'd cry. Then you'd sigh—and he'd kill."

Would he indeed? The Russian wondered as he sat in the darkness, waiting. He shifted his position on the narrow rough stone plataeu that formed the top of the pyramid.

Would he really kill for such a reason? The killing part would be easy, of course. He owns so many lives already. Not with his two hands, but those lives are his, all right. Just as mine belong to me. But that was all business, and this . . . to do something like that out of passion? It seems incredible, but as Chalice says, we are two different men. In any event, necessity now rules and we shall soon see.

He knew first from the creaking of the chain—a faint sound, for the links were taut, but it carried in the silence of the night. For a time that was the only sound, and long before he heard any other he was able to see in the blackness below a shape of darker blackness moving up the steps of the pyramid, moving cautiously but firmly. The silence puzzled him, for he had expected to hear the scuff of shoes on stone, and then he realized that Mancuso was climbing barefooted. The Russian waited patiently as the blob of darkness coalesced into a wiry body working hard over hand up the chain, agile feet following. Then Mancuso was up and over the top, standing to stretch cramped muscles. Vasily watched from the other side of the small plateau, masked in shadow. Then he said softly:

"Well, Eddie? Silent upon a peak in Darien?"

Eddie tensed, took one step back, and crouched. He whispered, "What's that?"

"Keats, Eddie."

"I don't know anyone named Keats."

Vasily sighed. "I should have know better."

"How do you know my name, Keats?"

"Please, my name is not Keats."

"Then what is it?"

"Sit down. You must be tired from the climb."

The crouched figure did not move. "I'll stand. Start talking, and start with the name."

"Gladly. But I don't want any rash reactions when you hear it, and so I'll tell you first that I'm unarmed and I mean you no harm. Do you understand?"

"I hear you."

"Then hear this, and think about it. If I had wanted to, I could have taken you when you came over the top. One push, and you would have been splinters and jelly a hundred feet down. True enough?"

"I still hear you. Go ahead."

"My name is Vasily Borgneff."

56

*"Madronne,"* Eddie murmured. He was silent for a moment. "So Macy's finally meets Gimbels."

"Gimbels? I would have said Bloomingdale's, myself. Yes, Macy's meets Bloomingdale's. Much better."

Eddie lowered himself gingerly and sat with his legs crossed, hands clamped on the stone. "Borgneff . . . I'll be damned. I never thought it could happen. What is this, a truce? You want to defect? I'm the wrong guy to talk to, I'll tell you straight out."

"Call it a conference—a conference to test out a theory of mine. A truce is for enemies. We've never been enemies, Eddie."

"Okay, I buy that. But the people we work for aren't exactly kissing cousins."

Vasily dismissed this with a wave of his hand. "Politics. Ideology. We're not politicians. You and I are specialists. No more, no less."

"You could call it that."

"Good. Then this is a conference between specialists, without reference to ideologies. Communist, capitalist, Russian, American, that has nothing to do with us. You agree?"

"I've never been a flag-waver. I work for the money."

"Excellent. We have a common ground. Now we may go on."

"Then get going. You're taking long enough. What's the point of all this?"

"It's really quite simple. I am going to save your life. Does that sound terribly dramatic?"

Eddie chuckled. "Yes. Considering who you work for, and who I work for, and considering the business we're both in—it sure does."

"I'm glad. It was meant to sound that way. Because if my theory is correct, you are going to save my life as well."

"Stop blowing bubble gum, Borgneff. Put your cards on the table."

"Very well, but bear with me. Now I must tell you a story."

Vasily spoke tersely and quietly, almost as if to

avoid being overheard, although they were as alone as two men could be under the fragile quarter moon and in the shadow of the face of the rain god. He told the story simply, as one professional to another, telling Eddie exactly what had happened on the Devil's Ridge at Grindelwald. When he had finished, he looked inquiringly at Eddie for comment.

"Cute," said Eddie. "A very nice touch. I'll have to remember that one."

"No," Vasily protested. "It was crude, and I was lucky. And this is not a critique, and I am not asking for compliments. I've told you my story. Now . . . let me hear yours."

Coldly, precisely, Eddie said, "What makes you think I have a story to tell?"

"Your people have tried to extract you just as mine have tried it on me. Tried and failed. I know that for a fact, but now I must know the details."

"Exactly what facts do you know, and how did you get them?"

"There will be time for that later. For now, accept my request on faith."

"That's a heap of faith you're asking for."

"Believe me, my friend, I am trying to save our lives."

"I'm going to have a hell of a lot of questions to ask later on," Eddie said, but in the same quiet tones that the Russian had used, he told Vasily what had happened in his Manhattan apartment.

"Saxitoxin-D," said Vasily, musing. "How interesting. I developed that strain myself eight years ago."

"I had a barrel of it in my lab back in sixty-four."

Vasily inclined his head. "I was unaware. Of course, I bow to the master." Then, in a brisker tone, "So, now we know each other's secrets. We are both on the run. The next question is why. Why are our organizations trying to kill us? Any theories?"

"Simple. I want out."

"You asked for retirement?"

"No, that's the damnedest part of it." Puzzled, Eddie stood up suddenly and began to step off the few

58

paces around the plateau. "I knew they'd never allow it, so I didn't bother asking. I figured the only way to get out would be to . . ." He hesitated, looking at the Russian obliquely.

Vasily nodded his encouragement. "Please go on. It will not sound absurd to me. You see, I am faced with the same problem."

"Absurd. Yeah, that's the word for it, all right. It was okay just thinking about it, but to say it out loud . . . absurd. Okay, in plain language, I figured that the only way for me to get out clean would be to extract the entire O Group."

"The Five Group in my case."

"You mean you figured it the same way?"

"What else? It was the only satisfactory solution."

"You're swift. But it's good to know that there's one other cold-blooded bastard in this world."

"Those who live by the sword . . ." Vasily shrugged, and the words trailed away. "As a matter of professional curiosity, would you mind telling me your plans for the extraction?"

"My plans? Zilch," Eddie said flatly. "Zero. I have no plans. I said that I thought about it. I didn't say that I was going to try it."

"And what stops you?"

Eddie whirled on him, pirouetting gracefully. "Christ, haven't you figured it out yet? Look, we each came up with the same idea at the same time. Early retirement. Plenty of bread in the bank, the world's big, papers are a snap to get hold of. Now, I know damn well you didn't put an ad in *Pravda* to tell your people about it, and neither did I. But your people found out about you, and my people found out about me. How? Have you thought about that?"

"I have," Vasily said softly. "But I want you to tell me."

"It's the fucking computer, that's what it is. CYBER or whatever you call it in Moscow."

"We also call it CYBER."

"Then you agree with me?"

"Of course. Regrettably, my conclusions are the

59

same as yours. The Moscow CYBER can predict every move I make up to a point. Your CYBER can do the same for you."

"Which is why I have no plans," said Eddie. "I'm screwed, and so are you."

"What odds do you calculate?"

"None. Look, before I figured CYBER into the picture I knew I had long odds to beat, real long odds, but I was willing to give it a try. But not with the computer working against me. That makes it a suicide mission."

"Then what will you do? Run for the rest of your life?"

"What choice do I have?"

"The choice I am about to offer you." For the first time Vasily stood, stretching himself, towering over the shorter man. "You're right—it would be a suicide mission. For you. But not for me."

Eddie cocked his head to one side. He was silent for a long moment. He seemed to be listening to some distant music heard faintly. He smiled tightly and said, "Go on."

"The CYBER at Williamsburg is programmed against you, not me. All I would need from you is information. For example, the profiles of the four remaining members of the O Group. Give me that and I will do the job for you. It will take time and careful planning, but I can do it. No one, in fact, could do this particular job better."

Eddie nodded slowly. "And all I have to do is the same job for you."

"Yes, at Zhukovka."

"Me? Go there? How could I do it? You must be kidding."

"There are always problems. They will be solved."

"*I'm* the problem," Eddie said glumly. "I never . . ." But even as he started to say it, he realized that it was no longer a fact. He had killed a man. Kelly, who would have killed him. And Colonel Parker, Erikson, Arteaga, Rakow—all were dedicated to the same end. There was an enemy, and it was no longer faceless.

60

"When I left New York, I lost my lab." He frowned. "I've got nothing."

"You have what is in here," Vasily said, tapping his forehead. "And so do I. Money is no problem. We both have that."

"And a base?"

"Here in Mexico. I know a place." He waited a moment, then said, "Do you have an alternative?"

"None I like. But I've got plenty of questions."

"Ask them."

Eddie asked, and Vasily answered. He spent the next half hour feeding him facts about the *dachniki* at Zhukovka, detailing strengths and weaknesses, profiling individual members of the unit, and suggesting methods for their elimination. He spoke quietly but persuasively, presenting his plan the way a gifted salesman would present a product. At the end of the half hour he said:

"There's more, of course. That's just the beginning. It would take me weeks to brief you properly."

"And I would do the same for you?"

"Yes. An elegant solution to an inelegant problem. Will you do it?"

After the slightest pause, Eddie said, "It's the craziest thing I ever heard, but it's the best shot there is. I've got to take it. Yeah, you've got yourself a partner."

"Excellent. In that case, shall we descend? There is much to discuss."

The Russian walked to the western side of the pyramid and stared down into the darkness. He grasped the chain and went over the edge. He took three quick steps down and stopped. With his head still visible, he said, "Follow me down. Step carefully in the dark."

They went down in tandem, Vasily first and Eddie close behind, each holding on to the chain and feeling cautiously for footholds. The chain was wet, slippery with the moisture of the night; the stones were slick as well. The darkness now was absolute, the light of the stars extinguished by the bulk of the looming pyramid. Vasily had taken no more than a dozen steps when he suddenly stopped. Eddie closed up, above and behind him, close enough to touch.

"Keep going, don't freeze," Eddie said.

"It's not that. I just remembered that you had some questions you wanted to ask me."

"You better believe it. How did you know I'd be up here tonight? How did you know what happened in New York?"

"Do you really want to know the answers?"

"Don't bother," he said grimly, "I figured it out myself. You bought the girl. You're smart, Borgneff. I hope you paid her plenty."

"I paid Chalice nothing. Nothing at all."

Eddie snorted. "Sure, she did it for love."

"Why not?" Vasily tightened his grip on the chain and braced his feet. "After all, I *am* her lover."

The silence was so complete that it screamed in the night, hummed in the air, quivered between them like a struck string.

"Chalice?" There was a touch of wonder in Eddie's voice.

"I've known her for almost a year. Not as long as you have, but long enough."

Again the screaming silence. Then Eddie said, "You're a heavy gambler, aren't you?"

Vasily chuckled. "I have that reputation. It is a particularly Russian vice. Mine is a severe case."

"You're rolling high stakes now."

"The highest."

"One push, one kick, and you're gone. Blown away. Dust."

"I'm in your hands."

"You put yourself there. Why?"

"As you said, I'm a gambler."

"Not good enough."

"Perhaps I wanted to test another theory of mine. Chalice once said that if you ever found out about us, your first reaction would be to kill. I don't believe that. Particularly not now."

Eddie's words came as little bitter drops. "And that's

what you're counting on. If I blow you away I lose my last chance to get out clean."

"What I'm counting on is your good sense. I'm not trying to take the girl away from you. She's there for both of us."

"You prick. You cold-blooded prick."

"What is it going to be, Eddie? The dice are rolling."

Vasily, tensed and braced, felt movement above and behind him, and then the pressure of a bare foot in the small of his back. He sucked in breath, then forced himself to breathe it out. Another breath, another, and then the pressure of the foot relaxed, and was gone.

"Get going," Eddie said. "We can't stay up here all night."

# 7

The Mexican dogs began barking before dawn—first the strays on the square in the center of town, then the pets penned into jungled yards, the chorus finally joined by the wild pack that ranged along the cobbled road that led out of San Miguel de Allende. Their yowling split the stillness of what was left of the warm Mexican night, and as the gray edge of dawn appeared, the wails were augmented by a cascade of church bells tolling madly, an ornamental counterpoint of roosters greeting the day, and, in the case of Eddie Mancuso, the cracked voice of a drunken Otomi Indian singing of *amor* as he wandered down the road with his wood-laden *burro*.

Eddie sat straight up in bed, sweating and furious at being awakened. It happened that way every night, and neither alcohol nor Valium nor the ear stopples that always fell out while he slept could get him past the crazed cacophony of the Mexican dawn. It woke him that way every morning, and once awake he stayed awake, jaded, unrested. And now, hungry.

He crawled out of bed wearing only shorts and T-shirt, eyes half shut as he stumbled across the tiled floor and down the stone staircase toward the kitchen at the bottom of the house. He passed through a series of gardened patios, and beyond them in the fields saw his sheep stirring lazily, his rabbits in their hutch making breakfast on alfalfa. The sheep and the rabbits were silent, but they were part of the dawn, and he glared at them.

In the kitchen a pile of crisp tortillas lay on the shelf next to a bowl of mangos and avocados, guavas and oranges. He stared down at the fruit with bleary eyes, trying to decide. All the fruit was good, and the oranges were particularly sweet and delicious, but it took fifteen minutes of passionate squeezing to produce a decent glassful. He thought longingly of a container of Tropicana, of Egg McMuffins, of lox and bagels from Zabar's, and in a final burst of self-pity wished heartily for that simplest of luxuries, a glass of water he might drink directly from the tap. In the end he heated a can of tomato soup, spooned it up with a dried tortilla, and washed it all down with a bitter cup of black coffee.

With the hunger pangs eased, he decided to try for more sleep. As he climbed the stairs he hurried past Chalice's bedroom as he always did, hoping not to hear what he heard too often on his early-morning travels, but through the door came the clear squeak of bedsprings, then Vasily's mutter, Chalice's moan. He grimaced and ran from the sounds, pounding up the stairs and hoping childishly that the noise he made would distract them. Back in his room he stretched out on the bed, kicking away the damp and tangled sheets, and closed his eyes. He lay with his stomach knotted and his jaws clenched before dropping into a tossing, troubled sleep.

The house that Vasily had found for them in San Miguel de Allende was perched on a steep and cobbled road that twisted up from the village in the valley, leaving the narrow, dung-filled streets and then striking out arrow-straight across the brown desert to join the highway heading south to Querétaro and on to Mexico City, hours away. The house was built into the side of the hill, rising from a walled courtyard to a succession of brick levels that topped the crest. The walls continued down behind the house, on a slope dotted with prickly-pear cactus and chaparral, enclosing the shed that they used for a workshop. The shed was private, and within the walls grew just enough withering grass to support the small flock of sheep that grazed there daily.

The people of San Miguel were puzzled by the sheep, but their curiosity was idle and prompted no questions that could not be answered with a shrug. The middle-aged European with the courtly manners and excellent Spanish, the sullen little American who seemed to glow with contained resentment, and the attractive woman who walked between them with such a jaunty step . . . ah, well, it was known that most *gringos* were *loco,* and if these three wished to keep sheep they were simply proving a point that all Mexicans knew. Besides, San Miguel was filled with American eccentrics: the young, guitar-strumming art students at the Instituto Allende, the retired elderly slowly shriveling in the fierce year-round sun, and the inevitable leavening of slow-talking dope dealers, would-be painters, sometime writers, divorcées, and booze mechanics; all on the run from something up North, even if that something was nothing more than boredom. They drifted into and out of town on the seasonal tides, and the three people on the hill were lost in their numbers. It was that kind of place.

Their cover story was simple: three old friends, all aspiring painters, come to San Miguel to capture on canvas the exotic panorama of the desert. At times they went to the various street *fiestas,* with fireworks and plumed Indian dancers, at times ate an indifferent meal in town, and at times strolled around the *zócalo* at sunset while the birds shrilled in the trees and the town band played off-pitch Verdi. But most of the time they stayed at home, working at their art.

With its rising layers of terraces and flowered gardens, its long, cool bedrooms floored with multicolored tiles, the house on the hill was large enough for three strangers to have lived there comfortably, and in the beginning the three could well have been strangers. The top tier of the house belonged to Eddie, the next below was Chalice's, and Vasily occupied the lowest level, close to the cobbled road. The Russian had assigned the quarters on the day after their arrival from the Yucatán, and they had accepted the arrangements indifferently. But if Vasily's intention had been to create a symbol—Chalice sandwiched between the two men—Eddie had made sure that the symbol remained only that.

For Eddie Mancuso was sulking. That was the only word for it.

He had been sulking since the pyramid at Uxmal, and his depression had deepened in San Miguel. Their second night in the house, a warm night made balmy by the drifting scent of jacaranda, he lay sleepless in his bed and heard the soft pad of bare feet on the steps outside. He stiffened, alert, but did not move. A moment later he saw her shadow cross the window glass, heard the click of the opening door, and smelled at once the fragrance of Diorissimo as she entered the room. He saw the familiar curves of her flesh through the wisp of white she was wearing. She sank to the side of the bed, sitting on the edge.

After a silent moment, Eddie said, "No sale, Chalice. I'm not interested."

Her finger touched his cheek. "I know you're angry and you're hurt, but I can't believe that."

"Why not? We didn't sign any contracts. All we had was some good times in the sack. Now it's over."

"I still can't believe it." One hand gently touched his shoulder, while with the other she made light, circular motions on his chest, stirring the curly black hair.

He felt the tingling in his shoulder and chest, but he forced himself to lie rigidly, his arms under the blanket, staring up at her. "Does Vasily know that you're here?"

"Of course he does." She was rubbing him with both hands now, making wider circles, swinging lower. She leaned over him, and through the gauzy fabric her nipples, stiffening, grazed his skin. "What I have with Vasily has nothing to do with you. And vice versa.

67

Can't you see that? I still feel the same about you. Nothing's changed."

"Not for you, maybe. But for me it has. You're wasting your time."

Disregarding that, breasts pressing, lips at his neck, she was all over him, hands fluttering lightly across the blanket covering his thighs. "I know you, baby. I know how your mind works, and how your body works, and I know . . ." She broke off with a delighted chuckle as her hand on the blanket found the thick, long protuberance between his thighs. Delight turned to triumph. *"Now* tell me you don't feel anything. . . ."

Sweat broke from his forehead. "The hell with what I feel. This is what *you* feel."

He drew his right hand out from under the covers, and the bulge in the blanket disappeared. In his hand was a pistol. It was pointed directly at her. She did not know that it was a Mauser, but she did know that it was the largest pistol she had ever seen.

He said coldly, "Here's my erection, ready to go off. I heard you coming two minutes before you got here. Anybody else, he would have been dead. Now, for the last time, will you get out of here?"

She stared at the pistol, fascinated. Then she shook her head. "You'd never use that on me."

"Move," he said, his voice tight, high. "On the count of three, you get it. Now move. One . . ."

Chalice smiled.

"Two . . ."

She puckered her lips, blew him a kiss.

"Three."

Her lips were still puckered when he pulled the trigger. A jet of water hit her face, a ramjet as heavy as a baby fire hose. It was the Vesuvius of water guns, the Mount Etna of toys, and it soaked her face, her hair, flowing down her breasts to her waist. She stood, spluttering, trembling, hands knuckling at her eyes.

"I'm sorry," Eddie said, chuckling. "I guess I came too quick, huh?"

Chalice fled, dripping water over the tiles and the

handwoven Indian rugs. Eddie heard her footsteps pattering swiftly down the stairs. Then the closing of a door, then silence. The smile vanished from his face; his laughter died.

Keep laughing, he told himself. That's the only way you're going to make it.

After that night he continued to sulk, speaking rarely to Chalice, and then always in a flat tone that refused any show of friendliness. To Vasily he spoke only of the mission, their work: designing and creating, fashioning new equipment, foraging for supplies, testing and retesting the nuts and bolts of their profession, and, most important, exchanging the tricks of the trade each had accumulated over the years.

"Lilies of the Valley," said Vasily. "You cover them with vodka and heat them on a burner. Then strain off the liquid and simmer what's left to a thick paste. The nerve toxin that results is both quick and fatal."

"I've heard of that one, but I've never tried it," Eddie said. "Did you ever use mountain laurel?"

"I'm not even sure what it is."

"*Kalmia latifolia.* Probably doesn't grow where you come from. Anyway, you put some in a glass jar and set it out in the sun for a day. Then you throw out the laurel and recap the jar real quick. What's left in the jar is straight sodium cyanide gas. Nice, huh?"

"Lovely. Just put the jar on top of a door. When the victim walks in the jar falls and breaks, and it's all over."

"Neat, too. No evidence, just some pieces of glass."

"Tell me, do you milk your own snakes, or do you buy the venom from dealers?"

"Always milk my own," said Eddie. "I may be a city boy, and cows confuse me, but milking snakes is my specialty. Rattlesnakes are easy. It's those damn boomslangs that are tough to do. The fangs are set so far back that you can't get at them."

"I might be able to help you on that one. Try pegging the jaws open and using a suction pipette."

"Yeah, that might work. If you can get the snake

to cooperate. Most of the snakes I know are touchy that way."

"What do you know about lasers?"

"Plenty. We've got this thing called Project Flash Gordon. The Air Force started it with a Marked Target Seeker system. Parker wanted me to take it a little further—use a gas amplifier and turn it into a heat source."

"What about using laser fusion in a device?"

"Hey, wait a minute. We've got eight individual hits to make. You're talking about something that would take out a blockhouse."

"Just thinking out loud," said Vasily, and went on to talk about methyl mercury as a tissue penetrant. Eddie countered with the advantages of using dimethyl sulfoxide, and they were off again, exchanging treasured secrets. They went on that way for hours at a time, and it was only during those freewheeling discussions that Eddie found himself able to relax. He had always respected Vasily Borgneff professionally, and now he found himself liking him as well. The Russian was the first person he had ever been able to speak to openly. They knew each other's worlds, and in the fertile ground of those long conversations on death and dying they each saw the seeds of a friendship sprouting.

He's okay, Eddie decided. No matter what else is coming down around here, this guy is okay.

He's a solid person, was Vasily's estimate of Eddie. He's a master of his trade, and he's good to be around.

But despite this relaxation, Eddie continued to sulk outside the workshop. He rejected the hopeful smiles of Vasily and Chalice just as he rejected everything else that was lovely all around him: the old Spanish-style house, the bountiful gardens of purple bougainvillea and red geraniums, the crystal air, and the fire-and-salmon-colored sunsets over the distant lake. Eventually he even rejected the food prepared by the two sober-faced, black-haired maids, one afternoon

70

pushing aside a fragrant plateful of *pollo mole poblano* in disgust.

"I'm finished eating this Mexican crap," he announced. "Once, just once, I want something made without chili peppers."

That afternoon he tramped down the long hill in the afternoon sun to the *supermercado* and filled two shopping baskets with canned hams and frankfurters, baked beans, assorted soups, cookies, and jarred fruits. He ordered two cases of Pepsi-Cola to be delivered, and then took a rattling taxi back up the hill. Thus supplied, he quit the dining-room table and ate his meals in his room—the ultimate rejection.

Thirty-eight years old, and Eddie Mancuso was sulking.

"I warned you," said Chalice, at breakfast with Vasily and heartily attacking *huevos rancheros* and *frijoles*. "I told you it would be this way."

"May I smoke?" Vasily, already finished with his spartan meal—one slice of smoked ham, one slice of dry toast, two cups of coffee—inspected thin Cuban cigars in a gold case. When Chalice nodded, he selected one and lit it. After a long puff, he said, "You once told me that if he ever found out about us he would kill. First me, then you. You said nothing about him behaving like a child."

Chalice shrugged. "Whose idea was it to tell him?"

"Uxmal was a gamble. It happened to work."

"You mean that he didn't freak out. But can he function?"

Vasily considered this seriously, frowning at the tip of his cigar. "Quite so," he murmured. "That's the operative question. And at the moment, the answer is no. Not at one-hundred-percent efficiency."

"Can you do with less?"

"I wouldn't want to bet my neck on it. Or his, for that matter. I've grown fond of Eddie."

"In that case, you're betting both your necks on a three-legged horse. He's unhappy, he's depressed, and ever since Uxmal he knows that there's no Santa Claus."

71

"Chalice, he had to be told. Of course, I expected a reaction. He is a romantic. I expected anger, perhaps a blow, even a challenge to a duel. All followed by an eventual acceptance of the facts. What I did not expect was a lovesick teen-ager." He cursed softly in Russian.

"I told you what he's like."

"Very well, and since you know him so much better than I do, what do you predict? Will Achilles continue to sulk in his tent, or will he come out? It rather depends on you, doesn't it?"

"Look, I *want* him," she said angrily. "I made him an offer and he shot me with a water pistol. Vasily, don't you dare start laughing. . . ."

"I'm not," he said, and made sure that he wasn't.

"Well, how do you think that made me feel?"

"Wet," he murmured, and then added quickly, "and humiliated."

"Damn right I was."

"Tell me, as a point of information only, how often does Eddie . . . I mean, when the two of you are together, how often is he accustomed to . . .?" He raised his eyebrows delicately.

"Often enough, and that's all I'm saying."

"Fair enough. I leave tomorrow for the south— I'll be away for at least a week. Time enough, I should think, for reconciliation."

"I'm not making any promises. It might not be water in the gun next time."

"Do it, Chalice." He rose from the table and smiled down at her. "Get our Achilles out of his tent before I return." The smile faded. "Because if he stays inside, we're dead, both of us. And possibly—under the circumstances—all three of us."

Mancuso, sulking, bent over the workshop table, a jeweler's loupe in one eye. In his left hand he held the stripped-down chassis of a Polaroid Pronto camera, in his right hand a fine-edged tweezer. From a metal tray he picked out a tiny screw and set it into a slot on the camera frame. He twisted his fingers, but instead of engaging, the screw slipped out and clattered onto the tray. He found it with the tweezers and tried again, his fingers barely moving, but even that gentle pressure was enough to pop the screw loose from the mounting. He frowned, tried a third time, a fourth. On the fifth attempt the screw engaged and turned. He set the camera down and examined his hands critically, still frowning. He had always been able to depend on his hands. At the sound of footsteps outside he quickly bent over the camera again, threading another screw into the frame. Mercifully, it engaged at once. He continued to work on the assembly, aware of Vasily's presence behind him. On the last two screws his hands slipped again. He did not raise his head until the mounting was complete.

Then he looked over his shoulder. "That's it. Finished."

"You seem a little tense, Eddie." Vasily's voice was solicitous. "Your hands."

"Nothing wrong with my hands."

"Really? You seemed a bit—"

"There's nothing wrong with my hands," he repeated flatly. "It's finished. I can adapt it to the Nikonos or the Leica, too. We can test it anytime."

"Very well. What's the range?"

"With a one-ounce dart, about thirty yards effective. After that she'll drift."

Vasily nodded his approval, then said, "Before we test the camera I think we should have a little chat, my friend."

"Sure, let's chat. I've got the list of supplies I need."

"Not about the supplies."

"Here's the list." He handed the Russian a sheet of paper. "You should be able to get most of the stuff in Mexico City, but I'm not sure about the *Amanita phalloides*. Can you get mushroom spoor in Mexico?"

"In Oaxaca, no problem," Vasily brushed the list aside, set it on the table. "I want to talk to you about . . . this situation."

"Listen, I've got a set of number-eleven tubes on

the list. Try and get the disposable kind. I hate washing tubes."

"You're being very foolish."

"Vasily, I need a hand."

"Of course you do, dear fellow." Vasily was obviously gratified. "That's just what I've been trying to tell you. You're tense—ready to explode. You don't really understand this situation. I take full blame for expecting that you would. That was . . . indelicate of me. The facts are the same, but I ask your forgiveness for presenting them as baldly as I did. I want to help you, Eddie."

"You dumb bastard, I don't mean that kind of hand." He shook his head in disgust. "I need a prosthetic, an artificial hand. The kind an amputee wears."

"Sorry." At once, Vasily was all business. "Left or right, and how far up?"

"Left. Above the wrist, and with an adjustable forefinger. Can you get me one like that?"

"In Mexico City. Consider it done."

"You want to know what it's for?"

Vasily smiled. "Not really. The last time I heard of that device being used was . . . let me see, yes, Warsaw, about three years ago." His voice shifted gears, and there was a cutting edge to it now. "Friend, maybe you don't want to talk, but you're damned well going to listen. If you keep this up you're going to get us killed. You know that, don't you?"

Eddie regarded him silently.

"Killed. Dead. Because in three weeks we go operational on this project and you're not ready for it."

Eddie still did not speak.

"Well, are you?" Vasily insisted. "Are you ready to get on that plane to Moscow? Are you ready to go up against men like Durin and Marchenko? These are professionals—the best. Are you?"

"I'm ready," he said finally.

"You're not. You're ready physically, and you're ready mentally—Lord knows you have all the skills

74

—but you're not ready emotionally. And you won't be until you come out of this shell you're hiding in."

"We made a deal. I'll do what I have to do, and I'll do it right. I'll do my part and I don't need you to tell me if I'm ready or not." Eddie's voice was bladed now, too. "This business with Chalice is separate. To you I'm just square little Eddie, very uncool, and you're the man of the world, very sophisticated and civilized. Well, that's bullshit. It may be civilized to you and to Chalice, but it isn't to me. I'm just an old-fashioned ginzo from the Lower East Side. That's where I come from, and where I come from nobody fucks my lady except me."

"But that's just it, Eddie. She was never your girl. Not yours, and not mine. And she never will be. That's the way she is."

"In that case, what's she doing here? This town is full of ass, all high-grade females. What the hell do we need Chalice for?"

Vasily's eyes narrowed as he tried to judge the seriousness of the question. Eddie was relatively calm, but Vasily's defensive instincts, never at rest, warned him not to strike too close to what he believed was the truth. And yet a curious sense of obligation to the man on whom his life depended, and who in turn depended equally on him, laid a check on his deviousness.

"I need her," he said quietly, "because she pleases me, and there are very few women who do. She remains a challenge. You can't own her, and you can't easily manipulate her. That makes her special. I rather imagine she has the same effect on you. So, given the present circumstances, when life may be short, I choose to have my cake and eat it too—even though there are attendant risks."

"What risks?"

"Come, come. The lady may not be privy to all our plans, but she knows more than enough." He shook his head sadly, and repeated, "More than enough. There is, however, a cure for that. If you find her presence here intolerable, she can simply be eliminated from our plans."

"And you think she'd go, just like that?"

"Eddie, I said eliminate."

The word had only one meaning in their profession, and the word, almost palpable, hung in the silence between them. Their eyes locked and held.

Eddie said softly, "Would you really do that?"

"If I had to. My life is at stake. So is yours. Wouldn't you?"

"No," Eddie breathed. "I couldn't. That's out."

"You could. And believe me, you would."

"No." The word came firmly.

"Forgive me, then. I had to show you the options." Vasily saluted him with a mocking forefinger. "And since you reject one option, I'm afraid that you're stuck with the other. You'll have to accept the situation as it stands. Accept it truly, without reservations. Can you do that?"

The question went unanswered. Eddie turned back to the table, took a slim flechette from the metal tray, and inserted it into the film compartment of the Polaroid. He examined the mounting, then closed the camera with a solid click. He took a greasy *sarape* from a hook on the wall and flung it over his shoulder.

"Let's go kill a sheep," he said. "I want to test this camera."

They went from the cool of the shed into the hot and silent morning, dodging cactus spines and thorny growths as they walked down the slope toward the herd of sheep. Eddie gave the *sarape* to Vasily.

"Roughly the weight of a KGB greatcoat," he explained. "Tie it around the biggest sheep you can find."

"A big one will be much too tough to eat," Vasily objected. "Kill a lamb, Eddie. That cute little one over there—what a tasty *gigot* that would make. Two of them, in fact, and two *épaules*."

"With our cook? I can taste it now, four chili peppers on the hoof."

"I'll cook it myself, I promise. I'll make a *gigot*

76

*à moutarde,* perhaps with a *farce aux herbes.* How does that sound?"

"The peppers sound better. Listen, the idea is to test the dart for penetration. For that I need a full-grown sheep. I could knock over that lamb with a toothpick."

Vasily nodded, defeated, and advanced toward the flock trailing the *sarape* behind him like a bullfighter's cape. The mass of sheep stirred and bleated softly at his approach. He circled around them and they began to move through the dust, making for the wall. Vasily launched himself forward and landed on the largest of the sheep, his arm around its neck. The weight of his body dragged the animal to its knees, but no farther.

*"Baaaaaaa . . ."*

"A little help here, comrade," Vasily called.

Grinning, Eddie laid the camera carefully on the ground and moved up to Vasily's side. Together they wrestled the animal to the dirt. Working rapidly, grunting, sweat popping from pores, they forced the *sarape* around the belly and neck, and tied it in place. The sheep resisted indignantly, delivering the ultimate protest with a jet of urine that splattered over Vasily's shoes. They straightened up, brushing greasy hands on their trousers, Vasily staring down at his ruined shoes.

"The next time, *you* play the cowboy," he said ruefully.

"The next time, wear boots. When did you ever see a cowboy in suede loafers?"

The sheep rose slowly, burdened by the *sarape.* Its head was framed by the curve of the garment, and the long, bony face stared out at them reproachfully. It blatted once, then hobbled away to join the flock.

Eddie picked up the camera. "Just about thirty yards. Watch."

He raised the camera to his eye and found the sheep in the viewer, centering the cross hairs on the rolls of fat and fleece around the neck. He pressed the trigger. The sheep jerked up its head; then the front legs collapsed and it fell to its knees. It stayed that way for a few seconds, then rolled over, stiff and still. The other sheep stared down incuriously.

"Marvelous," said Vasily.

"Wait. Watch."

Eddie reloaded the camera with another flechette, flicked a switch, turned, and pointed the lens at Vasily, who swallowed hard.

"Eddie, don't aim that thing—"

"Fuck around with my girl, will you?"

His smile hidden by the camera, Eddie quickly found the dead animal in the viewer and pressed the trigger. Although the lens was pointed at Vasily, the dart shot out from the side of the camera and thunked into the body of the sheep. Reloading again, he turned his back to Vasily, aimed, and fired. This time the dart came out of the other side, hitting the sheep a third time.

"Three-way action," Eddie said proudly, turning around. "What do you think of that?"

"Marvelous," Vasily repeated, but this time his voice was a croak.

"You should have seen your face."

"Bad, eh?"

"Well, some guys freeze up when you point a camera at them."

"You must admit that you caught me unaware."

"Want to try it again?" Eddie raised the camera. "Go ahead, smile."

Vasily forced a grin onto his face. From between tight lips he grunted, "How do I look now?"

"Sheepish."

Vasily's artificial smile turned to a real one of delight. "Mancuso, there's a side to you I never even suspected," he said, and the tension between them vanished.

They went to kneel beside the dead animal. Eddie removed the *sarape* and parted the wool at the neck. The ends of the three flechettes were grouped closely, dull metal on the greasy fleece.

"I congratulate you. It's a first-class device," said

78

Vasily, his voice sincere. "I assume you'll be taking it on your little trip?"

"Of course. Who ever heard of an American tourist without a camera?"

# 8

The next morning, after an early breakfast, Vasily left for Mexico City. Eddie and Chalice watched as he backed the Chevy pickup out of the garage and onto the cobbled street. Then he came back to the doorway to kiss Chalice's cheek and grip Eddie's shoulder in farewell.

"Remember, if anything goes wrong here, bail out," he said. "Then call me. You have the numbers where I'll be."

"Nothing's going to go wrong," Eddie assured him. "We've got good, deep cover. You just watch your own ass."

"I appreciate your concern." He stepped back to look at them both. He seemed about to say something more, then shook his head silently. He climbed into the truck, and from the driver's seat looked down at them.

"Back in a week," was all he said, and was gone. They stood and watched until the truck was out of sight, reluctant to leave the spot even when all they could see was a plume of dust on the road.

"It's a funny feeling," Chalice said. "Having him go like that."

Eddie nodded. "Yeah, you get used to having him around."

80

"You like him, don't you?"

Slowly, uncertain of what was proper to say, he answered, "I guess you could say that. I never had a chance to . . . well, I never had many friends. I had three sisters, but they all got married and left New York. You know how it is. And my mom and pop died five years ago." Then, to break away from the mood, "I could use another cup of coffee."

They went back into the house and sat in the *sala* drinking coffee, talking of the bullfights of the day before, a local *gringo* in trouble with the law, a fiesta soon to come—staying away from the deeper thoughts that troubled them. They both felt so easy and the time went so quickly that they were surprised when they saw it was noon. Making a pitcher of *margaritas* seemed the natural thing to do, and they each had two, sitting out now in the ground-level garden under the jacaranda. They debated having a third *margarita*, decided against it, and then, suddenly, neither wanted to stay in the house. They grabbed swimsuits, called for a taxi, and took the bumpy road out to the mineral springs at Taboada. They spent the rest of the afternoon lying in the warm-water pools, then on the cool grass, listening to the *mariachis*, eating grilled shrimp, and drinking chilled white wine.

Late in the afternoon Eddie fell asleep on the grass, and when he woke the tightness he had carried for so long in his gut was gone. He felt the absence of it, knew it at once, and smiled up at Chalice bending over him. The two strips of her bikini did nothing to impede his memory of her body.

"Time to go home," he said. She was smiling, too.

Back at the house they separated to shower and change, and when they met again in the *sala* Chalice was dressed for the evening in white chiffon. Eddie wore jeans and a T-shirt. Chalice hid a disappointed look.

"Something wrong?" Eddie asked.

"I thought we might go out," she said. "Sort of round out the day. One drink at La Fragua and then a plate of spaghetti at Mama Mia's."

"No. No, I don't think so."

"It doesn't make any difference how you're dressed —not in this town."

"Still no."

"All right, then we'll stay home," she said gaily, and whirled in a pirouette, hands in the air. "Same menu. One drink, and then pasta. You haven't lived until you've tasted my *fettuccine carbonara*."

"I'll manage," he said, his voice suddenly cold. "Look, I understand what you're trying to do, and I appreciate it. It's been a good day, a damn good day, up until now, and now is as far as it goes."

She dropped her arms, her face stricken. "Why does it have to stop now?"

"You know damn well why."

"You mean you still feel that way about Vasily and me?"

"Why should I change?"

"I was hoping you would. Especially after today."

"Like I said, it was a nice day," he said patiently. "But that's all it was."

Angry, she shouted, "Mancuso, you are one tough, stubborn guinea!"

"That's me." He nodded, as if complimented.

"And don't expect me to keep running after you, either. I'm finished."

"Thank God. I thought you'd never get the message." The words were hard to say. Angry and flushed, she looked as lovely as he had ever seen her. He cleared his throat and said, "Excuse me now. I've got some work to do in the lab."

He brushed past her, ignoring the sudden, involuntary movement toward him and the equally sudden withdrawal. He was almost to the *sala* door when he heard her at the telephone, calling for a taxi.

"You going out?" he asked without turning.

"I certainly am. And don't wait up for me, you son of a bitch," she flung after him.

"I won't," he muttered. But he did.

He didn't know at first that he was waiting. He spent the next two hours in the laboratory refining a solution of boomslang venom and testing the results by injection into rabbits. Shortly after eight, he buried the rabbits in the yard, washed his hands, and went to the kitchen for something to eat. He ignored the two maids chatting there and built himself a massive ham sandwich which he ate standing up, washing down the meat and bread with Double-X beer. Then he went back to the laboratory and worked on the spring attachments for a pair of hollowed-out heels. The springs were difficult to align properly, and the job took longer than he had thought it would. It was close to midnight before he was finished, and as he packed his tools away he was aware that for the past hour he had been listening for specific sounds: the grinding of a taxi engine coming up the hill, the slam of a door.

The hell with it. She's a big girl.

He went back to the kitchen for a beer to take upstairs. He drank the beer in his room, sitting on the edge of the bed, still waiting. Finally, he took off his shoes and lay on the bed with his clothes on and his eyes open. He lay that way until he heard the single tones of church bells striking one in the village. He forced himself to lie there for fifteen minutes more, then sighed at his own weakness and sat up. He changed into slacks and a tweed jacket, loaded his pockets, and minutes later was out the door and heading down the cobblestoned street toward the center of town.

La Fragua was the bar just off the main square where most of the *gringos* in town gathered to drink Oso Negro gin and congratulate each other on having discovered paradise. In the main room a four-piece band played listlessly for half a dozen students from the Instituto drinking cans of beer Mexican style, with salted rims and wedges of lime. In one of the smaller rooms an Irishman sang "Danny Boy" with drunken intensity to three dowagers from Duluth wearing hand-embroidered Mexican blouses and *rebozos*. In the smallest of the rooms two girls, one American and one Mexican, made frantic love to each other on a ban-

83

quette, incorrectly confident that they were concealed by the tablecloth.

Eddie found Chalice in the room with the great stone fireplace, its grate empty now that the winter was past. She sat at a table with three Mexicans, two men and a woman. Chalice saw him as he crossed the room, and she waved.

"Hey, sweetie, over here," she called, and her voice contained none of her earlier anger. She announced to the table, "This here is my little sweetie. Usually we're mad about each other, but right now we're just mad."

Eddie slipped into the seat next to her and muttered his prepared excuse. "Couldn't sleep, so I came down for a nightcap."

"Want you to meet my new friends," said Chalice, brushing aside his explanation. "This absolutely gorgeous young hunk is the well-known *torero* Señor José Cuervos, bull-killer extraordinary. Say hello, Joe. Sitting opposite him—now, hang on to this one—is a real live general in the Mexican Army, even if he is wearing mufti, which is civvies to all you ignorant civilians. General Herrera, say hello to my little sweetie. If you stick around long enough, I'll introduce you to my big sweetie. And last but not least—oops, bad manners, should have introduced her first—anyway, introducing the lady with the handsome boobs, weighing in at about one thirty-five, and wearing a minimal amount of underwear, if any, Señorita . . . uh . . . Francisca, or something like that."

"Holy Mother and the Marx Brothers, how pissed are you?" Eddie breathed as he nodded to the others.

"Not nearly enough."

"Is he really a general?"

"Bet your bubble gum. I can spot one at a hundred yards over open sights."

Cuervos, who looked barely out of his teens when seen up close, gave Eddie a friendly smile, put out his hand, and said in easy English, "Hi, good to meet you."

The general, middle-aged, mustachioed and moon-faced, wore a scowl that seemed engraved about his lips. He spread blunt hands in a sign of unfriendly refusal and said, "I excuse me. I no speak *inglés*."

Francisca was an ebony-haired, dark-eyed woman of about thirty, with lush lips that spread in an inviting smile. She obviously belonged to the general. "I speak a little," she said. She looked at Chalice and the smile faded. "Enough to understand."

Eddie said quickly, "Who's drinking what? It's my round, I'm behind."

An hour later he had finished off three double bourbons and had listened with admiration to a recital of the brief career of José Cuervos. The young bullfighter was engagingly open and frank about his abilities.

"I'm pretty good," he said with a disarming smile. "With the cape and with the sticks, I guess I'm one of the best around." Then the smile disappeared. "With the sword, it's something else, but maybe you know about that."

"I don't know anything about bulls," Eddie admitted. "What's your problem?"

The *torero* seemed embarrassed at having brought up the subject. He hesitated, then said, "It's just that I don't kill very well. Everybody knows it. The oldtimers, they're always saying that the young guys today don't know how to kill anymore. Well, in my case it's true. I don't know why, but it's true."

I should have such problems, Eddie thought sadly, and turned away to talk to Chalice. He ordered another bourbon and then, too quickly, another. Three drinks later he had danced with Chalice once, which had saddened him with memories; had danced with Francisca four times, which had excited him into a raging lust; and had endured with amusement the ever-deepening scowls of General Herrera. He asked Francisca to dance again, and she looked apprehensively at the general.

"What does he want now?" Herrera asked in Spanish.

"To dance?"

"Again? *Mierda,* he doesn't want to dance, he just wants to rub up against your *tetas.*"

"Rodolfo, please . . ."

"Let him dance with his own woman. Better still, let him take her home to bed."

"Hear, hear," said Chalice, who understood.

"What's he saying?" Eddie asked Cuervos. The *torero* looked uncomfortable and did not answer.

Chalice supplied her own interpretation. "He thinks you've been neglecting me. If he only knew . . ."

"Tell him to leave you alone," the general ordered Francisca. "I'm tired of supplying him with flesh to feel."

Eddie, confused in the bilingual crossfire, put his hand on Francisca's shoulder and asked, "Look, do you want to dance or not?"

"Maybe later," she answered.

"She wants to, but her old man says no," Chalice told him. "Are you going to take that jive from a Messkin?"

"Well, if he feels that way . . ."

Francisca appealed, "Please, I don't want trouble."

"Where the hell are your balls these days?" Chalice asked, her voice cutting. "If I were a man I wouldn't let any tin-pot Messkin soldier run me off a girl like that."

"Nobody's running me off anything, and take it easy on the Mexican business. You're not back in Texas now."

Chalice waved her hand airily. "Texas, Mexico, it's all the same thing."

"What is she saying now?" the general asked suspiciously.

Francisca, eager for any change in the subject, answered, "She says that someday Texas will conquer all of Mexico."

"*¡Qué puta sinvergüenza!*" the general exploded. "How much more do they want? They already have most of it."

Chalice turned on Francisca. "Listen, we took all

86

we wanted years ago. What's left ain't worth doodly-squat."

"Time out." José Cuervos rose and touched Eddie lightly on the sleeve. "Let's you and me go make room for some more whiskey."

Inside the men's room they stood side by side over the zinc trough, unzipped, staring at the blank wall before them. Cuervos cleared his throat nervously.

"Speaking as a new friend, Eduardo, may I give you some advice?"

"About Francisca?"

"The general is a very possessive man."

Eddie laughed. "You mean he's a Mexican."

Cuervos laughed with him. "I'm glad you understand. It would be much better if you did not pay so much attention to her."

"Why? Is he going to challenge me to a duel?"

Cuervos looked thoughtful. "No, I doubt if he would go that far. He would simply shoot you."

Eddie stood without moving for a long moment. "You're serious, aren't you?"

"Very serious." The two men zipped up and faced each other. "There have been incidents in the past."

"But he can't just go around shooting people, can he?"

Cuervos shrugged. "He's a general, and this is Mexico."

"I'll be damned," said Eddie, marveling at the idea of such casual manslaughter. "This is one hell of a country you have here."

Cuervos looked truly disturbed. "Please, Eduardo, be careful with this man."

"Don't worry, I will," Eddie assured him, but he knew that he had taken too much bourbon to be entirely careful. Not that he felt in any way drunk. The whiskey had only banked the fires of charcoal burning in his belly, but he knew that he was swaggering a bit as he crossed the room to the table. Still, he felt fine. Confident and fine.

Besides, he asked himself, who the hell is General Herrera? Just an old man with bad breath and a suit that doesn't fit right. I've got half a dozen toys in my pockets that could wipe him out. Two weeks from now I go up against four of the aces. What's Herrera compared to them?

With such thoughts in mind he approached the table, bent over Francisca's shoulder, and whispered in her ear.

"*¿Qué pasa?*" asked the general. "The dancing again?"

Eddie raised his head and looked at the man steadily. "Actually, I'm tired of dancing. I was asking the lady if she felt like getting laid."

Cuervos looked up at the ceiling, shrugged, and closed his eyes.

Francisca hid her face in her hands.

Chalice threw back her head and laughed, applauding gleefully, calling, "Way to go, little sweetie."

"What does he say, what does he say?" Herrera asked excitedly, but no one answered him.

Then the import of the words sank in and his face darkened. He reached inside his jacket and brought out a black, long-barreled pistol. The folds of flesh around his jowls quivered with anger, but his pistol hand held steady.

In a frozen moment of time Eddie heard the babble of voices in the room stop short, heard a chair fall over and crash, heard the dance music stop in a discordant jangle, heard someone, somewhere, curse loudly. Disconnected from these sounds, living only within the frozen moment, he made three imperceptible motions at the same time. His left hand, inside his jacket pocket, tightened round a ball-point pen adapted to spit flame. He shifted the weight of the right foot to his heel so that the explosive cap in the toe of his shoe was pointed directly at the general's knee. He straightened his right elbow, and a steel flechette, poison-tipped and spring-activated, slid out of its holster and into his palm. All this in seconds, while the general's jowls quivered.

He's not going to pull that trigger, not yet, Eddie

thought. He's got to make a speech first, tell me all about it.

"¿*Mi general* . . .?" It was Cuervos speaking tentatively, respectfully.

"¿*Qué*?"

The *torero* at once launched into a smooth flow of Spanish obviously designed to placate Herrera. The general listened impatiently, his eyes never moving. Eddie met his gaze with a grin. When Cuervos had finished, the general replied in short, abrupt sentences.

"I will translate," said Cuervos. "The general reminds you that you are in Mexico, and that there are certain things not done here. He said that you have no respect, that you treat this matter lightly, that you seem to find it amusing. He reminds you that honor is a serious concern here. He insists on an immediate apology. He says that if you do not apologize, he will shoot you on the spot."

Eddie listened abstractedly, his mind concerned with the options available to him, thinking: I can take him out easy with the pen, but I paid a hundred and seventy bucks for this jacket. Why the hell did I have to wear the good tweed tonight? Besides, the flame is messy, turn him into *chile con carne* in front of the ladies, not very polite. On the other hand, if I use the shoe . . .

Chalice's voice cut into his thoughts. The voice was low, but urgent and compelling. "Eddie, take him out now. Right now."

. . . if I use the shoe, that means noise. It also means that his leg comes off at the knee, which means a lot of blood, and I'm wearing my J. Press slacks. Christ, eighty-five dollars shot right there unless they have a decent dry cleaner here in town; damn difficult getting blood out of wool. Still, it's cheaper than losing the jacket . . .

"Now, Eddie, now."

. . . so maybe I'd better use the dart—nothing gets ruined that way; just open my palm and let the spring action do all the work—except, damn, when that boomslang venom hits his heart he's going to puke all over the place, and right on top of my Gucci shoes. Son of a bitch, the next time this happens I better be wearing hip boots and jeans.

"For me, Eddie. Do it for me."

For her? I'm not doing anything for her. I'm doing it because I . . . Jesus, what *am* I doing it for? How did I get into this mess?

"Eduardo," said Cuervos softly. "The general is waiting for your apology."

This is crazy. I can't touch him without ruining the best clothes I own.

"Eduardo?"

Besides, Vasily would be sore as hell.

"Please translate for me," Eddie said to Cuervos. "Extend my sincere apologies to the general. Make it as flowery as you like. Tell him I didn't know the local customs. Tell him I was drunk. Tell him anything you please. Understand?"

"I understand," said Cuervos, and turned to the general. While the *torero* rendered the apology in Spanish. Eddie looked at Chalice. She looked away. He looked at Francisca. Her face was still covered by her hands. He looked at the general. The general stared back contemptuously. When Cuervos was finished with the translation, Herrera tucked the pistol back inside his jacket. Then he spat on the floor to show what he thought of apologetic *gringos,* and nodded for Eddie to go.

"José," said Eddie. "Thanks for your help. I owe you one."

Then he turned and walked out of La Fragua and into the dark, moist early-morning air. He was halfway down the street to the taxi rank when he heard the swift click of Chalice's footsteps behind him. She caught him as he opened the door to the taxi, and climbed in after him. She was silent and contained during the ride up the hill, keeping stiffly to her side of the seat. Only when they were inside the house, and alone, did she turn on him angrily.

"Just answer one question," she said. "Were you holding anything?"

"Enough for an army."

"Then why didn't you do it, you gutless bastard?"

"What for? To entertain you? To top off the evening with a little blood?"

"I don't know what you're talking about."

"Come on, you were begging me to do him."

"That's just an excuse. You lost your nerve."

"Use your head, will you? What happens if I blow away Herrera? I also blow the mission wide open. Then what happens to your little sweetie? Not to mention your big sweetie. Vasily and me, we're both out of business, that's what happens."

They were both more sober now, the hard edges of reality cutting at them. Chalice said slowly, "I didn't think of that."

"Sure. You were high on blood and bourbon, and so was I." He held up two fingers an inch apart. "I was that close to doing him. *That* close."

"But you didn't."

"No."

"Because of the mission."

He laughed unsteadily. "Because of the mission, and because I didn't feel like ruining a perfectly good jacket."

She collapsed against him softly, muffling her laughter in his shoulder. She lifted up her face. "You nut—you lovable nut. If you were so concerned about your clothes, then why did you make a pass at Francisca?"

He was holding her now, her flesh pliant under his fingers. "Francisca's just a body to me."

"A lovely body."

He drew her close to him. "But not the body I want."

"I know," she murmured. "I know what you want."

"You do?" His nose was in her hair, inhaling. He felt the last of his resolve go fleeing.

"You want to get laid, that's what you want."

"Romantic, aren't you?"

"You're the romantic, Eddie, not me."

He held her off so that he could look at her. His

voice was sober and steady. "I want you. That's all I really want."

"That's easy," she said, and her voice was as steady as his. "I'm right here. I always have been."

"I know." Empty of outrage or anger, knowing only his need, he drew her to him again. "I only wish it didn't have to be this way."

She put a finger to his lips. "But it is."

"Okay, it is. I accept that. But I can wish." He took her hand and walked with her to the stairway that led to her bedroom. As they mounted the stairs he turned to her with a sudden gaiety. "Okay, I accept it all, but on one condition."

"What's that?" she asked, leaning against him.

"No more of this 'big sweetie' and 'little sweetie' business. From here on in it's an equal partnership."

They had a week alone together, a week without tomorrows, a week of softness to cushion the hard rock of Vasily's return. They spent the week much as they had spent its first day—afternoons lying in the warm pools at Taboada, nights lying between cool sheets rediscovering old pleasures and inventing new ones. In the mornings Eddie worked in the laboratory, but each day at noon he produced a pitcher of *margaritas* to start them up the spiral of their own particular day. It was a romantic sort of week, a pause in time just made for Eddie Mancuso, and he reveled in it. Even Vasily's return did not do much to diminish his contentment.

The Russian returned to San Miguel on Saturday afternoon, racing the truck up the hill with the horn bellowing flourishes, parking in the driveway with a cascade of gravel, and rushing into the house calling out for Eddie and Chalice. Lying in the garden, in the sun, they had heard the sounds of his coming and were up to greet him, the three of them exchanging bear hugs and grins in a warm round robin. The greetings over, they fell back from each other, and when they did it seemed only natural that Chalice remained within the crook of Vasily's arm, while Eddie slid down to sit on the grass.

Vasily looked keenly at them both, then smiled broadly. "Do I detect a new air of peace and contentment in the household? A touch of the triumph of Eros? Correct me if I'm wrong, but—"

Chalice stopped him by saying softly, "Be quiet."

Unsure at first of what to say, Eddie stared at the ground; then, determined, raised his head to look up at his friend. "Yeah, you could say that, but what's the sense? We don't have to talk it to death, do we?"

"Of course not." Vasily was at once contrite. "It's only that I was so pleased for you both."

"Then let's leave it that way. How was the trip?"

"Magnificent. I have everything we need, plus a few extra goodies that ought to delight you. Your mushroom spoor, incidentally, is in perfect condition, and I found some . . ." He stopped when Chalice, leaning against him, rested her head on his shoulder. He smiled an apology. "Actually, we can go over all that in a little while. Right now, well, the warrior is home from the wars, the hunter from the hill, and all that."

"Sure," said Eddie, not at all sure of the allusion, but very much aware that Vasily and Chalice wanted to go upstairs together. "Sure, I understand."

He watched as they mounted the steps, arms around waists, and was surprised that the sight caused no pain. He watched until they were gone beyond the curve of the stairwell, then he lay back on the grass and closed his eyes. He felt the gentle touch of the sun on his skin, breathed in the odor of fresh-cut grass, and, section by section, blanked out his mind until he fell asleep.

When he woke there was something between him and the sun, and for a moment he thought he was back a week at Taboada with Chalice bending over him, and smiling; but it was only Vasily standing at his feet.

"Did I wake you?" The Russian had changed to

casual clothing; his hair was still damp from the shower.

"That's okay." Eddie scrambled to his feet.

Vasily gripped him by the shoulders. "Now that we're alone, tell me the truth. Are you all right? I man, really?"

"If you mean my head, yeah, I'm okay. You said I had to accept it, didn't you? Well, I have, and that's all I want to say about it."

"You've said enough," Vasily punched him fondly in the arm. "Lets unload the truck."

They spent the next two weeks refining the work of the past month, preparing their witches' potions, memorizing lists of emergency telephone numbers and letter drops, and working into their new identities. Eddie Mancuso became Edward Morrison, Indiana farmer and delegate to the Twenty-second Annual Soviet Exchange Program for Agricultural Implements. Vasily was now Baron Artur Zitowsky, Polish-born and currently attached to the French mission to the United Nations. The new passports and identity cards were faultless, and at the end of the two weeks they were both satisfied that they had reached the outer limits of preparation. Vasily then declared them operational.

"You agree?" he asked Eddie. "Or is there anything else we can do here?"

"Not a thing. It's time to get moving."

"Very well, we leave Monday. You for Moscow via Terre Haute, me for Williamsburg via Washington."

"You know, there *is* one thing before we leave," Eddie said thoughtfully.

"Whatever you say."

"I want to go to the bullfight tomorrow. I owe a guy a favor."

Late the next afternoon they sat close down behind the *barrera* at the *Plaza de Toros* of San Miguel, Chalice between the two men, drinking beer from cans, chewing sunflower seeds, and watching José Cuervos butcher his first bull of the day. The ring was crowded with tourists and *aficionados,* although now,

94

in April, the *toreros* with any reputation had departed for the summer season in Spain, and those who were left were as much the culls and rejects as the bulls they fought. Of them all, only Cuervos displayed a natural style and grace.

"His only problem is that he can't kill," Vasily told them, lecturing. "Other than that, he has all the equipment: fine hands, lovely capework, and he plants his own *banderillas*. But when it comes to killing he's a butcher, just like the rest of them. If he could kill decently he'd cut two ears every time."

"Two ears?" Eddie asked. "Is that good?"

"One ear, two ears, the tail, and then they start on the hoofs," Vasily explained. "It's how the public shows its approval of his work."

"Not a bad system. Maybe we could work out something similar in our line."

"It's a thought," mused Vasily. "Personally, I'm not much of a one for trophies, but a few ears, tastefully mounted, perhaps on a walnut base . . ."

"You're being grotesque, both of you," said Chalice, as a flourish of off-pitch trumpets announced the next bull of the afternoon.

From the sports page of *La Prensa de San Miguel*, as translated:

> . . . rare and moving event to see the coming of age of a young matador whose skills have always been apparent to the discerning eye of the *aficionado,* but who, until now, has suffered from the one fault common to a generation of *toreros,* namely, the inability to kill cleanly and well. Today's events at our *plaza* showed clearly that José Cuervos, the pride of San Miguel, has undergone this passage of arms and now, as he leaves triumphantly for Madrid, may well be ranked with the young masters. True, with his first bull of the afternoon Cuervos was anything but masterly, and although his *faena* was touched with elegance, his sword work was as ineffectual as ever. Once, twice, three times and more he stabbed at the bull, drawing plenty of red but never coming close to

95

the vital spot. As happened in his last appearance, it took a clumsily pierced lung to bring the *toro* to its knees, and the *estocada* to achieve the final release . . .

Thus, a disappointing afternoon drew to a close, but all was redeemed by a brilliant performance given by José Cuervos with his second bull of the day, a cathedral of an animal from the ranch of Paco Medina. The bull came out on railroad tracks, took the cape well without showing any preferences, and charged the cavalry bravely, accepting two solid lances. As is his custom, Cuervos planted the sticks himself, placing three pairs of shorts to the delight of the crowd. When it came time for the capework, the pride of San Miguel opened with a *paso de muerte,* followed by a series of linked naturals that had the crowd singing, and finished with a *media-veronica* that fixed the Medina frozen in place. It was with the sword, however, that Cuervos provided the emotion of the afternoon. As he addressed the bull and sighted along the blade, it must be confessed that those observing expected nothing more than the usual clumsy hacking and stabbing. But today was the beginning of a new era for José Cuervos. He crossed the *muleta* with his left hand, leaned forward, and at that moment . . .

Some seconds before, Eddie Mancuso rose from his seat in the first *tendido* and raised the Polaroid to his eye. All around the arena, dozens of foreign tourists stood with their cameras ready to record the moment of truth. He focused on the scene directly below him, the *matador* sighting in over the horns, crossing the *muleta,* leaning forward; and then as the sword began its descent he pressed the trigger. The sword skidded over the horns and slid in off-target—a typical Cuervos thrust. The dart from the camera hit dead center on the hump of muscle behind the neck—the killing spot. The bull's head dropped, his knees buckled, and he fell forward at the *torero's* feet. He was cut off from life as cleanly as if someone had thrown a switch.

Cuervos stared down, unbelieving. The crowd was

stunned into silence. Then from a back row a voice made raspy by *mescal* called out, "*¡Qué torero es!*"

The crowd found its collective voice, the roar of it cracking over the sand. "*¡Olé!*"

"*¡Diestro!*"

"*¡Torero!*"

"*¡Olé!*"

To these cheers, and to a shower of hats, flowers, cigars, wineskins, and *sarapes,* José Cuervos trotted around the ring in triumphal procession. When he reached the position below the president's box, he halted and waited respectfully for a decision. It came with a flourish of trumpets.

"Two ears," said Eddie. "Not bad."

"Wait, there's more," said Chalice. "They're cutting two ears *and* the tail."

"That's my boy."

Vasily turned to him, speaking quietly. "You know, I worry about you, Eddie. That sentimentality of yours. One of these days it's going to get you into deep trouble."

Eddie shrugged, slipping the camera back into its case. "I owed José a favor. When I owe, I pay up."

"Well, you certainly did today. Without your help it would have been just the usual butchery." He shook his head sadly, and then added the universal complaint of all *aficionados.* "It's shameful, but nobody knows how to kill well anymore."

Eddie looked at him indignantly.

"Present company excepted," Vasily added quickly.

# 9

*Getting close to Suvarov won't be easy, Eddie, but it
can be done. Tell me, what do you know about farming?*

*You mean cows, and horses, pigs? The cows are
the ones with the horns.*

*I was thinking more of planting. Wheat, corn and
barley.*

*Listen,* tovarich, *have a heart. When I was a kid on
Mulberry Street my grandfather used to grow oregano
in a cheesebox out on the fire escape. That's what I
know about farming.*

*I see. Well, you'll have to learn.*

*Why? Is this guy Suvarov a farmer?*

*No, but he is the ultimate Russian. He is in love
with the rich earth of Mother Russia.*

*That's his business. Me, I dig concrete.*

*Try to understand. Suvarov adores everything Rus-
sian: the vodka and the black bread, the smoked
herrings, the pickled cucumbers and the steaming sam-
ovar. He is one of those Russians who make a grand
ceremony out of picking wild mushrooms every Sunday in the springtime. Now do you understand?*

*Keep talking.*

*It may seem strange to you, but it is a custom all
over Russia. Families have their favorite spots in the
forest where they go to pick the mushrooms. Under a*

*certain tree, beside a certain stream . . . you see? Each man keeps his favorite place a secret, but it just so happens . . .*

*Yeah, it just so happens that you know where Suvarov scores. Where?*

*Approximately five kilometers from the dacha at Zhukovka, in a secluded glade not far from the border of Soviet Model Farm Number Forty-two. What do you think?*

*Maybe. What else can you tell me about him? What about the women in his life?*

*There is only one, his wife. Nedya Ivanova is the center of his life. He adores her.*

*Nedya Ivanova Suvarov. It sounds familiar. Why should I know that name?*

*You've probably seen it in your files. She is also KGB. Not only that, she also holds the title of Heroine of the Soviet Union.*

*Big-time stuff. What outfit?*

*Fourth Division, Second Directorate.*

*The family that slays together stays together. She sounds like a sweetie.*

*He loves her. I truly think the man would die for her.*

*He may have to. So what about all these cows and horses?*

*Eddie, this is modern Russia we're talking about. Tractors, and combines, and reapers, and . . . harrows, I suppose. Yes, at this time of year it would be harrows. . . .*


"This next model is a tandem harrow developed in our factories at Novosibirsk. As in all double-action harrows, the gangs in the first section throw the soil outward and the rear-section discs cut the ridges in half, thus working the soil twice over. Please notice that either section of the harrow can be angled from zero to twenty degrees, as opposed to the rigid, or non-angling, harrow which is popular in certain parts of the United States. In addition . . ."

The Intourist guide was a Russian woman built on

Amazonian lines. Full-bosomed, full-hipped and stern-faced, she spoke perfect English in an impressive voice, but despite her air of command she was clearly nothing more than a watchdog over the various delegates to the Twenty-second Annual Soviet Exchange Program for Agricultural Implements.

"I also ask you to notice the concavity of the discs on the harrow," she continued. "On this particular model the concavity is slightly more than four centimeters deep, which aids the inverting ability of the unit. Now, on this next model, if you will all follow me . . ."

Beside the guide stood the Chief Tractor Driver, a short and weatherbeaten man in high boots and a Little Russian blouse that folded at the neck without buttons. His eyes were bright and his nose was red and runny, and he did not try to conceal the bottle of vodka tucked into the top of his boot. He rattled off specifications and statistics in a bored voice, and the Amazon translated them into a low bellow that echoed across the open spaces of Model Farm Number Forty-two. The members of the exchange program followed her now, crunching through the freshly turned earth to view the next of a dozen pieces of machinery lined up at the edge of the field.

Eddie Mancuso lagged behind the others. They were a mixed bag of Asians, Europeans, and South Americans, all anxious to ask him questions about Yankee farming methods, questions for which his crash reading course in agricultural equipment had left him almost totally unprepared. They gathered around the guide to inspect the next model, a small offset harrow, and as the Amazon resumed her pitch Eddie let his eyes wander over the pleasing contours of Model Farm Number Forty-two, the checker board of its green and brown fields placed in a gentle geometry under a blue sky so pale that the clouds blended into it. Beyond the final field, the second-growth scrub of oak and pine worked itself up into a full-grown forest that dropped away with the land to the lazy curve of the Moskva River below. Surrounded by pastoral solitude, it was hard for him to believe that he was only thirty miles west of the Kremlin and less than five miles removed from the *dachas* at Zhukovka. He breathed deeply of the nippy springtime air.

Being out in the country isn't bad, he admitted to himself. It isn't bad at all for a joint without any telephones or pizzerias. It's sort of like Central Park without the muggers. Or like opening day at Yankee Stadium if you're sitting down close to the foul line. Except that at the Stadium they don't spread cowshit over the outfield.

He started to smile as he flashed the thought of Reggie Jackson racing in from right after a short fly ball, up to his ankles in liquid manure, and he felt the bubble of a giggle rise in his throat. He swallowed sharply, cut off the giggle, and his smile changed to a frown.

Nerves? he wondered, and then answered his own question. Nerves . . . sure, why not? Got a right to a few nerves standing here in the middle of Russia, a million miles from home, with phony papers in my pocket and enough merchandise tucked into the heels of my shoes to fill a good-sized cemetery. Who wouldn't be nervous? One of those animals from O Group, maybe; but me, I'm no field agent and I'm scared. Agricultural expert, sure, it sounded good back in Mexico, but here on the line all it takes is the wrong answer to some bright question and right away that Amazon is hip that I don't know a bull from a bass fiddle. One slip like that and I'm finished before I even get a chance to make my run.

Been too easy up to now. Good papers from Vasily's man in Mexico City, legitimate visa, membership card in the exchange program, and then that smooth flight over with all those 4-H types from Indiana and Nebraska drinking bourbon and talking about hay balers and tension bars like it was a different language. Easy, just like Vasily said it would be, going through Customs at Sheremetevo Airport with a gang like that, bus to the hotel, honored guests of the Soviet Union, and all the time I'm walking soft with my heels

**101**

screwed on tight. Easy until now, but now it's for the money. Once I get up on that combine there's no way back, so I've earned my nerves. And it looks like it's time to earn them again.

"I now wish to call your attention to this magnificent product of Soviet technology, the seven-ton, three-hundred-horsepower combination harvester-thresher capable of coverting one acre of grain in slightly less than thirty minutes."

The Amazon had led the group on to the last of the machines on display, a massive combine, and now was busily reciting its glories. The emphasis of her lecture had undergone a subtle shift from the purely agricultural to the vaguely ideological, and with his services no longer needed, the Chief Tractor Driver now sat perched on the seat of the combine staring dolefully over the fields. Without bothering to look around, he took a drink from his boot bottle. As he wiped his lips with the back of his hand his eyes crossed with Eddie's, and he lowered one eyelid in a broad wink. Startled, Eddie winked back, and then worked his way around the edge of the group to where the driver was sitting. Behind him, the guide droned on:

"In a few minutes we will give a demonstration of this machine, and those of you who are interested will be invited to ride on the combine as it travels over the fields of the model farm in an exactly straight line, at a uniform speed, for a distance of five point seven kilometers in each direction. However, before the demonstration begins it is necessary that we understand the historical importance of the combine harvester from the socialist point of view. First of all, it must be remembered that before the invention of the first automatic reaper by the Russian peasant Boris Marmolinski, in the year 1821, the time required to harvest one acre of grain was forty-six hours . . ."

"Bullshit."

Away from the group, Eddie looked up. The Chief Tractor Driver sat high above his head, smiling down.

He spat over the side of the machine and repeated, "Bullshit. Good English, no?"

"The best," Eddie assured him.

"Work two years John Deere factory stateside, one year International Harvester. Talk plenty. Chesterfield Cigarette Company sixpacka Schlitz watcha doin' later baby? Speak bullshit English."

"You do okay."

"You bet." The driver nodded vigorously, snuffled his nose, and wiped it on the sleeve of his blouse. He tossed his head in the direction of the guide, who was still addressing the group. "Maybe I talk bullshit English but I no talk bullshit like that one talk bullshit. You get me?"

"No," Eddie admitted. "You lost me on the curve."

"Look." The driver was patient. "I talk bullshit English. That one talk good English. But that one talk bullshit like Russian boy Boris Marmolinski inwent first weeper. Bullshit. American Cyrus McCormick make first weeper. Babies know this. You bet, American first, but . . .what is? *Nasha luchshe!* Ours is best. You get me?"

Eddie got him, but before he could say so, the Intourist guide broke off her spiel and came tramping over to them kicking clods angrily, sinking her furtopped boots ankle deep into the soil at each step. By the time she got to Eddie she had controlled her temper, and she said in a reasonable voice, "I'm sorry, but it is bad practice to address the workers directly. Whenever you have a question please tell it to me and I shall be happy to translate."

Then she turned to the driver and fired off a burst of staccato Russian. The driver yawned, nodded, wiped his nose again, and answered in one laconic sentence. The guide stiffened, opened her mouth, closed it again, thought for a moment, then turned and marched back to the group. She resumed her lecture as if uninterrupted, picking up on the next word.

"What did she say?" Eddie asked.

"She tell me no talk with *chuzhoi*, foreigner. She say is *nekulturny*. Also bad socialism."

"And what did you say?"

"I tell her go fawk herself."

"Jesus! Can you do that?"

"You just see me do it." The driver took the bottle from his boot, pulled out the rag stopper, and offered it. When Eddie declined he took a slug for himself and replaced the bottle. "You right. Too strong. Listen, mister, here on this farm I make eight hundred fifty ruble every month, drink vodka all day long, tell KGB lady go fawk herself. You know why? Because when goddamn bullshit cultivator break down only Mikhail can fix. Same thing harrow machine, same thing combine, same thing manure spreader. Fawking machines always breaking down and only me, Mikhail, can fix. Fancy engineers from Moscow Institute come, you think they fix? Bullshit they fix. Only Mikhail fix, because I work two years John Deere factory stateside."

"But I thought you said that yours were the best."

"*Nasha luchshe!* The best. Me! Best goddamn tractor mechanic in Soviet Union. I have to be because bullshit machines keep on breaking down."

Eddie stroked the steel flank of the combine. "How about this one?"

"This one, she's okay. Number one machine. You come for ride?"

"Oh sure." He reached into his pocket for the nasal spray. "Wouldn't miss it for the world."

While the driver beamed approval, Eddie inserted the spray into one nostril, pressed, and did the same with the other. At once he felt the modified chlorine biting deep into his nasal pasage, and instant tears leaped into his eyes and rolled down his cheeks.

The driver, concerned, yelped, "Hey, what is?"

"Hay fever," Eddie explained. "Terrible this time of year."

"You farmer with hay fever?" The driver found it hard to believe.

"It runs in the family. Back home they call me Crybaby Morrison. They call my father Tearful John, the sorriest farmer in Campbell County, Indiana. Poor

Daddy, he used to cry even when he milked the cows." He used the spray again, and this time almost gagged when the chlorine hit. A fresh wave of tears covered his face.

"Goddamn," said the driver. "Maybe better you don't come for ride. Is plenty dust, plenty hay out there."

"Don't worry about me. Crybaby Morrison never quits."

"Attaboy, Yank." The Russian reached down a callused palm. Eddie grasped it, and was at once jerked high into the air, levitated upward and over into the cockpit next to the driver, who gave him a boozy blast of breath and a friendly nudge as he grunted, "Velcome aboard."

Five minutes later, three other volunteer members of the various delegations were perched in position on the fenders and chassis of the combine, ready for the demonstration ride. Below them on the ground the Intourist guide gave final instructions, admonishing them to sit quietly, observe the operation of the machinery, and above all to avoid disturbing the driver.

She concluded by saying, "We shall meet you back here after the demonstration, which will last exactly one hour and twenty-seven minutes." Then, looking up at Eddie, she said, "Mr. Morrison, is something wrong? You are crying. Are you ill?"

Goddamn, thought Eddie, if she thinks I'm sick she pulls me off the combine, and then I'm screwed.

Before he could think of an answer, the tractor driver interrupted, saying something to the woman in Russian. She seemed surprised, but nodded. The driver chuckled, spat, and put the combine into gear. The machine moved forward slowly, the harvesting blades whirring and the interior belts rattling. A cloud of swirling dust rose up at once. Looking back through it, Eddie could see the Amazon staring after them. Then the dust thickened and she was out of sight as the combine proceeded down the edge of the field at a steady, stately pace.

"What did you tell her?" Eddie asked the driver.

"I say you got tears in eyes from sight of bee-yoodi-ful Russian motherland."

"And she believed that?"

The driver shrugged. "Who knows? She very good communist. They believe all kinds shit like that."

"Terrific."

"Maybe so, but sometimes with woman like that is better just tell her go fawk herself."

The demonstration route ran for more than five kilometers along the eastern border of the model farm, a straight and undeviating course through the last of a crop of winter wheat so overgrown and soggy as to be worthless for food. The crop had value only as part of the demonstration; otherwise it would long since have been plowed under. Because of this, no storage truck accompanied the combine to collect the harvested grain that spewed loosely from the elevator and added to the storm of dust and straw that surrounded the machine. The result was a cloud so thick and dark that it was just possible to see through it the contours of the land, the growth of the forest off to the right, and to the left the harvested fields that stretched away. After the first ten minutes, the driver reached under the seat and brought out a pair of goggles to protect his eyes. The eyes of the others on the combine soon were red-rimmed, their heads bowed and bucking into the storm. Despite their discomfort, the delegates were eager to see how the machine functioned, and they chattered among themselves as they observed the process.

Only Eddie was indifferent to the workings of the combine. He sat with his head hunched over, his tearing eyes regularly checking the minute hand of his watch, then moving to scan the right-hand edge of the cultivated field. Just beyond the edge of the field and the split-rail fence the forest began, and he searched for the signs that Vasily had given him: a blasted rock and a shale-strewn gully that opened onto an avenue of trees leading down toward the river. Halfway down that avenue and fifty meters off to the left would be a clearing in which stood a solitary oak, ancient and royal in its bearing. The tree was unique and could not be missed; must not be missed, for round its thick base after every rain in the season rose the wild mushrooms so prized by Captain Pyotr Suvarov.

He checked his watch on the seventeenth minute after departure, and thirty seconds later saw the blasted rock and the gully beyond it. He at once took a massive dose of spray, and tapped the driver on the shoulder. The driver turned, and Eddie pointed to his flooded eyes.

"Stop," he yelled. "I have to get off."

The driver looked at him incredulously, not sure that he had heard right.

"The hay fever!" Eddie dabbed at his eyes in anguish. "The dust is killing me. Let me off!"

"Goddamn, I told you plenty dust."

"I can't take it. I've got to get off!"

"No stop," the driver shouted. "Is forbidden! No stop, no turn."

"But I can't breathe. I'll die."

"Umpossible. Is forbidden to die."

"You can't stop me from dying. I'm an American."

"Umpossible," the driver repeated, shaking his head emphatically. "Is orders. No stop, no turn. Straight lines only. If not . . ." He drew a finger across his throat.

"Tell them to go fawk themselves."

"No joke. Is orders. Go up, go back, one hour twenty-seven minutes. No bullshit, no stop."

The tears had collected in a pool under Eddie's chin. The discomfort was real and urgent. He looked down at his watch. Through the torrent pouring from his eyes he could see the second hand coming up on the twentieth minute.

"That's your problem," he screamed. "I'm getting off here. Pick me up on the way back."

"Is forbidden!" The driver made a grab for Eddie's arm as he stood up and braced himself against the guardrail. The other three delegates, riding the fenders, glanced back curiously.

Eddie looked at the ground rolling by slowly, and

107

said, "You know, I really hate to do this. I hate to quit."

"No quit, Crybaby, no quit."

"Sorry, but they don't call me Crybaby for nothing," he said, and launched himself over the rail.

He landed rolling on one shoulder, and stood up at once. He reached for a handkerchief and dabbed at his streaming eyes. Once they were clear, he could see the driver staring back at him helplessly. The combine could not stop, the combine could not turn. Locked into his course by the rigidity of his regime, the driver was a prisoner of the machine. He shook his fist once in despair, and then the rolling cloud of dust obscured him.

Eddie scrambled. Over the fence and behind the rock, down the gully, slipping and sliding on the loosely strewn shale, up on his toes to preserve heels as he sped downhill propelled by the pumping terror in his gut. Out of the gully and into the trees, flashing down the needle-covered floor of the forest striped with alternate layers of sun and shade; and then the sweat began, popped out on his skin, and he knew it was the sweat of fear. Twenty meters, thirty, fifty, and he saw the space in the trees off to his left. He cut hard, almost fell, staggered through branches that whipped at his face, vines that pulled at his feet, and skidded into the clearing breathless.

The great oak tree was unmistakable, the earth around it rich and black and loamy. Eddie slumped at the base of the tree, his back against the trunk. He closed his eyes and counted to one hundred, forcing himself to count slowly. Then he opened his eyes and crossed his left leg over his right. He gripped his left shoe with his left hand, and with his right hand he twisted the heel sharply. The heel came off in one piece. It was a normal-looking heel save for the patch of plastic over the top. He peeled off the plastic, and from the hollowed heel removed a minute flask. Holding the flask carefully, he raised himself to his hands and knees and crawled around the base of the tree, searching.

In three places he found old and shriveled mushrooms, the harmless and delicious *Agaricus campestris*. There the new mushrooms would grow overnight with the rain, and in each of those three places he squirted the ground with the contents of the flask, holding his breath and turning his head aside to avoid breathing in the spoor of the deadly *Amanita phalloides*.

When the flask was empty, he crawled some distance from the tree before replacing it in the hollow heel and returning the heel to his shoe. Then he kept on crawling until he was out of the shade of the oak, away from the loamy soil and back onto the needle-carpeted forest floor. He stood up and checked the soil for footprints; there were none. He turned away and without looking back began the return hike up to Model Farm Number Forty-two. When he reached the field he lay down in the stubbled stalks of wheat, closed his eyes, and let the sharp edge of the sun warm his face.

Twenty minutes later he heard the engine noises and the slapping blades that signaled the return of the combine. He raised himself on one elbow to observe its approach. He frowned at the sight of the dust cloud, and sighed as he reached for the nasal spray. By the time the combine came chugging past him his face was once again covered with tears. He ran alongside the slow-moving machine, grabbed at a fender guard, missed, grabbed again, and hauled himself aboard. He climbed up beside the driver and resumed his former seat. The driver was silent at first, looking at him with grave disapproval, before he finally said:

"That goddamn bullshit thing to do. Make big trouble."

"Look, I'm really sorry," Eddie said contritely. "I'm not trying to make trouble, but I had to get off. That dust was killing me."

"Sure, and now maybe dust kill me."

"You don't mean that."

"Okay, now no. Ten years ago, you bet. Now maybe lose good job."

"I don't want you to lose your job," Eddie said, and waited.

The driver waited, too. Then after a while, he said, "Look, them three." He nodded toward the other delegates. "I speak them people. They no tell. Me, I no tell. How about you? You tell?"

"Of course not." Eddie's smile was genuine. "Why should I tell?"

"Good. Is deal." The driver reached across and shook Eddie's hand enthusiastically. "No tell. No make trouble, not for you, not for me. You scratch my back, I scratch yours. Okay?"

"Okay," said Eddie, and took a deep breath. *"Ty mne i ya tebe."*

"Hey, where you learn that?"

"From an old friend," said Eddie, grinning. "Speak bullshit Russian, yes?"

That evening Eddie Mancuso, freshly bathed and barbered, dined at his hotel, the Rossiya, an establishment catering particularly to visiting foreign dignitaries and businessmen. He drank a modest two hundred grams of vodka as he nibbled at the *zakuski,* the hors d'oeuvre that are the soul of a Russian dinner, and then picked at an overdone steak. He gave up on the steak, thought fleetingly but longingly of finding a Burger King in the neighborhood, and then contented himself with Crimean strawberries for dessert. After coffee he strolled through the lobby filled with foreign visitors, examining the newspaper rack, staring sternly at the impenetrable forest of Cyrillic letters. He addressed himself to the concierge, an amiable young man who was anxious to please.

Eddie asked casually, "Can you tell me what the weather will be like tomorrow? I can't read Russian or I'd look in the newspaper."

"You wish . . .?"

"The weather report for tomorrow."

"I am afraid I do not have that information." The concierge sounded truly regretful.

"Well, could you look in the newspaper for me?"

"I am afraid the newspaper would not contain such information."

"How about the radio?"

After a moment's hesitation the young man said, "May I ask, sir, why you wish this information?"

Because, you dumb bastard, I want to know if it's going to rain, because rain means mushrooms, and that means a score on the hometown board.

Thinking this, he said, instead, "Just wanted to know what I should wear tomorrow."

The concierge seemed relieved. "Ah, in that case, sir, may I suggest that in the morning you simply observe out of your window. If the weather is fair, light clothing will suffice. If there should be rain, then galoshes and a heavier garment would be necessary."

Eddie glared at him indignantly. "I could have figured that one out myself. Now, listen, all I—"

"Steady, old boy." The speaker was a member of the British delegation standing nearby. "You won't get anything that way. New here, are you?"

Eddie turned to face him. "Yeah, just blew into town on the fast freight from Smolensk."

"Er . . . yes. Well, at any rate, there's no use trying to get that sort of information out of friend Ivan here. You see, in this country the weather report is meteorological information, which is a military secret. That's why Ivan is so close-mouthed. He's convinced that you'll send it straight on to the Pentagon. Fair and clear, send on the bombers, that sort of thing."

"Are you serious?"

"Oh, quite. Just look at Ivan's face. He knows how absurd it is, but he also knows that I'm right."

Indeed, the concierge's face reflected his embarrassment. "Forgive me, but I do not make the regulations," he said stiffly. And then, unbending a bit: "As for the weather, I believe I can safely say that it will rain during the night." He tapped his elbow

111

meaningfully. "Arthritis. It always hurts here before rain."

The Englishman cackled gleefully. "Now, there's a Moscow weather report for you. What's the matter, lad? You don't look very happy."

Eddie, not happy at all, felt the sharp end of a disquieting thought prodding at his mind. "If they don't print weather reports," he said slowly, "then what *do* they print in these newspapers of theirs?"

"Very little, actually. Mostly ideological stuff and production figures. And the sports, of course. Couldn't do without that."

"But what about news? You know, things like wars, earthquakes and plane crashes, and . . . well, accidents. Disasters."

"They don't print things like that," the Englishman said flatly. "No news is good news, and Ivan doesn't believe in upsetting the masses. You know, you definitely do look unwell. Have you been drinking the water? They say it's all right, but I prefer the bottled stuff myself. . . ."

Eddie, whose stomach was fine but whose mind was now churning, nodded his thanks silently and turned away. He walked in a daze to the elevator, rode up to the fourth floor, and claimed his room key from the *dezhurnaya,* the woman on duty as floor clerk. He thanked her automatically, walked down the corridor, and let himself into his room. Once there he slumped into a chair, ignoring the buzzing of two pesky flies and the sharp smell of paint. He slapped a fist into the palm of his hand as his daze turned to anger.

"Goddamn Vasily," he muttered. "Thinks of everything, but that's the one thing he didn't tell me. The newspapers. I've planted the spoor, but now I'll never know if it worked. I figured I'd know from the papers, but . . . what the hell do I do now?"

He sat in the chair for over an hour, thinking furiously, raging at his ignorance; and he was so engaged with his thoughts that at first he did not notice

112

the sound of rain beating on the windows. When he realized what it was, he smiled, but bitterly.

That takes care of the mushrooms, he thought. But I'll never know if they worked.

He knew everything he had to know just four days later. He spent those four days attending exchange-program meetings in the mornings, and in the afternoons walking the length of Gorky Street and then over to the Sadovo Ring Road, where the black market hustlers in records and tapes worked the sidewalks. For the morning meetings he wore the usual conservative business suit, but for the afternoon walks he changed into jeans and a leather jacket, a turtleneck jersey, and charcoal-gray Adidas track shoes. On the first afternoon he had three offers for the shoes from well-dressed young Russians, and two offers for the jacket. The second and the third days were much the same. On the afternoon of the fourth day, one of the Russians took him aside and asked him what the game was.

"Who're you, and what game are you talking about?" Eddie asked, straight-faced.

"Call me Wolf." He cocked his head to one side and grinned. "The way I see it, you come around here every day and you don't want to sell any clothes, so I figure maybe you've got something else to sell. Like music."

"Why music?"

"Because this is the place for music. Everybody knows that, and everybody knows that for music you see me, Wolf."

"All right, I see you."

"What have you got?"

Eddie looked him over from top to bottom: the suede jacket, the brushed-cotton jeans, the pseudo-Texas boot. "Nothing that you can afford."

Wolf flushed. "Try me."

"How about some Coltrane for openers? A little Miles Davis? Some MJQ?"

"Cassettes in good condition?"

"Who said anything about cassettes? I've got the original records."

"Discs?" The Russian gave a quick little intake of breath, and then whistled softly. "How much?"

"Two hundred dollars each. I have twenty-five of them. That's five grand total. Cash."

"Does it have to be in dollars?"

"What the hell would I do with rubles?" Eddie shook his head in disgust. "Who're you kidding? You don't have that kind of money."

As he turned to go, the Russian put a hand lightly on his sleeve. "Wait, please. You don't understand. No one has that kind of money in dollars. In rubles, yes, even certificate rubles. You know, the kind that you can spend in the special stores?"

"Dollars. Cash." Eddie stood, waiting. "Well?"

"It's too big for me," Wolf admitted. "But I might know somebody. I'd have to inquire."

"Forget it. I'm looking for a quick deal."

"Please, again you don't understand. The Russian's smile was quick and anxious. "You're asking something very unusual. You're looking for a collector who can spend big money, and in dollars. There aren't many people like that."

Don't I know it, Eddie thought, and said, "How long would it take?"

"A few days. The man I have in mind . . . well, he's difficult to get hold of."

"I can give you two days," Eddie said grudgingly.

"How do I reach you?"

"I'm at the Rossiya, room four twenty-three. Call me."

Wolf looked doubtful. "Those telephones. They're tapped, you know."

"You don't have to spell anything out. Just give me a time and I'll meet you."

The Russian thought it over and nodded. "And my commission?"

"Five percent. After the deal is closed."

"In dollars?" Wolf asked quickly.

Eddie laughed. "Yeah, in dollars."

114

He turned and walked away briskly, not looking back. That sets the bait for Comrade Durin, he thought happily, and then not so happily: But I wish I knew about Suvarov.

That evening he dined as he always did at the Hotel Rossiya, stoking up on the *zakuski* as a hedge against the uncertainties of the rest of the meal. He was halfway through a piece of roast veal with mushroom sauce when the Englishman stopped at his table.

"Mind if I sit with you?" he asked. "The place is full tonight."

Eddie, chewing, waved his acceptance with his fork. The Englishman slid into the chair opposite and looked with interest at his dish. "Bloody brave of you eating mushrooms," he observed. "Although I daresay the ones they serve here are all right."

The meat lumped in Eddie's throat. He swallowed, hard, and it went down. In a choked voice he asked, "What's so brave about eating mushrooms?"

"Ah, then you haven't heard." The Englishman was the pleased purveyor of fresh news. "The word's gone round that some toadstools have turned up. Poisonous, you know. Actually killed one person out at Zhukovka."

"One person." Eddie kept his voice low and steady. "Did you read this in the newspaper?"

"No, of course not," the Englishman said impatiently. "They don't print things like that, but the news gets round unofficially. The town has been buzzing with it all day."

"This person who died . . . do you know who it was?"

"Certainly do. Quite a big shot out in *dacha* country. Named Suvarov. KGB type, and all that."

"Suvarov." Eddie savored the name.

"Damned shame popping off that way from a poisoned mushroom. Not that I have any great sympathy for the KGB . . ."

"Suvarov." He said it one more time, contentedly.

". . . but all the same, it was a hell of a way for the lady to go."

115

Eddie turned cold. "Did you say . . . *lady?*"

The Englishman was irritated again. "Of course I did. I said it was a big-shot KGB type. Nedya Suvarov, Heroine of the Soviet Union, no less. Suvarova, as they have it. I dare say they'll give her a jolly big funeral."

Eddie closed his eyes. His first thought was: Sweet Jesus, I got the wrong one. I blew away the wife.

His second thought was that Vasily was going to be very upset.

# 10

*Let's go to Erikson. What can you tell me about him?*

*Well, he's a big, tough redhead. A twenty-year army man—four years in Nam with the Green Berets. Right now he's the number two man in the O Group and the number one honcho. He makes things move. What else? He likes his work . . . you know what I mean? He digs the pain and the killing. He's sick. What's so funny?*

*Your moral indignation. What are his weaknesses?*

*He doesn't have any.*

*Nonsense. Everyone has. What does he do for relaxation?*

*He kills people.*

*What about women?*

*He kills them too.*

*I meant, what does he do when he wants a woman?*

*He's married. Except . . . wait a minute. Yeah. There was some noise a while back about a hooker up in Washington. He was seeing her pretty often, and I think he hurt her. Let me think. It was a while ago. There was something kinky, I mean really kinky, going on there. I never really understood it, but I'll tell you what I remember. . . .*

The colonel's lady returned to Virginia. No questions were asked, no explanations for her absence

117

were offered, and the colonel's Williamsburg home was a happy one again. Each evening when he left his desk at the O Group building he knew that she would be waiting across town for him with a pitcher of martinis and a welcoming smile, and he also knew that when he slumped wearily in his chair at the end of the day she would kneel beside him, her cool hand stroking a blessing on his skin. Once again she was ready to cook for him, cluck over him, cater to his whims; and when they made love in the night she was patient and gentle, showing her pleasure and returning it so bountifully that often as he drifted off to sleep he murmured, "Thank you, Catherine, thank you."

But if the colonel's nights were now a contented dream, his days continued to be part of the ongoing Mancuso nightmare. Each morning the CYBER chattered and spewed forth the results of its overnight computations, and each morning the colonel met in executive session with his number two, Red Erikson, to pore over the printouts. The results were uniformly favorable, the probability against Mancuso's success remaining comfortably high; but on the fifth morning after his wife's return the colonel frowned as he read the report, tapped the sheet with the stem of his pipe, and looked up to see if Erikson was keeping pace with his reading.

"Red, how far have you gotten?"

"I see it, Colonel."

"Page two, third paragraph?"

"I see it."

. . . so that while the predictability of Mancuso's operation remains unchanged, the accumulation of new internal evidence now shows the potential emergence of a procedural pattern. This pattern indicates that Mancuso is likely to strike next against the most vulnerable member of the O Group complex in order to test the capacity of his abilities. Statistically (see appendix CYBER VI-B-27 for formulae) the profile of the target member most closely resembles that of Romeo Arteaga, and under the circumstances it is suggested that maximum security protection be afforded this member, and that . . .

"Get hold of Romeo," said the colonel.

Erikson still stared at the printout. "Jesus, the spick," he said wonderingly. "Why him?"

"Get him."

Erikson swiveled in his chair, punched buttons on the phone, and spoke into it softly. Then he handed the instrument to the colonel. "He's in the house. Upstairs."

The colonel spoke into the telephone, listened for a long moment, and then his voice grew stern. "No, I know how you feel, but it's an order. I want you on ice, locked up, right now. Yes, here in the house, effective at once. I'll be up to explain it to you later."

He replaced the receiver and stared at Erikson through coils of smoke. "It's okay when we're alone, but I'd be careful about my language around Romeo if I were you. He offends easily."

"You mean calling him a spick?" Erikson chuckled, and his shoulders shook. "Colonel, he's a knife man, nothing more, and the day I can't take a knife man is the day I buy the chicken farm. What I don't understand is, why him?"

"CYBER says that on his home ground he's the most vulnerable. Elsewhere it would be different. It makes sense for Eddie to try him first. But that doesn't mean that the rest of us can afford to relax."

Erikson stretched and yawned. "I'm always relaxed, Colonel. And I'm not going to let that little dago change the habits of a lifetime. Relaxation is my middle name."

"You know what I mean. I don't want anybody getting careless."

"Have you ever seen me careless?"

"Everybody gets careless sometime. I just don't want you starting now. It's a battle, Red. Think of it that way. And it's a crazy sort of battle because we can't afford any casualties. Not even one."

Erikson stretched again, and grinned. "The only battle I've got right now is with the income-tax people, and they're giving me more grief than Eddie Mancuso ever will. Those people play tough."

"I told you how to handle them. Stall."

"Oh, I'm stalling, all right, but I sure don't enjoy kissing their asses up in Washington."

"Ride with it. After the flap is over I'll fix things. We have the connection."

"That's a guarantee? No interest? No penalties?"

"Not a penny." The colonel grinned faintly at his dependable number two, the bulk of him sprawled at ease in the armchair. "Income tax. Christ, Red, you're unbelievable. Worrying about an income-tax audit at a time like this."

"That's why I'm still in one piece. I know when to worry and I know when to relax."

But he was still worried the next afternoon as he pounded up Constitution Avenue in Washington, his brisk pace keeping to the shade of the building line, avoiding the sun. The cherry blossoms around the Tidal Basin had fallen from the trees, the brief spring had fled, and summer had struck the city unseasonably early in April. A more leisurely walk would have been in keeping with the weather, but fifteen years of army living had bred in Erikson the habit of the military style: shoulders braced back, chest flung out, paunch pulled in, arms swinging smoothly. Even the rhythmic click of his leather heels on the hot pavement made him feel alive and vital. The sweat on his skin did not bother him. Sweat cleansed the blood, he believed, and helped to discharge the natural aggressions that built up within him like an unfailing battery charge after nearly a lifetime of combat. He picked up the pace, thinking with pleasure of the shower he would take at Tina's place.

And to hell with the entire Washington bureaucracy, the Internal Revenue Service in particular, and most definitely and emphatically to hell with Mr. Henry H. Bedney, the auditor in charge and the frog-faced bastard so intent on nailing him to the cross for back taxes. How can anybody in a secret service

120

pay proper taxes? They carry me on the books as a GS-9—eighteen lousy grand a year, with the rest of it under the table in cash—and now the pencil-pushing idiots at the IRS want to know how that kind of a salary can add up to a sixty-thousand-dollar home without a mortgage, a new car every two years, two sons at VMI and a daughter at Vassar, and an investment portfolio at the Lombard Odier Bank in Geneva.

Well, my wife is very economical with the household money. That's what I should have told him.

The thought of his wife clipping nickels and dimes from the grocery money to help pay for the new Oldsmobile was funny enough to make him laugh, and he almost did. But he was still too close to the interview, just minutes away from having left Mr. Henry H. Bedney behind his cheapie plastic desk in his cheapie cardboard office, and there was no room for laughter yet. There was room only for the memory of M. Henry H. Cheapie licking the point of his pencil and asking his probing questions as he went down the list of income and expenses. Erikson all the while trying to answer politely but in fact thinking of nothing but Tina Lee and what he was going to do to her once he got to her apartment. In his mind he constructed every twist and turn he would make with her, while as if from a distance he heard his own voice explaining politely that he spent very little money on personal expenses, and that it really was much more economical to trade in a car every two years to avoid repair bills, and more of the same, and then the thoughts of Tina faded and all he could think of was the electric clamp he had used on the Charlies at Da Nang and how handsome it would look attached to the balls of Mr. Henry H. Asshole. Who finally had nodded wearily to show that the interview was over, and had told him to come back again the following week, and not to forget the bank statements and the records.

"I won't forget," Erikson had said, still deferential. "I'll bring them all."

"Make sure that you do."

"I will, I will, sir," Erikson had said, and as he added the *sir* had thought fleetingly of a triangular steel spike that the team once had used for rectal persuasion.

Now, booming up Constitution Avenue, heels clicking, forehead sheened with sweat, he felt the anger building up again. The walk was good for him, far better than taking a taxi, although it was almost half an hour before he reached the Watergate Complex, where Tina lived. His blood was still pounding as the elevator glided upward, still pushing at his brain as he pushed the bell on the door of apartment 16-G.

Tina Lee, wearing a flowered *cheongsam* and a demure smile, answered. Her eyes were the pure almond shape, and the perfect bow of her mouth was only faintly touched with pink. Her slender body and gentle hands were in contrast to the fingernails sharp as knives.

"Stanley." She murmured the name she knew him by. "Stanley . . . so nice."

Looking at the Chinese girl, Erikson felt the familiar surge that came whenever he was with an Oriental woman. They had gotten into his blood in Nam, in Taiwan, and in Tokyo, for they understood his needs, any man's needs, far better than any other kind of woman could. His wife would never have understood those needs; in truth, he would not have wanted her to. What he had with Tina and with her darker-skinned sisters was part of a separate life he had come to crave as once he had craved the electric clamp and the dentist's drill at Da Nang, and although he rarely thought of it now, he knew that the pleasure she gave him was somehow connected to the pleasurable thrill he had felt with the palms of his hands pressed lightly on the kneeling Charlie's shoulder blades, the roar of the chopper loud in his ears, the wind whipping in through the open hatch, the other two Charlies bound and gagged and watching helplessly as he gave the gentle push to the first one that sent him toppling out of the hatch, pinwheeling, fluttering, screaming and plunging into the jungle treetops far below.

"Stanley . . . how hot you look. Perhaps a shower first? And then a drink?"

He glanced around the cool and shadowed room. "Your friend?"

"In the bedroom. Everything is ready. Just remember, you pay him nothing. I take care of it all."

He nodded his agreement. "Bombay gin, with plenty of ice. I'll shower first."

He went directly into the small bathroom off the hall, stripped off his clothes and folded them neatly, draping his suit on the ready wooden hanger. The cold water bit hard into his flesh. He turned the hot water up as high as it would go, then the cold again, and let it flail him. He let his shoulders droop, felt his gut relax. Looking down, he saw how white his flesh was, close to the color of the tiles. Out of shape, he thought. Got to jog a little. Kelly jogged, and shit, it didn't help Kelly. Now Romeo's under the gun. Does Romeo jog? The hell with it. I'm here to relax. Hey, Mr. Henry H., the two hundred I pay Tina, is it tax deductible?

He came out of the bathroom with the towel knotted around his waist. Tina was waiting with the cold gin, stirring the ice with a long red fingernail. She gave him the glass, kissed his cheek lightly, and together they went into the bedroom.

"This is Big John," Tina said as they entered. "He is someone special."

Erikson stopped in the doorway, staring. Big John was tall and broad, black and naked, save for a purple mask that covered most of his face. He stood with his thick arms crossed over a muscular chest, a riding crop gripped tightly in one hand. Behind him was an umbrella stand filled with other crops and silken whips. The black man stood without moving. Even in repose his cock looked like an ebony length of garden hose. Erikson shivered. He raised the glass to his lips and drank off the gin in one searing gulp to cover the shaking motion. Then he set the glass aside, dropped the towel from his waist, and said to the black man:

"Take the mask off, nigger."

123

Big John stiffened, then at a sign from Tina his shoulder muscles relaxed. He raised the mask from his face. It was a young face, the lips slightly curled in a derisive smile.

Erikson nodded. "All right, put it back. I'm funny that way. I like to see who I'm dealing with."

He turned to face Tina. She stood calmly by the side of the bed. He closed his eyes and took several deep breaths. Then he opened his eyes and spoke in a voice far different from the one he had used before.

"Chink cunt," he said softly. "Fucking yellow bitch."

Tina said nothing; she bowed her head. Erikson put his left hand under her chin and forced her face up again. With his right hand he slapped her cheek. The blow left a mark. He slapped her again.

"Slant-eyed, stinking cunt!" He slapped her a third time, and in a continuation of the motion grasped the neckline of the *cheongsam* and pulled. The gown split open down the front. He stared at her small, pointed breasts, then struck her across the face again. His voice was ragged now, his breathing short. "I killed you before and I'll kill you again. I killed a hundred like you . . . a thousand."

"Yes," she said, and her own voice was weak. "Do it, Stanley. Kill me again."

He struck her one last time, and for the first time she screamed, the high voice echoing in the sound-proof room.

Then her right hand flashed out, the long nails extended. Carefully avoiding his face, the claw struck down and across his chest, leaving five red furrows. The left hand flashed and raked five more. Then she doubled over her tiny fist and hit him in the pit of the stomach. He staggered back from the blow. She hit him again, her eyes gleaming now, her breasts quivering as she swung. He fell on the bed, face up, and she lunged after him, ripping away the tatters of her dress. She jumped on him and straddled him with strong thighs.

"Wait," he gasped. "Wait. Don't."

He raised his hands to ward her off, but she brushed them aside and went to work on his face, slapping with

124

hard, stinging blows. He whimpered. She slashed at his chest again, drawing more blood.

"Don't," he moaned. "Please don't. . . ."

Tina reached behind her and below: his cock was not quite erect. Still straddling him, she raised herself up, leaned forward, and took his earlobe between her teeth. She bit down hard. Erikson screamed, arched his back and bucked upward, throwing her off him. He rolled over and onto her, grabbing her wrists as she struggled. Then the struggling ceased and the weight of him held her still. They lay like that, their faces touching, their breathing ragged, for what seemed like a very long time.

Then Tina said in a quiet voice, "John . . ." and they heard the whistle of the whip.

He felt the pain of the first stroke as an explosion between his buttocks. The whip sang again, and the pain climbed up his back. After the third stroke he felt the blood run over his scrotum and down his legs. He bit his lip to keep in the scream, and drove forward. Fully erect, he drove through Tina's thighs and found the wet opening. Once inside her, he looked up at Big John. The black man's eyes were calm and uncurious as he struck again. He too was fully erect. Erikson waited four more strokes; then through the pain he grunted, "Now, now."

He heard the clatter of the whip as it fell to the floor, heard the bedsprings squeak at the extra pressure, smelled the cinnamon scent of Big John, felt the weight of the body above him, and then the probing fingers as his cut and bleeding buttocks were spread. He screamed once more at the familiar, pleasing pain of penetration, and then the three of them were locked together, rocking in one rhythm, driving themselves and each other toward the goal that at first seemed so far away and then was so suddenly close, and closer, and then was upon them and into them, rising to explode as they all came together, two spurting, two receiving, and all of them gasping at the end.

Erikson slid out of Tina, limp. Within him he felt Big John's hardness stir. "That's enough," Erikson said in a different, calmer voice. The stirring stopped, and he felt the sad relief of withdrawal. He closed his eyes, resting his head on Tina's breast. He heard and felt the movements around him, and when he opened his eyes again the black man was gone. Alone with the girl, he wept silently, the salt of his tears running over her skin. The weeping afterward was part of it for him and had nothing to do with the pain. By the time he had showered once more and Tina had tended to his savaged flesh he was feeling fine again, telling the girl tales of Kowloon and Saigon, and making arrangements for another visit the following week.

Tina marked the date on her calendar while she smiled dutifully at the stories. She had heard them all before, and her mind was occupied with thoughts of her next appointment.

After Erikson had left she bathed, put on fresh scent, and dressed herself in another *cheongsam*. Then she checked the calendar book again: Baron and Baroness Zitowsky. She said the name over several times to be sure she had the pronunciation correct, and had time for no more than a puff on a cigarette before the doorbell rang.

The Zitowskys were an impressive couple, even to someone like Tina whose clientele included a sizable portion of the Washington diplomatic corps. The baron was not only well built, but witty and urbane, while the baroness possessed the full-fleshed form of beauty that the slimly built Chinese girl adored in other women. Impressive was the word for the Zitowskys, and an hour later she was even more impressed as the three of them lay relaxed and intertwined on the king-sized bed, their bodies totally drained. Tina was the first to move, stirring in the baron's arms, reaching down to caress the head of the baroness between her thighs.

"Lucky me," she murmured. "Three times in an hour. That usually doesn't happen three times in a month."

The baron propped himself up on an elbow to look

126

at her. "Is having an orgasm considered unprofessional?"

She shrugged. "It just doesn't happen. I give pleasure. I rarely get it. I don't often meet people like you."

"I'll bet you say that to all the boys."

"And girls," said the baroness, looking up from between Tina's thighs. In one lithe movement she slipped out from under and came up the bed to lie next to the other girl. She nuzzled a breast on the way, nipped at soft shoulder flesh, and said, laughing, "In that case you can give us a discount."

Tina laughed, leaned over, and kissed her lips lightly. "I'm the one who should be paying."

"Now that," said the baron, *"would* be unprofessional." He pressed closer to her, and she could feel his hardness beginning again. On the other side the baroness did the same, pressing softness on softness.

Tina looked from one to the other. "I have another appointment soon, but I could call and break it."

"Wouldn't think of it," said the baron. "Unprofessional again."

Tina Lee smiled. "No extra charge."

The baroness kissed her tenderly. "You have a living to make. And we really have to go."

Tina looked at her dejectedly. Inside her, all the last shreds of professionalism were gone, but she knew enough not to press them to stay. "Well, you know my telephone number."

"We'll call," the baron assured her. "Perhaps next week."

"Wonderful." Tina Lee almost clapped her hands in delight. "We'll make a party out of it, do something special. Is there anything special you like?"

The baron was quiet for a thoughtful moment, then said, almost reluctantly, "Well—there *is* something. I hesitate to shock you . . ."

"The last time I was shocked was when it snowed in July."

The baron told her carefully and in detail what he wanted to do. She listened, frowning slightly, but nod-

127

ding as he spoke. When he was finished, she said, "That doesn't sound terribly shocking. It sounds like fun."

The baron sighed. "And I thought I was being so decadent."

The baroness hugged the Chinese girl. "Do you think it can be arranged?"

Tina pretended to think, but she had already made up her mind. "I think I know just the man. I'll have to . . . do some shuffling around, but . . . yes, I can do it."

"Oh, lovely. When?"

"How about a week from today? About three in the afternoon? I'll have to charge you more than—"

"Please," the baron said. "That's not a problem."

"You're a darling," said the baroness, and the baron smiled his agreement.

The baron and the baroness were not the only ones who thought of Tina Lee as a darling. To Red Erikson, as he strode up Constitution Avenue one week later, she was not only a darling, but the wise and wonderful woman who understood so well the demons that rode him. And right now the demons were riding hard. Score another one for Mr. Henry H. Bedney, with his Thom McAn shoes and his button-down drip-dry shirt with the pocket full of fifty-nine-cent Bics. Two more hours of probing questions with that toadlike tongue flicking out to lick the pencil point, those puffy eyes that could spot an error in a column of figures at twenty paces, and that whining, insistent voice.

"Well, sir, unless you can substantiate these figures —and frankly, I don't think you can—it looks to me as if you're going to wind up owing Uncle a pretty penny. Yes indeed, a tidy sum when you come to include the interest and penalty."

God damn the man. Owing Uncle? How about what Uncle owes me? Over twenty years of active service and I wind up getting pushed around by Mr. Henry H. Punk who never stepped on an ant in his life, gets his kicks out of terrorizing helpless taxpayers. Christ, but I'd love to waltz him around a little, just to set him straight. See this hand, Henry H.? I kill with that

128

hand. See this boot? I kill with that, too. See this finger? I use it to pluck out eyeballs. I kill, Mr. Henry H. I kill our country's enemies so that assholes like you can sit behind your plastic desks and intimidate loyal Americans. That's my job—I kill, and I get paid for it, and not the lousy eighteen grand that they put on the record. Three times that much, Mr. Henry H. Taxman, and if you think I'm going to pay tax on the cash you're out of your tree. That's part of the perks, Mr. Taxman, part of the bonus for putting my ass on the line day after day for twenty years, and if you think any different maybe you and I, we'd better have ourselves a little session in the Bamboo Room. Ever heard of the Bamboo Room, Henry? No, the walls aren't made of bamboo, but they've got lots of lovely slivers of the stuff, all shapes and sizes guaranteed to fit under fingernails, into nostrils and ears and anuses, and any other opening available. Yeah, you'd just love the Bamboo Room, Henry. I could waltz you around all day in there.

Blood pumping, heels clicking, sweat pouring, he charged up Constitution Avenue toward the only center of sanity he knew, the thoughts of Tina cooling him and spreading calm. Through the glass doors and up in the elevator like a camel racing for the waterhole, his shaking finger pressing on the bell, and then she was there in the flowered *cheongsam* and everything was turned around and right, all right for now and later. Just right.

"Stanley," she murmured. "How nice."

"Christ Jesus," he said, his voice a croak. "Thank God for you."

"Come in, come in. You look so hot, and I have a surprise for you."

First the ritual of the flailing shower, the massive glass of Bombay gin and ice, and then she led him toward the bedroom, her quick fingers already working at the towel around his waist. As they crossed the threshold, she said, "And this is my surprise. Isn't he lovely? We're going to call him the baron."

Erikson turned on her. "Where's Big John?"

"I'm sorry, dear, but he couldn't make it today. I'm sure you'll find the baron a happy substitute."

"A white man?"

"Really, Stanley, does it always have to be black? There are white men with big cocks, too."

Erikson glanced across the room. The baron stood in the classic position, arms crossed over his chest, the whip clenched tightly, the mask in place. He was older than the usual stud, but his body was still good, and the girl was right about his being well hung.

"Besides," said Tina, "he's a genuine Polish baron."

Erikson wasn't listening to her. He growled, "Take the mask off."

The baron lifted the mask to reveal his face. Erikson studied him carefully. The face reflected only an incurious lust. Satisfied, Erikson signaled to replace the mask, and turned to Tina.

"He knows what to do?"

She nodded. She had already assumed the passive position, chin lowered and her eyes cast downward.

"You fucked it up," he said flatly. "I wanted the nigger and you fucked it up, you dumb Chink cunt."

Then without any further preliminary he struck her across the face, knocked her to the bed, and was at once caught up in the familiar cycle of pain and pleasure, blow and counterblow, smack of flesh on flesh, that filled him with a savage joy pressing on the bubble of his manhood, increasing the pressure, expanding the bubble and the pain until the pain was all of him stretched to the breaking point, stretching and entering the girl beneath him.

He waited for the whip, but it did not come. He twisted his neck to look up. The baron stood over him. Only his eyes showed over the mask, and they seemed so soft and gentle for the role he was playing.

Erikson gasped, "Now."

Beneath him, Tina said quietly, "The whip."

"As you wish," said the baron with a sigh, and struck.

Erikson screamed, then Tina. They both screamed

130

at the second blow, and the third. After that there was no more screaming.

Erikson felt the touch of the whip as a dull and painless thud on his flesh, and even then was startled by the strangeness of the feeling. He tried to cry out, but he had no voice, no breath. Beneath him, Tina's skin was cold on his, her eyes were glazed, and her mouth was frozen in a rictus of fear. He felt an unendurable cold invading his body, starting at the loins and spreading upward. He fought to breathe, felt his eyes flood with blood, and in the final moment before terror overtook him completely had time to wonder at what had gone wrong. It was wrong, all wrong to happen like this. The machine had said so, and the machine never lied. The CYBER said Romeo. The CYBER said the spick was next. CYBER said. CYBER said . . . and in the flash of light before the ultimate darkness he knew what had happened.

Vasily sighed, stripped off the mask, and wrinkled his nose in distaste. Behind him he heard the sound of the closet door opening, and then Chalice was beside him and staring down at the scene on the bed. Her face was calm, but her bare body was covered with a film of sweat.

"What did you use?" she asked softly.

"A mixture. Hydrogen cyanide and rattlesnake venom. Very effective."

"Good God." She looked at the bodies.

"One more down. Three more to go."

"One?" Chalice's eyes widened. "You're not counting the girl."

"The girl was a civilian. Civilians get killed in wars. Bombs drop on innocent towns. It happens."

"I liked her, Vasily."

"You hardly seem to be mourning her." Then, pushed by curiosity, he asked, "How do you feel?"

"About Tina?"

"About all of it."

She would not look at him, and her answer was faint. "Sad, I suppose, but there's more than that.

There's a joy in it, too. Do you know what I mean?"

"I know only that they're dead."

"Then we're different. There's always been a joy in it for me. A completion. A fulfillment. Like watching a lovely sunset. The sun goes down, but it comes up again the next morning. Always."

She turned to face him now, and he saw that her nipples were erect and her hands were clenched at her hips, as if to keep them from straying.

"The hell with your sunsets," he said. "You're excited."

"Of course I am. That's why I wanted to watch."

"And do you feel completed? Are you fulfilled?"

"Not the way you mean."

"And am I supposed to remedy that? Am I supposed to make love to you now with two dead people in the room?"

With the hint of a smile, she said, "I had a little something like that in mind."

Without moving the rest of his body, he reached out and slapped her sharply across the face. She flushed, bit her lip, but she did not cry out. In a low voice, she asked, "What was that for?"

"I have dealt in death for many years. I have learned to respect it. I suggest that you do, too."

She nodded as if in agreement, but he saw that his words had been meaningless to her. He leaned over and kissed the cheek he had slapped.

"Get dressed," he said. "There will be plenty of time for that later."

# 11

On a chilly April morning after the death of Nedya
Suvarova, the four remaining members of the Five
Group met in the office of Colonel Fist at the *dacha*
in Zhukovka. Four men met, but only three took active part in the discussion around the desk in the colonel's office. The fourth, Pyotr Suvarov, sat apart from
the others in a deep armchair, his head in his hands,
his shoulders shaking as he sobbed uncontrollably.
He had been sobbing that way for twenty-four hours,
since the news of the death of his wife. He had not
slept in that time. The unit doctor had tried to sedate
him, and the other members had plied him with vodka
and cognac, but to no effect. Sleep had not come to
him, and now, totally exhausted in his grief, he sat and
sobbed.

The gasping sobs were an irritant to Colonel Fist.
He frowned at the sound of them, and shook his head
as if to clear it. Major Marchenko cleared his throat
sympathetically. Captain Durin stared straight ahead,
unsmiling but with a hint of hidden amusement about
his lips. The colonel tapped his pencil on the desk.

"Let us see if we can arrive at a consensus. Does
either of you believe that Nedya Ivanova's death was
accidental?"

Marchenko started to speak, but the colonel in-

133

terrupted him. "No, follow procedure. Juniors first. Durin?"

Igor Durin said hesitantly, "If the colonel pleases, Captain Suvarov is actually junior to me."

"Very well." The colonel hauled himself to his feet and went over to the armchair where Suvarov sat, his face hidden in his hands. "Pyotr, you heard the question. What is your opinion?"

Suvarov did not answer. His sobbing grew softer, but he was unable to speak.

"Captain." The colonel's voice was sharp. "I asked you a question."

Suvarov looked up. His eyes and nose were red, and his face was streaked. "Colonel, forgive me," he whimpered. "I can't believe it. I cannot accept it. She's gone."

"You have our deepest sympathy. Nedya Ivanova is dead, but you are alive, Pyotr, and I have asked you a question."

"You don't understand. She was everything to me." He buried his face again. "She was the center of my life."

The colonel's hand shot out, gripped Suvarov's thin, graying hair, and yanked his head up. "*I* am the center of your life. And then this group, and then the service, and then the Party, and then the Soviet state. Now, answer me."

"I cannot help myself," Suvarov sobbed. "I beg you to understand."

"Control yourself." The colonel released his hold and returned to his desk. "You see how he is. His opinion is meaningless. Durin, proceed."

"Yes, sir." Durin studied his glossy fingernails for a moment, buffed them once on his sleeve, and asked deferentially, "May I inquire about the computer, sir? What conclusion has CYBER come to?"

"You take no chances," the colonel said wryly. "Very well, you're entitled to know. The machine's report is negative. It calls the death of Nedya Ivanova an accident. Definitely not the work of Vasily Borgneff. In fact, its latest projection shows that Borgneff's

134

next logical target would be Major Marchenko, not Captain Suvarov."

Durin shrugged. "In that case, I must agree. An accident."

Colonel Fist grunted. "Very daring of you. Marchenko, what do you think?"

The handsome major shifted his athletic body in the chair and cleared his throat again. "The CYBER is a machine—an unusual machine in that, theoretically, it does not make mistakes. Therefore, naturally, I respect its judgment." He paused thoughtfully. "But I am not a machine. I am a man over forty years of age, and I have not lived as long as I have by believing in coincidences or accidents."

"Then you consider this as part of an attack by Borgneff?"

Marchenko looked unblinkingly out of his cool blue eyes. "Every instinct that I have rejects the concept of coincidence. Every instinct tells me that the intended victim in this mushroom business was Suvarov, not his wife. However, I must say in all seriousness that if Vasily Borgneff were within fifty kilometers of Moscow, I, of all people, would know of it."

The colonel looked at him with interest. *"You,* of all people?"

"Ivan Nikolaevich, you are the respected leader of this organization. But I am the one in daily operational control. Everything flows through my hands. Everything. Every entry point is under surveillance. A thousand men, women, and children are looking for him. I repeat: If Borgneff were here, I would know. And he isn't."

The colonel leaned back in his chair and stared at the ceiling. "I thank you both for your opinions. I myself am caught between the two of you. CYBER does not make mistakes, that much we know—or at least, believe. But like you, Major, I do not believe in coincidences. Somehow Borgneff has done this. When he learns that he has failed, he will try again. We must be ready for him."

The colonel rose and went back to where Suvarov

sat, standing over the sobbing officer. He looked down at him with distaste. "Amazing," he muttered. "When I think of the things I have seen this man do. And now, because of one woman, a wreck."

Gently, very gently, the colonel put a hand under Suvarov's chin and raised the blotched face. He gazed into the red-rimmed eyes, and said in a lower, mellower voice, "Pyotr, we all know what you are going through. We all sympathize."

Suvarov nodded dumbly.

"Nedya Ivanova was a magnificent woman. She was not only a Heroine of the Soviet Union, she was a heroine to us all."

"She was the only woman who ever comforted me."

The colonel controlled his distaste; his voice remained mellow. "Because of the great respect we all had for her, I want you to know that her death will not go unacknowledged. Too often the members of our service go unmourned to their graves. It is the nature of our profession—security demands it, but not this time. Your wife will be mourned, I assure you. I propose to have a state funeral held for her in the hall of the Ministry of Justice. What do you think of that?"

Marchenko and Durin looked at each other in surprise. Suvarov grasped the colonel's hand; he looked as if he might kiss it, but thought better of the idea. "I thank you, sir," he said. "I thank you deeply. Not for myself, but for poor Nedya."

The colonel disengaged his hand. "I will call the Kremlin to make arrangements. I am sure that Leonid Ilyich will not deny me this small favor."

As he left the room, the colonel nodded to the other two. They followed him into the corridor. Once there, he addressed himself to Marchenko. "The ceremony will be on Friday. Your job is to make sure that this killer turned milksop is in proper shape to attend. I want him looking like a model Soviet officer as well as a bereaved husband—do you understand?"

"I do, Colonel."

"As for you, Durin, I want you in charge of security

136

at the ceremony. You know how Borgneff works. Take every precaution necessary . . . up to a point. Do you follow me?"

Durin obviously did not. Puzzled, he said, "If the colonel could be more explicit."

"Very well, if I must. I worked with Vasily Borgneff for over twenty years, and I can assure you that if he is behind this new attack he will be at that ceremony Friday. No matter where he is now, he will be there. To try again. And frankly, I don't want him frightened off. I want him to make his attempt."

"And Suvarov?"

"You see what the man is like now. Worthless to us. Let Borgneff take him if he can. Just so long as Borgneff is taken as well. Now do you understand?"

"Perfectly, sir."

Thus it was that although the manner in which Nedya Suvarova had met her death went unreported in the Moscow papers, on the following day both *Pravda* and *Izvestia* announced the plans for a memorial funeral service to be held in the grand hall of the Ministry of Justice, a ceremony in keeping with the deceased's honored position as a Heroine of the Soviet Union. The public was advised that the body would lie in state on Friday from ten in the morning until three in the afternoon, during which time citizens would be able to pay their respects.

The concierge at the Hotel Rossiya was pleased to translate the *Pravda* announcement for the sad-eyed Mr. Morrison, and in fact was impressed by the American's apparent concern to the extent of deciding that compassion was an international attribute and that all men truly were brothers. He would have been less impressed had he known that Eddie's melancholy sprang purely from a battered professional pride. Neither sadness nor remorse had anything to do with it. Nedya Suvarov had been as much a serving KGB officer as her husband, and as such her life had long been up for grabs. She bought some early retirement accidentally—those things happened; but on the score-board of results Nedya was dead, her husband was still alive, and Eddie Mancuso had blown an assignment.

He thanked the concierge for the translation, took the elevator to the fourth floor, claiming his key from the *dezhurnaya,* and walking down the long corridor aware of the smell of fresh paint in the air. The door to the room opposite his was open, the pungent odor flowing out from it. Cans and brushes were stacked on the floor, but the painters were absent.

Long socialist lunch hour, Eddie thought as he unlocked his door. He slumped in the chair to ponder, stared out the window at the Church of the Conception of St. Anne, which occupied his section of the Moscow skyline, and proceeded to kick his ass around the room. When he got tired of that, he began making excuses for himself.

"Who could figure it that way?" he asked the empty room. It's supposed to be Suvarov's own secret mushroom patch, so how the hell do I figure that Sunday morning, maybe, he rolls over in bed and says, Hey, sweetie, I'm really whacked out this morning. You know how it is—long, hard week arranging to kill people, like that Colonel Fist is a tyrant in the office, seven copies of everything. So how's about you go out and pick the mushrooms today, huh? Give the old man a break.

Or something like that.

All right, excuses don't help. What now? I've got one ace going for me, the funeral. Suvarov has to come out for that. So I can take him at the ceremony, but how? The camera? It's a sure thing they don't let anybody in with a camera. The hand? Yeah, I can take him with the hand, but for that I have to get up close, and once I take him they take me, which is not exactly the purpose of the operation. Besides, I can't afford an open kill. It has to look natural, at least for a while, so that I can go after the others. But how?

How would Vasily do it? This is his turf, what would he use?

He sat and thought about that for a while, trying to think as Vasily might, but the process was fruitless. He was a stranger on foreign ground without a working knowledge of the people and the customs of the place. He could think of a dozen workable gadgets that he might have chosen at home, but here in Moscow all doors were closed to him. There were no friendly machinists or cooperative druggists to supply his needs. He was wholly on his own, and helpless. He sat back and sighed, wrinkling his nose at the irritating odor of fresh paint. A quick movement on the floor caught the corner of his eye, and as he swung his head he saw a cockroach scurry across the strip of wooden flooring beyond the carpet. The roach slipped into a crack in the wall, and was gone. Seconds later another roach followed, then another.

It's the painting across the hall, he told himself, tenement-wise in the ways of the roach. New York or Moscow, it's the same, I guess. When the painters move in, the roaches move out.

Paint? Roaches?

The edge of something scratched at his mind, then slipped away. Paint and roaches. Go together. Why?

He sat up suddenly in the chair. His chin came up as well, and he started to smile. The smile changed to a frown as he checked the details of the idea now expanding in his mind like a supernova. He checked each point, then checked them all again. He made his mind a blank, let the idea rest, and then opened up and went through it one more time.

"Only if they have the strips," he muttered. "They should, it's a deluxe hotel—but who knows in this country?"

Almost as if he were afraid to test his theory, he stood up very slowly and walked to the edge of the carpet. He ran his foot along the border. Nothing. He did the same thing a few feet farther down. Again nothing. On the third try, he felt something long and flat under the carpet. He knelt down and flipped back the edge. Under the carpet was an oblong strip of plastic.

"Eddie, my boy, you've still got the touch," he said softly. He picked up the strip, examined it, and grinned at the English printing that read SHELL NO-PEST.

Moving quickly, he worked his way around the edge of the carpet, feeling and reaching. He found four of the strips of pesticide. On a sudden thought he looked in the clothes closet and found four more hanging as fly killers. With the eight strips clutched in his hands, he stood in the center of the room and looked around until he found what he needed. Taking a vase from the bedside table, he discarded the flowers. He emptied the water down the bathroom sink, and dried the inside of the vase thoroughly. Then he went back into the bedroom and slipped the strips of pesticide into the vase one by one. The eight of them filled the container.

"Phase two," he murmured.

He left the vase on the table, went to the door, opened it, and peered out. The corridor was empty. Leaving his door open, he skipped across the hall to the opposite room. The painters were still out to lunch. He was into and out of the empty room in less than a minute, and when he came out he was carrying a two-liter can of paint thinner. Back in his room, with the door locked, he poured the thinner into the vase until the plastic strips were covered. A quick trip across the hall to replace the can, and phase two was complete.

"Phase three," he said as he tried to figure the rate of evaporation. He decided on twelve hours as a minimum and eighteen as an optimum. He picked the vase up carefully, opened the closet door, and set it down behind his suitcase. He looked down happily at the soaking strips.

"DVDP," he said, pronouncing the letters the way a lover would murmur the name of his beloved. He wondered if Vasily would have thought of the roach strips, and decided against it. He's got the wrong kind of background. To know about cockroaches you either have to live in New York or a luxury Moscow hotel.

He spent the rest of the afternoon working on his nasal spray. He toook the mechanism apart, cleaned

140

the tube of residual chlorine, and then went to work with his pocketknife and cigarette lighter. The folding knife contained, among other things, a diamond-edged blade. The lighter's charge could be boosted to the temporary strength of an acetylene torch. He used the two tools to cut down the nasal-spray tube; when he was finished it measured less than an inch and a half. He cut the spray mechanism in half as well, repacked it into the tube, and filled it with water. He tested it in the bathroom, filling it and emptying it three times before he was satisfied. Then he took it apart again, dried it, repacked it, and went to stand in front of the hall mirror.

You're going to have to be quick as a snake, he told his reflection. Quick and accurate.

He spent the next hour practicing in front of the mirror: reaching into his left jacket pocket, palming the spray, and bringing it out with his hand flat at his side, the tube unseen. He worked steadily, pausing only when the telephone rang.

"Yeah?"

Wolf's voice said, "Do you know who this is?"

"I know you. When and where?"

The voice gave an address, and added, "It's off the corner of Arbat Street, very easy to find. Saturday at six."

"What name?"

"No name."

"If there's no name, I'm not interested."

"All right: Igor. Just ask for Igor."

"Does Igor know the story?"

"He knows everything." The voice became concerned. "You won't forget my commission, will you?"

"You'll get it," Eddie said, and hung up.

He went back to practicing before the mirror, thinking, It has to be Durin. Igor Durin. I take Suvarov tomorrow, Durin on Saturday, and then I go after the big brass. *If* that stew in the closet works. It damn well better. It's about time I did something right on this run.

He put the nasal spray aside and went to the closet

141

to get the records from his suitcase. He stacked them on the bed. The slip jacket of the top record read, PIANO MUSIC OF CHOPIN BY WILHELM KEMPFF. The record inside was the Billie Holiday 1956 Carnegie Hall concert. The second jacket announced three Beethoven sonatas played by Vladimir Horowitz, but the record was vintage Louis Armstrong. The rest of the discs were similarly disguised. He flipped through the stack until he came to four recordings by the Modern Jazz Quartet. He picked one at random and examined it carefully, nodded, examined the other three, and then compared the four rigged records with several that were untouched. He could see no difference between them. Again content, he packed the records into an attaché case and slid it under the bed.

That evening he enjoyed his meal at the Hotel Rossiya for the first time since his arrival, eating the *zakuski* with an extra vodka, and devouring a goulash which, in other days, he would have rejected. Also that night, for the first time since his arrival, he allowed himself to think of Chalice as he lay in bed on the edge of sleep. The desire was strong in him, and he tried to count the number of days since he last had seen her, last had had her. He fell asleep still counting.

He slept soundly through the night and awoke as the first touch of gray reached the windows. He started to get out of bed, then forced himself to lie down again and be patient. He stayed in bed that way for another hour, dozing and waking, checking the bedside clock. Then at seven o'clock he rose and forced himself to go through his bathroom routine slowly and carefully. Only after he was shaved, and bathed, and dressed for the day did he allow himself to open the closet, take out the vase, and set it on the table.

The vase was apparently empty. The plastic strips were gone and the paint thinner had been totally evaporated. What was left in the container was a thin, oily sludge that covered the bottom. The sludge appeared both innocent and commonplace.

"Dichlorovinyl dimethyl phosphate," Eddie said

142

with a chuckle. He did not stumble over the complex syllables. He knew the words well.

Standing in the grand hall of the Ministry of Justice, Captain Igor Durin reviewed the security arrangements for the lying-in-state ceremony, and was satisfied with his work. The hall was a long, narrow, and high-ceilinged room with only two doors, one at either end. The open casket had been placed on a bier in the center of one long wall, surrounded by flowers, banked with greenery, and guarded by armed sentinels from the various services. Opposite the bier, against the other long wall, stood the official mourning party, the KGB contingent led by Colonel Fist, seconded by Major Marchenko, and between them the pale but composed Suvarov. The shape of the room allowed for an easy flow of traffic as the double line of viewers entered from the south door, filed forward slowly past the casket, and then exited at the other end. Uniformed KGB troops guarded each door and stood in positions of observation down the line. Outside the hall, where the line extended as far as the street and into it, more troops maintained a disciplined order, collected handbags and packages to be returned later, and kept the visitors moving at a steady rate. At no point during the process was a visitor left unobserved.

From his concealed position well behind the casket, Durin watched the procession filing past, wondering not only at the large number of visitors but also at the diverse types of people who had come to pay their last respects. Some he recognized as *apparatchiks,* party members present for political purposes. Others were obviously visitors from sister socialist republics, and curious foreigners from Western trade delegations; but the bulk of the mourners were ordinary Soviet citizens with nothing better to do with their time than honor a dead woman of whom they had never heard before, and all because she bore on her breast the star of a Heroine of the Soviet Union.

Durin checked his wristwatch. Just after two, less

143

than an hour to go, and already by his calculations over two thousand people had passed through the hall. Two thousand pairs of eyes into which he had stared from behind his screen, two thousand faces he had studied, recorded, and rejected. There were only a certain number of ways in which a man could disguise his appearance, Durin knew them all, and certain basic characteristics always remained. After over four hours of continuous observation he was certain that Vasily Borgneff had not yet appeared in the hall. He was equally certain that should Borgneff appear he would know him at once.

From behind the screen, Durin could see down into the open coffin and the body lying there in the dress uniform of the KGB. She had been an attractive and intelligent woman, Nedya Ivanova, and there had been a time when he had seriously considered . . . but the thought was indecorous for the occasion, and he dismissed it. Besides, the word on the woman was that she had been totally devoted to her clod of a husband, just as he had been to her. Durin allowed his eyes to flick across the room to the official party. Suvarov's face was set, and there were no tears, but every once in a while he would rock back and forth on his heels, as if about to crumple to the floor. Marchenko stood close to him, close enough to catch him if he fell.

Durin thought: A hell of a job for the major. If Borgneff does try something, Marchenko is right in the line of fire.

He peeked again at his watch. Two thirty, another half hour to go. A long and monotonous duty, and one that was obviously unnecessary. The computer had said so, but because an old fool like Marchenko preferred to trust his instincts, poor Igor Durin must stand on aching feet peering into thousands of strange faces. When there were so many other things he could have been doing, like relaxing in his nest off Arbat Street, feet up in the air, a bottle of brandy by his side, and some Charlie Parker on the stereo. Something like "Embraceable You," where he takes that six-note phrase and noodles it around five different ways, up and down, inside out, and then comes back to rest on the same six notes. Thinking of that, he wondered what the boy, Wolf, had come up with this time. It sounded good—early Louis, MJQ, Horace Silver, and all the rest—but five thousand dollars? *Dollars!* For some Yankee capitalist entrepreneur squeezing money out of honest Soviet citizens. There were laws to deal with such people, and for a moment he toyed with the idea of applying those laws, of buying the records from this so-called businessman and then arresting him for illegal trading. And reclaiming the money. The idea lasted only for a moment; the scandal would be too great. No, better to pay the money and get the goods. *If* the merchandise was worth it.

Thinking such thoughts did not distract Durin from his duty. As the line moved slowly forward he carefully scrutinized each face that passed at a distance before him, male and female alike, staring, recording, rejecting; and at the moment found himself looking into the eyes of Eddie Mancuso. He was not looking for Eddie Mancuso, he was looking for Vasily Borgneff.

He stared, recorded, and rejected. His eyes went on to the next in line.

Because of that, he failed to see the quick motion of Eddie's hand, although the four service sentinels at the bier, and a dozen other officers standing nearby, did not see the motion either. The hand moved only inches, traveled those inches in seconds, but during those seconds the concealed and converted nasal spray ejected an almost invisible mist of lethal DVDP that settled on the lips and nose of the corpse of Nedya Ivanova Suvarova. Then the line moved on.

At exactly two forty, the people still on the line outside the Ministry were told that no more visitors would be admitted. By that time Eddie was outside the hall and walking briskly up the street. At three o'clock the last of the visitors had passed by the casket, and then had exited through the far door. By that time, Eddie was sitting in a taxi on his way back to the Hotel Rossiya. When the last of the visitors had left the hall,

145

Durin gave the signal for the doors to be closed and locked. Colonel Fist left the group of official mourners and crossed to where Durin was standing.

"Well?"

Had he not been in uniform, Durin would have shrugged. Instead, he contented himself with saying, "The computer was correct. No sign of Borgneff."

"We were obliged to try," the colonel said, unruffled. "Let's put an end to this farce. Do you know the drill from here on in?"

"The casket is to be closed and pallbearers then take positions," Durin recited. "The official mourning party forms behind the pallbearers according to seniority. The casket is then borne to the hearse waiting in the courtyard, after which—"

"All right, carry on," said the colonel. He turned. "What's this now?"

Suvarov had broken down. For five hours, with the public looking on, he had contained his grief in a soldierly fashion, but now the sobs welled up in his chest, and before Marchenko could restrain him he had rushed across the room and stood staring down into the open casket.

"Nedya," he groaned.

Marchenko, beside him again, growled, "Stand at attention. You are still on duty."

At a signal from Durin, two of the workmen began to lower the lid of the coffin.

"Not yet," said Suvarov. "Please."

He bent over the coffin and looked tenderly at the cold, stiff features of his wife. He was silent for a long moment; then he whispered something no one could hear, and leaned forward to press his lips on hers in a final farewell.

Colonel Fist grunted impatiently, while Marchenko looked at his watch. Durin tried not to look amused.

Suvarov straightened up, gasped, screamed once in a strangled voice, and fell stiffly to the floor.

For the time of two heartbeats there was silence, and then the pounding of feet and hoarse voices calling out. Colonel Fist knelt at once beside the stricken man.

With quick hands he checked for signs of life. He found none. He announced flatly, "You may call for a doctor, but he's dead."

Durin stared down, horrified. "A heart attack. Is that possible?"

The colonel looked up at him, his lean face twisted with disgust. He pointed to Suvarov's lips, and the yellowish foam that covered them. "Does that look like a heart attack?"

Durin said weakly, "But it has to be—he couldn't —there was—"

"No sign of Borgneff." The colonel stood up. "Those were your words, weren't they? No sign of Borgneff."

He drew back his clenched fist and hit Durin in the face. Durin kept his hands at his sides. The colonel hit him again, then spat at his gray uniform, turned, and strode away.

The news crossed Moscow within an hour. Eddie heard from the concierge at the Hotel Rossiya.

"The official story will be a heart attack," the concierge confided. "But some people are saying that he died of a broken heart. Do you think that is possible?"

"Anything's possible."

"Do you really believe that? In your country do people die of broken hearts?"

"Only at the racetrack," Eddie said. "Or sometimes during the football season."

# 12

*Tell me about John Rakow, Eddie. Describe him for me in one word.*

One word? He's a criminal. Why are you smiling?

*Your choice of the word. How many of these people are law-abiding citizens?*

Rakow is different. The others are either military types or they have a political axe to grind. Rakow is a thug, a hood.

*Any prison record?*

He's been lucky. He got busted for boosting cars when he was a kid and did some state time, but as soon as he made the street he hooked up with Vinnie Galliano's people and then he was set. They take good care of their people in Boston. Rakow went up the ladder real quick. By the time he was twenty he was one of Vinnie's top hit men.

*No other prison record?*

Just once. The feds got him for extortion. It was a bum rap, but it was the best they could do. They socked him away for eighteen months in one of their country clubs out in Pennsylvania. Rakow used to tell us how he went out under the wire once a week to eat a pastrami sandwich and get laid. Those Boston people, they take real good care.

*How was he recruited?*

*The feds again. They tied him into the hit on the Francusi brothers, and he was facing ten years for conspiracy at some tough joint like Lewisburg or Atlanta. That was when Parker stepped in. He made him the offer, and Rakow bought the package. Now he works on the side of the angels. Full immunity, top pay, and all the fringe benefits. He even gets Blue Cross. You don't get Blue Cross working for Vinnie Galliano.*

*Training?*

*What are you talking about? Rakow was a top gun. He knew all the tricks before he came to the Agency. All they had to give him was one advanced course in heavy explosives at Fort Gulick down in the Canal Zone. After that he was operational.*

*Next question, the usual. Women?*

*Problems, but simple problems. He's got a wife in Boston who won't give him a divorce. He's got a girlfriend in Williamsburg, divorced, with a young kid. He usually spends the weekends with her. That's all —nothing kinky like Erikson.*

*Mr. Rakow sounds like a dull boy. What are his interests?*

*He keeps himself in shape lifting weights. He likes to gamble a bit, dice and cards. Things like that. Like you said, he's dull. Johnny Rakow's idea of a good time is to take his girlfriend and her kid out to Busch Gardens on Sunday afternoon.*

*Indeed? And what is Busch Gardens?*

Boston Johnny Rakow wore an undershirt in all seasons. He also wore a hat the year around. To Rakow, an undershirt and a hat were two of the signs of being properly dressed. Without either, he would have felt like a bum. Bums went hatless. Bums wore their shirts next to their skins. Boston Johnny was many things, but he was not a bum. He even slept in his undershirt. Despite many rumors, however, no one had ever caught him sleeping with his hat on.

On this Sunday morning he slipped from bed wearing undershirt and shorts, moving carefully to avoid waking Helen. He padded across the carpeted floor to the closet and pulled a set of dumbbells from out of the litter of boots and shoes. He put the dumbbells aside and without giving himself time to think, did fifty push-ups and fifty sit-ups. He then did three sets of curls, ten reps each, increasing the weight ten pounds with each set. It was a good pump, and he felt the blood surge.

Once showered and dressed, he went down to the kitchen in the Sunday-morning silence. Helen was good for at least several hours more of open-mouthed snoring slumber, and seven-year-old Terry had learned early on not to make noise on the weekend mornings when Uncle Johnny had spent the night.

Rakow took his first cup of instant coffee out onto the front porch and stood sipping at it as his hooded eyes swept up and down the street. He ignored the crisp, green lawns, the magnolia trees, and the twittering birds. He was interested only in the two cars parked at either end of the short street, both black late-model Fords. There had been a time, in the old days in Boston, when the sight of two strange cars parked that way would have sent his blood racing, but not now. Now he was immune. Even his old boss, Vinnie Galliano, had gotten the word: Hands off Boston Johnny Rakow. He's one of ours now.

Besides, he knew the six men who sat in those cars. They were killers, all right, but they were Agency killers, additional troops sent down from Langley, and their one function right now was to keep John Rakow alive. The protective coverage had been Colonel Parker's idea, and had gone into effect directly after Erikson's death.

"I'm changing the procedure," the colonel had said. "From now on, no more hiding. We stay out in the open, keep to normal routine. We make Mancuso come to us. When he does, we'll be ready for him."

"Like Erikson was?" Romeo asked.

"Erikson was careless," the colonel snapped. "He must have been to let Eddie get that close. It's not going to happen again. I've ordered blanket protection for all of us: three teams of six men each, twenty-four-hour coverage. All eighteen men have Eddie's photo and they've seen his film clips. If Mancuso comes within a mile of us, they'll take him out."

"A mile isn't very much," Romeo observed.

"Hey, I've got an idea," said Rakow. The other two looked at him strangely. Ideas rarely came from that quarter. "How's about we all take a little vacation? Like, I could go down to Miami, and Romeo could head out to the Coast, and the colonel could maybe go up north for a while. Mancuso can't follow all of us, can he?"

"After what happened to Erikson I'm not sure what that little bastard can do." The colonel shook his head. "No, we play it my way—which happens to be the machine's way, too."

"CYBER says so?" Romeo asked.

"CYBER says," the colonel confirmed.

That was good enough for Rakow. He had total respect for the powers of CYBER, the kind of respect that other men reserve for heroes and idols. Three times CYBER had intruded on his life, each time with a demonstration of awesome ability.

The first time that CYBER affected his life had been just after the O Group had moved from Langley to Williamsburg. The move had not been a popular one with O Group staff. They saw it as a banishment, removing them by three hours from their favorite Washington playpens. Colonial Williamsburg, with its restored houses, its quaintly costumed residents and its hordes of tourists, was a poor substitute for the excitement of the capital.

Rakow was the only one of the Group who did not see it that way. He took a long, hard look at Williamsburg through his angle-sharp eyes and toted up what he saw. He saw a tourist-laden town filled with easy spenders. He saw the second-oldest college in the country filled with well-heeled kids. He saw a countryside around the town filled with prosperous farms. And he saw a business community that thrived on catering to the tourists, the students, and the farmers.

Seeing all that, he put his nose to work to find out where the action was. It took him less than a week of street-wise searching.

The Greeks and the blacks had the town carved up for gambling. Most of the Greeks operated with Baltimore connections, and they ran the plush joints out along the Interstate. The blacks were all local people, and their action was limited to serving the brothers with numbers and dice, red dog and cooncan. There was no crossing over the line; any invasion of territory, by either side, was met quickly and violently. As a means of avoiding friction, the division was logical. It was also highly inefficient.

Rakow saw this at once. Trained in the syndicate methods of Vinnie Galliano, he realized that a combined operation was bound to result in lower running costs, a bigger bank, and higher odds to attract the bettors. The problems of racial balance did not bother him at all. He knew that when profits are high enough, skin color becomes secondary. He also knew that it would take just one strong man, schooled in the system, to effect the combination and make it run smoothly. From what he could see, there was no one of that caliber in Williamsburg. Only Boston Johnny Rakow.

He thought about it. That's all, just thought about it. He didn't ask any questions around town, didn't seek any advice. He stayed away from the Vine Leaf Café, where the Greeks hung out eating *avgolemono* and *feta*-cheese strudel. He stayed away from Tiger Sam's, where the brothers held court over chittlins and grits. He kept his own counsel, and thought about it. That's all.

Colonel Parker called him in a week later. His statement had been short and pointed. "You're a public employee on the public payroll," he said. "That means no outside business enterprises—none at all. Is that clear?"

"No, sir, it isn't. I don't know what you're talking about."

"I'm talking about your bright idea to muscle in on

the local gambling here. I can't allow it, Rakow, so forget it."

"Colonel—"

Rakow's protests were cut short as Parker flipped a computer printout across the desk. "Read it. It's all there."

Rakow read it. The printout was a detailed report on the gambling situation in Williamsburg, an analysis of the weaknesses in the system, and an estimation that John Rakow would attempt a combination and takeover of the two groups within thirty days. The takeover had a success probability factor of 87.6%.

"Well?" asked the colonel.

"It's a bum rap. I was just *thinking* about it, that's all."

"No more thinking," Parker said in dismissal, and Rakow left the office shaking his head.

His respect for CYBER was born that day. It was augmented on a day several months later when the colonel again called him in for a private meeting. Again, a printout copy lay on the desk.

The colonel read from it without preliminaries. "Mary Beth Ferguson, age twenty, a sophomore at William and Mary, member of Kappa Kappa Kappa sorority. On the seventh, twelfth, fifteenth, and twenty-second of this month. What about it?"

Rakow felt himself grinning foolishly. "Well, you know how it is."

"Yes, I imagine I do. These Virginia girls haven't met many Boston hotshots, have they?"

"Maybe that's it," Rakow admitted. "They like the way I talk. Do you think I talk different, Colonel?"

"No, I'm used to it, but I think you talk too much. The Ferguson girl's father is a state senator with his eye on Washington. She's already told him that she's madly in love with a Yankee from Boston."

"Where does she get that Yankee stuff? I've been a Red Sox fan all my life."

Parker looked again at the printout. "And to complete the picture, CYBER predicts that if this affair continues, in exactly seven weeks Miss Mary Ferguson will announce her pregnancy. First to you, and then to her father."

"That's a bum rap," wailed Rakow. "She told me she's on the pill."

"Then either she lied, or CYBER did, and you know what we say around here?"

"Yeah."

"CYBER doesn't lie. Break if off," said the colonel, dismissing him, and again Rakow left the office shaking his head.

Any doubts that he might have had left about the infallibility of CYBER were put to rest after he met Helen. Helen Wykowski was different from the other women he had known in recent years, different from the hard-edged girls who hung around with the mob guys, different from the curious Virginia coeds. Helen was his kind of woman, straight from his own background. She liked what he liked. She enjoyed bowling, beer, ten-cent pinochle, and simple, conventional sex. Her favorite meal was a well-done steak and a baked potato with sour cream dressing. She sang "Peg o' My Heart" in roadside taverns. She watched *Kojak* avidly, and the soaps religiously. She thought Archie Bunker was a philosopher. She cried when she saw *Love Story*. She was his kind of girl. She was, in fact, not too different from the wife he had left in Boston, but he would never have admitted that, not even to himself.

The wife in Boston was named Lorene, and before Rakow met Helen she had been nothing more than an expensive irritant in his life. For the six years they had been separated it had been well worth a thousand dollars a month to keep her in Boston and out of his sight. But now, with Helen pushing him to get married, Lorene had grown from an irritant into the major obstacle to his happiness. For Rakow was basically a family man. He liked the idea of marrying Helen, just as he liked the idea of playing daddy to little Terry. He truly believed that he would be totally happy for the first time in his life if Lorene would give him a divorce. But the perverse bitch refused to hear of it. No matter how much he bullied her, no matter how much he offered in compensation, Lorene refused. No divorce.

It was then that his little fantasy began to take shape. Thinking about it idly, he realized how easy it would be. A quiet trip to Boston once a week to map out her pattern, and set up the hit just the way he would have on a regular job. Then, with any one of the dozens of devices he had at his fingertips, he could eliminate his most pressing problem without a trace. And even if he made a slip—that could always happen—there was always the O Group to back him up and give him cover. The fantasy grew more elaborate every day, occupying more and more of his waking and thinking time until he knew that it was not just a fantasy but a very real possibility. He made a firm decision to put the idea into operation. That afternoon he received the usual summons from Colonel Parker.

The usual computer printout was tossed across the desk at him, and there it was again, a detailed blueprint of his fantasy plan, up to and including a success probability factor of 93.0%.

"Another bum rap?" the colonel asked acidly.

Rakow mumbled, "It was just an idea I had. Sort of like practicing for the real thing."

"John, you are just about the dumbest man I have ever had in this squad."

"I don't know about that, Colonel. That ninety-three percent makes me look pretty good."

"That's what I mean by dumb. When are you going to realize that CYBER is way ahead of you? That ninety-three percent just shrank to zero."

"You mean you won't let me kill her?"

The colonel winced. "I wish you wouldn't use language like that."

"Okay. Extract."

"Certainly not. What would this office be like if everybody used the agency to settle their personal problems? Chaos! Anarchy!"

"Look, I never asked for any favors before—"

"And don't start now. What makes you think you're

so special? We've all wanted to get rid of our wives at one time or another."

"But all I want is a normal life. Love and marriage, you know?"

"Okay on the love, but no marriage," said the colonel in dismissal. "CYBER says so."

For the third time Rakow left the office shaking his head in wonderment, and it was the last time he ever tried to stay ahead of CYBER. The three incidents had given him an almost holy respect for the power of the machine, and now, standing on Helen's front porch in the Sunday-morning sunshine with the covering agents parked at both ends of the street, he nodded approvingly at the colonel's arrangements. Playing it out in the open this way, daring Mancuso to come to them, might seem like a high-risk proposition to most people, but CYBER had ordained it, and that was good enough for John Rakow.

Two hours later, he sat at the breakfast table with Helen and the boy making plans for the day. The plans were not really necessary, since they did the same thing every Sunday: a ride out on the Interstate to the Busch Gardens amusement park. The Gardens was a complex of replicas of European villages, and it was Rakow's Sunday pleasure to sit in front of the café in the Bavarian Village, drink the dark German beer, eat *Münchner Weisswurst* with potato dumplings, and listen to the music of the oompah band. The fact that he did this every Sunday without fail did not diminish the pleasure for him. Once, only once, Helen had suggested that they try the Italian Village, eat pasta and listen to Verdi, but when Rakow frowned she had quickly withdrawn the suggestion.

The Sunday passed uneventfully, just as dozens of others had passed for them. The only change in routine was the protective coverage; but the men were good at their job and Helen never noticed them. Rakow, of course, did, noting the neat bracket they provided on the drive down the Interstate. Once within the Bavarian Village, the coverage split up, the leader heading for the kitchen to check out the food, the others taking up defensive positions at tables, on the mall, and in the shops. Rakow glanced inside the café to where the lead agent stood by a window. The agent gave him an imperceptible nod to indicate that the food and beer had been checked and were safe. Rakow relaxed, stretched out his legs, pushed back the brim of his hat, and ordered from the waiter. When the food came, he and Helen ate voraciously, bending over their plates and shoveling in thick slices of sausage. Terry pushed his *Weisswurst* around with his fork and then, as he did every Sunday, asked for a dollar.

"I can't eat this, Uncle John, really I can't," the boy complained. "Hot dogs aren't white. I want a real hot dog."

Rakow gave him the money and watched as he ran across the green to the mobile hot dog stand, pleased to see an agent peel off and follow the boy. He divided the uneaten *Weisswurst* with Helen and they finished it together, smiling at each other contentedly and delicately dabbing grease from their lips.

"I got to go on a diet," said Helen, sighing. "If it isn't the beer, it's the food."

"I got no complaints. I like a woman I can grab ahold of."

Helen looked down at herself complacently. "Well, there's plenty to grab, all right, but ten pounds more and you wouldn't be so happy."

"Ten pounds is nothing. I can work ten pounds off anytime."

"Hey, what do you think I am, some kind of a horse?"

"Yeah, my kind of a horse. A filly."

"Some filly," she said, but she was pleased.

The rest of the afternoon passed quietly, with only three minor incidents to mar the routine. The first was when a crowd of William and Mary students came roaring through the Bavarian village waving full beer steins and singing, incongruously, "The South Will Rise Again." They weren't drunk, just high-spirited and boisterous, but their path led them close to Rakow's table. The cover reacted smoothly, three agents wandering over to place themselves casually between the students and the table, and the other three joining the crowd, jostling, stumbling clumsily, and finally funneling the boys around the corner and out of the way. Rakow nodded his approval.

The second incident came when a tourist set off a cannon cracker on the green. Helen started at the loud noise, as did most of the other people in the cafe. Rakow did not move, nor did any of the agents. They knew the difference between a cannon cracker and an explosive device. Properly trained, they were not distracted. Five of them kept their eyes on their subject, while the sixth went off to check the origin of the sound. He returned within minutes and gave the all-clear sign. Rakow nodded approvingly again.

The third incident occurred late that afternoon as they were leaving the Bavarian Village, Rakow and Helen contentedly weary, Terry still burning energy wildly. An old man selling balloons was posted at the gate. With his white mustaches drooping and his *Lederhosen* shiny with wear, the old man was as German as the sausage and the beer. He had only half a dozen balloons left on his strings, and as Rakow passed by he thrust one out hopefully. Terry was instantly alert.

"Can I have one, Uncle John? Can I have one?"

Rakow nodded, and gave the old man a dollar. The old man handed the balloon to the boy. As he did this, three things happened in quick succession.

One of the covering agents, walking close by, stumbled and fell. He fell against the boy and knocked the balloon from his hand. It drifted free.

A second agent yelled, "I've got it," and grabbed the string.

A third agent, walking in the opposite direction, brushed against the balloon with a lit cigarette. The balloon exploded with a harmless pop.

Terry looked up with a stricken face. Rakow nodded approvingly, and said to the old man. "Give the kid another balloon."

The old man said anxiously, "You pay, *ja?*"

Rakow exchanged a dollar for the second balloon, and gave it to the boy. The agent with the cigarette was full of apologies. Rakow waved them aside. "Accidents happen," he said, and let one eyelid droop in the slightest of winks.

Sunday evening went as uneventfully as the day had. By eight o'clock Terry was asleep in bed, and Rakow and Helen were happily placed in front of the television set, well supplied with beer and pretzels. At ten o'clock, Helen flipped through the *TV Guide* and asked, "Do you want to watch the movie? It's Robert Redford."

"Not much. Come on over here."

"Honey, it's still early," she said reproachfully.

He reached over and grabbed a handful of the flesh around her hips. "See what I mean? I like girls with handles."

"Hey, you lug, that hurts," she said, but she came to him willingly.

Terry slept soundly in the bedroom upstairs. His toys were piled in heaps on the floor, and a nightlight glowed on the bedside table. The bathroom door was open to admit even more light, and the hallway door was open, too. The new balloon was tied to the back of a chair.

Just after ten o'clock the balloon began to deflate, slowly and silently. The deflation took nearly twenty minutes. During that time the VX gas spread gently through the bedroom, reaching the boy quickly. He died in his sleep, knowing nothing.

The colorless, odorless gas moved through the house, out the bedroom door, and down the narrow staircase. By the time it reached the living room, Helen and Rakow were hard at work on the couch—she a bouncing mound of soft white flesh, and he wearing only his undershirt and thick wool socks. Their breathing, already labored from exertion, now came in gasps. Rakow shook his head as if to clear it.

"Don't stop," Helen urged him. "Don't stop now."

"Long day," he muttered. "Too much beer."

"Getting old, that's what." She heaved herself up, bucking against him.

"No, not that." He knew it wasn't that, although he was never to know what it was. Still braced between her thighs, he rested his head on her shoulder, and died.

Helen survived him by seconds. She felt him spurt within her as his muscles relaxed in death, and for a flash of time she was furious that he had come before her. The fury was her last emotion, and then she was gone as well.

Up in Terry's bedroom, the deflated balloon lay limply on the floor. At ten-thirty the rubber began to contract on itself, and within five minutes had formed itself into the shape and size of a peanut. When it reached that size, it exploded in a flash of green flame. The balloon and string vanished; the fire crept across the carpeted floor.

It was almost an hour later when the agents deployed around the house saw the flames come shooting out of the lower windows. Again they acted smoothly, three men running for the building, two men breaking away to cover the grounds, and the last man patching in the radio to the Williamsburg Fire Department. They acted as they had been trained to act, with speed and precision; but by that time there was nothing at all left for them to do.

# 13

*What about Igor Durin?*

*Eddie, the best way I can describe Durin is to com-
pare him with Suvarov. The two of them are opposite
faces of the Russian personality. Suvarova is a tradi-
tionalist who is madly in love with two females, his
wife and Mother Russia. Igor Gregorivich Durin, on
the other hand, is a modernist who is in love with nobody, but who has a wild infatuation with the products
of Western technology. Bench-made shoes, Cardin
shirts, things like that. He even drives a new Mercedes.*

*How does he get away with that?*

*No difficulty. Brezhnev himself has a stable that in-
cludes a Rolls-Royce Silver Cloud, a Cadillac, and a
Lincoln. What's good enough for Leonid Ilyich is certainly good enough for Igor Gregorivich.*

*Likes to drive, huh? Fast?*

*He is noted for it. Yes, I see what you mean. You
might be able to use your pop-off wheel, but how
would you get it into the country?*

*I might be able to rig one once I get there. Tell me
more about Prince Igor. It sounds like he enjoys the
good life.*

*According to the stories, his private life is quite lav-
ish. He's supposed to have a little* pied-à-terre *tucked
away somewhere in one of the old quarters of Moscow.*

*Any idea where?*

*Sorry. All I know is that it's extravagantly furnished with all the modern accessories, things that the average Russian only dreams of. An English refrigerator, a freezer chest from West Germany, a French color television set, an American microwave oven, and a stereo rig beyond description. That's about all I can tell you.*

*You're doing fine. About the stereo . . . what kind of music does he dig?*

*Jazz, American jazz. Durin is reputed to have the finest, most extensive black-market collection of jazz in the Soviet Union.*

*Bingo. Look, how does this sound? I bring in maybe two dozen discs, most of them straight, but three or four I'll have rigged . . .*

*What were you thinking of using?*

*Something simple. A variation of the potassium chlorate compound cut with Vaseline. I rub it into the grooves of the record very fine, can't be spotted . . .*

*Will it have enough of a kick?*

*Kick? You got any idea how many hundreds of feet of grooves there are in a long-playing record? It should be enough to take out a small room.*

*Detonation?*

*The needle, buddy. Once the record starts spinning, the friction heat takes over, and then . . . ka-BOOM.*

*Yes. Yes, I see. . . . You know, Eddie, I've been in this business for over twenty years. But there are still times when you frighten me.*

Igor Durin knew. At the precise moment that Colonel Fist struck him in the face, he knew how Suvarov had died and who had killed him. It was as if the blow had jarred his mind, had rattled his brain free of preconceived notions, and had opened him up to receive a shaft of startling insight. The process was not deductive—two and two did not suddenly make four—but rather an intuitive leap to an inescapable conclusion. The leap did not provide him with details. Names, places, and motives remained to be filled in. But in that moment of insight he was morally certain of two things.

162

The computer was right. Vasily Borgneff was not in Moscow.

The computer had been incorrectly programmed. Someone else was doing the killing for him.

The fact that he had been publicly struck by his commanding officer did not offend him. He was a member of a harsh service, and had himself struck subordinates in moments of rage. He ignored the amused glances of the other officers in the hall, ignoring as well the almost sympathetic look that Major Marchenko sent his way. He signaled for his junior lieutenant to carry on with the ceremony, and then beckoned for his duty sergeant to join him. He drew the sergeant away from the others and gave him a description of Wolf, the music man.

"You can find him where the black-market people hang out on the Sadovo Ring Road," he told the sergeant. "He's always there. Bring him in."

"To Zhukovka, sir?"

Durin hesitated. On the one hand, if what he had in mind was true, then Colonel Fist should be told at once. On the other hand, should his theory be inaccurate (he could not bring himself to say wrong), then he had no desire to look like a fool. There was also a third hand: the hand that had struck him. Although he was not personally offended by the blow, he knew that his professional reputation had suffered badly, and what better way to recoup the loss than to prove his point single-handed? To interrogate Wolf at the *dacha* would mean bringing the colonel into the action, and he was not quite ready for that yet. A far better place would be Lubyanka Prison, where he could work privately, yet officially. With that in mind, he said to the sergeant:

"Not Zhukovka. Bring him to Dzerzhinsky Street. Put him in an interrogation room and hold him there." He looked around him, at the disappearing funeral cortege, at Suvarov's body still lying on the floor, at the uniformed troops awaiting his orders. "Hold him. I'll be over as soon as I get this mess cleaned up."

The mess took several hours to organize, and it was

not until late in the evening that Durin finally sat facing Wolf the music man across a desk in a basement room in Lubyanka. The boy was nervous. He had been picked up, brought in, and kept waiting for hours without knowing why. Now he squirmed in his chair and he could not keep his hands still. His eyes darted round the bare-walled room, and his forehead was damp.

Well and good, thought Durin. He has every right to be nervous. Guilty or innocent, an invitation to Lubyanka unhinges them all.

He went directly to the point. "This man who has records to sell. Tell me about him."

Relief showed on Wolf's face. His imagination had conjured up darker deeds for which he might be questioned. "The American? What do you want to know?"

"Specifics. Weight, height, appearance. All you can tell me."

"He's short, maybe one meter seventy; couldn't weigh more than sixty-five kilos, seventy tops. Has a sort of swarthy skin, you know, like a *zhid*, except that I don't think he is. I can always tell a *zhid*. No, this is a Mediterranean type. Greek or Italian, or something like that."

Durin nodded his approval. "Now, I want you to tell me exactly, and I mean exactly, the conversation that took place between the two of you."

The accounting took longer than the description. Words, and the memory of them, were difficult for Wolf. Had he been asked to quote a specific riff from a Beiderbecke solo, he could have done so with ease, but words were a problem. Frowning with the strain of recollection, he gave the best account of the conversation that he could, prompted along by Durin's searching questions.

When he had finished, Durin again nodded with approval. "Not bad, Wolf, not bad. But not terribly good, either."

"It's all I can tell you, Comrade Captain."

"I doubt it."

"Look, sir, I don't know what this is all about, but

you know how it is with me. I'm always willing to help if I can, but I've told you all I know. After all, it's just a question of a couple of records."

"Illegal records. Black-market records. There are laws about that, you know."

"Excuse me, Comrade Captain, but I have broken those same laws for you several times in the past."

Durin did not comment. He stared coldly at the young man, and Wolf's familiar attitude shriveled. He knew that he had gone over the line. He gripped the arms of the chair and waited. When Durin finally spoke, it was in a sharper voice.

"He's asking two hundred dollars each for these discs. Doesn't that seem high to you?"

"A bit," Wolf said cautiously. "But after all, they are collector's items. I doubt if you'd find a single one in Moscow. Tapes, yes, but not the original records."

"Still, two hundred, and in dollars. It seems very high. After all, how many collectors are there, big collectors, who could raise that much in dollars?"

"Very few."

"Less than that, I'd say. If you asked my opinion, I'd have to guess that there is only one collector in Moscow who could do it. Me."

"That's why I came to you, Comrade Captain."

"Indeed you did. And did it never occur to you that your Mr. Morrison intended you to do exactly that?"

Expressions flashed across Wolf's face: shock and disbelief, followed finally by fear. "Comrade Captain, I don't know what to say. . . ."

"Then say nothing. I think it is almost certain that your Mr. Morrison is a foreign agent. I am equally certain that he is using you to get to me. What I don't know is why. I was hoping you could tell me."

"I've told you everything I know. Everything. I swear it."

"Quite possibly," said Durin, and his voice turned soft, almost tender. "But you see, Wolf . . . I have to be sure."

The boy stared at him, frozen in fear.

"Perhaps Mr. Morrison is using you. I hope so.

On the other hand, perhaps you are working with him. I hope not. But either way, I have to know. And there is only one way I can know with certainty."

Durin pressed the buzzer on his desk. The duty sergeant entered, and stood to attention. Durin said to Wolf, "I'm sorry about this," and he sounded truly sad.

To the sergeant he said only, "Take a team and break him."

The breaking of Wolf the music man took most of the night. Not that he had anything to tell, and not that he resisted the telling. After an hour of severe and intensive interrogation it was apparent that he was hiding nothing, but Durin had to be sure. He ordered the interrogation to be continued and went out for a late supper.

When he returned, he bypassed the interrogation room and went directly to Files Section. There, while his team was methodically taking Wolf apart by the nerve ends, he called for the files on the O Group at Williamsburg. He compared the description that Wolf had given him with those of the five O Group members. None of them fitted. He then matched the description against those of former members of the Group, with no results. He moved on to the Langley echelon, with no success. He continued the search, checking every known active agent in the American service who might be capable of organizing the Suvarov job. At the end of the search, he was convinced that the man he was looking for either was not an American, or was not a professional.

"An amateur? Is it possible?" he mused, and in that moment the answer fell into place. "No, not an amateur, a professional. But a professional designer, not a professional agent."

He called for the file on Eddie Mancuso, and studied it carefully. When he had finished, he was convinced that Mancuso was the man at the Hotel Rossiya. What he could not understand was why the American was working with Borgneff, but that knowledge, he was sure, would come in time. What mattered

166

now was that he had his man. Again he thought briefly of informing Colonel Fist, but the thought was never a serious one. Mancuso had a lot to answer for, not the least of which was the public humiliation of Igor Durin.

He went back to the interrogation room to see what was left of Wolf the music man. The boy was unconscious, barely breathing. Most of his teeth were gone, and all of his fingernails. Blood ran from every natural orifice in his body and some that were newly created.

"Anything?" he asked the sergeant.

"Nothing new. The same story over and over."

"Good enough. I thought as much. Get him out of here."

"Disposition?" the sergeant asked.

"Terminate," said Durin. He looked at the clock on the wall. It was Saturday morning, almost time for breakfast. He sat down at his desk to make his plans for Saturday afternoon.

The private retreat of Igor Durin was a house off the corner of Arbat Street in a quarter that Muscovites like to compare to the Saint-Germain of Paris, a district of twisting streets, well-worn buildings, markets, and cafés. It was a narrow, single-storied building, a relic of the days of Tsarist Russia when the area was favored by the court nobility. The exterior of the house was dull and drab, the facade needed paint, and only the brass fittings around the doorway supplied a touch of liveliness.

The interior of the house, by contrast, was modern in every way, with thick carpets and baseboard heating, indirect lighting and smoothly sliding doors. The living room looked as if it had been furnished from the pages of Western magazines, as indeed it had been. Chrome and glass glittered, a solid mahogany bar occupied most of one wall, and deep, inviting lounges formed sharp angles in the room. The draperies were folds of velvet, the paneling was oak, and behind a curious arch of steel in one corner the music system gleamed, a composite of the finest components.

Durin stood at the bar pouring Hine cognac into fine crystal. He was proud of his private nest, and he expected others to admire it.

If Eddie Mancuso was impressed, he did not show it. The room was extraordinary for Moscow, but in New York it would have been considered somewhat garish, and in California rather tame.

"None for me." Eddie waved aside the cognac. "Let's get down to business."

Durin sipped from his snifter and sighed appreciatively. "The American businessman. Rush, rush, rush. No time for the niceties of life."

Damn, but he sounds just like Vasily, Eddie thought, and made a mental note to apologize to his partner.

He opened the attaché case and stacked the records on a block of quartz that passed for a coffee table. Durin picked one up and looked at the jacket curiously. It read VIENNA WALTZES, but the record inside was Duke Ellington.

"For the Customs, no doubt. Any trouble with them?" Durin asked, and then answered his own question. "No, of course not. You came in with an agricultural delegation, didn't you?"

"You've been peeking."

Durin smiled. "I have access to certain . . . facilities."

"Actually, your Customs people went easy with us. They didn't seem to care what we brought in."

"Those are their instructions." Durin leafed through the records, nodding approval at each discovery. "These trade delegations bring in good business, and I can assure you that when it is necessary, communists can be businessmen, too."

"You're not doing so bad yourself. You should make a bundle selling tapes of these discs."

Durin's grin grew broader. "I see you are wise to the ways of our world."

"As you said, it's business. Let's get going. You have the cash?"

"I have the cash." Durin was no longer smiling. "But you are moving too quickly. Surely you do not expect me to buy a . . . what do you call it? . . . *svinya*, yes, a pig in a poke. Tell me, I have often wondered, what exactly is a poke?"

"Beats me."

"A pity. I thought you might know, being a farmer. At any rate, no pigs in the pokes for me. First we must test the merchandise."

"Look, I don't have much time."

"Not enough to play one record?"

"I guess I can spare that much," said Eddie, carefully casual. Equally carefully, he took a record from the top of the stack and held it out. "Here, try this Jelly Roll Morton."

Durin did not move to accept the disc. "An excellent choice. Put it on, won't you?"

"You'd better do it. I might wreck your machine."

"The set is simple to operate. The volume is on and the levels are set. Go ahead."

"I'd rather you—"

"I insist."

Eddie shrugged, and walked across the room. In order to get to the stereo rig, he had to pass through the steel arch. He heard a buzz, and then a hum. He looked back at Durin. The Russian was smiling again.

"Where did you get it?" Eddie asked. "From the airport?"

"No, this metal detector is a bit more sophisticated than the airport model. If you were carrying any sort of weapon, the alarm would have rung." He added apologetically, "As you can see, I have a weakness for gadgets."

Eddie said sourly, "In my country, the farmers stopped carrying guns as soon as the Indians got good." He put the record on the turntable and moved the pickup arm over. The music of "Dead Man Blues" filled the room with classic New Orleans ensemble playing reproduced with startling clarity. Durin's rig was a first-class, professional piece of equipment with all the devices.

After a few minutes, Durin held up his hand and said, "Fine, that's enough. Let's try another one."

"Sure." Eddie went to the stack and took another record from the top. "Thelonious Monk?"

"Is that the quartet with Coltrane? Yes indeed—and would you mind being a disc jockey again?"

Not good, Eddie thought. That smile is as phony as a politician's handshake. Either he's supercareful with everybody or, somehow, he's made me. Definitely not good.

Again he put the record on, again the music swelled in the room, and again, after a few minutes, Durin asked for a change. He played three more records that way, each for only several bars. He took all of the discs from the top of the stack. Finally, after the fifth record, he said, "Look, I've got to get going now. You've heard enough."

"Indeed I have. No pigs, no pokes. At least, not from the top of the pile." Durin tipped the stack over and pulled out the Modern Jazz Quartet from the bottom. "Let's try just one more. This one."

Eddie shook his head. "No time. Where's the money?"

"Right here." Durin tapped a drawer in the bar. "What's the matter? Don't you like the MJQ?"

"They're terrific, but I'm still going. Let's have it."

"Not quite yet." Durin's hand went into the drawer and came out with a Luger. "Again I must insist. I want to hear that record, Mr. Mancuso."

Blown, thought Eddie. And if I put that music on, all we'll hear is the choir of angels. Okay, here we go —a brand-new ball game.

"Morrison is the name," he said.

"The name is Mancuso. Put the record on."

Durin held out the disc. Eddie kept his hands by his sides. Durin nodded, unsurprised, and said, "I thought as much. How many records are doctored?"

"Four."

"And what would happen if we played one?"

Eddie said easily, "Comrade, it would blow us both right through the roof."

170

The respect in Durin's eyes was genuine. "We've heard about you, of course. We knew you were good, even better than Borgneff, but these records . . . a masterpiece."

Eddie shrugged aside the compliment. "How did you make me?"

"Luck and instinct. If it wasn't Borgneff, it had to be you. I saw you yesterday. I looked into your eyes. At the funeral."

And I never saw him, Eddie thought. Vasily, maybe you're right. Sometimes I think I'm in the wrong business.

Durin reached for the bottle on the bar and poured himself another cognac, but his eyes never moved and the Luger stayed steady. "Mancuso, you're finished. You see that, don't you?"

"Things look dark for the visiting team."

"You are being sensible. Good. But I can't imagine what possessed you to come here unarmed."

"I didn't."

"What? Oh, the records. Yes, that's your sort of weapon, I suppose."

"What happens now?"

"Right now? A little conversation. As for later, well, we both know the answer to that." Durin eased himself into a comfortable position leaning with his back against the bar. "What I want most to know is why you are doing this for Borgneff."

"No comment."

Durin looked surprised. "I thought you were going to be sensible."

"I'm not in the mood for conversation."

"That's absurd. You know we can get whatever we want from you eventually."

"Maybe so."

"You know it is so." Durin shook his head, perplexed. "Mancuso, we are both professionals; we both know how useless this is. I appeal to you as a colleague. Don't cause yourself unnecessary pain. In our business, a clean death is a bonus on the contract. Take it."

"Maybe I'm not ready to close the contract yet."

"What did you have in mind? You admit that your position is hopeless."

"Hopeless, but not impossible. Tell me, Durin, I don't know if Russian kids play the same games as American kids, but when you were a boy did you ever play cowboys and Indians?"

Durin stared at him wonderingly. "What in the world are you talking about?"

"Did you?"

The wonder changed to impatience. "Of course we did. We called it Bolsheviks and Mensheviks."

"And the Bolsheviks always won, right?"

"Right."

"And then you shot all the Mensheviks, right?"

"Right."

"Yeah, that's the way we did it too. The cowboys always won. Then we'd shoot the Indians. Used to make a little fist and stick out a finger, pretend it was a gun. Bang, bang. That's what we used to yell. Bang, bang, you're dead."

"Exactly, exactly." Durin was enjoying himself now. "That's what we did, too."

"So you see, old colleague, that's why I can't oblige you with a little conversation. Because the good guys always win, and the way I see it I'm one of the good guys."

Durin laughed—a deep and hearty rumble. "And so what do you do now? You point your finger at me me and say, Bang, bang, you're dead?"

Eddie smiled ruefully, and shook his head. "It sure would be convenient if I could," he said. He raised his left hand slowly, forefinger extended, and pointed it at Durin's face.

Durin laughed. Eddie laughed with him.

Then he squeezed the rubber bulb inside the artificial plastic hand. A jet of hydrochloric acid shot from the tip of the forefinger directly into Durin's eyes, blinding him instantly. The Russian screamed and clawed at his face. The Luger dropped to the floor. Eddie scooped up the pistol and pressed the muzzle to Durin's temple. He pulled the trigger. The report was a flat *crack,* and Durin fell. Eddie looked down at him.

"Bang, bang," he said. "You're dead."

And thought: So am I unless I move fast. He made me at the funeral yesterday, but did he tell anybody else? Maybe yes, maybe no. He should have, but he was a conceited bastard and maybe he wanted all the gravy for himself. If he told, they would have been here today and it wouldn't have been one on one, but I can't take the chance. The hell with the others for now. It's time to get out.

After that he moved rapidly, taking the four MJQ records and loading them onto the changer. The digital clock in the base of the turntable read 4:15. He set the timer on the record changer at 4:45 and pressed the delay button. He detached the artificial hand and left it next to the turntable, then looked around the room, checking for details. He smiled when his eyes came to the open drawer in the mahogany bar. He reached in and pulled out five banded stacks of hundred-dollar bills.

"An honest man," he said to himself. "He really had the cash."

Then he was out of the room, and out of the house, turning the corner onto Arbat Street in the last of the afternoon sunshine. He walked rapidly to Arbatskaya Place, debated taking a taxi, and decided against it. He kept walking, crossed Gagarin Street, and went down into the Kropotkin Metro station. Fifteen minutes later he was back at the Hotel Rossiya, and at four forty-five, when the needle came down on the Modern Jazz Quartet's version of "Softly, as in a Morning Sunrise," blowing a chunk out of Arbat Street and turning the area into a replica of the South Bronx, Eddie Mancuso was vigorously explaining to both the concierge and the Aeroflot clerk why it was vital that he be on the night flight to Paris. The concierge assured him that such a rapid booking was impossible. The Aeroflot clerk agreed.

"A good communist can also be a good business-man," Eddie quoted, and pulled out Durin's roll.

The concierge and the clerk took a look at the roll and went into a huddle. The clerk used the telephone and then they huddled again. Half an hour later the roll had been substantially reduced, but Eddie had a confirmed seat on Aeroflot's flight 4-A to Paris.

He was fine until just after takeoff, and then his hands began to shake. They shook all the way to Paris. During the flight he tried to draft a cable to Vasily, but his hand could not hold the pen. After he had landed at De Gaulle, taxied into the city, and checked into a hotel, he went to work on a bottle of bourbon. Somewhere below the shoulder of the bottle his hands stopped shaking. He had one more bourbon to be sure, and then wrote out the cable in large black letters, sending it off to the Washington letter drop.

SCORE YANKEES 2 REDS 0. GAME TEMPORARILY SUS-PENDED BECAUSE OF EXTREME TERROR. MINE. MEET ME WHERE THE SHEEP AND THE ANTELOPE PLAY, AND BRING COURAGE. YOURS. (SIGNED) CRYBABY MORRI-SON.

He fell off to sleep then, knowing he was drunk, and not caring.

# 14

The old Indian had been standing in front of the door for ten minutes without moving a muscle, and the sight of him made Andy nervous. The former Green Beret who stood portal guard at the Colonial Squad headquarters was not normally a nervous man. A nervous man could not have held his job, which was to scrutinize all visitors through a closed-circuit viewer. For those who belonged, the door was opened; for those who did not, it remained closed. Dozens of times each day a tourist would knock at the door, thinking that the house was part of some exhibit. The knock was never answered, and eventually the tourist would wander away. But not today. Today the old Indian had knocked, and had waited, immobile, for more than ten minutes, and for the first time since he had come on the job, Andy Washington was nervous.

He was not the only one. The members of the Colonial Squad at Williamsburg below the level of the O Group—the service and supply troops, the technicians, the guards, the low-grade assassins—knew that the times were out of joint, but they didn't know why. They knew that something horrible had happened to Kelly in New York, that something obscene had happened to Erikson in Washington, and that something tragic had happened to Rakow in the Williamsburg

175

fire, but that was all they knew. They knew nothing of what Colonel Parker now privately referred to as the Mancuso Offensive; but knowing as little as they did, the troops were aware that all leaves had been cancelled, that communications traffic had doubled, and that security precautions had trebled in the past two weeks. Without any other knowledge, this was enough to make them nervous and edgy, and Andy Washington was no exception.

He looked again at the television screen. The man who stood at the front door was like no tourist he had ever seen. He was old, and he was an Indian. His face was leathered and lined with deep furrows, and his hair, although still black, had been thinned by the years. His body was lean right down to the bones, his jeans and his vest were shabby with hard use, and he wore a single eagle feather stuck into the band of his Stetson. His face was expressionless. He stood there and waited.

Andy turned to Billing, his backup man. "Did you ever see anything like that? He's been standing there for close on to twenty minutes."

Billings, who read books, asked, "Do you think he's a chief, Andy?"

"He's a fool, that's what he is, standing there like that. Makes me itchy just looking at him."

"I read somewhere that only chiefs can wear eagle feathers."

"If he'd only move, or smile, or scratch his ass."

"Indians can stay still like that for hours. They teach them when they're babies."

"That's no baby out there."

"It's like riding a bicycle. Once you learn how, you never forget."

"Damn old man, looks more like a hundred."

"Comes in handy when they're stealing horses."

"You think that's what he's here for? You think he's come to steal our horses?"

Billings looked at his partner in surprise. "Andy, you know we don't have no horses here."

176

"Sure, *I* know it, and *you* know it, but does that goddamn Indian know it?"

Billings thought about that one, then shook his head. "That isn't it. He knows we don't have no horses here."

"How'd he get so smart?"

"Oh, Indians are clever. All he has to do is look around and see. There ain't no horseshit outside."

"Goddamn, that's right," said Andy in apparent admiration. "You're smart enough to be an Indian yourself."

Billings waved aside the compliment. "It's just that I read a lot. I try to keep up on things. Like that feather he's wearing. I think maybe it's turkey, not eagle."

"Say which?"

"What the chiefs wear. Turkey feathers."

"He's a turkey, all right," Andy muttered. "Got me a turkey outside standing there like a statue, got me a turkey in here don't know cotton candy from horse-apples. Got me more goddamn turkeys than the Salvation Army come Christmas."

Billings said thoughtfully, "On the other hand . . ."

"Yeah?"

"Maybe he figures we hid the horseshit."

"That does it," said Andy, undone. "That turkey out there, he's going to fly."

He flung open the door and stared into the furrowed face, the dark, unblinking eyes. The Indian spoke, moving only his lips. "Mighty slow service, son."

"Sorry, sir, but this is private property. You'll have to move along."

"Don't I get to take the dollar tour?"

"No tours here, mister, nothing like that. Now how's about we get moving, huh?"

"Looks like you weren't expecting me."

"Not you, not nobody."

"Maybe you'd better call Colonel Parker and tell him I'm here."

"No colonels here, mister. No tours and no colonels."

"You don't want to con a poor old Injun, son. That ain't right. Next thing you'll be wanting to buy up my oil wells."

"Mister, you're trying my patience."

"All I want is in, son."

"There *ain't* no in, I told you that." Andy stepped out onto the porch. "Look, what does it take to get you moving?"

"Can't rightly say. They haven't invented it yet."

"Do tell?" Andy smiled. "You sure are one salty old man. I hope I get to be that salty when I'm your age."

"If you live to be my age," the Indian said calmly.

Andy chuckled and shook his head. He reached out to take the Indian by the arm. He intended no violence. He wanted only to help the old man down the stairs. His fingers barely touched the Indian's sleeve, and then he was in the air, flying. Trained in the arts, he knew as he flew that he had been thrown *harai tsurikomi ashi*. He twisted in the air, landed lightly, and came charging back up the stairs.

*"Kiai!"* the old man shouted. He dropped his left shoulder and moved his left arm. Andy went flying again. This time he did not land lightly, and after he landed he lay without moving.

The Indian turned to Billings, who stood in the doorway staring in disbelief. "It was Colonel Parker that I wanted. See about it, will you?"

Billings gulped, nodded, and slammed the door shut. He grabbed the telephone, punched bottons frantically, and got through to the colonel. He tried to keep his voice calm.

"Colonel, sir, this is Billings, on the gate? Sir, I know this sounds crazy, but I've got an Indian outside who insists on seeing you."

"Did you say an Indian?"

"Yes, sir, a very old Indian. At first we thought maybe he was trying to steal our horses, but—"

"Our *what?*"

178

"Well, anyway, he may not be no horse thief, but he just beat the crap out of Andy Washington."

"An Indian? An *old* Indian?"

"Yes, sir."

"And he took Andy Washington?"

"Andy's just a-laying there."

There was a moment of silence. Then the colonel said slowly, "Oh, my God." He hung up.

A moment later he came racing down the corridor, brushed past Billings, and opened the door. His eyes took in first the weatherbeaten face before him, then shifted down to Andy's body, still lying motionless. His eyes came back to the Indian. He did not look happy.

"Howdy, Fred," the old man said. "That's a good boy you have there. I had to throw him twice."

"Tom. Tom Crowfoot."

"In the flesh, what's left of it. Piss-poor sort of welcome you hand out here."

Behind him, the colonel heard Billings stir with indignation at the familiarity. Billings was unaware that he was standing in the presence of a living legend, not to mention the one man who could always make Frederick Parker feel like an erring schoolboy.

Thomas Crowfoot, a full-blooded Oglala Sioux, was a name spoken of with awe in intelligence circles. No one knew his actual age, but he was an ancient who had spent more than forty years with U.S. Army Intelligence, then the Office of Strategic Services, and finally the Agency. It was he who had flatly told John Kennedy that the Bay of Pigs was a doomed operation. It was he who had arranged the exchange of the Russian spy Rudolf Abel for U-2 pilot Francis Gary Powers. The fine touch of his hand had been felt in covert operations in Guatemala, Iran, Chile, and a dozen other global hot spots. Long past retirement age, he held no rank and needed none. Wherever he went, Thomas Crowfoot was in charge, and anyone who disagreed could be easily convinced by a single telephone call to the White House. Not that anyone had ever disagreed.

Parker stammered, "I—we—that is, we weren't expecting you, Tom."

"So it seems. Probably thought I was dead by now."

"Oh, no, of course not."

"Bullcacky. You'd dance on my grave. Reckon I should be dead, at that. But I'm not, and you're stuck with me. Do I get in, or do I have to throw somebody else down the stairs?"

"No, no. I mean, yes, come in." He turned to Billings. "Have Andy taken care of and put another man on the gate."

The colonel led the way to his office. Once on familiar ground behind his desk, he was able to compose himself into the model of a proper senior officer. He squared his shoulders and said, "Now, Tom, what can we do for you here?"

Crowfoot, slouched in a chair opposite, smiled faintly. "You can start by saving us both some time. Eddie Mancuso has got you in the buffalo dung up to your nose. I'm here to get you out of it."

The colonel's composure vanished. Hesitantly, he asked, "Are you relieving me?"

"Hell, no, I don't want your job. I just want to clean up the mess."

"Langley sent you?" The colonel received a cold stare for an answer. "All right, I'm not questioning your authority. It's a mess, all right. Have you been briefed?"

"I've read the dayreps and the KGB intercepts."

"How about CYBER?"

"Your machine says that Mancuso is doing the impossible. That doesn't make me eager to read printouts."

"But CYBER doesn't lie."

"I've heard that holy writ before. Sure, CYBER doesn't lie, but no computer is any better than its input."

"I'll vouch for our programming all the way down the line."

"I'm sure you would. That's why Mancuso has you by the old shorties. Do you know what computer peo-

180

ple say about this kind of programming? Garbage in, garbage out. That's what they say."

"Are you calling my programming garbage?"

Crowfoot said firmly, "I am. You people with your blind faith in machines. CYBER says that Mancuso is out to destroy the O Group, so when three of your people get the axe you automatically assume that Mancuso did it."

"Certainly I assume it. It's only logical." The colonel's voice changed. "I mean . . . it *is* logical, isn't it?"

"Maybe to you, but not to me. Garbage in, garbage out. Eddie Mancuso isn't killing your people, Freddy."

"He isn't?" The colonel's voice rose to a wail. "Then who is?"

"Vasily Borgneff."

"You were frightened," said Vasily.

"Out of my wits," Eddie agreed.

"You panicked."

"Like a pregnant schoolgirl."

"You ran."

"Like a turpentined cat."

"And you've probably compromised the entire operation. We're finished."

"I don't think so. I think we can still pull it off. But I guarantee you one thing. No matter what else happens, I'm not going back to Mother Russia."

They sat in the *sala* of the house in San Miguel. The house seemed strange to them after weeks away from it. The maids had been dismissed, the furniture was draped with dust covers, and, more important, the absence of Chalice robbed each room of dimension.

"At first I couldn't believe your cable," said Vasily. "I was so close to success—only two more to go. Then you panicked and ran, and I had to run too."

Eddie whipped a cover from an armchair and sank into it, sighing. "What did you expect me to do? I was blown. Durin made me. Maybe he told the others

181

and maybe he didn't, but I wasn't going to hang around to find out."

"The answer is obvious. He told no one. If he had, you never would have made it to the airport."

"That's easy to say now, but I didn't know it then." Eddie hesitated, obviously seeking approval of his actions. "What would you have done? Would you have stayed in Moscow?"

Vasily frowned. "The question is unfair to both of us. I'm Russian, I could have gone underground for a while. You couldn't." He shook his head. "I suppose you had no choice."

Eddie breathed deeply in relief. "Then we're still partners?"

"For what it's worth, yes. But I don't see what can be done. So much of the operation depended on timing, on speed, on catching them off balance. And now the timing is gone."

"But we're more than halfway home. We've each got only two more to eliminate. We can't stop now."

Vasily smiled sadly. "We may have to. Don't you see, with the element of timing gone they've probably figured out by now that we're working together."

"Of course they're working together," said Crowfoot. "Our KGB intercepts tell us that the *dachniki* have lost Krasin, Suvarov, and Durin. In the same space of time you've lost Kelly, Erikson, and Rakow. It's obvious what's been happening. Mancuso and Borgneff have swapped assignments. You've been set up to bushwhack little Eddie, and all the while the Russian has been operating right under your nose."

Parker chewed the back of his hand. "Are you sure of this?"

"Do bears crap in the Kremlin?"

"Makes me look like a fool, doesn't it?" The colonel started on a knuckle.

"Don't worry about that part of it. Langley doesn't expect miracles from you."

"But they do from you?"

"Hell, I'm just an old Injun scout with a good sense

182

of smell. Even I don't have the whole thing figured out yet. For instance, how did Borgneff and Mancuso get together in the first place? Be interesting to know, wouldn't it?"

"It certainly would," said Parker with a bit of force in his voice.

Crowfoot looked at him speculatively. "We'll find out, eventually. Right now we've got bigger bones on our plate than that. We've got to get a counteroperation going."

"Do you have any plans?" The appeal was pathetically apparent in his voice.

"Hell, no, Freddy. A few ideas, maybe, but no plans." Crowfoot stood up and stretched. "If you feel like being helpful, you can show me where your teletype room is. I want to have a chat with our friends at Zhukovka."

The colonel's voice went up a notch. "You want to talk to the Russians?"

"Why not? Let's see what that old dry-gulcher and bushwhacker Comrade Colonel Fist has to say about all this."

"Tom . . . are we allowed to do that?"

Crowfoot looked at him pityingly. "I can see why you're still a colonel, son. At a certain level there's always communication between opposite numbers. There has to be. Tell you the truth, old Fisty and I get along real fine, always have. The man knows a thing or two about enjoying life. One time in Budapest —ah, hell, that was a long time ago. You just tell your man to get Fist on the teletype circuit for me."

"Tom, I wouldn't even know how to go about it."

"Tell him to patch it through the blue line at Langley. They'll know how to handle it."

"Let's assume that they know we're working together," said Eddie. "I think we can still do it."

"We'd have to give up our original plans."

"Damn right. They'd be waiting for you in Williamsburg, and like I said, I'm not going back to Moscow. So we make new plans."

Vasily looked at him skeptically. "It took us weeks to develop the original mission."

"I've already got something in mind for Fist and Marchenko. The Americans would be your problem."

The silent house had been too depressing for them, and now they walked through the fields behind the sheep pen, heads down and hands in pockets, shoes kicking tufts of grass. They were both sharply aware of Chalice's absence, although so far neither had spoken of her.

"Check me out on this," said Eddie. "Do you remember when we compiled the dossier on Fist?"

*. . . that's about all I can tell you about Colonel Fist, Eddie, except that he's a tennis nut. He and Marchenko play several times a week on his private court at the dacha.*

*Nothing unusual about that.*

*Only one thing. Like most Russians, he refuses to play with Soviet-made balls. He claims they have no bounce. The ball he prefers is a Wilson. As a matter of fact, it's becoming something of a joke at Zhukovka.*

*You mean his tennis is that bad?*

*No, I mean the balls. Everybody at the dacha knows of his preference for Wilson balls. It's become a standard routine for agents returning from a tour of duty in the West. They always bring him a can of Wilson tennis balls as a gift. It's illegal to import them, of course, but the Customs never check KGB luggage.*

"Yes, I remember that," said Vasily. "The colonel's balls. An old joke at the *dacha*. What did you have in mind?"

"You know all the KGB station heads in Western Europe. Could you work out who's the next one due to go home on rotation?"

"Certainly, but why?" And then, "Oh."

"That's right, a switch. I prepare a can of tennis balls, and one of his own men brings it home to him."

Vasily stopped, and leaned against a fence rail. He pulled a blade of grass from the earth and chewed

184

on it thoughtfully. "It's all right as far as it goes, but there's no quarantee that Fist would be the one to open the can."

"You're right," Eddie said ruefully. "We'll have to think of something else."

"No, let's not give up on it so quickly. Actually, there's an idea I've had for some time that might fit in with this. I'd like to show you my notes on it."

They went back to the laboratory. Inside the shed, Vasily took a thick notebook from the shelf, paged through it, and extracted a sheaf of papers. He handed them to Eddie.

"Tell me what you think," he said.

Eddie went through the notes carefully. They were covered with equations and diagrams. When he had gone through them the first time he looked at Vasily sharply, then went back and started again at the beginning. The second time through, he checked random equations with a pocket calculator. Finished again, he folded the notes and gave them back to Vasily.

"I'm not going to insult you by asking if it's really possible," he said. "But I never dreamed you could make one that small."

"It's a question of ratios," Vasily said, and launched into a complex explanation. Eddie nodded as each point was made. At the end, he held up his hands in surrender.

"Enough," he said. "I believe you. Anyone else, I would have said he was nuts. But not you."

"Thank you." Vasily said it solemnly, but he was close to laughing with boyish pleasure. "As nuclear devices go, it's nothing fancy. It's atomic, it's primitive, and it's low-yield. But we could fit it into a can of tennis balls, and it could do the job. No matter who opened the can, it would take out the entire *dacha* stone by stone."

"Not to mention parts of Moscow," Eddie said drily. "It could also start World War Three."

"I take it that you're not in favor of the project?"

"I'm not in favor of wiping out a few thousand innocent civilians, if that's what you mean."

"Ah, well." Vasily sighed, and returned the notes to the shelf. "Let's keep it on the back burner for a while and concentrate on the Americans first."

XXXXXRTE424+4L WMBG VIA LANG TO ZKA VIA MOSC.

CLEAR ALL. READY TO SEND.

ZKA VIA MOSC.
READY TO RECEIVE. GO.

CROWFOOT TO FIST.
RED CHIEF SENDS GREETINGS TO CHIEF RED.

FIST TO CROWFOOT.
HOWDY, INJUN. STATE REASON FOR POWWOW.

OUR MUTUAL PROBLEM. MANCUSO AND BORGNEFF.

UGH!

OUR REACTION ALSO. AGENCY ASSUMES THEM IN CA-HOOTS AGAINST BOTH OUR TRIBES.

KGB RELUCTANTLY AGREES. RECENT EVENTS CONFIRM THEORY.

AGENCY SUGGESTS THAT TRIBES JOIN FORCES. CUT THEM OFF AT THE PASS.

WOULD PREFER TO CUT THEM OFF ELSEWHERE, BUT THE PASS WILL DO.

DO YOU AGREE TO JOINT WAR PARTY?

AFFIRMATIVE. RED CHIEF SPEAKS WISDOM. WHAT DOES CYBER SAY?

WE ARE BYPASSING CYBER FOR NOW. SUGGEST YOU DO SAME.

GLADLY. CYBER SPEAKS WITH CROOKED TAPE. WILL YOU BUY IT BACK?

NEGATIVE. AGENCY SUGGESTS GRAND POWWOW SOON-EST FOR STRATEGY. IF AGREEABLE, WHERE AND WHEN?

MY WIGWAM IS YOUR WIGWAM. ONE WEEK FROM TODAY AT ZHUKOVKA?

AGREED. LOOKING FORWARD TO MEETING. PLEASE STOCK ONLY FRENCH COGNAC AND IRANIAN BELUGA. NO CHEAP DOMESTIC STUFF.

ONLY DOMESTIC STUFF WILL BE PRIMA BALLERINA, KIEV STATE BALLET COMPANY, WHO STILL MENTIONS RED CHIEF FONDLY.

THIS TRANSMISSION IS BEING MONITORED. PLEASE OBSERVE CONVENTIONAL USAGE.

SORRY. SEE YOU NEXT WEEK. CHIEF RED OUT.

RED CHIEF OUT.

XXXXXRTE424+4L WMBG TO ZKA.
TRANSMISSION ENDS.

"Assuming that we decide to send the tennis balls to Zhukovka," said Vasily. "And assuming that it works, that still leaves us Parker and Arteaga."

"That's your department. I've done enough work for today. Let's eat, I'm starving."

With the maids gone, Vasily had taken over the kitchen and had spent the afternoon happily banging pots and pans. Now, in the evening, they sat down to a meal of *linguine* with clam sauce, salad, and garlic bread. Eddie wrapped some of the *pasta* around his fork and tasted it gingerly. Then he smiled.

"Hey, that's good *linguine*," he said. "Just like my mother used to make. What did you put in the sauce?"

"Nothing special," Vasily said hastily, and changed the subject. "As far as the Americans go, I can see only one method of operation open to us. We'll have to try a lure."

Eddie nodded, chewing. He swallowed, and said, "It's risky. One of us surfaces, and they go after him. The other one hangs back and picks them off. Very risky. There's a dozen ways it could go wrong." He

187

dug into his dish again. "This clam sauce is terrific. Very tasty, very Italian. What did you say you put in it?"

"I didn't." Vasily looked away. "I agree that it's dangerous, but what else can we do? The only way we can get Parker and Arteaga out of Williamsburg is to lure them out. It's like big-game fishing. One of us has to be the fisherman, and the other one has to be the bait."

Eddie looked at him suspiciously. "I don't like the way this conversation is going."

"Please! I only thought that considering how expert you are at scuba diving—"

Eddie stopped chewing, a forkful of *pasta* poised in midair. "I thought you didn't have any plans."

"It's not really a plan, just a glimmer of an idea."

"Yeah, sure. You've got me up on the end of a hook, that's the idea. All right, let's hear the rest of it."

Vasily said casually, "No need to go into details now. We can discuss it on the plane down to Cozumel."

"Cozumel, huh?" Eddie went back to chewing *linguine,* determined to be just as cool. "It's just the glimmer of an idea, but we're going to Cozumel. To go diving, no doubt."

"For *you* to go diving."

"And when does this happen?"

"Tomorrow morning. Eat your *pasta,* don't let it get cold."

Eddie obediently rolled another forkful. "This is one hell of an equal partnership. One fisherman and one piece of bait. It's a damn good thing that the fisherman knows how to cook *linguine.*"

"Just an old family recipe," Vasily said modestly.

"Russian *linguine?* You still haven't told me what makes the clam sauce so tasty."

"You really don't want to know."

"Why not?" Eddie demanded.

"Chili peppers," Vasily confessed.

One week later, five men sat around an old oak table in the *dacha* at Zhukovka. The table was covered with paper files, ashtrays, the twisted filters of Russian cigarettes, empty teacups, and the crumb of a fruitcake recently consumed. Thomas Crowfoot studied a single sheet of paper, then let it slide from his fingers to the table.

"They're pulling a lure," he said. "It's obvious."

"Unquestionably," said Fist.

Major Marchenko nodded his agreement. Colonel Parker looked confused, but he nodded as well. Romeo Arteaga only smiled.

It was the second day of the conference. The first day had been given over to what Colonel Fist called a reunion of old colleagues. The mechanics of the reunion had been simple to the point of genius: a bottle of cognac and a bottle of champagne placed in front of each man, and an overflowing tureen of *beluga* caviar set on ice in the center of the table. Toast points, grated onion, lemon wedges, and chopped egg completed the arrangements. Only Major Marchenko bothered with the toast; the others happily spooned great gobs of the caviar directly from bowl to mouth.

By midnight, the two Russians had been falling-down drunk, Parker asleep, and Arteaga slumped in his chair giggling helplessly. Crowfoot, who had drunk glass for glass, then smiled gently at the sight and took the last bottle of champagne from the melted ice in the cooler. He swung it jauntily by the neck as he marched off, slowly but steadily, to the room where the prima ballerina of the Kiev State Ballet Company had been waiting impatiently for several hours.

Now, on the second day, Colonel Fist retrieved the paper that Crowfoot had dropped, and looked at it idly. He had read it twice before.

"Where and what is Cozumel?" he asked.

Marchenko answered him promptly. "A small island off the coast of Yucatán, in Mexico. Well known for underwater sports. Mancuso surfaced there three days ago. He's using the name of Morrison, the same name he used here."

"Almost as if he wanted to be spotted," said Fist.

"Not almost. He wants it, all right," Crowfoot said. "Any sign of Borgneff?"

Marchenko looked again at the paper. "None, but we can assume he's nearby."

"Why?" asked Parker. "He could be thousands of miles away."

Fist looked unhappily at his opposite number. "Tom, would you care to explain the situation to the colonel?"

"Glad to." Crowfoot tilted back his chair and hooked the heels of his boots over the rungs. "Fred, it has to be a lure. Short of an all-out assault, that's the only option they have left. Mancuso is the bait. They figure you and Romeo here will go after him. Borgneff waits in the background and picks the two of you off when you make your move."

"*Cabrones,*" Arteaga muttered. The others ignored him.

Parker asked slowly, "What do you think we should do?"

"I think we should oblige the gentlemen." Crowfoot looked over at Fist. "I had a joint operation in mind."

"Under whose command?" Fist asked.

"Yours and mine at the top. The field commander would have to be one of our people. Romeo is the logical choice. Major Marchenko could second him."

Parker flushed. "You seem to be forgetting something. I'm senior."

"That's just it, you're too senior," Crowfoot said smoothly. "This is a field job, Fred. Calls for a younger man."

Fist joined into diplomacy. "In addition, I understand that Mr. Arteaga is an an expert scuba diver. That skill might be called for."

Romeo said, "He's my meat, Colonel. Let me have him."

Parker sat back in his seat. "All right, I'll go along with it, but I want the record to show that I asked for the command."

"Nobody's keeping any records here, but I understand your feelings," Crowfoot said. "Now, for the

190

backup force, I think a dozen men should be enough. Six of ours, and six of yours, Fist. Naturally, they won't know the true identities of the targets, or the reasons for the hits. Agreed?"

"Agreed," said Fist. "The oldest ploy there is. The trapper is trapped, the fisherman is hooked. It should work." He looked around the table. "Any questions, any discussion? None? Excellent. In that case I suggest that Major Marchenko confer with Mr. Arteaga to work out the logistical details. That will leave the senior officers free to hold another reunion this afternoon."

Crowfoot grinned, and held up his hand. "Before you start popping the corks on the firewater, I have a piece of unfinished business to bring up."

Fist returned the grin, but slyly. "I was wondering when you were going to get to that."

"I assume we're talking about the same thing. How did Borgneff and Mancuso make contact in the first place?"

Fist nodded. "In the days when I still trusted CYBER, I put the question to the machine."

"And the answer?"

"The damn junk heap just laughed at me. All I could get it to say was INSUFFICIENT INFORMATION."

"I'm not surprised. What we have here is an unprogrammed factor. Until we know what it is, we'll be working blind."

"Then I suggest that we exchange dossiers. I give you Borgneff's, and you give me Mancuso's. Then we cross-feed both machines to see if we come up with a behavior pattern that would explain the contact."

Parker said quickly, "I don't think we could do that without editing the dossiers first. Security, you know."

Crowfoot yawned. "Security, my ass. Do you really think there's anything hot in those files that our friends here don't already know?"

"Or that you don't know about ours?" Fist added.

Parker said stiffly, "I was only pointing out the obvious risks."

"You've made your point, son, and your butt is

covered," said Crowfoot, not unkindly. "The responsibility is all mine."

"In that case, on with the reunion!" roared Fist. "Marchenko, get cognac and champagne, and a large plate of *zakuski*. Two plates. And tell them in the kitchen to put in lots of cucumber. I adore cucumber with cognac."

"With respect, Comrade Colonel, you know how the combination affects your stomach."

"To hell with my stomach. How often do I have a reunion with my old enemy Thomas Crowfoot? Quick, the bottles."

"Let's take it a little easy with the reunion today," said Crowfoot. "You keep forgetting, Fist. You're dealing with one ancient Injun here."

"I know all about ancient Indians." Fist's face split into a huge grin. "I had the pleasure of having breakfast with the lady from Kiev this morning. She tells me that the Oglala Sioux are like fine wines. They only improve with age."

"These Russian squaws talk too much," was Crowfoot's only comment.

# 15

*They call Arteaga the knife man, but he's a lot more than that. For example, he plays chess. All right, you're good, Vasily, you can beat me three times out of four, but Romeo could spot you a rook and trim your ass every time. Back in Havana they called him a budding Capablanca. So he's got the brains as well as the guts. He was the one who wrote the script on how to extract Castro.*

*I heard about that. Dimethyl sulfoxide and methyl mercury on Fidel's cigars, wasn't it?*

*That's right—the part he'd hold, not the part he'd smoke. Something like a sixty-day lapsed period. Fidel drops dead and there isn't a doctor in the world who can say what did it. When the State Department killed the operation I thought Romeo was going to cry.*

*What about his diving? How good is he?*

*He's a pro. I wouldn't stand a chance with him down there. Just remember that. If he gets to me, I'm finished.*

*He'll never get to you, I promise. It's my job to see that he doesn't. It's your job to be the bait.*

*I know. I feel like I've been practicing for it all my life.*

Eddie moved slowly along the jagged edge of the coral reef, drifting with the current, glancing up occasionally at the dark shape of the fishing boat sixty feet above him. The water was so clear that he could see down to the bottom, nearly two hundred feet, to where the reef sheered off to yet another level. A myriad of fish swam there in the stillness, singly and in schools: jewel-like blue-and-yellow Beau Gregories, gray groupers, banded angelfish, and awesome baracuda—like torpedoes with teeth. The sun poured down, blinding him whenever he looked up from the depths. Bubbles floated serenely, reassuringly, toward the surface. The world was as it should always be: calm and beautiful.

"Nice," he murmured.

"Repeat, please," Vasily said from the beach.

"Sorry, I forgot that the Wetphone was on." He spoke clearly into the Scubapro mask. "I just said it was nice down here, even for the bait."

"How is your air?"

"Three hundred pounds. Time to come up. Anything happening on top?"

"Nothing in sight but your boat."

Vasily crouched at the edge of the jungle that ran down to the beach, looking out over the still water. In his left hand he held the microphone attached to the surface unit of the Wetphone. Next to his right hand, propped against a coconut palm, was an SVD Dragunov rifle with a telescopic sight and ten Mischmetal bullets chambered below the breech. Misch metal, a blend of radioactive lanthanum and polonium, that could strike no more than an arm and send the victim into critical shock. If it struck a man's chest, there was nothing left to bury.

"This is the bait calling the fisherman," Eddie said through the Wetphone. "That's it for today, I'm coming up. Make sure to cover me when the boat pulls into the dock."

"Fisherman to bait. You won't see me, but I'll be there."

"The bait is grateful. What time do we meet tonight?"

"Ten o'clock, the beach at your hotel."

"Right. Bait signing off."

Eddie surfaced gently, spat out his regulator, inflated his BC vest, and snorkeled in lazy strokes toward the *Santa Ysabel,* the fishing boat that bobbed on the swell off Palancar Reef. The owner of the fishing boat, a cheerful, villainous-looking young man named Isidoro, hauled him aboard. The boat had been rented for two weeks at a good price, and the Mexican had asked no questions of the silent little American who broke all the rules by diving alone, carrying a spear gun with which he speared no fish, a Nikonos underwater camera with which he took no photographs, and a Wetphone with no surface unit on the boat. The *gringo* had said he was looking to photograph a hammerhead shark.

"I find for you," was Isidoro's promise, although he knew that the sharks were asleep for the summer in the caves near Isla Mujeres. To turn one's back on such a blessing—a tourist in the slack season—would have been sinful. A winter paradise, the island of Cozumel was packed with tourists and scuba divers from Christmas through Easter; but this was June. The tourists had been replaced by mosquitoes and torrential afternoon rains.

"*Hasta mañana,*" Eddie said to Isidoro when the boat reached the dock at the center of town. Nearby, Los Mariscos Café was nearly empty, with only a few stray tourists sitting in the shade drinking beer and eating turtle steak. Eddie checked them out carefully before hailing a taxi and setting out with his diving gear for his hotel. He was dutifully vigilant during the ride as well, but the vigilance was a matter of form only. Neither he nor Vasily expected the attack to come on land. He was too tempting a target, circling baitlike underwater each day. After all, went their reasoning, who would shoot a fish out of water?

He dozed through the rest of the afternoon in his hotel room, dined lightly, and at ten o'clock stood on the soft, warm sand of the beach, listening to the lap of the surf. A shadow moved among the coconut palms, and white starlight slanted off Vasily's bony

195

face. Eddie walked off the beach and into the trees, where the Russian waited.

"Which do you want first?" Vasily asked. "The good news or the bad?"

"Neither. I want to go back to bed and pull the covers over my head."

"The good news is that Arteaga is here."

"You call that good?" Eddie asked, but he was instantly alert. "Where did you spot him?"

"When you docked this afternoon. He was in a parked car across from Los Mariscos."

"Jesus, he could have popped me right then and there."

"He'd never do it that way. He wants you in the water. He wants you to disappear."

Eddie shivered. "You said something about bad news?"

"Your boatman, Isidoro. You've got to figure him as being turned. Arteaga spoke to him after you left, then they went off together in a rented car. You'll have to take care of him tomorrow."

"Tomorrow? You think he'll hit right away?"

"Why should he wait? He has you spotted, and he's got your boatman in his pocket. Yes, he'll hit tomorrow."

"Isidoro's no problem, just a complication," Eddie said thoughtfully. "But what about Parker? Any sign of him?"

"None, and I don't like it."

"Maybe he sent Romeo solo."

"Perhaps, but I doubt it. In any event, we'll have to play it as if Parker is here. We're not taking any extra chances."

"Okay, we stick to the game plan. Let's run over it one more time."

"Now? You should know it inside out by now."

"Come on, pal, be patient. You're the big, smart fisherman. I'm just the poor, dumb worm."

They spoke for another several minutes under the star-laden sky, and then they parted, Vasily walking down the beach to the Cabañas del Caribe, Eddie

196

going up the beach to the Mayan Plaza. Once in front of the door to his room, he took a six-inch plastic pick from his pocket. He did not use a key to open the door. A key, or any other piece of metal, or the forcing of the door itself, would have set off a nitroglycerin bomb built into a can of Old Spice shaving cream that hung from the inside doorknob. The plastic pick deactivated the detonator, and he was able to enter safely. Once inside the room he reactivated the device and checked a second, similar, bomb that protected the window from intrusion. Then he lay down on the bed and composed himself to wait for the morning. He had not expected to sleep, but he did.

Vasily, at his hotel farther up the beach, had no time for sleep. Once in his room he went to work taking plastic bags and jars from his suitcase and spreading equipment on the bed. In the bathroom sink, with his hands sheathed by rubber gloves, he ground up a kilo of potassium chlorate, sprinkling it with warm water to speed the process. From the bed he took three jars of common Vaseline. Mixing it with the potassium chlorate, kneading it and punching it as a baker makes dough, in ten minutes he had worked the ingredients into a lump of pliable paste, which he divided and pressed into a dozen thin plastic bags.

Then, from the suitcase, he took out three long strips of common fiber-glass insulation and a bottle of sulfuric acid. He dumped the acid into the bathtub, ripped up the fiber-glass into long, silky strands, and dropped them in to soak. Hardly enough for the purpose, if he wanted to interdict the area completely. He frowned, glancing around the room. There was always something. The mattress? He slit it open with a knife. It contained polystyrene foam in small, soft white chunks. He added three armloads of the foam to the fiber-glass in the bathtub. Still wearing his gloves, he stuffed the wet contents of the tub into two pillowcases and wrapped the rest of it in a blanket which he stripped from the bed. Outside, in the darkness, he loaded everything into the back seat of the

Safari. Then he set off for the beach opposite the tip of the Palancar Reef.

The island of Cozumel was in the shape of a fat sausage snuggled north to south against the Yucatán coast. A single narrow road ran around the perimeter of the island, from the hotels bunched on San Juan Beach on the northwest coast, past the yacht-club basin, then through the town, then south past the El Presidente Hotel and Chankanab Lagoon to the Palancar Reef. The interior of the island was a flat matting of scrub and jungle, with a few seldom-used dirt tracks, hidden Mayan villages, and a scattering of small ruined temples dating from the time before the Spaniards. Vasily reached the reef in darkness, but even as he began to unload the Safari, the weak light of the moon showed through the trees. A faint breeze rustled banana leaves. Battling his way through the brush and creepers, in ten minutes he reached the edge of the beach, sweating, breathing hard. The breeze had died, and the air was thick with heat. Just enough moonlight bled through the jungle mist for him to see.

He worked quickly, removing the doughy substance from the plastic bags and planting each lump a few inches below the cool sand in the open spaces between the palms, then tamping down the sand with his foot— smoothing it out in some places, deliberately leaving his footprints in others. His footprints from the other mornings were everywhere, and he made no effort to obliterate them; they would serve nicely as a guide for the trackers. Wet, the mixture of potassium chlorate and Vaseline was not yet volatile, but the first rays of the sun would begin to dry it. By nine o'clock, the full heat of the morning would harden it into *plastique*. Using a random pattern, he distributed the load of fiber-glass strands and chunks of polystyrene foam soaked in sulfuric acid. He scattered it from the edge of the jungle all the way to the waterline. Again, the sun would convert it lethally.

He smiled in satisfaction. With his homemade devices he had effectively denied the beach area to any potential intruder. His position for covering Eddie was now secure.

He drove back to his hotel in the starry darkness and parked the Safari off the road. He carried his room key in his pocket and was just passing the lobby desk when the clerk hailed him.

"Señor Victor? A message for you."

Vasily studied the scrawled handwriting on the small pink slip. It said, *I miss you. Call soon.* And that was followed by the area code for Washington, D.C., and a telephone number.

"You received this call?" Vasily asked politely.

"No, Señor. Our telephone operator."

"Is she here?"

"No, Señor. Gone home."

"It doesn't say when the call came in."

"Undoubtedly when you were out, Señor."

"Yes, undoubtedly." Vasily offered his warmest smile. "Would you place the call for me please?"

*"Ahorita,* Señor. Right away."

Vasily slid a hundred-peso note across the counter and it vanished instantly. "Please try to make it even sooner than that."

In his room he sat in a chair, arms folded, and waited. He was calm. The cooling breeze from the air conditioner swept across his cheeks. He waited for an hour, then called the desk. The clerk was apologetic.

"I am trying," he explained, "but there is only the one line that goes from the island. Please be patient."

"Of course," said Vasily, but there were chips now in the surface of his calm. He went back to the chair, tried to sit, but found that impossible. From the pocket in his suitcase he took out a portable chessboard and a book of problems. He laid out an ending, white to mate in four, and pondered over it. Lost in the dynamics of the problem, he was still aware of the passing of time. He fought against looking at his watch, and when he finally did, saw that it was almost two in the morning. He reached for the telephone. The clerk was still apologetic, but with a note of defensiveness in his voice.

"Señor, please to understand," he said. "This is not Mexico City here. This is Cozumel, and the telephone service is not very . . . *elegante,* you understand?"

Vasily understood very well that the telephone office was most likely staffed by one sleepy Indian girl who should have been tending bar at *cantina,* but he said only, "Yes, I understand. But please try again. It is important."

"*De acuerdo.*"

Vasily hung up the telephone but stood with his hand still on it, his eyes still staring down at it, his mind finally forcing to the surface the fears he had tried to bury.

It's trouble. and it has to be big trouble. She wouldn't call for anything trivial. And until I know what it is I can't make a move.

He tried to go back to the chessboard. but the problem, which at first had been intriguing, now only irritated him. He swept it away and laid out another ending, but he could not concentrate on the moves. He forced himself to lie on the bed with his eyes closed, breathing slowly. That actually worked—he dozed off for a while—but he was up again in fifteen minutes and pacing the floor. He debated calling Eddie and alerting him, but that would have gone against all the rules of security they had established. Tapping nervous fingers on the table, his calm now completely cracked, he knew that there was nothing he could do but wait.

He waited that way through the night, the tension growing hourly. Every thirty minutes he called the desk, and each time he was told that his telephone call was in progress. Despite his nervousness he kept his voice cool and polite when he spoke to the clerk, knowing that one flare of anger might be enough to cancel the call entirely. He watched the first gray cracks of dawn and then the rim of the sun coming up over the sea. He watched it rise, helpless, willing it to stop, begging it for time; but the dawn was established and the sun well up over the water when the desk clerk finally called with the triumphant announcement.

200

"Señor, we have succeeded. After great effort I am now able to proclaim that your *conferencia* is about to begin. One moment please for the city of Washington."

A moment later Chalice's voice came on the line. She wasted no time with politeness. "My God, what took you so long? I've been waiting all night."

"I've been calling all night. Quickly, what is it?"

"They know you're in Cozumel. Both of you."

Vasily took a deep breath. "They know *I'm* here?"

"That's right—both sides do. Ours and yours. They've figured out your next move, and they've got their own little surprise planned. This is an open line. How freely may I talk?"

"As freely as you wish. If you don't tell me, I'm dead anyway."

"They're working together in a combined operation, six of ours and six of yours, with the Cuban in command. Yours is a lure, theirs is a counterlure. That's all I know. He wouldn't tell me any details."

"The usual source? He's there in Williamsburg?"

"Of course."

"I was hoping he would be here."

"No, he's up here safe and sound. Darling, don't you think this calls for a change in your vacation plans? Why not try the mountains instead of the ocean?"

"My thoughts exactly. I must jump now. Many thanks, my love."

He hung up to the sound of her chuckle, but there was no joy in his voice as he called the desk and asked to be put through to Eddie's hotel. The sun was high, his watch read after seven o'clock, and there was no time now to worry about security.

Chalice left the hotel room, ordered her Thunderbird brought up from the underground garage, and paid her bill. It was full morning in Washington as she slid behind the wheel and worked her way through the streets of the capital. The drive back to Williamsburg took three hours. In no hurry, she kept well within the speed limit, switched off the air conditioner, and let the cool morning breezes flow through the windows. The noonday sun was high over the Virginia landscapes as she pulled into her driveway. Her husband was waiting for her in the living room. His gray and weary face reflected a sleepless night and an anxious morning.

"Where have you been?" he asked.

"Washington," she answered truthfully. "I felt like dinner and a show by myself. Do you want to know where I ate? Do you want to know what show?"

"No." He shook his head slowly. He did not believe her, but honor and anger had left him by now. "I wish you wouldn't do things like this, Catherine. I worry."

"Still?"

"Yes, still."

"That's sweet, Freddy." She came to him and let him put his arms around her. She kissed him firmly. "I think it's time for bed. For both of us."

He returned the kiss and looked down at her. She moved against him. Against all his wishes, he felt his desire rising.

"Well?" she asked. "Bed?"

He nodded dumbly and let her lead him toward the stairs.


Vasily listened, drumming his fingers lightly against his cigarette case. The telephone buzzed and stopped, buzzed and stopped, with that peculiar, inexplicable monotony that somehow tells the caller after the second ring that it will not be picked up, that no one is there.

The polite but tired Mexican voice said, *Señor, no contesta."*

"Are you certain you're ringing the right room? Two oh four? *¿Dos—cero—cuatro?"*

"*Si, señor, pero no contesta. Señor Morrison ha salido."*

"How long ago did he leave?"

"*¿Quién sabe?* Ten, maybe fifteen minutes."

For the second time in moments Vasily hung up

the phone and stood staring at it. Eddie on his way to dive, perhaps already on the boat, and no way to warn him that the odds had changed. From even money, two on two, they had gone to six-to-one-underdogs. He resisted the impulse to pull the telephone out by the wires and hurl it across the room, forcing himself to examine his options coldly. His mind rolled over them, but he could find only two.

There are no true options, he told himself, but only two unpalatable choices. Either I stay, or I go. If I stay and cover him, I am going against suicidal odds. Every instinct tells me to get out of here quickly. Borgneff's First Law of Survival. It's too late to try the ferry, but there are plenty of fishermen who would take me to the mainland for a price.

The trouble is . . . I like Eddie. After nearly fifty years of the business called living, he stands as my only friend.

The thought took him by surprise, yet he realized that it touched an area of truth. Eddie was his friend, and to abandon him would not be easy, but it would be in conformity with his lifelong principles. To attempt to save him, given the new odds, would be difficult, almost impossible, and probably fatal. Yet, as he voiced the choices silently, he knew that he was going to try.

I owe him that much, and I owe myself the opportunity to make the *beau geste*. Besides, Chalice would never forgive me if I didn't.

Smiling to himself, secretly pleased by his lapse into romanticism, he grabbed his two prepacked suitcases and raced down the stairs to the lobby. In minutes he had paid his bill to the yawning clerk and was into the Safari, driving along the broken, pitted road that led to the yacht basin. He kept his speed down, glancing often into the rearview mirror and scanning the sea as well as the road ahead. The sun was already hot, baking down. The breeze dried his sweat. Just before the yacht-club basin, a few hundred yards ahead on the road, he saw two Mexican workmen in the left-hand lane. One of them was tarring the road surface with a roller; the other held a tattered red flag in his hand.

Mexican workmen at seven-thirty in the morning?

Vasily took his foot off the accelerator and lightly touched the brake, shifting down into second gear.

The Mexicans looked up casually, and the man with the red flag waved it, beckoning him ahead. Both men wore *sombreros,* the white *guayabera* Mayan shirts, baggy white trousers, and sandals. But under their sombreros, even at that distance, Vasily could see that their faces were pale. Too pale.

He swung the Safari into a tight turn, braked, jammed to a stop, and backed up. Give them a chance, he thought . . . could be wrong. If they're workmen, they'll shrug and go back to their tarring. If not . . .

The man with the red flag suddenly dropped it to the ground, and from the brush two BMW motorcycles catapulted out onto the road, bouncing hard, engines backfiring and spitting. Vasily wrenched the wheel to the left, slammed the gearshift into second, and brought the Safari screeching around on the road, gunning it, right foot down to the floorboard. In less than ten seconds he was in third gear and up to fifty miles an hour, streaking toward the hotel. The wrong direction, he realized. And with nowhere to go. A few yards beyond the Mayan Plaza, the road ended. There was nothing but jungle to the right, the sea to the left. On those BMW's, they would overhaul him even before he reached the Cabañas del Caribe.

Gripping the wheel tightly with his left hand, with the other he reached behind and pulled one of his suitcases into the front seat. In the rearview mirror he saw the BMW's looming larger, the goggled heads of the riders tucked down behind the plastic shields. He spun the wheel hard and hit the brake. The Safari bounded off the road, and into the brush to the lip of the jungle. Then he was out of the car, hauling the suitcase with him, stumbling, running, a fresh pain shooting through one ankle. He kept the suitcase close to his body as the undergrowth tried to wrench it from his grasp. No shots so far. The jungle closed in around him. Suddenly it was darker, the turf underfoot soft and muddy. A monkey screeched, and a bright-green macaw fluttered over his head. He breathed in the foulness of the place as he ran, stumbled, and batted back the creepers and the vines.

Sorry, Eddie, he thought. I wanted to help, I truly did. But you're on your own now. And so am I.

Eddie, on his own, stood in the bows of the *Santa Ysabel* and scanned the smooth seas around him. The boat was alone on the sea with no sign of other craft, but he knew one would come, and soon. Two hundred yards across the water, the beach and the low-lying jungle also showed no sign of life, but he knew that Vasily was in there, waiting. Behind him, he heard Isidoro cut the engine and come running forward to drop the hook. The Mexican paid out cable until the anchor hit bottom. The *Santa Ysabel* coasted forward, then pulled up short, swinging with the current.

"*Bueno*," Isidoro said. "You dive now?"

"First a beer. You want a *cerveza?*"

"Beer is bad before dive," said the Mexican, but he licked his lips.

"One is okay. And you're not diving."

Eddie snapped open a can and handed another, unopened, to Isidoro, who smiled his thanks. The Mexican snapped open the can, tilted it to his lips, and swallowed.

"Hits the spot, doesn't it?" said Eddie. "You sold-out son of a bitch."

Isidoro didn't answer. His eyes rolled, and the can slipped from his fingers. He sat down heavily on the deck. His eyes closed, and his head tipped over to one side. Eddie checked the eyes to make sure he was out, then pulled him into the cockpit, propped him against the slats in a sitting position, and adjusted the *sombrero* on his head. Loaded with chloral hydrate and dead to the world for hours to come, Isidoro looked like every caricature ever made of a Mexican taking *siesta* in the noonday sun.

There was still no other boat in sight. Eddie unzipped the dive bag and laid out his equipment. He made a final check, tested his tanks, and then, after he had struggled into the Calypso and strapped on the weight belt and knife, he activated the Wetphone.

"This is the bait, calling the fisherman. How's it going, *tovarich?*"

He waited patiently for Vasily's reply, then spoke again. "Hey, come on in, don't be shy. Or didn't you pay your phone bill?"

No reply came from the jungle. Eddie peered toward the brush, shielding his eyes from the glitter of sun bouncing off the water. He was within range, and the equipment was functioning.

"*Santa Ysabel* calling. Confirm reception. Confirm reception, damn it."

Once again he checked the battery pack and the potting compound around the electronics. The batteries were fresh and the unit dry.

"*Santa Ysabel* calling. Say something, Vasily. Anything."

The waters lapped against the hull of the boat, and the mast creaked in the breeze. There was no other sound. He was alone on the sea. Nothing stirred on the shore.

Eddie sighed unhappily. This is terrific. What does the bait do when the fisherman is out to lunch?

He glanced over his shoulder, then slowly turned. A single fishing boat had appeared on the northern horizon. He could see the creamy white wave sliding by its bows as it bore down on him across the bright-blue water.

# 16

Sweating, gasping, his heart pounding fiercely, Vasily crouched behind the shelter of a stunted coconut palm. The jungle pressed in from all sides; twenty feet away lay only green darkness. He listened for footsteps, heard none, but knew that he had only minutes in which to prepare. He spun the combination lock on the suitcase and unloaded the hardware. He quickly assembled the Dragunov rifle and clamped on the magazine. From another compartment he took three pieces of white plastic and screwed them together so that they became a modified Schick hair dryer. From the third compartment he gingerly lifted out a box of Lipton's tea bags.

It took only minutes to distribute the tea bags in a wide circle around the coconut tree, but they were minutes of pounding fear. Back at the tree, he took deep breaths to calm himself, listened carefully, but again heard nothing more than the rustling of fronds overhead and the distant call of monkeys. Crouched on one knee, the rifle cradled in his arm, the hair dryer resting on the turf beside him, he settled back to wait.

A low, flat boom sounded from the emerald-green jungle; then another. The two echoes flew out over the silver-blue shimmer of water. Every muscle in Eddie's body tightened. Half blinded by the glare, his eyes strained toward the beach. He saw nothing.

"Vasily!" He shrieked into the Wetphone. "What's going on?"

He heard the same buzz of static as before. No voice, no response. He struggled into the harness, tightening the straps with unsteady fingers, feeling the weight of the tank tug at his back and shoulder muscles. The *Santa Ysabel* rode over thirty feet of water on the high shelf just outside the reef. Hefting the second tank, Eddie pitched it overboard, watching it tumble and then slide downward through pale-green water toward the bottom, a school of blowfish veering hastily from the lazy path of its descent. The water was so clear that he could see the white patch of brain coral where it finally quivered to rest. By then he had yanked on his fins, clamped the mask down over his face. He shot a quick look at the fishing boat now closing to within a hundred yards of him. There were three men on deck, all divers in wet suits, the hooked tips of their spear guns glinting in the sun.

Three?

For the first time he was truly fearful. He had expected Romeo, and possibly Parker to back him up. But three? Three divers who could go like sharks; three sharks against one clumsy dolphin. If there were three on board, how many more were there ashore? He began to understand why the Wetphone was silent.

He had just fixed the Nikonos camera to its harness, and was reaching for his spear gun, when he saw it happen from the corner of his eye. The figure of a man broke out of the jungle and onto the beach. Vasily? No. There was something strange in the way that the man sprinted awkwardly on the sand, kicking up gouts of it in flight. Then he suddenly twisted, stumbled, and a rifle spun from his grasp. He lay writhing on the white sand.

Understanding nothing, Eddie looked over his shoulder. The oncoming boat was within fifty yards, bearing down, bows slapping blue water, the wake frothing. The three divers bent within the shelter of the windward gunwale, using the coach roof as a shield. A machine pistol stuttered; chips of wood sprayed from the mast. Eddie jammed the regulator into his mouth, sucked sweet air, clamped a hand to his mask, and launched himself over the side.

The water closed over his head, and in seconds, he was in that other world, cool and lovely and green, silent except for the sharp, labored sound of his own breathing. His bubbles blooped and bleeped reassuringly upward toward the surface. He flipped over, waggled his fins, and shot downward too rapidly, feeling the pressure pound into his ears. He cleared them at ten feet, did it again at twenty, then finally tilted his head back to purge the mask of water. The fog cleared and he could see. A grouper with bulging eyes watched him warily, and three or four black-and-white-banded butterflyfish hurried prudently away.

At thirty feet he saw his spare tank resting on the brain coral, and beyond it a slanting bed of staghorn where the reef tumbled down and out in a series of tunnels and caves. He kicked himself downward, aware of the clear and brilliant water, cursing the brightness and the sun that was now his enemy. His choices were limited. If he sheltered in a cave he would be hidden, but immobilized. If he stayed in the open he would be mobile, but visible. He did not consider the choices; he simply acted. Panic drove him toward the tunnel, and he plunged for it as fish floated by, serene, undisturbed.

The two men on the boat with Arteaga were also Cubans, Santos and Jiménez, both certified NAUI divers trained at the Agency school at Key West. Like Eddie, the three had heard the explosions on the shore and had seen the man stumble and fall on the beach. Also like Eddie, they were totally confused. Arteaga spoke sharply into his radio.

"Come in Beach Ops, this is Boat Ops."

Thomas Crowfoot's thin voice came back clearly and calmly. "Go ahead, Boat."

"Our man just went overboard. We're about to go

in after him. What the hell is happening on the beach?"

"Continue with your mission, Boat. The beach operation has been temporarily disrupted."

"What's that supposed to mean?" Arteaga said angrily. "Unless you get Borgneff pinned down, we can't move."

"Borgneff is nowhere near the beach. Carry on," said Crowfoot, and signed off. He shook his head sadly, and reviewed the situation on the beach.

The point man, an American from TSD, had been the first to go. He had crouched behind a palm tree and his knee had touched the sand. Beneath that sand lay one of the now dry lumps of potassium chlorate and Vaseline that Vasily had sown at dawn. The home-made *plastique* charge exploded on contact. The American's left leg went in one direction; the rest of his body, smashed and shredded, flew against the tree. Less than a minute later, one of the Russians stepped on a second charge. He screamed wildly as the explosive tore upward and burst through his groin into his chest.

A third man, another Russian, vaulted up over the matted dunes onto the beach. He wore light summer clothing, and a breeze blew in off the sea. He was struck immediately by one of the razor-sharp strands of fiber-glass. It only touched his ankle above his shoe, but the pain threw him to the ground. He screamed too. He began to crawl back toward the jungle, and the heel of his hand came into contact with a tiny piece of polystyrene foam from the hotel mattress. He screamed again.

On the boat, Romeo spoke rapidly in Spanish to the other two Cubans. Santos tossed out the anchor, and the boat rode over it until it bit. The fishing boat pulled up short. Jiménez cut the engine.

"Now listen to me." Arteaga armed his spear gun and pointed inshore about thirty yards. "Look there. You can see his bubbles. Santos, you circle round from the direction of the beach. Jiménez, you come in from over there." He waved a hand toward the south. "I'll go straight in from here. He can't look in three directions at once. Take any shot you can get. You only have to wing him and he's finished."

The three divers spat into their masks, rubbed them clean, clamped them into place and tumbled over backward into the water. In a few seconds the surface was calm again and they were undulating downward with dolphin kicks. At a signal from Arteaga, they spread out to encircle their prey.

That prey was huddled in a coral tunnel forty feet below the surface of the water, sharing his sanctuary with a translucent jellyfish that waved its tentacles lazily, seemingly unaware of his presence. The tunnel hid him, but he knew that he was not truly concealed; his bubbles gave him away. It was only a matter of time before they came to him, and he could only wait.

He jammed the barbed point of his harpoon into the coral and unsnapped the Nikonos camera. The velocity of the dart that had struck down the sheep and then had given José Cuervos two ears and a tail would be sharply reduced by traveling through water, but the lethality could be equal. All he needed was a clear view. He pressed back against a ledge, gripping with his fins. He was out of sight of the tunnel opening, but when he pressed the button on the camera he could see at right angles through the viewfinder. The view area was narrow, and he moved the camera slightly up, then down, then traversed a short arc. The jellyfish swam into view, blocking the lens. Unthinking, Eddie reached out of his shelter with one hand and tried to poke it with his elbow. Instantly he felt pain, a sharp sting that spread upward toward his shoulder. Had he been able to, he would have cried out, but at that moment he forgot the pain as the jellyfish moved out of view and its place was taken by a slim black shape approaching cautiously. Jiménez came on slowly, spear gun poised, eyes huge behind the mask, bubbles rising through the turquoise water.

The Cuban had spotted the bubbles of the prey, had seen the bright-orange flash of Eddie's BC vest retreat into the tunnel. Now all he saw was the jellyfish floating away and the bulky shape of a Nikonos protruding from the ledge, pointing in the wrong direction. No spear gun was aimed at him. His hand tightened on the trigger of his own gun and he gave a powerful flutter kick with his fins, coasting forward.

When he was in the viewfinder, less than ten feet away, Eddie pushed the button. The flechette shot from the side of the camera. It took Jiménez in the shoulder, the little firecracker charge inside the dart exploding as it hit bone. The water turned from blue to red, blood flowing in thick, ropy threads in all directions. Jiménez flopped over, and the spear gun tumbled away toward the ocean floor.

Eddie's head emerged slowly from the tunnel, and he watched the Cuban float away on the current, the blood streaming behind him. He would have stayed that way, transfixed by the sight, but the jellyfish was back again, wobbling toward him through the water. With the pain in his arm as a reminder, he jerked back his head, ducking quickly toward shelter.

Something bright and sharp flashed by, inches away, then vanished, arcing down. A slender steel shaft. He whipped around in the water and saw Santos.

The other Cuban had entered from the other end of the tunnel and had come up from behind. He had fired from five meters, and would have hit had it not been for the jellyfish. He was already loading a second shaft. Eddie snatched at his own gun, freeing the barb from the coral. It was all reflex now; he had one chance, no more. As he brought the pneumatic gun up, it felt as if it weighed fifty pounds. Santos clicked the second shaft home. With his gun hip high, Eddie squeezed the heavy trigger. The powerful harpoon zoomed silently through the water, sliced across Santos' arm, and plunged into his chest. As he died, the Cuban pulled his own trigger and his second shaft slammed through the tunnel, through the baggy pink shape of the jellyfish, and then off into nothingness. Wide-eyed, Eddie watched as Santos drifted downward, regulator dangling to one side, blood streaming from his mouth like curdled red milk. He yanked hard, and the harpoon disengaged, sliding back to him on its nylon line.

He checked his air: half a tank left. The blood and adrenaline pumped through him in surges, elating him. Two down, only Arteaga to go.

He came out of the tunnel smoothly, moving fast and breathing easily, a small white shark. The water cleared from the murky blue of the tunnel to a dazzling, sun-suffused green. He turned in a tight circle, searching in all lateral directions, then up and down. He saw Arteaga far above him and out of range. The Cuban was flutter-kicking toward the dark shape of his boat. Eddie moved slowly upward, spear gun ready, prepared to take him when he dived.

But Arteaga didn't dive. He turned once, and Eddie, thirty feet below and behind, looked directly into his eyes. Behind the mask, Arteaga seemed to be smiling, and with one hand he waved, almost a salute. A moment later he was gone, stroking powerfully toward the boat. Eddie saw his feet grip the rope ladder that hung from the side; then the legs surged up and Arteaga vanished.

Within a moment Eddie heard the bark of the inboard engine as first it sputtered, then caught, and far above him he saw the silver flashing of the singles screw. The sound of the motor was no more than a dull, distant hum that was lost as it penetrated the fathoms of green water; even the fish were undisturbed. Then he saw the anchor chain tighten as the dark shadow of the boat moved forward several feet, then stopped. The screw continued to whirl, the engine idling in neutral.

Eddie watched the long line of bubbles ascending. They no longer bleeped and blooped merrily, but went up in a sad procession. The elation he had felt after the first two kills was gone, replaced by a numbing depression. Then he had been ready to take on Arteaga *mano a mano,* but now he knew he would never have the chance. He checked his air again: six hundred pounds of pressure left. That, plus the second tank resting on the brain coral, gave him no more than an hour of dive time. Bright, clever Romeo Arteaga, always four moves ahead in chess, was one move ahead once again. If Eddie swam, Romeo would follow the bubbles. If Eddie stayed still, Romeo would patiently wait. No *mano a mano* for Arteaga, not after losing two good men. He was simply going to sit up on top and wait until the prey ran out of air and had to surface. And there was nothing that the prey could do about it.

During the Vietnam War, the United States Army had sown untold numbers of antipersonnel devices known as Gravel Mines throughout the jungle areas of Southeast Asia. The tea bags that Vasily had distributed around the coconut palm were modifications of this device, manufactured by him in San Miguel from thermite, black-iron oxide, and granulated aluminum. The first Russian motorcyclist who stepped on a tea bag, less than fifty feet from where Vasily crouched behind the tree, had his right leg blown to jelly from the foot to the knee. That man was Major Marchenko.

Vasily broke from cover as soon as he heard the muffled *swat* of the explosion, followed by the scream of agony. He ran low, keeping to the mine-free aisle he had left open, suitcase in one hand, hair dryer in the other. It took him more than a minute to battle through the underbrush to the wounded man, who lay where he had fallen, moaning pitifully, bleeding to death. His weapon, a Makarov pistol, had been flung aside. Marchenko's eyes rolled in shock, then fastened on Vasily.

"Borgneff," he gasped. The Russian words broke painfully from his twisted lips: "Finish it. Kill me now."

Vasily stared down, swallowing hard. There had been a time when he had known the man well.

"Comrade, please." Marchenko was begging. "For the love of God, do it."

*For the love of God?* Vasily came close to smiling, as he thought: In the face of death, we are all of us

214

virgins. This man would have killed me, and not for the love of God.

*"Nyet, nyet,"* Vasily said softly. *"Ni spishitye. U vas mnoga vryemini.* Don't rush. You have plenty of time. Be patient, it won't take long to die."

He kicked aside the Makarov pistol and stepped into the fringe of the jungle, into the deep shadows. He clenched his teeth as Marchenko began to scream incoherently. Moments later he heard the quiet crackling of brush, leaves being swept aside, damp branches bending and tearing but not breaking. Then there was a hush, the deep uncanny hush of the jungle. Then movement again, a cautious tread. Twenty feet away, Vasily guessed. I need him closer. But if he sees me first and he's carrying a machine pistol, I'm a dead man. He forced himself to wait, until finally he saw a darker hulk than the shadows, something black in the bottle-green foliage. And then a second silhouette, struck by an errant ray of sunlight. There were two of them.

Close enough, and he raised the hair dryer waist high. He squeezed the trigger. A jet of red-orange flame spurted out, roaring, crackling, filling the jungle with terrifying light and sound, engulfing the black human shapes in its path. Again the screams came, again in Russian, but when he released the trigger and the flame swept back to leave only shadows, there was silence from the two charred bodies huddled under palm fronds.

Vasily picked up the pistol and turned back to where Marchenko lay. The blue eyes still stared up at him, but they were the eyes of a dead man. Vasily murmured, "I would have done it for you, comrade. But you were in a hurry, I understand."

Ten minutes later he had reached the main road, approaching it cautiously. The last of the Russians waited there, bent on one knee next to his motorcycle, a Kalashnikov AKM under his arm. Very quietly, Vasily fitted a box of the rimfire cartridges into the breech of the Dragunov. Gently, he slid the barrel between two banana leaves and notched the sights on the center of the motorcyclist's chest.

He sighed. After all he had done, it seemed such a prosaic way to kill.

He sighed again, but this time held his breath for a second, then squeezed the trigger. As if he had been snatched by a violent wind, the motorcyclist flew back five yards across the road and landed on the dirt shoulder, chest smashed, arms outflung, and unmoving.

Vasily rushed for the Safari, its front fender crumbled against the trunk of a dead tree. The engine caught on the first turn of the key. He bumped up out of the ditch onto the road, hesitated a moment, then shifted into second gear and turned in the direction of the Palancar Reef.

Thirty feet below the surface, on the bed of brain coral, Eddie's hands shook as he changed air tanks. He had not thought this possible underwater, but they shook with good reason. Caught by a mild wave surge, the second tank slipped away, bumping along the slope and down toward the blue-green depths. His eyes bulged out in panic. He had already taken the necessary deep breath, spat out his regulator, and detached it from the first, nearly empty cylinder. The only air he owned was in his lungs. He grabbed for the second tank, and his foot hit the camera, sending it floating off the ledge and down into the canyon. It was then that his hands shook. By the time he caught up with the tank and clamped his regulator to it, his legs had been badly scraped on the coral. He blew out the regulator and sucked deeply, taking in salt water that seared his lungs, and then at last the sweet fresh supply of air.

When his hands had stopped shaking, he figured his time again. No more than an hour. Above him, the propeller of Arteaga's boat turned lazily as the Cuban waited.

Fantasies crowded his head, complex plans for fouling the boat's propeller and making a run for shore, but he knew they were only dreams. The propeller was only four feet from the surface, and although a bullet would not be lethal at that depth, a spear gun would. He was still the prey, and nothing more. Wherever he moved, if he tried to circle the boat and clamber aboard, it would be simple for Arteaga to follow his movements and spot him as he broke the surface. He gripped his spear gun with one hand, and with the other eased the diving knife in its sheath. He was armed, but he had no one to fight with.

Arteaga checked his watch as he sat in the cockpit of the boat. Fifty minutes had passed, and he figured Eddie for ten minutes' more worth of air, at most. His eyes followed the bubbles that broke on the surface. They usually broke in the same place, although sometimes they moved off a few feet. He smiled coldly, and flipped off the safety catch of the Colt Commando. As soon as Eddie Mancuso was six inches from the surface, he was ready to rip his head off. The trail of bubbles began to move forward swiftly.

He's going to come at me from the bow, Arteaga decided. He'll try to hide under the boat, then surface fast. He switched on his radio.

"Boat Ops here. He's coming out. I've got him."

Crowfoot said calmly, "Be careful."

"It's like a shooting gallery. I'll leave the radio on. You can listen."

Almost immediately Crowfoot heard the faint and muted sound of an explosion come clearly through the radio. Another quickly followed.

"Beach Ops calling. Do you have him?"

He waited patiently, but there was no answer. Then there was a series of evenly spaced dry *snaps:* more firing. He was still patient, waiting for Arteaga to confirm the kill.

On the boat, the Cuban bent in the shelter of the coach roof on the starboard bow. The first shot from the jungle had missed his head by inches and torn away the handrail. If he hadn't been moving quickly toward the bow, he would have been dead. The second spot slammed through the coach roof, tearing out a chunk of wood the size of a fist.

"*¡Chinga el diablo!*" he muttered. He was pinned down, couldn't move. The pupils of his eyes dilated. Under him, the boat shuddered, and he heard the steady crack of the rifle. The boat shuddered again. That's a high-powered rifle, he realized. What the hell is the son of a bitch using in it?

The miniature, metal-cased cherry bombs loaded into the Dragunov thumped solidly into the hull at the waterline, splintering wood, exploding on contact, sieving the hull. Vasily fired with a leisurely regularity, but he could not see Eddie, and time was important. He slipped a fresh box into the magazine, sighting carefully through the telescopic sight until the cross hairs lined up on the stern. A hit on the gas tank would end it swiftly. He squeezed the trigger.

Arteaga felt the boat spin at least a foot as the impact of the cherry bomb sheered it around. On the third shot, the gas tank exploded, the stern of the boat disintegrating, smoke and flames licking up over the deck. The sea flowed through into the cockpit, fighting the fire, but the stern was settling, sinking, the boat already listing to port where the first charges had torn holes in the hull. Arteaga slipped into his tank harness and fins, clamped the mask down over his face, dropped the Colt, and snatched his spear gun. He launched himself out over the side.

He had never known the shock of water to be so painful. He couldn't understand it. The water seemed to tear at his vitals, ripping up into his body as though it were bladed. His sight cleared for an instant as soon as he was below the surface: everything was magnified through the glass of his mask, a green-and-red panorama. The green was water; the red was blood. His own blood. In front of him, staring through his own mask, was Eddie Mancuso. His hand was outstretched, as if in welcome. At the end of the hand was the half of a dive knife, and the knife was buried six inches deep into Arteaga's abdomen.

The regulator slipped from his mouth. Water flooded his lungs. The knife slid out smoothly, the world turned dark, and Romeo Arteaga drifted away.

Eddie broke the surface, jammed the snorkel between his teeth, and began to breaststroke toward the *Santa Ysabel.*

Vasily waded out through the surf. He handed Eddie the suitcase, then the rifle, and then hauled himself over the gunwale and onto the deck.

"Get us out of here quickly," he said. "You know, you could have come in closer to the beach. I'm soaked."

Eddie spun the wheel, still in his glistening wet suit. He laughed. "So what? So am I. And I'm also alive."

Vasily came up to the cockpit. He looked down at Isidoro, snoring happily. Then he looked over the side as they passed the spot where the other boat had settled to the bottom.

"Did you get Arteaga?" he asked.

"Him and two others."

"Marchenko's dead. Plus three more Russians in the jungle and a couple on the beach."

"Russians? Jesus, what the hell hit us?"

"A combined operation. Six CIA and six KGB. We were mousetrapped. I tried to warn you, but—"

"How did you find out?"

"Chalice."

"*Chalice*? How the hell did she know?"

"I tried to warn you, but by the time I got the word—"

"From Chalice?"

"Exactly. You had already left for the boat and there was nothing I could do. After that, things got rather hectic."

"But how did Chalice know . . .?"

Vasily waved the question aside and lowered himself to the deck with a weary grunt. He sat cross-legged on the planking and told Eddie what had happened in the jungle. He told it quietly, and without dramatics, but his face showed the strain that his voice ignored. Eddie listened soberly, nodding.

"You could have split," he said when Vasily had finished. "You didn't. Thanks."

"A moment of weakness." Vasily smiled faintly. "A sign of advancing age. Don't count on it happening again."

"About Chalice. Are you going to tell me?"

"All in good time." Vasily closed his eyes in concentration. "Right now the important thing is to figure out how we get back to the mainland."

Eddie stared at him peculiarly. "Have you had a hard day at the office, dear?"

Vasily opened his eyes and said impatiently, "Come, come, start thinking. What do we do? Those people are bound to have the ferry and the airport covered."

"How about using a fishing boat?" Eddie asked quietly.

"A boat? Ah, yes . . . a boat." Vasily flushed, and tapped the decking with his fingers. "Apparently I'm more fatigued than I thought. Well, don't act so superior. I would have figured it out eventually."

"Sure you would have," Eddie said politely. "I just saved you some time. Any idea which way is Mexico?"

Vasily waved a languid hand toward the west. "Turn left at the corner and go that way. Then open up a couple of beers while I tell you about Chalice. It's about time you knew, and there's a lot to tell."

# 17

The Eastern Air Lines L-1011 began its descent at Tampico, winged down through the blue air over the central Mexican plateau, penetrated the brown layer of smog that hung suspended over the valley of Anahuac, and then rolled to a smooth halt at Mexico City airport. The colonel's lady smiled and charmed her way through Customs without so much as a handbag being opened for inspection, picked up her thirty-day tourist card at Immigration, then threaded through the jostling crowd toward the exit gate and the car-rental counters. Fifteen minutes later, as she tipped the porter twenty pesos for loading her luggage into the trunk of the Volkswagen, she felt a light touch on her arm. She turned to face Eddie Mancuso. A tight little smile of greeting played upon his lips, but when he raised his sunglasses under his *sombrero,* his dark eyes—puzzled, a little wary, and filled with a childlike sadness—betrayed him. He looked tired, as if restful sleep had eluded him for too long a time.

"Hello, Chalice."

"I didn't expect you, darling. Was it wise to come?"

He shrugged slightly. "Maybe not. But I blend in. And I had to talk to you first. Before Vasily."

She nodded her acceptance of that. "Do you want to drive?"

"You drive. I'm a little beat."

Their route crossed the southern fringe of Mexico City on the Viaducto Alemán and then joined the ring road, passing through the miles of slums and brightly colored housing projects. One thousand Mexicans from the provinces arrived in the city every day, looking for work that wasn't there, and the result was a suburban world they called *el cinturón de miseria*—the belt of misery. Once past it, the four-lane highway lanced through rain-washed desert and gently sloping mountains northward to Querétaro. Chalice drove smoothly, while Eddie smoked one cigarette after another, snugged deep in the cocoon of his thoughts. Finally he broke his silence.

"Vasily told me about it. He didn't have much choice. You're a hell of a woman, Chalice. Or do you prefer Catherine?"

"Chalice will do. My cup doesn't runneth over, but I keep hoping. I knew he'd tell you," she said lightly. "It was just a matter of timing."

"How long has he known?"

"Didn't he tell you that too?"

"Sure," Eddie said, managing a chuckle. "I'm just checking up on him. I'm the dummy. You can tell me anything and I'll believe it. At least, I used to believe it."

"He knew from the beginning," she said. "It didn't matter to him. As a matter of fact, I think it amused him more than anything else, once he'd decided the Agency wasn't behind it. You know how he is. He realized I couldn't hurt him, and I suppose he thought that one day I might be useful. He was right. It worked out that way, didn't it?"

"But you never told *me*."

"Why should I, Eddie? You would have run like a deer. And I didn't want you to run. I wanted to have it all, and you were a big part of my all. You still are."

She looked straight ahead as she drove, speaking quietly, and he wanted to believe her.

"What does your husband know?"

"Just that I go away. That there are probably other men. That there's no other way for me."

"And if we kill him?"

"I've accepted that," she said.

There was a flat finality in her words that chilled him.

"You might say," she went on, "that he dug his own grave. He broke all his own rules. Freddy's the most discreet man in the world, except with me. I suppose that's how he thinks he can hold on to me. He told me about you four years ago, and once he told me, I knew I had to meet you."

He remembered: a fine late-September day in Central Park, playing touch football with the Sunday-morning gang, and after the game the girl with the smiling violet eyes who had clapped her hands with delight when he threw the final touchdown pass. It had all seemed so natural, accidental and yet fated.

*Chalice. That's an odd name. Yes, I chose it myself. My father had a pet name for me; he called me Cupcake. He had eyes just like yours. But you can't be a grown woman with a name like that, can you?*

"I arranged all that," she said now. "I met Vasily the same way at Gstaad, skiing."

"I don't understand you."

"Does it matter? I never asked you to understand me. I just asked you to let me live my life and take me as I am. If you couldn't have done that, I wouldn't have stayed around. I wouldn't be here now. And you'd probably be dead. You and Vasily both."

He mulled the truth of that, then said, "Okay. But it's not quite good enough. Not anymore. I need to know who you are. I need to know what makes you tick."

"Oh, Eddie," she said, and her sigh was a whisper of sadness. "I spent nearly five years on the couch trying to figure that one out. It cost me a fortune, but it was worth it. And do you know why? Because after five years I finally realized that understanding yourself isn't all that important. Because you never can, not fully. All you can do is pick a convenient position, a half-truth you can live with. Then, if you're lucky, you can con yourself into believing that you're a free human being, and not just a freak."

"I never called you a freak, Chalice. It's not the kind of word I use."

"The word doesn't bother me. Underneath the masks, everybody is a freak about something. Vasily says that I'm a freak about death. Well, maybe I am. People start to die as soon as they're born. It's the one sure direction in life. My father taught me that. He was a soldier, and he knew."

"I'm not exactly ignorant on the subject myself."

She heard his words, but they drifted past her. They were driving through flat desert now, country like the deserts of her youth, and against the backdrop of the arid land she saw the figure of her father, the general, the warrior. General Malcolm Ripley, Jr., The Ripper. That's what the men had called him, half out of love, half out of fear. The Ripper, leading a tank battalion in Europe before she was born. The Ripper, with a regimental combat team in Korea when she was a child. Korea, with her mother dead, and little Catherine living at the post near El Paso, passed along through a series of housekeepers she hardly remembered. Waiting, just waiting for the warrior's return, waiting for him to come back and soothe her, laugh with her, stroke her hair and smile out of his dark eyes surrounded by the tiny wrinkles and call her, "My sweet Cathy, little Cupcake . . ." And tell her that whatever she wanted she could have. "A horse? A white horse with a black mane? Oh, I don't know if I can arrange a black mane, unless I get a bucket of paint, but a white horse, yes. For Christmas, my darling . . ."

The men loved him, but not as much as she did. That love was special, and perfect. "There's no one but you, little Cupcake. You're what I come home to. You're the only one." *The only one . . . the only one.* And later she knew that she had never loved anyone as much as she had loved that man.

How long does such love last? He gave her the

white horse, and she loved him. Then he gave himself a new wife, and for a time the love died. A wife? It seemed impossible. Those wrinkled eyes, that steel-gray hair, belonged to a patriarch and a warrior, not to a lover with a young wife. If the horse had been intended as a balm to soothe her, then it failed. No balm could ever soothe the sadness of her loss.

But she accepted it, and tried to be the quiet, obedient stepdaughter who kept out of the way. That's what he wanted: a good girl. *"My good little girl, my Cupcake. You know I still love you too. You know that, don't you?"*

Love you too?

It wasn't enough. The woman, Grace—dark-haired, slight of body, almost frail—was kind to Catherine. No one could fault her. They would shop in the PX together, go to the movies, ride through the desert and the trails above Shadow Mountain. But when the bedroom door closed, Catherine knew it was all a lie. *There's no one but you, Cupcake.* That was a lie. And he had never lied to her before.

The panorama of the Mexican desert, as she drove north now with Eddie through the state of Hidalgo, the green plain that would turn to brown dust when the rains ended, and the blue-purple mountains that bulked to the west in a never-ending, rippling line, brought it back to her easily—the morning that she and Grace had ridden up Shadow Mountain into the backcountry.

How strange, that such things happened on fine days, under a warming sun, a cloudless sky, rich shadows streaking the earth that sloped off the narrow trail. Grace rode well, sitting an English saddle with ease, comfortable with her chestnut gelding. At peace with her world, she laughed as they rode—a silvery laugh that echoed back from the canyon wall—and perhaps it was the laugh that lit the fuse. The happiness that rode on the wings of that laugh was a challenge to Catherine, and in that moment it seemed to her that Grace was the possessor of everything worth having, everything as yet denied to her: a fragile beauty, a contented life, a womanhood beyond the reach of a teen-age girl, and an adoring husband. Not just any husband, but General Malcolm Ripley, Jr. Grace had it all, Catherine had so little, and so she killed her.

Not badly, not bluntly, but at a place where the trail skirted the lip of the canyon, the gelding shied. Perhaps a lizard, perhaps a snake—Catherine never knew. But what she never forgot was the sight of Grace checking at the reins, sawing as the chestnut slid on loose shale. Catherine, up in the stirrups, reached over to help, to catch at an arm, a rein, anything to hold in case the chestnut plunged.

*"I tried, Daddy. I tried."*

The flanks of the horses touched, and the girl grabbed hold of the woman's arm. For a moment she pulled, helping, saving. And then, in a savage reversal, she pushed with all her sinewy young strength, shoved outward, and at the same time kicked at the chestnut's belly with her boot. Grace opened her mouth to scream, but no sound broke above the scraping of hoofs and the chestnut's frantic whinny; so surprised—and then the horse and rider were tumbling, cartwheeling, down through the brush and rocks into the canyon fifty feet below.

*"Daddy, it was horrible."*

He held her in his arms when he got there, spiraling up the trail in a jeep following the ambulance, the old warrior weeping, crushing her to him tightly, for now she was all he had left. When she was smothered that way, all the pain ebbed away, replaced by a pleasure that her mind could not define. Her body quivered; her spirit soared. In time the edges of the memory crumbled, the images faded, and although she could recapture the pleasure at any time she pleased, even now she was no longer sure if she had pushed or pulled that day on the trail high on Shadow Mountain.

Just past Querétaro, they turned off the four-lane highway onto the narrow road that twisted through the mountains toward San Miguel de Allende.

"I'm tired too," Chalice said. "I'm very tired."

"You want me to drive now?"

"Not tired that way. When this is over . . ." She hesitated, then glanced at him for the first time in an hour. "What happens now?"

"Good question. That's all we've been talking about. Well, not quite all, but it's the big thing. Since Cozumel, everything's changed."

"Because they know."

"That's right, because they know. And it's all been programmed into the computer. So . . ." He let it hang there, turning to light another cigarette, avoiding looking at her. The desert sped by: a laden *burro,* children playing in the dust, a clutch of adobe huts. "I want to quit," he said finally. "And Vasily wants to go to war—all or nothing. I can't see it. For me, it's the end of the line."

"If you run, they'll find you."

"I suppose so, sooner or later. I'll take my chances. I didn't go into this to make it my life's work. The other thing, what I did before, that was bad enough. It was a job and they paid me well and I didn't ask too many questions. I didn't think ahead. I didn't see that I could never get out of it. And I made this deal with Vasily because there was no other way. But where does it end?"

"You can end it," she said softly. "That's what I came to tell you. There's a new man running things in Williamsburg. His name is Crowfoot."

"Tom Crowfoot?" Eddie was momentarily roused out of his lethargy. "An Indian?"

"That's the one. He and Freddy went over to Zhukovka to set up the Cozumel operation."

"Crowfoot. He's the best, and we beat him. Not bad for two amateurs." He looked at her from the corner of his eye. "Of course, we had some help."

She smiled. "They still don't know how you did it. Crowfoot is furious, and Freddy has no idea that he's the leak. Now they're scared, and they have to meet again. Crowfoot, Freddy, and Fist."

"Where?"

"Williamsburg. They're back to using CYBER again, so it had to be either Williamsburg or Zhukovka. This time it's the Agency's turn to play host."

"Do you know when?"

"Yes." She slowed the speed of the car and touched his arm lightly. "All three of them together. You'll never get a better chance."

"We could never get inside. You know their security."

"From the outside, then."

"Blow it all away? The whole unit? Christ, you're getting to sound like Vasily. He had an idea for Zhukovka, a miniature atomic bomb planted in a can of tennis balls. Did you ever hear of anything so crazy?"

"It doesn't sound crazy to me. Could you use it at Williamsburg?" Then she frowned, and shook her head slightly. "No good—Freddy doesn't play tennis. Could you do the same thing with golf balls?"

"You're not listening to me," he said, depressed again, the weariness back in his voice. "Do you have any idea how many people have died so far in this operation? I counted them up the other night. I make it twenty-one, although maybe I missed a stiff or two somewhere. Twenty-one fucking bodies, and now you want me to take out an entire office complex. Forget it!"

"All right, I'll forget it," she said slowly. "And you'll run. And they'll find you. And whatever future you and I might have had together will go down the drain. Wasted. Just like you."

"Future? You and me? What future?"

"The two of us together. Wherever you want to go. Once this is all over."

"Say that again."

"You heard me right the first time."

"Stop the car."

She braked in a long deceleration that brought them to a stop at the side of the road. She switched off the key and half-turned on the seat to face him. He took her into his arms.

"You and me?" he asked. "Just the two of us?"

"If you still want me that way. All to yourself."

"And Vasily?"

"He won't object. Not if it's what I really want. He's probably guessed it already."

He stared at her for a long moment, reading her face intently. Then he released her from his arms and said, "Start the car."

"What is it?"

"I don't know. I have to think. I just don't know."

"But we can do it," Vasily said calmly, although his gray eyes were glittering with resolution. "Not with the tennis balls. With the laser. I told you a time would come when we'd need something big and we could use the laser. We can do it."

They were alone in the shed behind the house on the hill, Vasily straddling a chair, Eddie pacing back and forth on the tiled floor. Outside, the afternoon rain beat down on the earth as a parade of thunderheads moved in from the mountains to the west.

"You have to be out of your mind," Eddie said. "I mean, if we could do it—I'm not saying we could, but *if* we had a way—do you know how many people work in there? Lower-level people, secretaries, clerks, technicians. There must be more than a hundred."

"Chalice says that the meeting will be on a Sunday."

"So it's half-staff, then. Fifty people. Fifty people who never did anything to me. Do you realize how many people have died so far . . ."

Vasily restrained him with a raised finger. "Spare me the statistics, please. Chalice told me of your conversation in the car. Twenty-one, you said? I hadn't counted them up, but I take your word for it."

"And it doesn't bother you?"

Vasily slid by the question. "Look at it this way. With the score already so high, what difference will a few more make? Keep your mind on basics, Eddie. You have to get rid of Parker and Crowfoot."

Eddie grunted. "And you have to get rid of Fist. It would work out perfectly for you."

"Perfectly," Vasily agreed. "By the time the people in Moscow sort things out they'll have forgotten all about me, if anyone still cares. They'll be blaming the Agency, and the Agency will be in shreds. You might even think of this as a gesture for suffering humanity."

"Humanity? What about Rakow's girl and her kid? What about that hooker in Washington? What about Wolf the music man? Weren't they part of humanity?"

"They certainly were." Vasily said it smoothly, as if these arguments all were words he had heard before, words for which he had fashioned answers over years of constant phrasing. "And they are also part of the past. The future is what counts now. Your future. And Chalice's."

"More bait."

"The best kind. If you quit now, you'll never have her. Not the way you want her."

"And you? She said that you'd agree."

"What choice do I have? It's her decision, not mine." He raised his hand in a lazy benediction. "Dear fellow, you hardly need it, but you both have my blessing."

"We'll need it, all right. You know how sick she is."

"Yes, of course. That's something you'll have to live with."

"Maybe not. All this killing . . . it's gotten to her. Just like it's gotten to me. I'm hoping that when it's all over, maybe she'll change."

Vasily turned away to hide his expression. "When it's all over. That's a pleasant thought to dwell on. Do you know yet where you'll be going?"

"I've got a few ideas. You?"

"Of course." He laughed. "Don't ask me where, and I won't ask you either. Much better that way."

"What if we called it quits right now? Would that change your plans?"

230

"My plans aren't subject to change. If you quit now, for my own sake I'd have to do the job alone."

Eddie looked at him, startled. "You could never handle it."

"I'd have to. As long as Fist is alive I have no peace. A minimum amount of peace is necessary when one reaches my age."

"Your age, my ass." Eddie said it scoffingly, but with affection.

"Thank you, but I'm ten years older than you are. It's a paradox, but life becomes rather more precious the older one gets. Perhaps because it passes more swiftly."

"I still don't see how you can do it alone."

"It's a matter of technique, instincts, and a little bit of luck." He smiled. "I'm certainly a technician, and I must say that over the past few months my instincts have been developing rapidly. As for the luck . . ."

"The luck runs out sometimes."

"That's also a possibility. One never knows."

"How do you plan to do it?"

"With the laser. Use it as a heat source and project it. If the pulse length is short enough, the thermal shock will take out the entire building. What do you know about exothermic chemical reaction?"

Eddie looked thoughtful. "Enough to know that you'll need ruby or neodymium if you want to use a Q-switch. You'll have to get the pulse down to ten nanoseconds, and suppress feedback from the mirrors."

"One day I'll learn not to ask you questions like that." Vasily shook his head admiringly. "I can get the neodymium. Have you worked with a Q-switch?"

"I know how to do it," Eddie said impatiently. "That's not what I meant when I asked what your plans are. I know you can build the damn thing, with or without my help. But there are thousands of tourists swarming around Colonial Williamsburg this time of year. How the hell are you going to wander out onto the green with a laser slung over your shoulder and point it at that building? You'll start a riot, or maybe a small war."

"I won't start a war, I'll just take advantage of one. The War of the American Revolution. The mock battle between the colonial militia and the British Army. All I'll need is one of their cannon."

"The cannon," Eddie murmured. "Yeah, sure. You could load it into the cannon."

"How do you think I should dress? As a British officer, or an American? I think the British uniform is more my style, don't you?"

"Yeah, it matches the red in your eyes. How do you figure to get to the cannon?"

"You're going to tell me how. I assume you know where they're kept?"

"And the uniforms and muskets, too."

"Then there you are. You've answered your own question."

"It's impossible to do it alone."

"Not impossible. Difficult, yes, but not impossible. Of course, I'd prefer to have you there with me, but—"

"I'll be there," Eddie said grimly. "You know damn well I'll be there. You knew it all along, didn't you?"

"Certainly. You pay your debts."

"That's right. I would've been feeding the fish at Cozumel if you hadn't been on that beach. I guess I can do the same for you."

"Start work tomorrow?"

"The sooner the better."

Vasily laid a hand on Eddie's shoulder. "Thank you, my friend. You won't be getting any sentimental speeches from me, but thank you. When all this is over—well, if circumstances were different, I'd take you with me to where I'm going. I'd teach you to play a decent game of chess, and we might grow old and quarrelsome together. But that can't be. When this is over, our paths diverge."

Eddie nodded.

"But you'll have your lady for company. Go to her now. She's probably waiting for you."

Eddie nodded again, started to say something, then shook his head, and left.

I gave him my blessing, Vasily thought. I should have given him my sympathy as well.

He smoked a last cigar, pondering the frailty of man, and the need for love in whatever disguise it came. He decided that he was glad he was ten years older. He walked through the field of cactus to the house, enjoying the clear starlight and the soft night air.

"Technique, instinct, and luck," he said to himself, and to the far-stretching stars. "Except that I don't really believe in luck. For if I did believe in it, I should also have to believe that we've already used up far more than our earthly share."

# 18

It was the last lap of the journey, and both Eddie and Vasily knew it, were glad of it, and hungered for it to be over and done with. They drove north through the six hundred miles of dreary, unchanging Mexican desert in the Chevrolet pickup with the camper top, their equipment broken down into simplest components and scattered in cartons and suitcases, disguised as souvenirs, and buried in hollowed-out copies of pre-Columbian statuary. They joked a lot on the drive, and insulted each other in the easy camaraderie that had grown between them; but behind the light-hearted mood was the tense desire to be finished. At Matamoros they crossed over into Texas without incident, stood a perfunctory search there by U.S. Customs, and late on a Sunday afternoon pulled into a Holiday Inn outside Lake Charles, Louisiana. There they stopped for two days to reassemble the laser.

On the same day that they left San Miguel, Chalice flew back to Williamsburg with firm instructions. There would be one more telephone call to the Madison Hotel in Washington. That would be on the following Saturday, to confirm that on Sunday, Crowfoot, Parker, and Fist would be in conference behind the deceptive frame-and-shingle facade of the building they believed impregnable. After that call she was to return to her home in Williamsburg, and wait.

And on Monday, Eddie thought wistfully, we'll be thirty-five thousand feet above the Pacific and heading out to a world where they'll never find us. No more hunters, no more hunted.

With the laser assembled, they left Lake Charles and bounced across the South, staying at a succession of identical motels. Somewhere in South Carolina they stopped to make final preparations, and Eddie explained how the mock battle at Williamsburg worked.

"It's just another tourist attraction, but it's a good one," he said, sprawled on one of the twin beds. "The battle goes off about eleven in the morning. There are maybe a hundred soldiers, just local people and college kids. Half of them are dressed as militia, the other half as British soldiers. If we move fast enough, they won't know what's happening. How are you coming?"

Vasily sat on the other twin bed, busily sewing the costumes together. The local tailor in San Miguel had made them, shaking his head in bewilderment and muttering pleas to various saints when the two crazy *gringos* had brought in the scarlet cloth and the sketches of what they wanted. Then, when they had tried them on and been satisfied, Eddie had insisted on picking them apart at the seams and scattering the pieces in the suitcases among his trousers and sweaters and shirts, worried that the Customs officials at Brownsville would think twice about two grown men traveling with eighteenth-century British military uniforms. After a few protests, Vasily had agreed. Now he stitched and sewed, grunted and cursed.

"In my old age, I have become a seamstress. *You* were the one who insisted on taking these apart. *You* should sew them together."

"You sew, I reap," Eddie said, straight-faced.

"You mean you sit there and watch television while I stitch away like an old woman. Thank you, my friend. I won't forget this."

"Get those seams straight," Eddie said. "Not too tight under the arms. I hate it when a jacket's too tight under the arms."

"Why? Does it squeeze your brains? Here." Vasily tossed the red tunic and breeches across the bed. "Try them on."

Struggling into the tunic, Eddie looked at himself in the mirror. He tightened the belt and adjusted the tri-cornered hat. After a minute of gazing, turning this way and that, he screwed his face up in an expression of horror. Simulated sobs broke from his throat.

Startled, Vasily asked, "What is the matter?"

"We . . . good Gawd!"

"What is it?"

"We've . . . we've lost India!"

On that same Friday morning, Thomas Crowfoot punched the blue button on CYBER and began to read the printout that the machine silently and effi-ciently spewed, page by page, into the output tray. Colonel Fist and Colonel Parker stood nearby, watch-ing as the old man scanned the dark-gray print.

Into the machine, Crowfoot had first fed the physi-cal descriptions, provided by Colonel Fist, of every woman with whom Vasily Borgneff was known to have been seen—even for a single evening—over the past ten years. The machine was then given the same data relative to Eddie Mancuso. NO KNOWN REPETI-TIVE SEXUAL RELATIONSHIP AT PRESENT, CYBER had said back in February, and its Zhukovka counter-part had echoed the phrase in its printout on Borg-neff. And yet Crowfoot had suspected, and then seen, what the others had missed.

A woman in Barcelona eight months ago, with whom the Russian had spent two nights at the Hotel Colón: tall, dark-blond hair, in her middle or late twenties, believed by the KGB's Madrid desk to be Scandinavian. A brief and casual affair, nothing more, with no investigatory follow-up recommended. And then the Mancuso dossier: a tall, dark-blond woman, age twenty-six to twenty-eight, whom the subject had apparently picked up at a sidewalk cafe in Christian-sted, St. Croix, in March of 1976. A woman answer-ing the same description had been seen leaving his

236

Manhattan apartment on a Monday morning approximately ten months later. No positive identification. The reports had been filed away with thousands more, considered too insignificant to be fed into CYBER's memory bank.

Crowfoot had then programmed CYBER with the physical descriptions of all Colonial Squad and *dachniki* female personnel. Results: negative. He pondered that problem for two more days, and then punched in the computerized dossiers of all close relatives, including wives, daughters, and suspected mistresses, of all O Group and Five Group members. That process took less than fifteen minutes; the first file to be matched against the known description of the woman who had appeared both in Barcelona and St. Croix was that of Mrs. Frederick Parker, born Catherine Alexandra Ripley.

"Well, there it is," said Crowfoot, and tossed his copy of the printout onto the table.

Fist did the same with his, looked at the two Americans, shrugged, and walked to the other side of the room, disassociating himself from what was to come. Parker's face turned red, and then a sickly white. He struggled to maintain a semblance of dignity, although in that moment he knew that his career and his marriage were both ended.

Finally, he said, "It's—it's hard to believe, Tom."

"Harder for you than for me."

"What are you going to do?"

"What would you do in my place?"

"You mean—extraction?"

"A perfect example of a colonel's mentality at work. That may be necessary later, but first I want to have a little powwow with your wife. Any objections?"

"None," the colonel said grimly. "Let's go."

"Not you, Freddy. I'll see her alone."

That evening he sat across the coffee table from the colonel's wife in the half-timbered house in Williamsburg, shuffling papers and sipping sherry as a faint smile played upon his lips. But his eyes were coolly calculating. Catherine Parker drank Scotch with ice and water, and her long, red-tipped fingers were steady on the glass, her eyes unswerving as the old man told her what he knew.

"You understand that your position is untenable," Crowfoot finished. "I won't inquire into your motives right now. If I had more time, perhaps . . . but in fact they truly are of little interest to me. I need information. All you've got. If you won't give it voluntarily, we'll use scopolamine. You know what that is, I'm sure. The larger doses are dangerous, but they ensure the telling of the truth. Actually, we'll have to use the scopolamine in any event, to make sure that what you say now is accurate. But it would certainly be in your interest, Mrs. Parker, to make this first stage of confession a truthful one. It would make me feel a whole lot more kindly toward you later on."

Chalice considered carefully. "And may I ask how it will all end for me?"

"That depends," Crowfoot said. "But you do see that you have no options."

"It would seem that way."

"Good. I'm interested only in the present, since there's a certain urgency. Where are they now?"

"In Mexico. En route to Virginia."

"You've told them about Colonel Fist being here?"

"Yes."

"And they're coming here to . . . ?"

"To kill all of you."

"How unfriendly. How do they plan to accomplish such an ambitious act?"

"I don't know. They didn't tell me."

"Oh, dear." Crowfoot sighed. "Please don't lie to me at this stage of the game, Mrs. Parker."

"Why should I lie? You told me about the scopolamine. I know you meant it. I don't know their plans."

"Do they plan to infiltrate the building in some way, or reach all of us individually?"

"I don't know, Mr. Crowfoot."

"I tend to believe you, but we'll still have to verify. How can we contact them? Do you know their route?"

"They left Mexico in a Chevrolet pickup truck, but they may have abandoned that and picked up something else. They're going to call me at a number in Washington on Saturday. That's to find out where you all are."

"And if they were to succeed, Mrs. Parker, what were their plans? And yours, if I may be presumptuous?"

"I was going to leave with one of them," Chalice said calmly. "With Eddie Mancuso."

"Well!" Thomas Crowfoot smiled. "That may still be possible." He stood slowly, conscious of the creaking of his bones and the ache in his knees. "We can go now, if you're ready. I apologize for this. You do see that it's necessary. No," he added, as Chalice turned toward the staircase. "Please don't go upstairs. Not even out of my sight. It's a warm night. Come as you are, my dear."

By midnight, Crowfoot had administered the injection of scopolamine, had gone through the questioning again in somewhat greater detail, and had assured himself that Catherine Parker was telling him the truth. While she rested and was brought gradually back to a normal state, he sat at the colonel's desk, the lights dimmed, the air conditioner softly humming, to consider the situation.

He reached a decision.

His first step was an order that neither Colonel Fist nor Colonel Parker was to leave the building. There were apartments on the first floor where they would be comfortable for several days. And safe, which was even more important. The building was impregnable to intrusion by two men, and the only danger lay if either Parker or Fist should venture outside it. That would not be allowed until the second and third stages of his plan were completed.

The woman is a psychopath, he realized. She cannot be trusted. But she can be easily manipulated if one turns the right key. He believed now that he knew the key.

When Chalice's mind was functioning again, he fed her sandwiches and two cups of coffee, and then sat with her in what had been her husband's office. She smiled at him wanly.

"Are you satisfied that I told you the truth, Mr. Crowfoot?"

He nodded, and then said, "I want this all to end, my dear young woman. It has been exceedingly costly to this Agency and to our Russian friends as well. If you cooperate, it can be brought to a peaceful conclusion. And if that is indeed the result, then you will be free. Both you and your friend Mr. Mancuso. I can't answer for Borgneff's future. I'm sorry to say I must defer in that matter to the judgment of the man we know as Colonel Fist. You do understand that, don't you?"

"Yes."

"We're arranging for the telephone call from your friends to be routed to this building. For the moment, although it may be a slight inconvenience, you'll stay here. You'll take the call here. You may speak freely. You may tell them everything that's happened. And then I would like you to arrange a meeting, under what we used to call, in more civilized days, a flag of truce. I would like to offer them amnesty."

Chalice laughed quietly. "Do you think they'll believe it?"

"Probably not, but it would certainly be worth their while to listen. I'm sure they are ingenious enough to construct adequate safeguards for themselves—they seem to be very adept at that. I'll accept any reasonable conditions. I'll even talk to one of them if they prefer not to come together."

"Either one?"

"No," Crowfoot said. "If it's one, it must be the American."

"He might just do it, you know."

"I hope so. I'm being perfectly sincere. I want this to end. And," he added, "I know you won't be disappointed with the outcome."

240

By Saturday afternoon, on the ninth floor of the Sheraton Beach Hotel at Virginia Beach, Eddie and Vasily had assembled the finished laser. Eddie snapped the Q-switch and polarizer into place and then delicately inserted the lithium niobate frequency doubler. They had miniaturized every component as much as possible without sacrificing the necessary demolition power. With a lint-free cloth, he wiped the last coating of isopropyl alcohol from the optical mirrors. The device slid into a thin protective aluminum tube, so that it looked like no more than a four-foot length of pipe.

"Done."

"My congratulations," Vasily said. "Do you know, if you had taken a different fork of the road twenty years ago, you would have been in Stockholm now, receiving a Nobel Prize? Have you ever thought about that?"

"Sometimes," Eddie admitted. "I was a dumb kid and they grabbed me young. Once I showed them the blowback silencer, they knew they had a whiz kid. I called it the Little Devil. You know what I'm talking about?"

"Oh, yes. We heard of you even then. It was very impressive. Do your people have this little gadget yet?" He tapped the aluminum casing.

"Yeah, that's Project Flash Gordon. He was a comic-strip hero before my time, when they called these babies death rays. But they haven't gone any further than we've gone, and what they've got is too big and bulky. Fine for tanks, but two men couldn't carry one."

"Shall we test it?"

"On what? Listen, when you throw that switch and that mother heats up, anything gets in the way is going to be pulverized. This isn't Mexico—you blow up a sheep or a building in the United States, someone complains. It will work. Take my word for it."

"Look . . . out there." Vasily pointed from the broad window. The beach was crowded with hundreds of bronzed young men playing volleyball and ogling the bikinied girls who sprawled decoratively on the sand and splashed in the surf. Several hundred yards out in the Atlantic a series of small black marker buoys bobbed on the dark-blue water, setting the safety limits for the swimmers.

"Just one of them," Vasily cajoled.

"All right, all right," Eddie said. "If it will make you happy."

He moved the laser to the small balcony of his room, sheltered on either side by walls from the adjoining balconies. He activated it, then turned to Vasily and said, "Just one. Don't get carried away."

Looking through the tube and adjusting the sighting mechanism, Vasily pressed a switch. A thin red beam of coherent light, no more than two inches in diameter, sliced through the warm air of the summer afternoon at the speed of $10^8$ m sec$^{-1}$ with a power density of 50 megawatts per square centimeter. The beam danced on the waves, then moved toward the buoy as Vasily spun the elevating lever. For a moment, but only a moment, a clear red circle of light showed on the distant black surface. Then the buoy silently disintegrated. A second later the waves closed over what was left of it, a bit of hissing pulp. Vasily pressed the switch, the beam vanished instantly, and he looked at Eddie with a large smile of satisfaction.

"Once again, I bow to the master."

"Well, the master is going for a swim, and then he's going to take a little *siesta*. It's going to be a long night."

At nine o'clock, as the last light of the summer evening began to fade, they set out from Virginia Beach in the rented station wagon. An hour and a half later, dressed in the anonymous coveralls of repairmen, they walked quickly through the balmy darkness of Colonial Williamsburg, heading toward The Magazine on the green. A few lights still burned in the buildings that housed the Colonial Squad, and from the Governor's Palace came the faint strains of a Mozart quartet. The daytime tourists had long since gone, the restaurants and colonial-style shops were closed, but a few summer-session students sauntered singly or in pairs, arms entwined, across the green en route to the campus of William and Mary. The two men, despite the bulky package they carried, attracted no attention.

"The security guards are only here during the day," Eddie explained. "At night there's a patrol car that wanders around, but you can see it coming a mile off. It's like a small town. People actually live here."

With Vasily standing behind him, quietly whistling Mozart in the darkness, Eddie picked the padlock on the side door of The Magazine. Once inside, using the beam of a pencil flashlight, he quickly located the cannon, standing in two neat rows: ten cast-iron replicas of eighteenth-century artillery.

"They're on wheels," Eddie said. "They roll them out and set them up. They just shoot air and a big puff of smoke."

"Not tomorrow," Vasily murmured.

With his own flashlight he inspected the muzzle and powder hole. He grunted something to himself in Russian.

"Are they okay?"

"Yes, yes—just as you described. It's fine. It will fit perfectly." Carefully, he slid the long tube that housed the laser down the barrel of the cannon until it locked into place. Reaching into the touchhole, he satisfied himself that he could press the activating switches. Then, with a pocket knife, he made a deep, V-shaped identifying scratch on the butt of the cannon.

"If we only knew," he said, rising up. "If we knew they were in there right now, we could blow away the building and be gone in minutes."

"It's a temptation," Eddie admitted. "But we have to play it by the book. Chalice said Sunday, and that's what it is. If we screw it up now we don't get any second chance. Let's go."

They drove out of Colonial Williamsburg, down Second Street to the highway, and over to the James York Plaza Shopping Center. They found a telephone booth near the entrance to the Plaza, and Eddie dialed the Madison Hotel in Washington while Vasily sat behind the wheel with the engine running. In the pale light that came from the roof of the booth he saw the strain on Eddie's lips, saw the knuckles of his hand on the receiver whiten. He knew then that something had gone wrong, but he held himself in and waited. When Eddie had been on the telephone for five minutes, he tapped the horn lightly. Eddie looked up, nodded, talked for thirty seconds more, and hung up. He ran back to the car, jumped in, and slammed the door.

"Move it out, move it out fast."

Vasily came down sharply on the accelerator. The car leaped forward, shot out of the shopping center to the highway and across to the eastbound lane. Vasily wrenched the wheel around, and said loudly, "Which way?"

"Take the next side road. Drive down it and stop."

Vasily came screaming around the corner of Peniman Road and slammed on the brake. He killed the lights, but kept the engine running. "Tell me."

"They've got her. They know everything. That call never went to Washington. It was patched into the Squad switchboard. She's right here in Williamsburg."

"Speak calmly. Tell me exactly what she said."

Eddie told him. He told him about the CYBER match-up, about the scopolamine, about the conference with Crowfoot. "They want a meeting in half an hour. Crowfoot and me in an open area, the Sunken Garden at the college. I know the place."

"What did you say?"

Eddie took a deep breath. "I said I'd be there. Not you . . . just me. And I said that unless he came alone, or if anything happened to me, you'd blow him right into the Happy Hunting Ground. You'll have to cover me with the Dragunov."

Vasily nodded, then said slowly, "There is no sense to this, Eddie. There is nothing to be gained. Chalice doesn't know what we plan to do. We are not yet harmed. We can still do things exactly as we planned."

"And then what do you think happens to her?"

"That is . . . unfortunate."

"Yeah. And it can be avoided. They want to let

us off the hook, make a deal. I want to hear what it is. Will you cover me?"

"Crowfoot is an old man who may be quite willing to join his ancestors if he's under orders. Or they may want only you, Eddie. After all, it's Crowfoot who proposed this, not Fist. Have you considered all that?"

"Sort of." Eddie moved uncomfortably in the seat, rubbing his hands together nervously. "I can't let Chalice twist in the wind. And maybe they mean it. If they do, we can get this all over with tonight. I want to see the man. I'm going there, Vasily."

## 19

The architectural pride of The College of William
and Mary, the building designed by Sir Christopher
Wren, stands in the College Yard overlooking Duke
of Gloucester Street and the original Capitol exactly
one measured mile away. Directly behind the Wren
Building lies the Sunken Garden, which is not a garden
at all but a deep, regular grassy depression in the
ground approximately the size of a football field. During the day it is a bright and open space filled with
students strolling, studying, plotting sexual escapades,
and flipping football and frisbees. At night it is a dark
and empty void filled only with shadows.

Eddie and Crowfoot faced each other at the eastern
end of the Sunken Garden. The darkness was complete; each could see the other only dimly. The night
was silent as well as dark. An occasional car passed
by on Richmond Road, a cricket chirped, a church
bell tolled a lonely hour; but that was all.

"Go ahead and talk," Eddie said. "Just remember
that you're lined up in the cross hairs of a Dragunov
with a telescopic sight and an N2P2 light intensifier.
I don't have to tell you what that is. So that if anything happens to me—"

"I understand all that," Thomas Crowfoot interrupted him gently. "Nothing will happen to you. I've
kept my word."

246

"Then talk."

"You treat me as an enemy." The old man sighed. "In view of all that's happened, I suppose it's understandable. But I think it can be changed."

"I'm not coming back," Eddie said. "I'm finished with the Agency. I wanted out and they sent Kelly after me."

"They acted too quickly." Even in the darkness his eyes sparkled like agates, his ancestry written in them. "On the other hand, you can't blame them. The computer's judgment of your plans was accurate. They had no choice."

"I had less."

"I agree. I'm not here to turn you around. They don't want you back. It would be an uncomfortable arrangement. You would be acting very unwisely if you thought you could have any more dealings with them, especially with Colonel Parker. He wanted me to have you killed, you know. His attitude is, well . . . fixed."

"And your attitude?"

"You understand that I have considerably higher authority than that of Colonel Parker. I have authority that goes even slightly higher than that of the people at Langley."

"Okay, you're God. So read me the commandments."

The old man's lips curved in a thin smile. "I have no commandments," he said. "Only a proposal and the power to implement it. I propose that we end this little war. As I've told Mrs. Parker, it's been very costly to us, and to the people at Zhukovka as well. You and your friend are a formidable team. We underestimated you. We don't anymore. We are not being altruistic or forgiving, you understand. Just realistic."

"Tell me something," Eddie said. "I'm armed. I could put you away in two seconds if I wanted, and then I could walk away. What's to stop me from doing that?"

"Nothing at all. If you want to run for the rest of

your life, do it. Parker will find you. He has strong motives. I wouldn't advise it, Mr. Mancuso. It's not in your best interest. And then," he added softly, "there's the woman."

"What about her?"

"Ah, you see, that depends on you."

"You think I care?"

"Oh?" The old man looked surprised. "I thought you did. Was I mistaken?"

He knows, Eddie realized. He knows everything. He's smart and he's holding all the cards. If I won't play it his way I have to throw down my hand and walk away from the table, alone. And they'll bury Chalice and then come after me.

"You want a truce," Eddie said.

"A truce is temporary. I want peace. Amnesty on both sides. Stop hunting us and we'll stop hunting you."

"Did you bring a pipe to smoke, or a hatchet to bury?"

Crowfoot chuckled.

"What about Borgneff?" Eddie asked.

"I speak for the Russians too. Borgneff is included in the arrangement. Go where you like, live as you please. To be on the safe side, I would advise that you leave the country. You probably meant to do that anyway. We won't look for you. We're not interested. You're free."

"And what are the guarantees?"

"They would be meaningless. What would you accept? Documents? Affidavits? You know that's not possible. There's nothing I can give you except my word. If you knew me better, you'd realize that I've never broken it."

"I want the files destroyed. Taken out of CYBER. Mine and Borgneff's."

"It will be done."

"And I want the woman."

"That's understood." There was nothing smug in Crowfoot's tone. He was sympathetic, almost paternal.

"Will Parker buy that?"

"Don't worry about Parker. His usefulness to us, I'm sad to say, has come to an end. A man who wants to kill you is one thing. You can always reason with him, as I'm doing with you. A man you can't trust is quite another."

"You're going to retire him?"

"With prejudice," Crowfoot said. "To protect you. By protecting you, we protect ourselves."

Eddie looked into the dark, suddenly expressionless eyes. The old man means it, he realized. That's the way they always did things, and there's no reason for them to change. He shivered a little, even in the warm night.

"All right," he said. "I'll just have to talk to Borgneff. You understand that, don't you?"

Crowfoot nodded. "And suppose he doesn't agree?"

"I've agreed. I'm the one the Agency's worried about. Isn't that enough?"

"I'm afraid not. The Russians have bought the package, too. They can't be sent home empty-handed."

Eddie understood. "I'll talk to Borgneff," he said.

"If he doesn't agree," Crowfoot said, "there's a simple solution."

"Oh, no," Eddie said sharply.

"Think about it. He's been with the opposition all his life. You mean nothing to him. He's used you, just as you've used him. That usefulness is at an end."

"Listen, I don't want to talk about it. If he agrees, how do I reach you?"

"You know the Colonial Squad number here in Williamsburg. "I'm going there now. I'll be there through Sunday evening, or until we hear from you."

Eddie hesitated. "And Chalice?"

"Mrs. Parker will be there with me. Once you call, if you give me the right answer, she'll be released. You can meet her wherever you like. We'll never contact either of you again. You have my word."

"I'll call you."

"Think about Borgneff," Crowfoot said.

With a last grim nod, Eddie backed away on the grass of the Sunken Garden until he was sure the darkness obscured him. The old man never moved, just raised his hand in a small gesture of farewell.

*Think about Borgneff. . . .*

The words repeated themselves over and over again, like the refrain of a song that demands to be hummed and refuses to quit the mind. Sometimes they came softly with the rush of the warm night wind; sometimes they shouted above the chorus of crickets that poured through the open windows of the car. Vasily drove, hands casually flexed on the steering wheel, and Eddie sat beside him, hunched, tense, smoking a cigarette. The silent buildings that bordered the highway to Virginia Beach sped by in the darkness.

"No," Vasily repeated. He was perfectly at ease, voice betraying no emotion. "It would be a mistake . . . and one that we would always regret. They lose nothing, and we gain nothing. They count on our keeping to our pattern because we've been successful at it, so they've taken the correct measures to protect themselves. Right now, behind their concrete walls, they consider themselves safe. Such an opportunity won't come again, and to miss it would be a sin against survival. One is always punished for such sins."

"He gave his word," Eddie said stubbornly. "I believe him."

"Your trust is touching," Vasily remarked. "Forgive me if I don't share it. Eddie, when we first met on top of the pyramid at Uxmal, you took me at my word. You challenged me, but in the end you trusted me. You were lucky, because we had a common interest. You have no such common interest with a man like Crowfoot."

*Think about Borgneff. He's used you, just as you've used him. That usefulness is at an end.*

"Why would he meet me, then?" Eddie asked doggedly. "Why would he risk it? They could have tried to get to us through Chalice. Christ, she was on scopolamine! They might have been able to do it, but they didn't. He met with me instead. He didn't have to do that."

"He told you he no longer underestimated us." Vasily flicked his headlights at an approaching car. "That may have been one of the few true things he said. Perhaps he remembered what happened at Cozumel . . . he wouldn't want that to be repeated." He sighed patiently. "I know the mentality, Eddie. I've dealt with it all my life, and I know it better than you. He's lying. I beg you to believe me."

"He has no stake in this. He's going to extract Parker. That was no lie."

"I don't doubt it for a moment." Vasily turned slightly, so that his cool gray eyes looked for a second into Eddie's. Then they shifted and bore once again on the bright glare of the highway. "But will he do the same to Fist? I'm afraid that's beyond his power. And I can assure you, whatever your people do, the file at Zhukovka will never be closed while Fist is alive. They will come after me. That is something I cannot tolerate."

The lights of Virginia Beach showed ahead, sparkling like ropes of jewels in the darkness. A drizzle fell, speckling the windshield. The smell of salt air filled the night. Vasily turned off the main road toward the beach and their hotel.

"What about Chalice? If we take out that building, she goes with it."

Vasily swung the car into the parking lot, eased it into an empty space, and switched off the engine.

"I see no choice," he said quietly.

Gripping the Russian by the arm, his voice low and hard, Eddie said, "I thought we were both cold-blooded bastards, but you win the prize. I always knew it, but I didn't know how cold. You were even willing to kill her in San Miguel, and you knew who she was, what she was risking to help us. And she *did* help us. You say that Crowfoot remembers Cozumel. Well, I remember it too. Damn it, we'd both be dead back there if it wasn't for her. Doesn't that mean anything to you?"

"Please let go of my arm," Vasily replied coolly,

251

"and then listen to me. There's nothing you can do to save her life. Chalice is already dead."

His face paling, Eddie released the grip. "What the hell are you talking about?"

"I mean that while it's possible, just faintly possible, that they might allow *you* to walk away, that same privilege is not going to be extended to the lady. Don't you see it? Compared with what she knows, you know nothing. When her husband told her about the Squad's operation against us, he signed her death certificate. Over the years, how much else do you think he's told her? You don't know. I don't know either. Perhaps even Crowfoot doesn't know—but he can't take the chance. Chalice is unstable. She could talk to anyone. She could go over to the other side—and I'll remind you that in this game there are more than just two sides. They want you safely out of the way, so if by some chance they do keep to their bargain, they'll let her come to you. But then one day, one bright sunny day, wherever you are—in Bali or Cozumel or Paris, it doesn't matter—she'll be at the wheel of a car and it will go out of control. Or she'll fall ill, mysteriously. There will be no cure. A heart attack, a touch of botulism. Do I have to tell you the ways they can accomplish it? She's dead, Eddie . . . *dead*. It's a terminal illness and there's no cure for it. What we do this morning, if she's in that building, will only hasten the inevitable. At the least, it will be more merciful—on you as well."

"I don't believe any of that," Eddie said.

"Because you don't want to. You believe what it suits you to believe. You always have."

Sharing the hotel elevator with two couples who had stumbled in bleary-eyed from the discotheque, Vasily broke into polite chatter about the weather, the idle threat of rain, while Eddie lapsed into a rocklike silence.

Behind it, his mind churned. If I were smarter, he thought, I'd know what to do, what to believe. But I don't see it. Maybe Vasily was right: maybe Crowfoot was lying. The one obligation these people never had

252

in their whole lives was to tell the truth. So he's lying. Assume that. In which case, we leave them in peace and go away and they come after us. If he doesn't keep his word and they bury Chalice in Williamsburg, I know the score and I go after them again. Crowfoot can't afford to have that happen, so he's got to keep that part of the bargain. Which boils down to this: if I trust him, I get Chalice. And Vasily's wrong—they won't come after her, because if they get her, even the way he described it, I'll know it wasn't an accident and I'll come right back at them. Back to square one, me against them, where they don't want to be.

Think, dummy. Vasily doesn't give a damn about anyone except himself. Crowfoot was right; he never did. Chalice is in there. If we go through with this stunt and get away with it, she dies. And all the information is still locked away in the Zhukovka CYBER—maybe even up in the computer bank at Langley by now. Crowfoot would cover himself. Maybe someone else in the Agency knows, some guy who'll never let go. Take out a whole unit like the Colonial Squad and they won't sleep until they find out who did it and then bring him in from the cold to the heat. Zhukovka will tell them. They sleep in the same bed, and they always did. And Chalice dies.

In the end, there it was: Chalice dies. I can't do that, Eddie decided. Whatever the risk, I can't do it. No way, not for Mrs. Mancuso's little boy from Mulberry Street. Shove it, Vasily.

*Think about Borgneff.*

Oh, the old man was clever. He planted seeds and let them grow. He didn't need a computer to figure this one out. Just that smart old Indian brain, eyes that picked your mind apart like a cheap lock, and let the other guys do the dirty work. But he was wrong there. I couldn't do that. Could I?

In Vasily's room, the Russian faced him. His leather suitcases were neatly packed, waiting only for the straps to be buckled. A Brown Bess musket stood against the wall. Vasily was ready to go.

"Well?" he asked.

"I'm not going," Eddie said. "I'm going to call the old man and tell him it's a deal."

Vasily frowned, pursed his lips, then slowly nodded his head up and down. "Because of Chalice."

"That's it."

"And you expect me to accept that?"

"You owe her, Vasily."

"And you owe me. You always pay your debts—you told me that. Now it's time to pay me."

"If she wasn't in there, I'd do it."

"Is it useless to argue with you?"

"Yeah," Eddie said. "Don't waste your time."

Sitting on the edge of the bed, Vasily took out his gold cigar case. He selected one, lit it, and puffed leisurely. His eyes were contemplative, the muscles of his face relaxed.

"What did Crowfoot tell you to do with me, Eddie?" he asked quietly.

"Do?"

"Come, come. He must have foreseen that I might not agree to this so-called amnesty. We're friends, Eddie. We've been through a lot together. Don't lie to me now."

"He just told me to think about you. That if you wouldn't agree, there was a simple solution."

"To kill me."

Eddie grinned. "Yeah. That's what the old guy had in mind."

Vasily smiled back at him. "And what do *you* have in mind?"

"I wouldn't do it," Eddie said. "I couldn't. Like you said, I owe you. And I'm funny that way: I don't kill my friends." He spread his hands. "I haven't got a damn thing on me, *tovarich*. No camera, no prosthetic. I had a pack of cigarettes with me when I met Crowfoot, in case he tried to pull some stunt. They would have blown him into oatmeal. I left them in the car. I didn't even want to be tempted."

"I've never known anyone like you," Vasily said softly. "Not in this business, anyway. Chalice was right

. . . you're sentimental. It's a dangerous virtue, Eddie."

"It's the only one I've got."

"But now you stand in my way. Have you considered that I may not be quite so sentimental? Not as principled as you?"

"You won't kill me," Eddie said flatly.

"Why not?"

"You couldn't live with it "

"That may be wishful thinking. I told you—you believe what it suits you to believe. I could live with it. The question is whether or not I choose to do so."

"Why don't you flip a coin?"

Vasily smiled, and the smile grew into a throaty chuckle, and the chuckle into deep laughter. His bony face looked almost cherubic. Slowly the laughter subsided, but he was still smiling, and he raised his thin cigar in a salute.

"A coin won't be necessary," he said warmly "In such grave matters, one must never let fate decide. One must always choose, and the choice must be founded on enlightened self-interest. That has always been my rule—and, as you see, it has allowed me to survive a great many crises." He sighed. "But one must never be a slave, even to a rule, and so for the first time in my life I intend to break it. I suppose . . . somehow . . . we will all survive." He laughed again. "You see? You've converted me, Eddie. You were right. I like you too much, and I couldn't live comfortably after killing you. Friendship has its rewards."

Eddie grinned at him. "So we'll call it off. We'll take the offer."

"Yes, yes, but quickly, before I change my mind."

Tersely, he issued instructions. Eddie was to make the telephone call from a public booth in the hotel lobby. Vasily checked his wristwatch. "It's two thirty. No mention of the laser, if you please. We will have to retrieve it in case some innocent fool reaches inside the cannon and disintegrates half the colonial militia and a few hundred tourists. I don't think we would be easily forgiven." He pondered a minute, his eyes grow-

255

ing somber, then laid a hand lightly on Eddie's shoulder. "Arrange for a delivery of Chalice this evening. Just after dark. Pick a crowded street in downtown Washington and tell them to let her out of a car. Tell them that if she's followed, the entire arrangement is cancelled. Tell her to keep walking in a random pattern through the downtown area, and we'll contact her."

"Tell *her?*"

Vasily raised his eyebrows. "You've got to hear her voice, Eddie. You've got to know she's all right, that she's really there. Forgive me if my trust in Mr. Crowfoot is not quite so deep as yours."

"No, you're right," Eddie said. He put out his hand and clasped Vasily's.

"I'm a fool. Make your telephone call," said the Russian.

Squeezed into the booth near the reception desk, Eddie went through the cross-checks of identification, heard the scrambler go into gear, and then Crowfoot's reedy voice was on the line, murmuring pleasantries, then politely waiting.

"It's a deal," Eddie said.

Crowfoot's sigh came through audibly. "Good. I'm very pleased . . . for everyone's sake. Borgneff is included?"

"I said it was a deal."

"Did you have to go to extremes?"

"No, damn it, I didn't. And I wouldn't have."

"I'm surprised. Not that you wouldn't have, but that you didn't have to. You're a very lucky young man. Tell me what you want done with the woman."

Eddie spelled out the instructions, and then said, "I want to talk to her."

"She's asleep."

"Get her."

While he waited, he reached into his pocket for his cigarettes. He had left them upstairs. He drummed his fingers nervously on the table next to the telephone.

In another minute he heard Chalice's husky voice.

He heard the weariness in it, the defeat and the deep anxiety.

"Listen, kid—are you all right?"

"I'm all right, Eddie."

"It's going to work out. Trust the old man. He's going to let you go this evening. Do what he tells you. You understand?"

"Yes. Thank you, Eddie."

"I love you. It's crazy, I never said it before, and this is a hell of a time to start, but it's true."

"I love you too, Eddie."

"Tell them not to follow you. Remind them that that would be a big mistake. Where's Parker?"

"Asleep, somewhere in the building. They all are. I'm afraid of him, Eddie. He's gone a little crazy. I think if he could do it, he'd kill me."

"You just stick with the old man. Tonight it'll all be over. Give me Crowfoot."

Crowfoot came onto the line again.

"Two things," Eddie said. "If anything ever happens to her when she's with me, any accident, anything, I'm coming back. After you and everyone else. You got that?"

"No accident will happen," Crowfoot said. "I give you my word. You said two things."

"Yeah, I want something else. Call it a gesture of good faith, a little payment in advance. You said you were going to extract Parker. Is that still on?"

"Yes. That's on."

"Do it now. Do it so that she—Chalice, Catherine, his wife—knows about it. Sees it, or just knows for sure that it's been done, I don't care which. I want her to tell me tonight that Parker's dead. That's a condition for the deal."

"I understand," Crowfoot said. "I see no reason why we can't oblige you. Is there anything else?"

"No. That'll do. That's plenty."

"Good luck to you, Mancuso."

"Thanks," Eddie said.

Crowfoot listened to the empty hum of the line,

257

then gently replaced the telephone on its red cradle. He turned to the woman. A beautiful woman, even now, with tangled hair and the deep shadows under those haunted violet eyes. He could understand her hold on a man. In his own youth he had known such women, had made love to them and allowed them the illusion that they controlled him and that he had irrational need of them; but none had ever held him. Which is why, he thought, I am seventy-two years old, body and soul alike uncrippled. With Eddie Mancuso, he knew it was different. So vulnerable. A miracle that he had come this far unscathed. But he would learn, sooner than he realized, sooner than he wanted to. A pity about that, perhaps. Would there be forgiveness? It was beside the point, Thomas Crowfoot decided.

"Come with me," he said to Chalice.

Together they descended in the noiseless elevator to the first floor of the building that housed the Colonial Squad. Andy Washington sat hunched at his desk in the vestibule over a cup of tea. He looked up inquiringly.

"Our guests are asleep?" Crowfoot asked.

"Yes, sir."

"You have a man at the door to each apartment?"

"Yes, sir."

"Who's watching over Colonial Parker?"

"Heath, sir."

"Call Mr. Heath and ask him to come up here, please."

Before Heath arrived, Crowfoot asked, "How are you armed, Andy?"

"Walther PP nine-millimeter short."

"Silencer?"

Andy slid open a desk drawer and took out a slender black tubular silencer. At a nod from Crowfoot, he slipped the Walther PP from his shoulder holster and screwed the silencer firmly onto the barrel. Chalice watched, her tongue sliding over her lips. Heath, a lanky blond young man, stepped out of the elevator.

"Keep your eye on things, Mr. Heath," Crowfoot said politely. "We won't be long."

A few minutes later, flanked by Andy and Chalice, he stood outside the gray steel door in the basement of the building. Cool air flowed from the noiseless air conditioners. The corridor was bright with yellow sodium light. Crowfoot took a steel ring of keys from his pocket and gave them to Andy.

"Take them," he said. "Find the right key, please. Unlock the door, and then kill Colonel Parker. Not a head shot. We'll have a public funeral, and he has some friends in Washington."

Andy nodded impassively. "You'll stay, sir?"

"Oh, yes," Crowfoot said. "The lady and I will both stay to verify."

Inserting the correct key into the lock, Andy opened the heavy door. He stepped inside. The studio apartment was dark, but Andy flicked a switch and light blazed through the room, illuminating every corner. Colonel Parker's clothes, in uncharacteristic disarray, were strewn on a leather easy chair. The colonel himself flopped over in the double bed, then sat up, blinking in the glare. Andy leveled the Walther PP with two hands, and the two shots that struck the colonel's chest made no more sound than that of a fist thumping a plank of wood. Blood soaked the colonel's pajamas and the sheets. The dead eyes stared in disbelief.

Chalice let out her breath.

Crowfoot held out his hand for the pistol. Andy gave it to him, butt first. The old man said, "Thank you, Andy. Clean up, please. And you, my dear, come with me. We need to have a drink and some conversation."

He led her to his office and seated her across the desk from himself. He laid the pistol on the desk between them, then reached into a bottom drawer and came up with a bottle of Bell's and two glasses. He poured the drinks ceremoniously. Chalice slugged hers down; Crowfoot sipped at his. Then he unscrewed the used silencer from the pistol and tossed it into a basket. From the same bottom drawer he took out a fresh silencer and laid it on the desk. He refilled Chalice's glass, and took another sip from his own.

"I know it's been a trying night," he said, "but there's still one more piece of business we have to discuss."

Vasily was waiting in the room, smoking a cigar and gazing moodily out the window into the darkness. The drizzle still fell, cloaking the beach in layers of pale-lemon mist. At the light tap, he opened the door.

Eddie crossed the room and dropped heavily into a chair.

"Done. He bought everything."

Vasily nodded with satisfaction. "You spoke to Chalice?"

"She was right there."

"And the others?"

"Tucked away, safe and sound."

"How did you arrange the pickup?"

"Crowfoot will let her out in front of the IRS building on Constitution Avenue in downtown Washington. He'll do it himself. Tonight, at ten o'clock."

"Good, Eddie."

"Let's get the hell out of here."

Glancing around, he saw that he had left his lighter and his cigarettes on top of the television set next to an ashtray. He fumbled at the nearly empty pack. The lighter flared, the tip of the cigarette glowing cherry-red. With the first deep puff, as he moved toward the door, he felt weakness in his knees. He stumbled and turned. The lamplight was dancing crazily, and the image of Vasily looming over him began to blur. Unaccountably, the carpet struck his knees.

The Russian's voice came from far away.

"I'm sorry, Eddie. It won't hurt . . . just a little headache later. You were right . . . I couldn't kill you, not unless I had to. And that wasn't necessary. But I couldn't let you stop me. Couldn't let . . . Goodbye, Eddie. . . ."

Moving smoothly to the bedside table, he took a hypodermic needle from the drawer. Eddie lay on the carpet, legs twitching, eyes still open, trying to move, but his limbs felt like blocks of concrete. The injection, Vasily calculated, would put him to sleep for eight hours or more, and by that time the job would be done. The Colonial Squad and Colonel Fist would be only a memory. Bending, he slid the needle expertly into the vein of Eddie's arm. The dulled brown eyes fluttered once, then closed.

For what remained of the night, Vasily worked on the Brown Bess musket, stripping it down to its components and interchanging parts with the Dragunov and the Sterling L2A3 submachine gun he had carried disassembled in his suitcase. By the time he had put the musket back together, it had become a light semi-automatic carbine chambered for 9-mm parabellum cartridges. Any armaments expert would have seen at a glance that it was something more than an antique Brown Bess musket, but there would be no armaments experts in the battle at Williamsburg. He peeled back the covers of the bed in the other room, took off Eddie's shoes, and laid him comfortably beneath a sheet and single blanket. Eddie snored gently, peacefully. "Yes, sleep," Vasily murmured. "And when you wake, it will be all over. One day, my friend, you will be grateful. . . ."

On the door to the room he hung a DO NOT DISTURB sign. Downstairs in the lobby, under the name of Richard Victor, he paid his own bill and said to the desk clerk, "My friend Mr. Morrison will be staying an extra day. He's had rather a late night and doesn't wish to be disturbed. If you'd be kind enough to make sure of that . . ." Sliding a ten-dollar bill into the clerk's ready palm, he received a gracious smile.

In the coffee shop he breakfasted on poached eggs, toast, a pot of strong tea. The drizzle had stopped, although bloated gray clouds rimmed the horizon and the surf toiled restlessly on the beach. Church bells began to ring for early Mass. A bellman loaded his suitcases into the station wagon. Before eight o'clock, Vasily was on the road back to Williamsburg.

261

# 20

Eddie dreamed . . . dreamed that he was a boy again,
playing stickball on the cluttered side streets of summer off Avenue B . . . *Good hit! Run, Eddie, Run!*
Dreamed of Martin and Luther and King, taking the
quick pass from the quick black hands, fake and up
and in . . . *two points.* Games, always games. Us
against them. Even in the water, bubbles ascending,
the rainbow-colored fish grouped above and below,
hostile troops darting at him while he searched for the
trigger of the spear gun that wasn't there; searched,
then gave up, let the sea soothe and wash over his
body. No need to fight. Don't have to play the game.
Sleep is good, sleep solves it all . . . can't win,
can't lose. Just sleep.

His eyes opened to the narrowest of slits and let gray
light pass through to the pupils. Even that hurt. Gray
light . . . why was the light so gray? His eyes opened a
little more, so that pain bounced down from the brain,
up from the hollow sockets, down and up, down and
up, doing a crazy little circuit that made him want to
give up, let sleep take him, let the soothing sea claim
him.

But he forced the eyes to stay open, absorb the
ghostly light. Forced himself to think where he was, to
hear the ghostly voices. The reedy falsetto of Crowfoot.

*Good luck to you, Mancuso.* Chalice's husky, weary tones. *I love you too, Eddie.*

He remembered.

Oh, Vasily. Oh, you son of a bitch.

Very slowly, he raised his head, while the sockets of his eyes gonged and clanged with pain. No other sound penetrated. He moved his left arm inch by inch across the pillow, damp from sweat, until his wristwatch swam blurrily into view. The hands of the watch formed a narrow V. Five minutes to one. That couldn't be. Night? Morning? Something was wrong there. Finally he saw it. Five after eleven. And there was light bleeding through the curtains that faced the ocean; so it was morning. Five after eleven in the morning.

Oh, no. *No.*

Whatever the cost to his body, his brain ordered it to move. He staggered out of the bed across the carpet to the bathroom, shedding his clothes. Under the shower, the cold water beat on him like arrows of ice. He wanted to scream. *You son of a bitch, I trusted you. Can't trust the old man? It was you I couldn't trust. You!* He turned off the shower, shivered terribly, reaching with trembling hands for the big brown bath towel and, strangely, still heard the beat of the water. Like rain.

In the bedroom, still shivering and leaving a trail of water behind him, he forced open the curtains and looked out, blinking, at the steel-gray sea. The rain beat steadily down from a pearly sky.

He picked up the telephone. Again, the brain did the work while the body fumbled. He asked for the Information Center at Williamsburg. The musical tones pained his eardrums. His voice, when he spoke, had the hoarse growl of a three-day drunk. He asked about the weather, and was told that it was raining in Williamsburg.

"What about the military show on the green? Has it started yet?"

"Course not. Can't run that thing in the rain."

"Do you have any idea when it will start?"

"No idea at all, mister. Soon as the rain lets up, I reckon. Could be an hour from now, could be five minutes."

"Thank you," Eddie said, hanging up.

In ten minutes, unshaven and with bloodshot eyes, he was at the Hertz counter in the lobby. The black girl in the crisp red uniform looked at him warily.

"Yeah, I know," he said. "But here's my credit card. Look, sister, you'd do it for O. J. Simpson, so do it for me. My wife's just been taken to the hospital."

A gleaming blue Ford Fairlane screeched to a stop in front of the hotel in five minutes and Eddie, hands shaking, head pounding, sunglasses shutting out the weak gray glare of the morning, slid behind the wheel. *Run, Eddie, run....*

And while Eddie ran, Vasily cursed the rain; cursed it in Russian below his breath and more volubly in English, for he was not alone. He stood on the wet grass in the shelter of The Magazine, dressed in the hand-tailored lobsterback uniform of the King's Own Foot, in company with two other soldiers, both students at The College of William and Mary. Inside, the cannon also waited for the rain to stop. There was always an unknown factor, always something that one couldn't count on, could rarely foresee. In this instance, that something was as prosaic as the weather.

"It's the same old story," he said. "You can talk about it, but there's nothing you can do about it. What did they do back in 1776? Wait for the sun to shine before they fought the revolution?"

"If they were getting paid by the hour at a union rate," one of the students said, scratching his beard, "I'll bet that's exactly what they did. What's your hurry?"

"I've got to catch the midnight flight to Rio," Vasily said, grinning.

"Take me with you. I've never been there." The bearded student laughed, and put out his hand. "I'm Dave Lehman, and I don't think we'll have to wait much longer. It looks like it's clearing up."

264

And indeed, the stubborn sun had punched a hole in the grayness that was broadening into a wide patch of blue sky. Almost as soon as Lehman spoke, the last drop of rain pattered down, and a bar of gold light spread across the meadow. The grass steamed sweetly in the sudden warmth.

"Twelve forty," Vasily said, glancing at his watch. "How long before the shooting starts?"

Tourists began to emerge from the restaurants and buildings on the green. "Here they come," Dave Lehman said. "We can start to wheel out the cannon. I'd say by one o'clock we'll charge, then the militia will charge, and by three o'clock we'll be a beaten army. At four we get paid." He laughed and turned to Vasily. "Then at midnight you can fly to Rio."

Eddie prayed as he raced along I-64 toward Williamsburg at eighty miles an hour. He prayed for time, he prayed for rain, and he prayed that the state police were sleeping late that morning. He watched the elephant-colored sky thin away into a porcelain blue, watched the friendly rain clouds lumber eastward, and he prayed even harder. He was hungry, and the sockets of his eyes still ached, but his anger had cooled and given way to calculation. There was one way, and only one.

Once in Williamsburg, he swung the car into the Merchants Square parking lot on Henry Street, cut the engine, and flung open the door. Out on Prince George Street, several soldiers in red British uniforms ambled along on their way to Market Square, while a single young soldier in colonial buff followed behind, his musket at the trail and his powder horn looped over his shoulder.

"Excuse me," Eddie called as he approached. "Can you tell me where the Governor's Palace is?"

"Sure, straight ahead."

"Can you do me another favor? I've got a map of Williamsburg here, but I can't make head or tail out of it."

"What are you looking for? I can probably tell you

where it is." The tall colonial soldier bent forward. From under his road map, Eddie took a small nasal spray and squeezed it once, gently, so that the mist shot forward into the young man's face.

Minutes later, streaming sweat and dressed in the buff militia uniform, Eddie locked the doors of the car, leaving the front windows open an inch so that the student slumped on the floor of the back seat wouldn't suffocate. The tricornered hat came down almost to Eddie's eyes, the pants were baggy and the buckled boots two sizes too big. Gripping the musket, he hurried down Prince Goerge Street and across the Palace Green. British soldiers were already moving into formation on Market Square opposite the buildings of the Colonial Squad. There were no signs of cannon yet, and he didn't see Vasily. Across the way, the militia had begun to muster in ranks, pouring powder and loading muskets.

Eddie's eyes darted around the square, assessing the various shops there. Basketmaking, Spinning and Weaving, Bootmaker, Cooper. His eyes passed over all these and settled on the Deane Shop and Forge. The blacksmith had business; he was shoeing a horse. The fire in the forge showed dull red in the shadows of the smithy, and the clang of hammer on iron beat a steady rhythm. Eddie's eyes narrowed, he nodded, then he ran for the door of the shop.

"Shoeing nails?" the blacksmith said. "Now, what would you want with a pound of shoeing nails?"

"Souvenirs," Eddie mumbled hastily. "Um, paperweights . . . ah, carpet tacks."

"*Carpet* tacks?"

"Great for hanging pictures, too."

The puzzled blacksmith shook his head as he filled a paper bag with the metal pegs, then gaped as Eddie laid a ten-dollar bill on the anvil, grabbed the sack, and ran.

Outside the shop, among a press of people obscuring his view, he tore his handkerchief, wadded it, poured gunpowder from the horn down the barrel of the musket, and followed that with a handful of nails. He

266

rammed them tightly with the rod, and was setting the flint in the lock when a small boy looked up at him in wonder.

"Mister, will that thing really *shoot?*"

"I'll bet my life on it," Eddie told him.

Then he heard the first ragged volley from the green and, craning his neck to look over the crowd, he saw the cannon.

In The Magazine, a squad of British soldiers began trundling the cannon to the door, hauling them by the limbers, two men-to a gun. Vasily quickly picked out the cannon with the deep V scratched on the butt. Grasping the rope attached to the limber, he waved Dave Lehman to his side. Together, they worked the cannon out onto the grass, Vasily pulling, Dave bracing the barrel to keep the gun from careening out of control. The sun beat down strongly now; the grass was soaked, and in the humid heat a mist swirled up from the green. The mist partially obscured the maneuvering of the troops, but the frame-and-shingle building of the Colonial Squad showed clearly. Vasily and his helper bumped the cannon across the grass, the wheels jolting over stray rocks.

Vasily put a hand to his chest, and winced. "Hold on a minute," he murmured.

"What's the matter?"

"I don't feel so well. Please, let's just rest a minute."

The other cannoneers had passed them, heading for the southern edge of the green. That was not where Vasily wanted to go. Farther away, the line of British redcoats charged, firing at the colonial militia. A file of standing men fired while the file in front of them knelt on the wet grass to reload. Then the files changed places, the kneeling men straightening, pointing their muskets, and at an officer's command pulling the heavy triggers. The guns popped and banged wonderfully, acrid smoke rising into the mist. Children shrieked with pleasure; parents applauded politely as members of the militia sprawled on the grass, feigning death and injury.

How much they appreciate it, Vasily thought, and how deeply it touches them . . . and how little they understand.

A militia officer, head wrapped in bandages, shouted a command. His troops scattered to the flanks and began to fire their harmless charges at the redcoats. The thin red line stumbled, broke, fell back. Then the British cannon rumbled, great swirls of smoke pluming up from the muzzles. Again the militia fell back to rally and regroup. The crowd cheered the performance.

"Hey, come on," Dave Lehman said, puzzled. "Let's go! We can't just sit around, we're right in the middle of the whole damn battle."

"I'm really not well," Vasily said, his voice low and weak. "I was a fool to have done this." He slumped across the barrel of the cannon. "Please . . . get me a doctor."

"Oh, my God! Say, are you serious? You're not kidding me, are you?"

"No," Vasily gasped. "This is no joke. A doctor . . . please. My heart. There must be a doctor somewhere." He fluttered one hand toward the crowd.

"Stay right here," Dave Lehman said. "Don't move." He broke into a run toward the apothecary's shop.

As soon as he was gone, Vasily straightened up, laid down his musket, and began to haul the heavy cannon around into place. He was almost exactly in the center of the green, men lying on the grass all around him; the two armies firing, reloading, shouting hoarsely, the other cannon booming. Yelling soldiers ran by, and the smell of gunpowder bit sharply into his nostrils. Smoke drifted lazily overhead as he maneuvered the heavy limber to one side so that the muzzle of the cannon pointed toward the Colonial Squad building. He was about to reach into the touch-hole to activate the laser mechanism when he heard his name called.

*"Vasily, wait!"*

But that was impossible. He stiffened, controlled

himself, and refused to turn toward the source of the sound. The voice called his name again; it was no mistake. He wheeled and saw a single colonial soldier sprinting toward him, musket extended, weaving a path through the fallen men and around the other cannon. It took him only the briefest of glances to see, under the tricornered hat, the pale, hard, angry face of Eddie Mancuso.

Vasily reacted without thought, responding only to instinct and training. He dropped to one knee, snatched the modified musket from where it rested against the cannon, and leveled it in the direction of the charging soldier.

"Eddie!" he called. "Don't come any closer."

Thirty yards away, Eddie kept coming.

Vasily shouted at him: "Don't make me do it. Stay back!"

Eddie skidded to a halt. He had heard Vasily clearly the first time, but the musket pointing at him had seemed as harmless as the others on the field. Only now, as he came closer, did he recognize the odd configuration of the stock, the thickened barrel and notched sights, and know that it was no ordinary Brown Bess that was leveled at him. He knew immediately that whatever weapon Vasily had fashioned would blow him apart, and the warning message worked its way from his brain to his legs.

"Put that thing down," he called across the din of the battle. "Put it down and we'll talk."

Vasily's answer was a warning shot that screamed high and harmlessly over Eddie's head. He ducked quickly to one side, to where a group of colonial militia were bringing up a battery of their own cannon. Linstock touched powder, the carronade roared, and for a moment the smoke of the explosion obscured the field. Vasily vanished from his view.

Dropped prone on the grass behind the wheel of a cannon, Eddie raised his musket. As the smoke blew away in shreds, he saw the Russian bent to the base of the cannon. Aiming deliberately wide, returning the warning shot to drive him away from the laser,

Eddie yanked at the stiff trigger. The musket bucked.

Vasily heard the whine of metal weakly striking metal, ricocheting off the cannon barrel. Lips thinned, gray eyes cold as iron, he sighted along the tangent sights he had fitted to the Brown Bess and squeezed off two shots at the figure he saw veiled in the smoke and mist. This time he shot to kill.

A colonial soldier to Eddie's left, standing by the second cannon and priming his musket, screamed with pain and pitched to the turf. Blood flowed down the buff-colored trouser leg.

Eddie squirmed along the ground, musket clutched in one hand, his other hand clawing for a hold to haul himself forward. A bullet whistled past, struck a loose rock, ricocheting crazily. Men were shooting all around him, but except for the boy who lay moaning on the ground, not one of them realized that among the mock charges there were real bullets being fired. He knew then that there was not going to be any truce on that field; no time out for reasoning; but he called again in one last try.

"Vasily, don't! It's me. Eddie."

Again his answer was a bullet. This one plowed the ground nearby.

There was no time to press another charge of nails into the musket, ram it home, pour in gunpowder. Eddie launched himself forward at the figure in red crouched by the cannon. He threw his body to the left just as a 9-mm parabellum bullet plucked at his flowing white sleeve. He struck the grass, rolled, came up swinging the musket like a baseball bat. The wood of the stock connected with the barrel of Vasily's Brown Bess, knocking it to the side, and Eddie kept coming, driving his hundred and fifty pounds into the bigger man like a demented quarterback foolishly leading the interference. For a moment Vasily lurched, stumbled, then braced himself against the barrel of the cannon. His foot snapped out in a karate kick that caught Eddie on the hip and sent him spinning.

Even as he fell, Eddie thought, I can't do it! I can't handle him. Breath fled his lungs as his chest crashed into the ground, but he kept spinning, rolling, and his hand fastened on to a cold, wet rock, jagged, the size of a baseball. Grunting with fury, Vasily snapped the toe of his boot forward again.

Eddie squirmed, reaching out to catch the leg, and then the Russian was falling on top of him, eyes coolly murderous, one hand groping for the trigger of his rifle, and Eddie saw it. His arm went back; he twisted and struck. The rock in his fist took Vasily in the left eye, the jagged edge slicing through jelly and bone.

An animal bellow broke from Vasily's lips. With blood pouring from his eye, his hands found Eddie's throat and fastened on the larynx. The powerful fingers pressed deeper, looking for the leverage that would snap the cartilage and kill.

Nausea slammed through Eddie's nervous system. With his clenched right hand he struck a second time, and then a third time, and with the third blow the Russian went sliding away to the ground, unmoving. Eddie breathed deeply, rolled over, stood up.

"Vasily?"

The question in his voice went unanswered. The Russian was dead.

Eddie stared at the blood-soaked rock in his hand. After all the years, all the tricks, and all the devices, he had finally killed with the weapon of Cain, the oldest weapon known to man. He looked down at Vasily. The face was set, the eyes already glazed in death. He knelt and touched the cheek gently.

"Boy, we really screwed that one up, didn't we?" he whispered hoarsely. "We should have used a preheater to activate the laser, and a remote control on the trigger to ..."

His voice trailed away. His throat hurt too much for him to speak, and his eyes were blurred with tears.

He stood up and looked around. The battle still raged in mock fury on either side of him. Vasily's body was only one of many lying on the green. He ducked his head and broke into a trot through the drifting, bitter smoke, making for the parking lot and the car.

# 21

The black Chrysler cruised slowly up Constitution Avenue. The limousine pulled in to the curb and stopped behind the Post Office Building. For a moment there was no movement in the car; then the door opened and Chalice stepped out. The Chrysler pulled back into traffic. Chalice hesitated, then began to walk slowly along Constitution Avenue in the same direction. Eddie followed her from behind in the rented car. She walked aimlessly, circling the downtown streets at random. After twenty minutes he was convinced that there was no tail on her or on him, and that Crowfoot had kept his word. At a crowded intersection, as she waited for the light to change, he tapped his horn lightly, and opened the door near the curb. Chalice turned, saw him, and slid into the car. Twenty minutes later they had cleared the city and were heading south on Interstate 95. Until then, neither of them spoke. Only when they were moving freely on the highway did Eddie turn to her.

"Do you know about Vasily?"

She put her head back on the seat and closed her eyes. "Crowfoot told me. He said you called. He wants you to know that the laser has been removed. He knew you'd be worried."

"I had to do it."

"Vasily? Yes, of course you did."

"If you hadn't been inside . . ."

"You still would have had to. These things don't happen by accident." Her voice was strangely removed. "Freddy's dead, too. I saw it happen."

He nodded absently, trying to keep his eyes on the road, trying to fight the need for sleep.

"Where are we going?" she asked.

"Virginia Beach. I left everything there and I've got to pick things up. Then to sleep. Maybe for a day or so. After that . . . you name it. Anywhere. Except San Miguel. Too many memories there."

"He would have killed you, Eddie."

"I know. That should make me feel better, but it doesn't."

After that they drove silently, stopping only for gas, and twice for coffee which Eddie poured into himself to keep awake. By the time they reached Virginia Beach it was nearly three in the morning. A half moon had risen, silvering the edges of the clouds and casting a smooth, lambent light on the empty beach. He parked the car in the hotel lot and found his room key in the glove compartment.

"It's so beautiful," Chalice murmured. "Couldn't we walk on the beach?"

"If I collapse," he said, chuckling with weariness, "you'll have to carry me back."

"Just a little walk. To look at the moon."

"All right."

They walked in silence on the hard wet sand that sloped near the water's edge, listening to the rush of the night surf and watching the glitter of phosphorescence as the waves boiled and cracked far out near the jetties. The calmness of her mood puzzled him.

"What is it, Chalice? I know there's something. You'd better tell it to me now."

She stopped, drawing a little bit away from him. "Do you feel like making love to me now?"

"Right here? On the beach?"

"Yes."

He laughed and said, "I never thought I'd ever say no to you again, but I couldn't do it. I've had it for tonight. In the morning, cupcake. That's a promise."

"But suppose there is no morning?"

"Hey . . . don't even joke that way."

"I wasn't joking. You trusted Crowfoot, Eddie. You believed everything he told you."

"Yeah, I did." He was frowning. "What are you trying to say?"

"The old man is evil. He lied. He lied to me in the beginning, and then he finally told me the truth. But he lied to you all the way."

Quickly and nervously, Eddie glanced around in all directions. They were alone on the beach in the moonlight under scudding clouds. A dark cloud moved overhead and the silvery light was blotted out, taking the color from Chalice's violet eyes, obscuring her expression. But he watched, fascinated, as she unbuckled her leather shoulder bag, reached into it, and brought out a long black object: a pistol with the silencer firmly screwed onto the barrel. Even in the dim light he saw that it was a Walther PP.

Almost tonelessly, she said, "This is the gun they used to kill Freddy. I watched them do it. You know how I like that trip."

"I know, but we don't have to talk about that now."

"It's the same gun. Crowfoot gave it to me afterward. He told me to use it on you."

She pointed it at Eddie's chest. Her breath came quickly.

"Put that thing away," he said.

"Crowfoot offered you a truce, but he lied," she said. "The Russians would always have gone after Vasily, but you saved them the trouble. And Crowfoot would always have gone after you. But now he doesn't have to."

"Why not?" he asked, but he had already begun to understand.

274

"I've never killed anyone, Eddie, not really. Not since a long time ago, and that's too long a story to tell. I always wanted to again, and I never did. It was enough to be close to it, to people like Freddy, and then you and Vasily. But the old man knew I wanted to do it. He knew the time would come when I'd have to do it. Why do you think he let me go? Just to keep his word to you? You know those kind of people. You know what their word is worth."

"I'm getting the drift," he said.

"He didn't tell me until after he had Freddy killed. Then he told me that they couldn't let me go. I knew too much. They were always planning to break their word to you, but he couldn't let me live either. Not unless I did something for him, something that would save them a lot of time and trouble. That's what he told me after Freddy was killed. They thought it might be a long time before they reached you, Eddie, and you were smarter than you realized. If you caught on, you could make it difficult for them."

"And you could reach me fast . . . because I trusted you. And you could buy your way out by killing me."

Chalice nodded. "And then I'd be free."

The moon slipped out from behind the cloud, shining coldly down on the black barrel of the pistol and the long tubular silencer. With widening eyes, Eddie stared down at it. He knew now that it was not Chalice who pointed the gun, but Thomas Crowfoot.

"And then why won't he come after you?" he said casually. "I mean, after you kill me, if you do . . . what's to stop them?"

"Nothing. They probably will. But I've got money and a good long head start. I told Crowfoot we were flying south. That's where he'll look. I could run in the other direction, or I could even go east. Maybe even Moscow. I know the right people to see, and I'd have a lot to bargain with. I think they'll protect me. It wouldn't be such a bad life."

"Don't do it, Chalice." He could not keep his eye off the pistol bathed in silver moonlight.

She took a single step backward so that he was effectively out of arm's length. Eddie sighed softly, and her lip curled.

"Are you afraid to die, Eddie?"

He thought for a minute, and then said, "I'm just not ready for it, I guess. And it hurts a bit to think that I was in love with you . . . and you with me."

"Love doesn't count."

"No, I suppose with you it doesn't. But what *does* count? Life? Or death? Which is it you really want?"

"They're part of the same thing."

He smiled bitterly. "Then pull the trigger, Chalice. Get it over with."

"You take it well," she said. "I love that. I really do. I love you for that, Eddie. I could almost change my mind."

"But you won't. People like you never do." He stuffed his hands into his pocket and looked at her coldly. "Because you've got to get your kick. You've got to make your trip. Because you're a freak, a death freak, a . . ."

The pistol was pointed at the center of Eddie's chest, and he never finished the sentence. Her eyes flaring, Chalice squeezed the trigger. There was a muffled *pop*, the same wooden sound she had heard when her husband had died. The pop was the last sound Catherine Parker ever heard, as Thomas Crowfoot finally kept his word.

The Little Devil blowback silencer designed by Eddie Mancuso twenty years before, six inches of black steel with the same velocity that would have sped a bullet from the muzzle, detached itself and slammed back along the gun barrel and smashed through her chest just an inch to the right of her heart. The force hurled her three feet backward, and then she dropped to the sand and rolled slowly down the slight slope to the surf.

Water washed over her face, her hair, her limp hands. Her dead violet eyes stared up at the moon. For a moment, Eddie peered down into them, tryinig to fathom her expression. There was none.

276

"I hope you enjoyed the trip," he said sadly.

He walked slowly along the empty beach the mile or so to his hotel, and then took the elevator upstairs. First there would be sleep, healing sleep. After the sleep it would be time enough to start to run.

CLIFFORD IRVING is the author of five other novels including *The Losers*, which Robert Graves called "the best short novel I have read in 20 years"; four nonfiction books including *Fake!*, which Picasso called "a masterpiece"; and one hoax autobiography of Howard Hughes which the United States Government called a crime.

Born in Manhattan, he was graduated from Cornell and then spent most of his adult life in Europe, as he puts it, "living out (his) sensual fantasies." He has also traveled throughout Asia, sailed the Atlantic on a schooner, been a correspondent to Israel, written teleplays, movies and a prizewinning article for *Playboy*. He says, "I love my ladyfriend Valdi, my three sons, my ex-wife Edith, my friends and family, tennis, writing, good food and wine. I hate the IRS."

He lives now in Mexico and is currently finishing a long novel about Pancho Villa, Tom Mix and Lt. George S. Patton, Jr.

HERBERT BURKHOLZ made his mark as a serious novelist with his first two books, *Sister Bear* and *The Spanish Soldier*, then demonstrated his mastery of high entertainment in *Mulligan's Seed*. In writing of *The Spanish Soldier*, *The Washington Post* called it "boldly conceived and boldly executed with a breadth and audacity of vision that is all too rare," and *The New York Times* praised the author's "very apparent abilities at character, dimension, humor and setting." *The New York Times* called *Mulligan's Seed* "a fast-moving, ingenious caper."

Burkholz, who for many years lived in Spain and Mexico, is an active skier, a sailor of small boats, and an amateur chef of both high and low cuisines. In 1975 he returned to the United States to become Writer-in-Residence at The College of William and Mary in Virginia, and he currently teaches a Creative Writing Workshop at Hofstra University. He and his wife live in Manhattan, where he is working on his new novel.